SINGING THE CLASSICAL,

VOICING THE MODERN

Singing the Classical, Voicing the Modern

THE POSTCOLONIAL POLITICS OF MUSIC IN SOUTH INDIA

Amanda J. Weidman

Duke University Press *Durham and London* 2006

 Printed in the United States of America on acid-free paper ♾
Designed by Amy Ruth Buchanan
Typeset in Bembo by Tseng Information Systems, Inc. Library of Congress Cataloging-in-Publication Data appear on the last printed page of this book.

Duke University Press gratefully acknowledges the support of Bryn Mawr College, which provided funds toward the production of this book.

Portions of chapter 3 were previously published as "Gender and the politics of voice: Colonial modernity and classical music in South India," in *Cultural Anthropology* 18, no. 2 (2003): 194–232. © 2003 American Anthropological Association. ❈ Portions of chapter 4 were previously published as "Can the subaltern sing? Music, language, and the politics of voice in twentieth-century South India," in *Indian Economic and Social History Review* 42, no. 4 (2005): 485–511. ❈ Portions of chapter 6 were previously published as "Guru and gramophone: Fantasies of fidelity and modern technologies of the real," in *Public Culture* 15, no. 3 (2003): 453–76.

Contents

Illustrations

Acknowledgments

My first contact with Karnatic music came unexpectedly in 1990, when I happened to hear a concert of Karnatic violin. I remember being fascinated by seeing and hearing the violin—an instrument I had been playing for years—as it was played diagonally, its scroll resting on the seated player's foot. The performer that evening was Adrian L'Armand, a Western classical violinist who had spent time in Madras in the 1960s studying Karnatic violin. The Wednesday afternoons I spent at his house in Swarthmore, Pennsylvania, for the next two years, learning the beginnings of Karnatic music, opened me to a world of music and musicality that I had not known existed. Adrian is a supremely generous and gifted teacher. Over the years, I have learned much from him about music, the violin, improvisation, and teaching.

In India, I had the opportunity to study with four teachers who each gave me something different. My main teacher, whose name I withhold here for reasons of privacy, has a style of violin-playing unique in its elegantly understated virtuosity. She generously took me on as her disciple in 1994 and on my subsequent stays in Madras, allowing me to accompany her at her concerts and arranging performances for me. In the long afternoons I spent at her house, eating, napping, talking, and playing, she taught me to be a musician and, in her own way, forced me to become an anthropologist. The stamp of her character, both musical and personal, appears often in these pages. In Madurai, N. S. Saminathan, violinist and nagaswaram artist, taught me not only a repertoire of Tamil songs and secrets of improvisation, but also how to perform; then he arranged concerts for me in Meenakshi Amman Temple. His humor, iconoclasm, and intellectual interest in this project have helped me immensely. Also in Madurai, the midrangist C. S. Palaninathan gave me, with supreme patience, the gift of rhythm, teaching me how to "work out" rhythms, how to say them, and, most important, how to remember them. V. S. Narasimhan, a wonderful and original violinist, taught me with exquisite patience and accuracy in Madras and in the United States. With him, I learned the pleasures of dwelling on a single raga for hours.

My consultants for this project were many. For sharing their knowledge with me in Madras, Madurai, Tanjavur, Mysore, and Trivandrum, I thank: Anandi, nagaswaram artist; Subbu Arumugham, villupattu artist; M. Balasubramaniam, violinist; Sethalapathy Balasubramaniam, vocalist; Rajkumar Bharathy, vocalist; Theodore Bhaskaran; film historian; Srimathi Brahmanandam, violinist; R. Chandrakala, nagaswaram artist; V. Chandru, violist; P. T. Chelladurai, vocalist and principal of Tamil Icai Sangam College of Music; Mr. Das of Musee Musical in Madras; R. N. Doreswamy, veena artist; Dwaram Durgaprasad Rao, principal of Maharaja's College of Music in Vizianagaram; Dwaram Mangathayaru, violinist; Dwaram Shyamala, German teacher; L. R. Easwari, playback singer; S. Ganapathy, violinist; M. S. Gopalakrishnan, violinist; T. V. Gopalakrishnan, vocalist and mridangist; Kadri Gopalnath, saxophonist; M. Gunasekaran, clarinetist and band director; Randor Guy, film historian; S. Janaki, playback singer; Salem Jeyalakshmi, vocalist; Illayaraja, film music director; S. Kalpakam, violinist; A. Kanyakumari, violinist; N. Kesi, flutist; K. P. Kittappa, dance master; B. L. Kothandaraman, harmonium artist; T. N. Krishnan, violinist; Sampath Kumar Acharya, musicologist; Lalitha, violinist; the Maharani of Trivandrum; G. S. Mani, vocalist; R. Manimala, nagaswaram artist; T. Mukhta, vocalist; V. Murugan, instrument repairer; members of the Mysore Police Karnatic Band; Sarada Nambi, historian; Nandini, violinist; Dr. Omanakutty, vocalist; T. A. Thana Pandian, musicologist; Kovalam Narayana Panikkar, Trivandrum intellectual and artistic director; Sriram Parasuram, violinist; Ranganayaki Parthasarathy, veena artist; T. S. Parthasarathy, music historian; D. K. Pattammal, vocalist; M. Prameela, vocalist and music professor; Puratchidasan, author; H. M. V. Ragunathan, recordist; A. A. Raja, film musician; R. P. Raja, historian; N. S. Rajam, mridangist; S. Rajam, vocalist; Rajeswara Rao, film music director; R. Ramachandran, violinist; T. N. Ramachadran, book collector; V. A. K. Ranga Rao, record collector and dance critic; T. Rukmini, violinist; Saikumar, flutist; T. Sankaran, flutist; T. Sankaran, vocalist; K. Santanakrishnan, record collector; Sarada, violinist; B. V. K. Sastry, musicologist; Savitri Satyamurthy, violinist; V. R. Sekar, cellist; M. P. Sethuraman, nagaswaram artist; Sarada Shaffter, pianist; V. S. Sharma, historian; Thirupambaram Shanmughasundaram, vocalist; Sirkali Sivachidambaram, vocalist; S. Sivakumar, music editor for Dinamani; K. P. Sivanandam, veena artist; K. Sivatamby, historian; S. Sowmya, vocalist; Anuradha Sriram, vocalist and playback singer; M. S. Subbulakshmi, vocalist; V. V. Subrahmanyam, violinist; Surendran, violinist and music teacher; P. Susheela, playback singer; Dharmapuram Swaminathan, vocalist; Madurai V. Swaminathan, vocalist; Kala Tawker, literary critic; Aswati Tirunal, vocalist; Kunnakudi Vaidyanathan, violinist; L. Vaidyanathan, film music director; Valli, nagaswaram artist; Lata Varma, musicologist; M. B. Vedavalli, musicologist and historian; R. Vedavalli, vocalist; M. S. Viswanathan, film music director.

I gathered sources for this project at several libraries in Madras. I thank the staff of the Roja Muthiah Library, V. Geetha of Maraimalai Adigal Library, the staffs of U. V. Swaminathayyar Library and the Theosophical Society Library, and the Tamil Nadu State Archives. I am grateful to the staff of *Kalki* magazine for allowing me to photocopy music-related articles from old issues.

Many friends made my time in India enjoyable. The extended family of N. S. Saminathan—Sunderraman, Vasantha, Meenakshi, Murugan, Parvathi, Sivakumar, and Murugeswari—took me in as one of their own during my time in Madurai. I thank Padma and S. Anantharaman of Mahatma Gandhi Nagar, Madurai, for their hospitality and friendship and for their interest in my career as a Karnatic musician. Selvamani and family of Krishnapuram Colony, Madurai, provided hilarious times and fun adventures in and around Madurai, as did the "Misses Madurai," my fellow students in the American Institute of Indian Studies Tamil-language program, Faye Blazar and Susan Schomburg. In Madras, Chellamma and the late Sanmugham (*alias* Nilakantan) cooked me delicious meals, and showed me how to have a sense of humor about things. The members of the Madras String Quartet allowed me to play along with them and took me as a guest to the film studios. S. Sanmugham engaged me in many a long afternoon of talk on matters ranging from Tamil prosody to Derrida. S. Venkat shared his tremendous knowledge of the Madras music scene with me on many occasions.

The members of my doctoral committee at Columbia University—John Pemberton, Nicholas Dirks, Aaron Fox, Valentine Daniel, and Indira Peterson—all contributed helpful readings of this work when it was in dissertation form. Although they often had conflicting visions of how the project should progress, each of those visions has been beneficial. In particular, I thank John Pemberton for taking an interest at the very beginning and consistently pushing me to think originally about music, ethnography, and the voice.

I am grateful to the language teachers I have had over the years: Vasu Renganathan and Meera Narayanan at the University of Washington; S. Bharathy, R. Devi, and K. Sangita at the American Institute of Indian Studies Tamil program in Madurai; E. Somasundaram of the University of Madras; V. Narayana Rao at the University of Wisconsin; and Gary Tubb at Columbia University. I thank S. Ravindran and Perundevi Srinivasan for assistance with Tamil translation.

I have presented portions of this work in many places. The readings, comments, and suggestions I received on those occasions have helped me transform this work from a dissertation into a book. I am grateful to Bernard Bate for inviting me to participate in a conference and workshop on language and the historical imagination in South India, and to the members of that group for helpful comments: A. R. Venkatachalapathy, Steve Hughes, Rama Mantena, and Lisa Mitchell. I thank Bonnie McElhinny for inviting me to participate in a conference on language, gender, and political economy at the University of Toronto, and Richard Wolf for inviting me to present my work at a Radcliffe Institute workshop on musical culture in South Asia. Ann Anagnost, several anonymous readers for *Cultural Anthropology*, Sanjay Subrahmanyam, Beth Povinelli, Charles Briggs, Penny Eckert, Regula Qureshi, Steven Feld, Hajime Nakatani, Joshua Barker, Joel Kuipers, and Dan Neuman all gave me insightful comments on presented and written versions of parts of this work. I thank my colleagues in the study of Karnatic music—Matthew Allen, the late T. Viswanathan, Zoe Sherinian, and Beth Bullard—for arranging and participating in conference panels with me. My graduate-school comrades Dave Novak, Uma Brughubanda, Dard Neuman, Arafaat Valiani, Karin Zitzewitz, and Peter Cuasay gave me intellectual and social companionship and comments on my work, and Jen Gherardi tracked down photocopies of music manuals in Madras and sent them to me.

At Duke University Press, my editor, Ken Wissoker, and assistant editor Courtney Berger have made publishing my first book a wonderful experience. Three anonymous readers for Duke University Press commented thoroughly and insightfully on the various revised versions of this manuscript, enabling me to make connections among my chapters and clarify certain arguments that had eluded me for years.

Research funding and writing support for this project came from the National Science Foundation; Foreign Language Area Studies grants;

the American Institute of Indian Studies; Columbia University; and the American Association of University Women.

Portions of chapters 3, 4, and 6 were published in *Cultural Anthropology* 18, no. 2; *Indian Economic and Social History Review* 42, no. 4; and *Public Culture* 15, no. 3. I thank the editors of those journals for making it possible to publish these sections in their present form.

My family has been with me during every phase of this project, and I am immensely grateful for their love, support, and involvement. My mother, Bette, first taught me the pleasures of writing and reading, and how to take an interest in the poetry of life. My father, Burton, taught me intellectual curiosity, social awareness, and the patience to contemplate things in the world. My sister, Nadine, whose scholarship has been an inspiration for my own endeavors, really began to teach me when we were children, for it was in Tigerland, the imaginary world we created together, that I first learned—unwittingly—to be an anthropologist.

My husband, Ken Whang, has been with me through the last few years of this project. His discerning eye and knack for asking the right questions have helped me immensely. I am grateful for his love and companionship, and for his willingness to take a ten-day trip to India with me in 2004 so that we could share the people, places, and music that have been so important to me. The bright face of Sylvia Irene Whang, whose birth was a happy interruption to the revisions of this manuscript, has inspired me in the last phases, and it is to her that I dedicate this book.

Note on Transliteration and Spelling

My transliteration of Tamil words and phrases follows the Madras University Tamil Lexicon Scheme. However, many names and words are more recognizable in Anglicized forms which do not adhere to these transliteration rules. For instance, the word for music is transliterated from Tamil in the Madras University Tamil Lexicon Scheme as *caṅkītam*, but generally spelled sangitam. I have used the conventional, recognizable spellings for words from Tamil and other Indian languages that appear frequently, as well as for names of individuals and places, caste names, deities, and institutions. Where an author writing in Tamil provides a transliteration of his or her title, I have used the author's transliteration.

The spelling of the word *Karnatic* is a matter of some debate. While I have chosen this spelling throughout, other spellings that appear within quotes may include Carnatic, Karnatak, Karnataka, and *karṉāṭaka*.

Introduction

The West is the kingdom of the instrument; the East is the kingdom of the Voice.
—Margaret Cousins, *Music of the Orient and the Occident* (1935)

That "East is East and West is West and never the twain shall meet" is perhaps most applicable to music.
—T. V. Subba Rao, *Studies in Indian Music* (1962)

In the fall of 1994 I found myself in the dubious position of auditioning, unsuspectingly, before a music teacher who was determined not to take me as a student. As a student of South Indian classical music, I had sought out this particular teacher after hearing about the extraordinary qualities of her violin playing. I had announced my desire to study with her in a letter, which preceded my arrival in Madras by a few weeks. Since she was retired from her job as a staff artist at All India Radio, I assumed she would probably have time to spend with me, and I looked forward to apprenticing myself to her in the kind of disciple-guru relationship that is considered crucial to the education of any student of Indian classical music. I felt that once I had inserted myself into such a relationship, I would really have "arrived."

On a September morning I was shown into the front room of her house, greeted by her younger brother, with whom she lived and who asked me, in English, numerous questions: who had my previous teachers been, what part of America was I from, and what university did I attend. After about ten minutes, he showed me upstairs, where she was waiting. "Play," she said, after a wordless greeting. I played something I had learned from a previous teacher, and her face registered obvious disdain. When I had finished, she asked me to play it again and this time stopped me to correct me in a few places. Then, she and her brother and a family friend who was also present excused themselves and went downstairs. I could hear tearful voices and hushed negotiations in Telugu, which I did not understand at the time. Finally, after about twenty minutes, her brother returned and said that she had accepted me and that I should come the next day at 9 AM. As I was leaving, he mentioned that their elder brother, also a violinist, had unexpectedly passed away just a few days before my letter had arrived. He had fallen ill and died while playing a concert with my teacher, and she was now in a state of depression and had stopped playing her violin. Their long-awaited tour of the United States, which had been scheduled for that September and October, had had to be cancelled.

My teacher would subsequently relate the story of my arrival with great melodrama. At the time I had first come to learn with her, she said, she had been in the throes of a vow: she would never touch the violin again in mourning for her brother. She was prepared to reject me from the first. Relatives and concerned friends prevailed upon her to give me a chance. Having a student from America, they reasoned, was a great boon: handsome payment, prestige, and possible chances to go to America loomed in the future. Besides, the American tour she was supposed to make with her brother had just been cancelled, and here was America coming to her. Could she possibly think nothing of it? Affected by this line of reasoning, she thought that after all maybe God was sending her a sign that she should not abandon her violin. She decided she would give me a month, and if I demonstrated no improvement, she would be convinced that I was just an empty sign. According to her telling, on the twenty-ninth day, just as she was losing interest in me, I suddenly showed improvement. She consented to continue teaching me. On that same day, she decided that she would reconcile with her main disciple and adopted son, whom she hadn't seen in ten years after he had married against her wishes. She thus converted the prosaic story of beginning violin lessons into the kind of miraculous story befitting a guru and her disciple.

During the months, and eventually years, I spent studying with her, the exact nature of our relationship was under constant negotiation. She was frustrated by the ways I failed to live up to the ideal of discipleship. I did not live with her; I was in the United States for long periods of time; I had studied with other teachers; my research prevented me from being a single-minded and devoted student. I, meanwhile, wondered whether I was learning enough music and how I could convert the embodied musical knowledge I was gaining into anthropological scholarship. Just what kind of ethnographic practice was discipleship?

Before the rest of the Madras music world, however, we performed the roles of guru and *sisya* (disciple) more seamlessly. Perhaps we both sensed the need to prove our legitimacy. One evening, as we were preparing to leave for a visit, a friend of the family happened to be at my teacher's house. While my teacher was getting ready, I waited, impatiently, checking my watch to see how late we would be. She called out to me to fetch her "specs," and as I got up to do so, the visitor exclaimed with a smile, "You are a typical sisya." At the All India Radio station she made a point of not handling her paycheck herself, telling the director to "hand it over to my sisya." When people asked who I was, she would embark on the full story of how I had come and saved her from abandoning the violin, and how she had taught me "from the beginning," presenting my arrival as a miracle and herself as some kind of miracle worker who was able to make a Karnatic violinist out of recalcitrant Western material. Invariably she would inflate the number of hours we spent together to some extraordinary figure. When I questioned her in private about this and about why she insisted on saying she had taught me from the beginning when, strictly speaking, it wasn't true, she said that the story was more impressive that way and that it was an unnecessary bother to go into a whole explanation of my real history.

In the spring of 1998 a reporter for a Madras newspaper interviewed us for a feature story. When he asked how long she had been teaching me, instead of answering the question, she said, "This is not teaching. This is gurukulavasam" (a mode of teaching and learning in which the disciple lives with the guru for years while the guru imparts musical knowledge). We posed for a photo that was supposed to capture us in the act of gurukulavasam, sitting on a mat with our violins, each facing stiffly outward toward the camera.

I realize now that at that moment I *had* arrived, if not at what I had imagined the authentic role of the disciple to be, then at one of the central oppositions through which Indian classical music, at the beginning of the twenty-first century, has come to be defined. Gurukulavasam (*kurukulavācam*) refers to a method in which the disciple lives with the guru, learning music by a process of slow absorption and serving the guru as a member of his or her household.[1] At the turn of the twenty-first century, the term has acquired a certain semantic density; not only does it refer to a specific sense of fidelity, that of the disciple to the guru, but the enactment of gurukulavasam signifies, at a broader level, a fidelity to "tradition," an adherence to the element that makes this music truly

Indian. Gurukulavasam is imagined as the mode through which the essentially oral tradition of Indian classical music is passed on. This is in distinct opposition to the modes of teaching Western music, which, as the common stereotype goes, "can be played just from looking at a written score." Along with the contrast between orality and writing, a host of other oppositions are commonly drawn to differentiate Indian music from a generalized notion of Western music. Whereas Western music concentrates on technical prowess, Indian music is more "spiritual"; whereas Western music has become secular, Indian music retains its ties to its devotional origins; whereas Western music is primarily instrumental, Indian music is primarily vocal.

Such pronouncements resonate strongly with colonial and Orientalist discourses on India.[2] Lining up "written," "technical," "secular," and "instrumental" on one side and "oral," "spiritual," "devotional," and "vocal" on the other, they map "the West" and "India" as musical opposites, destined never to meet, as T. V. Subba Rao so confidently stated.[3] More precisely, such binaries orchestrate the ways in which Western classical music and Indian classical music, defined by their mutual opposition, are allowed to meet. Thus, Western students learn to approach Indian music as a great "other" classical tradition founded on diametrically opposite values, and they become disciples of Indian musicians because they seek the personal intimacy missing in their Western training; Indian musicians look to the West to improve their technical skills. These oppositions, and the discourse in which they are embedded, are central to the institution of classical music as it is now imagined in India. The emergence of this category of "classical music" and its definition in the context of colonialism, nationalism, and regional politics in South India are the subjects of this book.

In the last decades of the nineteenth century and the first decades of the twentieth, the musical field of South India underwent a series of profound shifts. Toward the end of the nineteenth century, musicians who had previously been supported by the patronage of royal courts or village temples began to move in increasing numbers to the colonial city of Madras (now Chennai) to take advantage of a new patronage structure: musical organizations and institutions run by a concentration of middle- and upper-class, high-caste (mostly Brahmin, but also Chettiar and Mudaliar) professionals working in the fields of law, medicine, civil service, education, and business. New kinds of public space came into being with the concert halls and academies established by this upper-caste elite, who were interested in what they termed the "revival of South India's classical music."[4] This "revival" depended on the selection, from a number of heterogeneous musical traditions, of particular sounds, performance conventions, and repertoire that would come to be identified with the indigenous "classical" music tradition of South India. In controlling the musical institutions of the city and the music-publishing industry, this elite influenced how classical music came to be imagined and defined. The new discourse on classical music—whose assumptions are taken for granted today—combined ideas about art and the artist with a notion of Indianness formed in opposition to the West. It suggested that music had a central role in defining what it meant to be modern while retaining a safely delineated realm called "tradition."

The idea of an indigenous classical music involved a complex maneuver. To be considered "classical," Karnatic music had to be modeled on the classical music of the West, with its notation, composers, compositions, conservatories, and concerts. The use of the English term *classical* for Indian music, beginning in the early decades of the twentieth century, placed it in relation to the art music of Europe. In Europe the term came into use only after 1800, in reference to a particular "golden age" of composers and as a marker of high status (Weber 1984, 175; Goehr 1992, 247).[5] Indian music, by contrast, never had a classical period; from its first use, the term was a marker of cultural status and authenticity whose original referent was not a historical period or particular style, but the West itself.[6] At the same time as South Indian elites emphasized the commensurability of Western and Indian classical music, however, they recognized that in order to be truly Indian, Karnatic music had to be different in reliable and enduring ways. Much of the discourse on music from the early twentieth century revolves around finding and articulating that which set South Indian classical music apart from its counterpart in the West.

The argument of this book is that the voice—the vocal nature of Indian music and its ties to oral tradition—came to stand for this essential difference. In twentieth-century South India the voice came to be associated with Indianness and not Westernness, originality and not reproduction, humanity and not mechanization, tradition and not modernity. What emerged in the twentieth century as a foundation for the idea of an indigenous Indian classical music was a particular *politics of voice* that depended on such associations. It was not just that a certain kind of voice came to be valued, but that the voice itself came to be privileged as Karnatic music's locus of authenticity, the preserver of its tradition in the face of modernity. A number of circumstances attended the emergence of this politics of voice: a current of nationalist thought heavily influenced by Western metaphysical notions of the self as a speaking subject; a social reform movement that stressed the virtues of domesticity and female chastity; the rise of an urban middle class, defined in part by an ideal of "traditional" Indian womanhood and in part by caste politics that privileged a Brahmin vocal tradition over a non-Brahmin instrumental one; the emergence of language-based identities; and the development of technologies of recording, amplifying, and disseminating the voice, such as the gramophone, microphone, and radio.

The valorization of the voice in Karnatic music is part of a distinctly modern set of ideas about music, the self, and Indianness. At issue here is the tension between claims to the primordial significance of the voice and the fact that such claims are made in particular historical and cultural contexts. When twentieth- and twenty-first-century musicians, musicologists, and listeners speak of the "fundamentally vocal" character of Indian music, they often invoke the authority of a "civilizational tradition." The importance of vocalization as a way of knowing, conceptualizing, and expressing music in present-day Karnatic musical practice is seen as a direct continuation of Sanskrit treatises on music, from the sixteenth century and earlier, that emphasize the importance of vocal sound to music making.[7] Imputing an essentially vocal character to Indian music that stretches into the ancient past, these claims have a distinctly Orientalist ring. Positing "Indian music" as an entity removed from history, they ignore the entailments of this music in the project of modernity. In doing so, they exemplify one way in which the voice is ideologized in discourse about classical music in South India. For it is precisely *within* modernity that the voice comes to occupy such a privileged position. In the context of the twentieth-century revival of Karnatic music as one of India's classical music traditions, precolonial Sanskrit treatises on vocal sound get appropriated by a set of discourses about the voice associated with colonial modernity and the emergence of bourgeois subjectivity.

Rather than approaching modernity either as a European invention or as simply a time period or a process ("modernization") through which all societies eventually pass—perspectives which essentially depoliticize the project of modernity—recent scholarship has argued that many of the institutions and ideas associated with modernity were linked to colonial modes of knowledge production and structures of power (Chakrabarty 2000; Chatterjee 1993). Modernity is thus not a purely Western or European project; on the contrary, it is constituted in and by the colonial encounter. “Staging the modern,” writes Timothy Mitchell, “has always required the non-modern, the space of colonial difference” (2000, xxvi). In order to perform its authority, modernity must constantly oppose itself to what it conceives of as nonmodern. Modernity in this sense is not a creation of the West but of an interaction between the West and the non-West. Its staging “does not occur only in the West . . . to be imitated later in the non-West. Its authority and presence can only be produced across the space of geographical distance. It is this very displacement of the West that enables modernity to be staged as ‘the West’ ” (24).

Modernity has been characterized variously as a set of institutions that constitute a civil society or public sphere; a set of technological developments that produce certain effects; a shift from feudal to capitalist modes of production; a set of ideas about the nature of time, history, society, and the individual. In this last sense, modernity can be seen as a discursive formation which has naturalized particular ways of thinking dependent on a series of familiar binaries: secular vs. sacred, content vs. form, rational vs. nonrational, mind vs. body, public vs. private, and, not least, tradition vs. modernity. Indeed, one of the most powerful ways in which the project of modernity operates is by defining itself as representative of rationality, progress, change, and universality, in opposition to “tradition,” a category which comes to stand for all that is irrational or emotional, stagnant, ancient, and local (Bauman and Briggs 2003). Such oppositions gain currency, of course, by being mapped as the difference between the West and the non-West.

The modern subject is one who ideally holds these poles—the rational and the emotional, the universal and the particular—in tension with each other; this tension is what produces the effect of interiority characteristic of modern subjectivity. Interiority, as Dipesh Chakrabarty has suggested, “comes to be constituted by a tension between individual-private experiences and desires (feelings, emotions, sentiments) and a universal-public reason” (Mitchell 2000, 63). As crucial to modern conceptions of the individual self as the rational, disengaged stance is the notion of an “inner voice” that stands for instinct and emotional life; in fact, as Charles Taylor has suggested, they developed together (1989, 390). The modern conception of the self, he argues, involves a localization *within* the subject of what was previously seen as existing *between* the knower or agent and the world (186); the self comes to be seen as a repository of inwardness (284), of inner emotions, ideas, and desires that need to be “expressed.” Modern subjectivity hinges on the notion of voice as a metaphor for self and authenticity, and on the various techniques—musical, linguistic, and literary—by which particular voices are made to seem authentic. The modern idea of art depends on this notion of expression as a creative, original, individual act, as opposed to imitation or mimesis, which comes to be seen as merely reproductive, belonging more in the realm of craft or tradition.

The fact that this inner domain of self, originality, and authenticity is figured as a voice is not coincidental, for such ideas of the self and art go hand-in-hand with a certain way of imagining language and the role of the voice. As Bauman and Briggs have compellingly argued, constructions of language and tradition played a central role in the modernist project: one crucial way in which the modern subject of the European enlightenment identified himself was by differentiating his own language—rational language, purified of unnecessary associations and suited to expressing supposedly universal concepts—from the language of lower-class "folk" or "masses," which was mired in custom and superstition (2003, 10–12). Purifying language in this sense, making it rational, meant emphasizing referentiality over all other functions of language; it meant drawing a line between content and form, and privileging the former. Thus, reason comes to be defined in opposition to rhetoric (27), just as poetry and "oral tradition" come to be defined in opposition to rationality and "literature" (70–72, 103–4).

These ideas about language combine two ways of imagining the voice. On the one hand, the association of voice with agency and sincerity is at the heart of notions of the rational subject; the voice in this sense is imagined as referring to, or directly expressive of, an individual, interiorized self. On the other hand, such a notion of voice is formed in relation to other voices that come to be labeled in their plurality "oral tradition"—those voices which call attention to performance, sound, and materiality and thus fail to privilege referentiality. The category of oral tradition and the association of orality with simplified cognitive, social, and political characteristics are central to the discourse of modernity (Bauman and Briggs 2003, 107).[8] Within this discourse, voice becomes a powerful trope of the modern, rational subject at the same time as its sonic and material manifestations are seen as standing for authenticity and tradition. It is precisely this dual imagining of voice that is at work in the twentieth-century definition of South Indian classical music.

In any work that takes modernity outside of the West as its focus, there is a tension between finding modernity and finding indigenous resistance to the culture of modernity, which Joel Robbins has characterized as the problem of "tacking back and forth between claims of convergence and divergence, homogenization and differentiation" (2001, 901). One would not want to view the narrative I present here as simply an imposition of the culture of modernity onto indigenous ideas and practices. However, it is equally risky to identify the institution of South Indian classical music as indigenous resistance to modernity, for such a move would erase the relations of power and regimes of knowledge production that have created the power and prestige of classical music in South India and enabled its passage to the West. Rather than identify a "local" or "alternative" modernity, I examine the kinds of claims *to* modernity that are made in a particular context. Deferring the question of whether such claims constitute imposition or resistance, I instead focus on the ways that claims to modernity are made by certain groups of people for specific purposes; claims to modernity in this sense are claims to power.

To say that the valorization of the voice in Karnatic music is a modern phenomenon is not to make an argument about the "invention of tradition." Such an idea unhelpfully sets up a choice between "invented" and "real" or "authentic" traditions. Indeed, as Marilyn Ivy has suggested, the idea of the invention of tradition also dangerously posits a world of discourse as separable from reality: "To say that all tradition is invented is still to rely on a choice between invention and authenticity, between fiction and reality, between discourse and history" (1995, 21). It forces one to separate what is traditional from what is imported, to see things in terms of an imposition of Western concepts and ideas onto indigenous musical material. In fact, the institution of classical music in South India—not only discourse about it but the very sound and practice of the music—has been produced in and through the colonial encounter. Thus the sounds, practices, and categories I discuss in this book are neither properly Western nor Indian, but specifically colonial in the sense that they position the West and India in relation to each other.[9]

Embedded within the specific arguments of this book is a more general claim. In identifying a particular politics of voice that emerged in twentieth-century South India, I am pointing to the need to treat the voice as a historical and anthropological object: something locatable within a particular time and place. I seek to bring the sonic, material aspects of voice into relation with issues of representation, subjectivity, and agency. Linguistic anthropologists have for several decades been concerned with "regimes of language" or "language ideologies," that is, bodies of culturally constructed knowledge about how language works and how it should be used. Language ideology "sets the boundary for what counts as language and what does not, and the terms, techniques, and modalities of citing and hearing" (Inoue 2003, 157).[10] Ideas about the voice (what it should sound like, where it comes from, how it relates to a singer's or speaker's body, its status in relation to writing and recorded sound, etc.) are undoubtedly part of language ideology, just as they are part of a perhaps broader regime or politics of voice that includes but is not exhausted by language. One might say that ideologies of voice, in many cases, set the boundary for what separates language from music, as well as for what counts as communication. Most crucial, ideologies of voice determine how and where we locate subjectivity and agency.

The voice has been most explicitly thematized as an object of study in psychoanalytic writing. Psychoanalytic theories of voice emphasize its primordiality, its privileged role in creating a sense of self. These notions find their clearest expression in Jacques Lacan's formulation of the voice as one of several "partial objects" which cannot be considered either part of the body or fully separate from it, but that are also partial because they represent only part of the function with which they are associated (1977). The very partiality of these objects is what gives them a primary role in creating a sense of subjectivity: "It is what enables them to be the 'stuff,' or rather the lining, . . . of the very object that one takes to be the subject of consciousness."[11] Responding to such formulations, recent work in musicology and in literary and film studies on the relationship between gender, voice, and embodiment has considered the place of the female voice in the Western cultural imagination and the stakes involved in its association with or disassociation from the female body.[12] Although much of this work provides a valuable critique of the ways the female voice has been essentialized either as seductive, dangerous, irrational, or alternatively as a site of women's potential liberation, its focus remains strictly within a Euro-American context and in relation to particular psychoanalytic paradigm. Building on these critiques, one might ask: how does the voice assume different significances in different times and places? What are the technologies by which experiences of voice are constructed and metaphors of voice made to seem natural?

While psychoanalytic approaches rely heavily on the assumption of the voice's primordial status, its prehistoric quality, social science has generally limited discussions of voice to the metaphorical level of self-representation. In anthropology especially, the voice, while not always explicitly thematized, has been identified as a vehicle of empowerment, self-representation, authentic knowledge, and agency. The assumption that underlies this metaphorization of voice, a central tenet of Western philosophy, is that the speaking subject is the ground of subjectivity and the source of agency. As media theorist Jonathan Sterne suggests, "Face-to-face conversation, embodied in mutual dialogue between speaking subjects, serves not only as the classic field situation for anthropologists, but also as the standard for judging the originality and authenticity of utterances and of communication in general" (2003, 20, 342). In this metaphysics the voice is fetishized, made to stand as an authentic source apart from the social relations that have produced it. In becoming strictly a metaphor for consciousness, voice and its opposites, silence and deafness, come to "inhabit our philosophic and political discourse as nothing more than clichés" (348).

Valuable critiques of fetishization of the voice have been made by postcolonial theorists and historians. In this regard, Gayatri Spivak's essay "Can the Subaltern Speak?" (1988) is programmatic in its critique of the ideological underpinnings of the project of recovering lost or subaltern voices. More recently, Mrinhalini Sinha has pointed out the problematic nature of the project of "allowing women's voices to be heard" as an antidote to male-dominated histories and historiography (1996). The desire for a "pure" feminist consciousness, she writes, "serves, in the end, to remove the feminist subject from the history of her production within interconnected axes of gender, race, class/caste, nation, or sexuality" (498). She suggests that one look instead at the ways women "come into voice" and at the particular voices that women assume. Such an approach, she maintains, "would have to take into account both the historical context which made possible the identity of the Indian woman and the particular strategies by which women learned to speak in the voice of the Indian woman" (479).

Sinha's approach is useful in that it shows the conscious construction of voice, the ways women learn to speak so that they will be heard in an arena already overdetermined by colonialism and nationalist politics. It shifts the focus away from the notion that the voice of the Indian woman was simply and naturally there, just waiting to be expressed, toward the idea that such voices were assumed strategically at a particular historical moment. Sinha thus illuminates much about the politics of gender, caste, race, and feminism at the time. At a theoretical level, she suggests that voices—here, the voice of the Indian woman—are socially produced, that the link between voice and agency or self-expression is complicated by questions of genre, audience, and historical location. However, she leaves the category of voice itself untouched. Indeed, the sense in which she and her historical interlocutors use the term *voice* is almost exclusively that of political self-representation, wherein voice is essentially a metaphor for representation in writing and in a middle-class, English-speaking public milieu.

Thus, while critiques such as these begin to challenge the notion of agency based on the model of the speaking subject, they do little to challenge the other part of that model, which has always treated the voice itself as secondary, as a mere vehicle for the expression of referential content. In order to move beyond the clichéd metaphor of voice as representation, one needs to focus on the sound and materiality of the voice, and to consider the way those sounds and material practices of voice are put into service in the creation of ideologies *about* the voice. In this regard, I find my concerns to be parallel to those of the media theorist Friedrich Kittler, who in *Discourse Networks 1800/1900* (1990) in effect historicizes the voice by considering the conditions of its production and dissemination. He traces the notion of an "inner voice," central to the emergence of what he calls modern subjectivity in the West, back to certain practices of reading, writing, and pedagogy. For Kittler, the inner voice, based on the aural memory of the mother's voice, which is associated with new family organization and new reading practices emerging in Germany at the end of the eighteenth century, is radically historical, not a psychological universal. Around 1900, when it became possible to record voices, Kittler argues, the concept of the inner voice and its accompanying forms of subjectivity were no longer available in the same way. The notion of a "discourse network" as a network that links bodies, sounds, writing and other technologies, and forms of authority very usefully draws attention to the fact that philosophical ideas are grounded in the material practices and technologies through which voices become audible.

Rather than starting with a universal concept of voice and its importance, then, I look for moments when self-conscious discourse about the voice arises. Rather than considering the voice as a natural means of self-expression, I ask how voices are constructed through practice and how music entails particular ideologies of voice. Musicology and ethnomusicology, as disciplines that focus on sound, have generally treated the voice as a means or technology for producing music. I propose that we reverse this idea and examine music as a means or technology for producing the voice, in both a sonic and an ideological sense. In doing so, we perform the critical anthropological move of denaturalizing the voice and thus open up the study of musical sound and practice as *productive* of particular subjects or subject positions, rather than merely *reflective* of social structures or *expressive* of identities. What new forms of subjectivity and identity are enabled by changing conceptions and practices of voice?

In addressing this question, I consider the material and sonic aspects of the voice in relation to the way voice operates as a culturally created metaphor. Focusing on regimes or ideologies of voice requires an examination of the relationship between sound or form, on the one hand, and meaning or function within a discursive realm on the other. It requires linking "a phenomenological concern with the voice as the embodiment of spoken and sung performance . . . [with] a more metaphoric sense of voice as a key representational trope for social position and power" (Feld and Fox 1994, 26). Recognizing the socially constructed nature of musical sound is essential to what Steven Feld, Aaron Fox, Thomas Porcello, and David Samuels call "vocal anthropology" (2004). In many cases, they suggest, song or musical sound allows for a "ritualized, explicit consideration . . . of the voice as the material embodiment of social ideology and experience" (332). In other words, it is the capacity of the voice to be both iconic (able to embody particular qualities) and indexical (able to point to or index particular subjectivities or identities) that makes it so powerful as a metaphor.[13] Precisely because voices are embodied and repeatedly performed, they can serve as deeply felt markers of identity, class, caste, gender, social position, and nationality. In this sense one can speak of a "politics of voice" as a set of vocal practices as well as a set of ideas *about* the voice and its significance.

The notion of vocal anthropology, as elaborated by Feld, Fox, Porcello, and Samuels, opens up a variety of productive ways to link the study of musical and linguistic sound with social identity through attention to the voice. While there is much in common between my project and theirs, my emphasis here is slightly different. Feld and his coauthors link the voice to both nature and resistance, assuming that the significance of the voice arises from universal human experience and identifying the larger purpose of vocal anthropology as the study of voices which express or embody resistant identities or which "talk back" to hegemonic power structures (2004, 341–42).[14] In part because I examine ideas about the voice associated with an art-music tradition that has achieved a kind of hegemonic status, I am wary of assuming either the link between voice and resistance or the naturalness of voice as a metaphor. Instead, I use the concept of "politics of voice" or "ideology of voice" to emphasize that practices of voice, while creative, are also a mode of discipline—embodied and performed—through which subjects are produced. I suggest that ideas *about* the voice and its significance are motivated by historically and culturally locatable practices of voice, rather than by supposedly universal bodily experience. And since ideologies of voice determine what voices come to be heard and how, understanding them as particular and changeable is essential to understanding the kinds of subjects and politics they both enable and silence.

The chapters that follow trace the emergence of a particular politics of voice by focusing on a series of moments when voice specifically comes into question or gets redefined. The first two chapters explore the staging of the voice in musical sound and performance practice. Chapter 1 concerns the career of the violin, which arrived in South India around 1800 in the hands of British and French colonists and was adapted to Karnatic music so successfully that by the early twentieth century it was regarded as an indispensable accompaniment to the voice—indeed, as an instrument capable of "reproducing" the voice. In the twentieth century, the violin came to be seen simultaneously as the modernizer of Karnatic music and as the preserver of Karnatic music's authenticity, as embodied in the centrality of the voice. What is the significance of having a colonial instrument in this position?

Rather than suggesting a history of Westernization, the story of the violin points to the emergence of a musical practice and discourse that is specifically colonial. In both its role as an accompanying instrument and its central role in experimental fusions of Indian and Western music, the violin becomes a key instrument for the negotiation of what is Indian and what is Western and of the relationship between them. I take into account the *instrumentality* of musical instruments, that is, the fact that they are not just vehicles for producing sound but also social instruments, instruments for thinking about music and its significance. In this respect I suggest the importance of engaging with performance and sound. Close engagement with performance, as Carolyn Abbate has noted in her subversive readings of opera, can disrupt the certainty of an authorial voice or a prevailing interpretation; opera as a text or musical score and opera as a performance produce very different notions of the authority of male and female voices (1991). Prevailing explanations and descriptions of Karnatic music emphasize the vocal nature of Karnatic music and relegate the violin to the status of mere accompaniment, a colonial add-on to an already existent musical tradition. In doing so, they disregard the complex mimetic relationship between violin and voice that emerges in performance, where the violin effectively functions to *stage* the voice—not merely to reproduce it but to produce it.

Chapter 2 moves to actual stagings of Karnatic music that took place in the newly developing contexts of urban concert halls and music schools in Madras in the early twentieth century. The emergence of Madras as a center of musical culture was a result of the shifts brought about by colonial rule. The annexation of princely states by the British and the consolidation of British authority over temples deeply affected patterns of musical patronage in royal courts and temples outside of Madras city in the nineteenth century. By the middle of that century, most of the princely states of South India had been effectively taken over by the British crown; although kings continued to rule in these states, their political power was diminished by the increasing centralization of the British colonial government. Tanjore, taken under British administrative rule in 1779, was officially annexed in 1856; Mysore was taken over in 1831.[15]

The consolidation of British rule in South India had direct consequences on the very nature of patronage itself. The old regime, as both Nicholas Dirks and Arjun Appadurai have noted, operated according to the principle of the gift: the ability to give gifts was a fundamental sign of a king's sovereignty, and gifts were the dynamic medium that constituted political relations (Dirks 1993, 179–80; Appadurai 1981, 63). Under British colonial rule, however, the flow of gifts was interrupted even as the British tried to keep the "little kings" in positions of apparent power as a kind of "native aristocracy." The little kings, under British administrative control, were settled permanently on their land as *zamindars*, or landlords, with the idea that they would collect revenue and act as middlemen between the British colonial government and South Indian peasants (Dirks 1993, 181). If the little kingdoms felt the effects of colonial interference by the late eighteenth century, so did Hindu temples, another center of musical patronage. According to Appadurai, the formation of the Board of Revenue in 1789 marked the increasing bureaucratic centralization of the colonial state and the change of the East India Company from a trading power to a political regime (1981, 109). With this came the decision that the collection and distribution of all temple revenues should be centralized. Whereas kings and temple trustees (*dharmakartas*) had once administered the affairs of individual temples as they saw fit, the colonial government was by the early nineteenth century auditing the use of temple funds, and temple-related disputes were increasingly brought before the Anglo-Indian judicial system. Dharmakartas were reduced to the status of public servants (ibid., 139, 165).

Madras City served as the center of colonial administration and grew as the status of princely states and temple cities (such as Madurai) diminished. As a result of the Karnatic wars in the late 1700s, the European military presence in Madras increased to several thousand; at the same time, the nonmilitary colonial population swelled in proportion (Neild 1979, 223). As a trading power, the East India Company had depended, for much of the seventeenth and eighteenth centuries, on "company merchants," who came from the traditional mercantile Chetty caste, for its supply of goods (Arasaratnam 1979, 20–21). Many of these merchants bought land in Madras city and built temples, acting as patrons of music (ibid., 23–24). After the mid-1700s, however, as the East India Company began to consolidate itself as a colonial power, local political influence and social prestige was transferred to a new class of men, the *dubashes*, who were employed by colonial officials to act as go-betweens, translators, personal servants, and brokers (Neild 1984, 4). Most dubashes were from the Vellala caste (landholding agriculturalists) and came to Madras from the surrounding villages to seek employment in the colonial administration (ibid., 12–13). As dubashes, they enjoyed considerable wealth and political power, in many cases acting as little kings in their own right. They built large garden houses in the suburbs of Madras, often serving as the dharmakartas of city temples (while retaining their ties to the temples in their native villages) and patronizing musicians and dancers (ibid, 16).[16]

By the early nineteenth century, as the character of British colonial involvement in South India changed to a more centralized bureaucracy, the dubashes lost their jobs and their privileged status (Neild 1984, 18). The reorganization of the East India Company between 1812 and 1832 brought its profits under the administrative control of the British Crown. During this period, and especially after the official declaration of the Crown's authority in 1858, Brahmins, rather than Vellalas, were actively recruited to fill civil service positions. Many of these Brahmins came from the Tamil and Telugu subcaste of Smartas, who had long claimed high ritual status as priests and scholars, and settled in the Madras neighborhood of Mylapore (Hancock 1999, 52). Madras High School was founded in 1841 to train a native elite, mostly Brahmins, in the skills needed for filling civil-service posts (Suntharalingam 1974, 62–63). Although traditional mercantile castes in Madras, such as the Chettiars, were clearly wealthier, Brahmins, working as clerks, lawyers, and publicists by the later decades of the 1800s, were beginning to claim political and social influence within the city. Meanwhile, musicians were moving to Madras from the princely states, particularly Tanjore, in great numbers between 1850 and 1920 in search of new employment.

Music was used by Brahmin elites to create a kind of public sphere in Madras and a sense of common outlook. By 1900, Smarta Brahmins in Mylapore had created a network of voluntary associations, the Radha-Krishna Bhajanas, which gathered in homes and community halls to sing *bhajans*, or devotional songs (Singer 1972, 200–205). Mary Hancock suggests that *bhakti*, individualized voluntaristic devotion, with its universalist ethos, was appropriated by Brahmins as a kind of expression of bourgeois nationalism, a "hallmark of new, nationalized, and self-consciously modern elite sensibilities" (1999, 57–58).[17] Music *sabhas*, private organizations that sponsored concerts, were another hallmark of such sensibilities. In Madras at the beginning of the twentieth century sabha owners became the new patrons of Karnatic music.

The rise of public concerts and commercial music making in Madras spawned new standards of taste, embedded in a set of conventions of voice brought about by the mechanism of the microphone and codified in the canonization of a group of saint-composers who have come almost exclusively to represent the voice of Karnatic music. Chapter 2 argues that the establishment of a canon depends not only on the selection and valuation of particular repertoire, but also on the establishment of techniques of physical staging and modes of listening—disciplines that are as embodied as they are intellectual. The emergence of concerts halls, music schools, and university music departments in the early twentieth century was linked to the emergence of new kinds of performing and listening subjects. Just as the concert hall entailed a new structure of presentation that demanded the clear separation of musicians from audience, the new concert format that developed demanded the separation of musical compositions from the contexts of their performance. The celebration of the saint-composer Thyagaraja as the primary voice of Karnatic music entailed a shift from compositions tied to contexts of performance to compositions that were imagined to have their origins in a personalized, timeless devotion. At the same time, the microphone, used in concert halls beginning in the 1930s, was not only a technology of amplification but also an instrument that enabled the emergence of new kinds of voices and performing subjects.

Chapters 3 and 4 discuss the emergence of a particularly modern ideology of voice inflected by both gender and caste politics in the mid-twentieth century. The discourse of social reform that arose in the late nineteenth century, associated with elite nationalist thought, was central to notions of what made music and dance "classical" and on ideas of their place in a new, urban, bourgeois order of things. Among social reform projects, those grouped under the "woman question"—sati, widow remarriage, child marriage, the *devadasi* issue—loomed large because the status of women and the status of the nation were linked in nationalist thought. The definition of the "devadasi system"—a general term for a variety of ways in which women were employed by temples as musicans, dancers, and ritual performers—as an object of social reform provides a particularly good example of the way social reform and cultural "revival" were intertwined. The Women's Indian Association (WIA), founded in 1917 by Annie Besant, Margaret Cousins, and Dorothy Jinarajadasa, was explicitly concerned with such issues; the advancement of India as a nation, they felt, depended on improving the status and situation of its women. Indeed, it was another WIA leader, Muthulakshmi Reddy, who authored the measures for the Devadasi Dedication Abolition Act. In the discourse of social reform the devadasi system came to be viewed as synonymous with prostitution, while the arts of music and dance practiced by devadasis were seen as needing to be rescued and placed in the hands of "respectable family women."

Chapter 3 is concerned with the emergence of a set of ideas about what constituted a "natural" or true voice, the relationship between the voice and the body, and the relationship between the singing voice and the speaking voice. This politics of voice was emergent in certain conventions of performance established in the moment when upper-caste, "respectable," "family" women, who previously did not perform in public, began to sing on the concert stage and make gramophone recordings. In discourse about these female musicians, the natural voice and the chaste female body were linked. Those female voices that represented India's classical music traditions were imagined as giving voice at once to an abstract notion of art and to the body of "Mother India." I draw a parallel in this chapter between the literal domestication of music as a sign of bourgeois respectability, its connection to a discourse about family values, and the interiorization of music within the body in terms of performance practice. The modern notion of the artist that underlay the revival of Karnatic music as South India's classical music depended on this new sense of interiority.

In the mid-twentieth century the idea of the "natural" voice was elaborated as well in the context of debates about the relationship between language and music and the role of language in music. Such debates emerged in the context of a broad current of Tamil revivalism, embodied in the Dravidian and non-Brahmin movements that arose to challenge elite nationalist discourse. Tamil revivalists rallied around the figure of Tamiḻttāy, or Mother Tamil, whom they imagined as needing protection from the onslaught of "Aryan" culture and languages.[18] Along with language, music became one of the central fields in which claims to Aryan and Dravidian difference and Brahmin and non-Brahmin difference were made in the 1930s and 1940s. The Tamil music movement—a demand that the classical music repertoire include more songs in Tamil rather than Telugu or Sanskrit—although not originally conceived as a non-Brahmin movement, came to be strongly associated with protest against the Brahmin domination of classical music.

Chapter 4 argues that the discourse about music's meaning that emerged in this context signaled a new set of discourses not only about the relationship between music and language but ultimately about the singing and listening subject. In the 1930s and 1940s, as the modern idea of music as a language began to dominate nationalist discourse, language became the central metaphor for articulating the relationship between voice and the singing or listening subject. Once this analogy had taken hold, the categories "classical language" and "mother tongue" increasingly dominated debates about how music should be defined and experienced, as did ideas about the "meaning" of music. Was music akin to a mother tongue or a universal, aesthetically motivated language? Was the voice best conceived of as an aestheticized instrument that required cultivation or as a transparent representation of oneself? Those on both sides of these debates sought to endow the singing voice with interiority precisely by comparing music to language; the concern with meaning relied on an opposition between real music and mere acrobatics, the threat of purely physical, automatic action, pure sound, exteriority. This discourse, relying as it did on the opposition between interiority and exteriority so central to modern concepts of the self, was essentially occupied with the problem of how to create modern musical subjects.

Central to modern self-definition is the notion of a rational, enlightened self who can appreciate but is not bound by tradition and is therefore an appropriate custodian of tradition. In terms of voice, this means that the modern subject is one who can quote, refer to, or preserve tradition while standing outside it; the quoting voice marks itself as modern at the same time as it marks the quoted voice as other than modern (Inoue 2002; Bakhtin 1981). This logic, in combination with certain technologies of preservation and recording, makes the notion of an originary oral tradition possible. The production of music and musical knowledge in South India in the twentieth century was shaped by the explosion of printing and technologies of sound recording and broadcasting. Far from being incidental technologies used to record or preserve oral traditions, printing and recording were crucial to the creation of a notion of oral tradition as an originary source that needed to be called on or preserved. In chapters 5 and 6, I examine various claims to voice and oral tradition that surround the composer and the guru, two figures central to the definition of Karnatic music as a classical tradition.

The notion of the composer, chapter 5 suggests, came into being in South Indian music only in the twentieth century, with the widespread use of notation and the printing of notation and music manuals. With the idea of the composer came other ideas: that of sole authorship, originality, and art for its own sake. Most important, the idea of the composer demanded notation, a way of preserving the original voice of the composer from forces that might change or alter it. Chapter 5 explores these ideas by looking at a debate about the legitimacy of a particular composer that erupted in the 1980s and working backward from this moment to examine conflicting ideas about notation from the early twentieth century. Notation was seen both as a guarantor of literacy, and therefore of classical status, and as a transparent and legible representation of orality, and therefore of Indianness. While an originary oral tradition came to be privileged as a sign of the Indianness of the music, the idea of the composer was crucial to proving its legitimacy as one of the classical musics of the world. A contradictory set of anxieties about the voice is at work here: the fear that the voice could be lost if *not* captured by writing coexists with the fear that the voice could be lost precisely by being *completely* captured by writing. Thus, along with the imagination of a pre-existent, somehow pure oral tradition also come the notions of the sublime and the ineffable, the idea that the real power of music cannot be expressed by notation or words.

These anxieties about the voice are elaborated as well in the uneasy coexistence of human embodiment and mechanical mimesis as models of authenticity in contemporary discourse about Karnatic music. In chapter 6, I explore the relationship between technologies of sound reproduction and the mode of learning from a guru, focusing on moments when ideas about voice and music and when practices of listening and performing seem to change in conjunction with technologies of recording and broadcasting. For elites interested in the "revival" of South India's classical music, gurukulavasam was problematic because it defied standardization and preserved idiosyncrasy, but it was also desirable because it seemed to embody a particularly Indian mode of disseminating and acquiring musical knowledge, an oral tradition that defied writing. Meanwhile, sound reproduction, correctly channeled, was seen as a potential tool in the project of developing a standardized body of theory and practice, of making Karnatic music commensurate with other great musical systems of the world.

The concept of sound fidelity, as Jonathan Sterne argues in relation to the history of sound recording in the West, is a social construct, reflecting more the way technologies were conceived than the actual relation of a sound to its source (2003, 219). In chapter 6, I suggest that the concept of sound fidelity in the South Indian context is imagined in relation to and through a distinctly postcolonial sense of fidelity to tradition. To be sure, the technologies of sound recording and broadcasting created disruptions in earlier modes of teaching, performing, and listening, but there is also a way in which desire for the traditional is projected out of the new technologies themselves. Instead of narrating the takeover of "tradition" by "modern" technologies, I demonstrate how ideas about tradition and authenticity were themselves formed in the encounter with such technologies. This is not to argue for technological determinism but rather to suggest a focus on the ways that technologies both shape and are shaped by local politics and forms of knowledge.

Finally: what is at stake in this project? The fraught nature of any research about Karnatic music was made clear to me one evening in Madurai, in 1998, when I was discussing the Tamil music movement with a musician friend. His father, a distinguished scholar of Tamil, had apparently been listening from the verandah as we talked. After about fifteen minutes, he stormed in and asked in anger what the point (*nōkkam*) of my researching this topic was. What kind of conclusion (*poruḷ*) was I going to draw from it? Was I going to tell how Brahmins had taken Tamil music and translated it into Sanskrit, and how the Brahmins never acknowledged their non-Brahmin teachers? Was I going to take a side? Or was it all just amusement (*vēṭikkai*) for my professors?[19] As I prepared to stammer out an answer, he drew himself up and uttered the following verse from the Tirukkural:[20]

Epporuḷ yār yār vāyk kēṭpinum apporuḷ meypporuḷ kāṇpaṭu aṟivu.
Epporuḷ ettaṉmait tāyiṉum apporuḷ meypporuḷ kāṇpaṭu aṟivu.
[Whatever thing from whosever mouth one may have heard that thing a true thing to see is knowledge.
Whatever thing in whatever state it may be that thing a true thing to see is knowledge.]

The tension and anger in his voice dissolved as he assumed the voice of the ancient Tamil sage Tiruvalluvar. The archaic and proverbial sound of the words, mysteriously different and yet recognizable as Tamil, removed them from everyday speech, evoking the ancient Tamil past. Their alliteratively poetic sound invited repetition and demanded interpretation; their allure was in the fact that they remained, even after translation, slightly ambiguous. These words imply that truth is not simply found but created actively by the knowing subject, who picks out what she hears or sees as the truth from many possible (and often conflicting) versions, both written and aural. Finding *mey* (truth) can thus never be mere vēṭikkai.

Although his anger faded, his message remained clear: any ethnography or history of Karnatic music had to come to terms with the exclusions that the consolidation of classical music had brought about. Many people with whom I discussed my project in Madras agreed that Karnatic music is "more classical" now than it ever has been before. By "classical," they meant exclusive, dominated by Brahmins and Brahmin ideals, associated with conservative cultural politics, composition oriented, standardized, rule bound. They meant that the classicalness of the music was not a given characteristic but an imposed set of values. As Karnatic music has become more exclusive, however, it has also become more available to the general public through new media: cassettes, radio, Tamil cinema. Framed within a thoroughly culturalist discourse, it operates in a larger public sphere precisely as a sign of culture, tradition, and conservative values.

If the consolidation of a discourse about classical music served nationalist purposes in the early twentieth century, it now serves the needs of a generation of South Indians who have migrated to the West. Karnatic music is now transported on a large scale to the United States, Canada, Britain, and Australia, where it has come to signify tradition and Indian culture. With the migration of thousands of upper-caste, mostly Brahmin South Indians to the United States in the last few decades, Karnatic music has also, through its identification with culture, become a safeguard of difference; it is there to insure that although East and West may meet, there will always be a realm in which they can be kept safely separate. Hindu temples, music schools, and music organizations have sprouted around the country to feed the growing demand of nonresident Indians for the music of their motherland. A new pattern of patronage has developed, with software engineers and doctors serving as temple trustees and sponsors for concert tours. Cleveland, Ohio, which sports a world-renowned music festival in honor of the South Indian composer Thyagaraja, whose attendance far exceeds that of the original festival in Tiruvaiyaru, has earned the half-joking title, "the Second Tanjavur."[21]

A by-product of this efflorescence is the association of Karnatic music with a pure, original, Indian Hindu culture. For instance, in 1997 the right-leaning magazine *Hinduism Today* featured a didactic centerfold presumably meant for the children of immigrants growing up in the United States.[22] Through a calculated juxtaposition of images it purports to show such children what "their" culture is really about and how it is different from Western culture: a disco scene with boys and girls dancing together in jeans is side-by-side with a picture of a woman dressed in a sari and facing her husband with hands together in the "traditional Indian greeting"; a picture of a marching band is placed beside a picture of a classical concert party; below, on the "Indian" side, are the words "the way Indian culture prefers it."

To answer the question so passionately thrown at me that evening in Madurai, then: the purpose of the project I have attempted here is to oppose culturalist appropriation by revealing the complex political encounters from which the institution of classical Karnatic music emerged. I focus on the appearance of particular practices of and attitudes about music that have become identified with the notion of classical music in South India to suggest that, far from being natural or purely aesthetically motivated manifestations of an essentially Indian sensibility, they are the products of a particular colonial and postcolonial history.[23]

If one of the goals of this project is to critique the formation of a musical canon in South India, it is equally concerned with the ways that music—especially that which is labeled "art music" or "classical music"—has been placed in our own academy. Indian classical music has a canonical place in ethnomusicology; its status as an art or classical music was what allowed many ethnomusicology programs in the West to argue in the 1950s and 1960s that their field was legitimate, indeed, commensurate with musicology. Ethnomusicology embraced the idea of a musical tradition that seemed to be framed in familiar terms—composers, compositions, concerts, virtuoso performers, a musicological tradition of its own—and yet utterly different in its musical sensibility and logic. By uncritically borrowing Indian nationalist and postcolonial discourse, ethnomusicology elided the colonial history that made the category "Indian classical music" possible.

While ethnomusicology was embracing Indian classical music as part of India's "great tradition," anthropology, at least in regard to South Asia, was busy developing its own canon around the "little traditions": those practices and traditions, mostly oral and nonstandardized, associated with the folk or common people rather than with elites.[24] Meanwhile, because of the way music has been framed in our academy and in our society at large as something to be studied and "mastered" only by those with specialized knowledge, anything relating to music or sound generally fell outside of anthropology's focus. Indian classical music was thus, like Western classical music, constructed as an object fit for musicological study but distinctly unfit for anthropological treatment.

One of the most important aims of this project, then, is to bring music, generally, and Indian classical music in particular, within the purview of anthropology. The project is by necessity both historical and ethnographic in its attempt to dislodge Indian classical music from the musicological discourse within which it has persistently been contained. Practices of musical performance and cultures of listening are crucial as domains in which modernity is staged and embodied and in which claims to authenticity are made. In the chapters that follow, I endeavor to show how India became, in the words of Margaret Cousins, "the kingdom of the Voice," and what such a claim might mean.[25]

1 Gone Native?

TRAVELS OF THE VIOLIN IN SOUTH INDIA

No other instrument is so powerful as the Violin.
—T. K. Jayarama Iyer (1965)

Unlike the golden age of India, which Orientalist accounts place in the precolonial era, the golden age of Karnatic music occurred, according to conventional accounts, at the peak of colonialism, the early to mid-nineteenth century. The so-called trinity of composers—Thyagaraja (1767–1847), Syama Sastri (1762–1827), and Muthuswamy Dikshitar (1776–1835)—who are said to have revolutionized the sound and practice of Karnatic music were all active during this period. Even more extraordinary is the fact that while they were composing their masterpieces, a new instrument was changing the sound, practice, and repertoire of Karnatic music: the European violin. Brought to South India circa 1800 by British and French colonial officials and visitors to the princely courts, the violin was taken up and, shortly after its arrival, adapted by South Indian musicians, who gradually altered its tuning, playing position, and technique.

This is no secret: although Karnatic music is unanimously described as a vocal music, the violin is one of its most visible and audible elements, found on almost every concert stage playing solo or doubling the vocalist's line. In twentieth-century South India, the violin not only became a vehicle for conveying Karnatic music to modernity but also came to be seen as essential to preserving Karnatic music's authenticity. These notions of modernity and authenticity, so crucially intertwined in the redefinition of Karnatic music as "classical," are played out in the central role that the violin has had in constructing the voice of Karnatic classical music. This chapter traces the career of the violin in South India from its arrival around 1800 to the present. How did a colonial instrument "gone native" come to be heard as the source of an authentic Karnatic voice?

In its early days in South India the violin was an instrument for Scottish jigs and reels, French dancing songs, and English marching tunes, rather than an instrument of Western classical music. In the beginning of the twentieth century, however, attitudes toward the violin changed, the old "fiddle" image was rejected in favor of a classicized "violin" whose counterpart was the classical violin of the West. The newly classicized violin was central to a discourse about modernity: the violin was seen as the vehicle for bringing Karnatic music into the modern age since it could reproduce the voice with more accuracy than the old-fashioned veena, with more sensitivity than the "mechanical" harmonium, and with a kind of social impunity the sarangi had never had. The defining aspect of the violin was its double character; it was Indian in its ability to reproduce the Karnatic voice, yet Western in its origins and form. These double capacities made the violin the ideal instrument for twentieth-century musical experiments: violin-and-piano, violin-and-Bach, violin-and-computer, and multi-violin concerts that enact and rearticulate the relationship between Karnatic music and the West.

Articulations

Descriptions of Indian music by European scholars in the nineteenth century and early twentieth century were primarily concerned with comparing Indian music with the music of the West. Such studies inevitably placed Indian music in a cultural half-state, as though waiting to be awakened. Though Indian music was relentlessly compared to the music of the West, the separation, usually opposition, between the two was scrupulously maintained. Indian music had to take its place in a historico-musicological tree of natural connections, but it was also to stand on equal footing with Western music as one of the great musics of the world. In contrast to such a vision, the violin and its passage to India represented the possibility that instead of separation and opposition, there could be mixing and influence. Western scholars of comparative organology in the late nineteenth century showed little interest in the violin's increasing popularity in India precisely because it threatened to undermine the neat family trees they were determined to draw to illustrate the relationship between Indian music and European music.

In his *Researches into the Early History of the Violin Family* Carl Engel's genealogy of the European violin depended on "an acquaintance with the musical instruments of foreign nations in different stages of civilization, extant at the present day" (1883, 3). With the European violin as the pinnacle, or endpoint, of "civilization," the "rude fiddles" in evidence around the world were to be taken as stages of development whose natural connections to each other could be traced. Following the evolutionary theory of the time, such "natural" connections were assumed to be based on function, not form. Engel hinted that ancient migrations were the cause of diffusion of fiddle types but considered present-day migrations unimportant, as admitting of possibly unnatural connections that gave rise to inauthentic imitations of the violin. "Shapes resembling the f-holes are occasionally to be met with on Asiatic instruments. . . . [T]he two sound-holes are sometimes merely painted upon them, without their being pierced into the sound board. What can be the origin and object of this fancy?" (19). Engel likewise mentioned the use of the European violin in India at length but then dismissed it as inconsequential.

> Nay, it is well known that in some of the seaport towns of Hindustan the European violin has actually been introduced although it does not appear to have obtained much popular favour. The rajas seem not to appreciate its really commendable qualities, to judge from the fact of their having ordered violins to be manufactured of silver instead of wood. . . . We have seen that the Hindus are not entirely unacquainted with the European violin. . . . There is now in Calcutta a Musical Academy, founded in the year 1871 by the Raja Sourindro Mohun Tagore, in which this instrument is actually taught, so that ere long we may perhaps expect in our public concerts a Hindu virtuoso astonishing his auditory with the performance of some of our brilliant violin compositions. However this may be, it can hardly be said that this European introduction has affected in the slightest degree the spirit of the Hindu national music. (16–17)

Engel thus dismissed the use of the violin in India as a mere superficiality, just like the f-holes painted onto "Asiatic" instruments. Such a dismissal hardly squares with the fact that the violin was, according to Charles Day in *Music and Musical Instruments of Southern India and the Deccan* (1891), rapidly taking the place of the sarangi in South India.[1] Strangely, however, this is the only mention of the violin in Day's entire work. His large section of illustrations and descriptions of South Indian instruments includes lengthy descriptions of the veena and its tuning but omits the violin entirely. The sarangi is described as the main accompaniment to the voice, yet the illustration of "a musical party" depicts a violinist, not a sarangi player (Day 1891, 98). It seems that for both Engel and Day, the present-day music of the violin seemed to threaten their ability to hear "echoes of an indigenous music . . . remaining in the Indian music of today; but not yet so clearly heard that we can say we identify here or there a refrain of an original or pre-historic music, although we may unconsciously be very near it" (ibid., x).

These accounts were pervaded by a longing for a pure Indian music unaffected by colonialism, a music impervious to its contemporary circumstances. Such a vision of Indian music continues to dominate Western scholarship even at the end of the twenty-first century. For instance, Gerry Farrell's *Indian Music and the West* (1997), a book about the West's encounter with Indian music in the nineteenth and twentieth centuries, also never mentions the violin. Farrell's approach seems to invest in an idea of "Indian music" as an essentially stable field free from the unstable realm of politics and the whims of "the West." Accordingly, his analysis allows only for the coming together of spectacularly different elements: the use of "Indian" motifs in Western parlor songs for piano; the use of the sitar in Western pop music in the 1960s. Such examples are certainly worth discussing, but Farrell's alignment of them seems to suggest that the story of Indian music and the West can be told completely in terms of such spectacular misfits, of misguided Western appropriations of a pre-existent and independent entity known as Indian music. If, as Farrell states, "at the very core of Western attitudes toward Indian music is the idea that it is in some way deeply unknowable," then his own position unwittingly seems to fall within such attitudes (9). His approach preserves a pristine place for Indian music as an entity that exists before and after two centuries of "misunderstanding" on the part of the West, an entity that went on "developing and adapting as it would, largely impervious" to the debates and appropriations to which it was subjected (54).

The career of the violin in India surely does not fit into a history that would prefer to leave Indian music untouched by the West or by colonialism. Following the violin in South India points to a different history, one that admits the centrality of the colonial encounter in the creation of what is now called "Indian classical music." Such a history does not amount to a narrative of Westernization, a story other ethnomusicologists have told.[2] The Westernization narrative implies that before the arrival of Westerners, Karnatic music existed as much the same kind of entity we know now, and that it was then selectively affected by Western musical practices and ideas. This narrative suggests that definitions of "Indian" and "Western" are unproblematic, and that the Western influences could be stripped away, leaving a pure core of Karnatic music. Certainly, the colonial encounter changed musical practices and discourses about music in South India. These practices and discourses are not Western, however, but specifically colonial. They position Karnatic music as India's classical music, definable and audible as such precisely because it is poised in opposition to the classical music of the West. Pervading this peculiarly colonial discourse is a structure of comparison that, as I have suggested, includes both a claim to commensurability and a claim to essential difference.

The King of Instruments

The first violins in India were probably brought to Calcutta in the 1760s for the Calcutta Harmonic Society, which played Handel, Corelli, and later Haydn and Mozart, and for the Catch Club, which played jigs and reels for dancing (Head 1985, 549). Musical instrument shops opened in Calcutta in the 1780s, and the Calcutta Band, an orchestra, was established in 1785 (551).[3] Yet although there must have been interaction between English and Indian musicians, the violin did not seem to play a major role. By contrast, in South India the violin's influence seems to have been immediate.

Exactly where the violin first came to South India and who first adapted it to Karnatic music are matters of some contention. One popular story holds that the violin appeared in Madras in the late eighteenth century, probably introduced by colonial officials with musical hobbies. Baluswamy Dikshitar (1786–1858), who was from a Brahmin family and the younger brother of the composer Muthuswamy Dikshitar, moved with his father to Manali, a village near Madras, around 1800 or slightly before. Attracted by the English band music at Fort Saint George in Madras, Baluswamy expressed a desire to learn European music. Manali Chinniah Mudaliyar, son of the dubash to the governor of Madras, trustee of the Manali temple, and patron of many musicians at that time, engaged a European violinist from Madras to give Baluswamy violin lessons (Raghavan 1944, 129). He had lessons for three years and also managed in that time to adapt the violin to Karnatic music, although there is no explicit mention of this in P. Sambamoorthy's account (1955a, vol. 1, 37). Baluswamy then returned to Tiruvarur, near the thriving royal court of Tanjavur, known as the principal seat of Karnatic music before Madras gained that reputation. The violin became known in South India through Baluswamy's performances. Indeed, the maharaja of Ettayapuram, a small state south of Madurai, was so taken with Baluswamy's violin music that he appointed him court violinist (*samasthana vidwan*) in 1824 (ibid.). Baluswamy's brother, Muthuswamy, later came from Tanjavur to Ettayapuram, and there had the chance to hear the violin and the European music his brother played on it.

Another popular story has it that the site of the violin's first transformation was the royal court of Tanjavur, where Maharaja Serfoji had appointed the Tanjore quartet—four brothers from what is now called the *icai veḷḷālar* community—as court musicians and dancers (Subrahmanyam 1980, 47).[4] Vadivelu (1810–1868), the youngest of the brothers, was a disciple of Muthuswamy Dikshitar and also studied Western violin with the missionary Christian Friedrich Schwartz, who had established a Protestant mission in Tanjavur in 1778 and developed a friendly relationship with the royal court (Seetha 1981, 103). Vadivelu later demonstrated the tunes he had learned from Schwartz to Muthuswamy Dikshitar, who composed songs based on them. Vadivelu also introduced the violin to the composer Thyagaraja, accompanying him while he was singing; sometimes Thyagaraja would ask just to hear the violin by itself (Subrahmanyam 1980, 48). When Maharaja Serfoji and the brothers had a disagreement over their rights in the temple at Tanjavur, the quartet was dismissed from Serfoji's court, but it was not long before they found another post in the court of the composer-king Swati Tirunal at Trivandrum in 1830. Vadivelu became an intimate associate of the king and taught violin to several court musicians there. In 1834 Swati Tirunal presented Vadivelu with an ivory violin inscribed with the eagle, emblem of the Trivandrum royal court, and a bow made from an elephant's tusk (ibid., 49).

A third version of the violin's entry into South India concerns the minister Varahappayyar (1795–1869), who worked for Maharaja Serfoji as the superintendent of all court musicians (Seetha 1981, 258). He eventually became Serfoji's trusted minister and when Serfoji wanted to enter negotiations with the governor of the Madras presidency, he sent Varahappayyar, who was noted for his proficiency in the English language (Jayarama Iyer 1985, 27). A musical negotiation seems to have resulted: the governor was hospitable to Varahappayyar and showed him his music room, which had violins and a piano. Intrigued by these instruments, Varahappayyar played Indian melodies on them, impressing the Western musicians, who then agreed to teach him a few violin techniques. "This news reached the ears of the governor . . . [who] being very music-minded asked him to play before him. In order to please him and have his political mission fulfilled, he agreed to play before the governor (otherwise he would have preferred to play it to his Maharaja first). He took the violin and played some Indian melodies to the pleasure of the governor" (ibid.). The governor presented the violin and a piano to Varahappayyar, who returned to Tanjavur and impressed the maharaja. Varahappayyar later taught violin to Vadivelu, who was the first to fully realize the potential of the violin, and more violins were then brought to Tanjavur.

While the three preceding versions of the violin's history in India could perhaps be correlated, yet another version places the arrival of the violin somewhat earlier and offers an alternative narration of its adaptation into Karnatic music. A musicologist in Mysore, to whom I had mentioned my interest in the violin's history in South India, commented that I had probably only heard the Tanjavur stories but that there was evidence—a woman pictured playing the violin in a dance party in a mural—to show that the violin had come to the Mysore area much earlier. The mural is located in the summer palace of Tipu Sultan, who ruled the royal state of Mysore in the last quarter of the eighteenth century. The musicologist R. Sathyanarayana dates this mural to 1784, presenting linguistic evidence to show the incorporation of the violin into the Kannada language: "Fiddle—Fittle—Pittle—Pitil—Piteel—Piteelu" (1993, 11).[5] The mural, he states, points to the fact that the violin was already in accepted usage in Mysore state by the time Varahappayyar, Vadivelu, and Baluswamy Dikshitar were born and thus was probably introduced by French army officers. The evolution of a distinctive school of violin playing in Mysore, states Sathyanarayana, points to the long tradition of violin playing there (12).

With this the written sources on the violin's entry into South India end, so understanding what this early violin sounded like, who played it, and how it spread requires a certain degree of speculation. From its earliest use in South India the violin seems to have been played by both Brahmins and non-Brahmins, traveling through political rather than caste alliances. In fact, in the case of Varahappayyar, the violin was used as a political bargaining chip: he played Indian melodies on the violin to demonstrate his diplomacy. Vadivelu's story shows how the colonial machineries of government, reflected in the policies of princely states toward their musician-officials, affected the movement of the violin around South India. The violin moved from Tanjavur to Ettayapuram to Trivandrum in the hands of court musicians seeking to improve their status, as it helped maharajas improve theirs; the ivory violin presented by Swati Tirunal was probably hailed then, as it is now, as a sign of his progressive and forward-looking stance (Venkitasubramonia Iyer 1975, 3, 159).

The violin traveled through other colonial machineries, such as the military and railroads. The grandfather and father of the well-known early-twentieth-century violinist Dwaram Venkataswamy Naidu (1893–1964) were both military men who played violin as a hobby and probably picked it up from English officials; Naidu's brother, the elder by approximately thirteen years, worked for the railroads in Vishakapatnam and used to acquire violins in his travels. The amateur violinist C. Subrahmanya Ayyar (1885–1960) used his postings as chief railway accountant in various parts of India between 1910 and 1940 to buy violins and to learn about the state of violin playing in India in general (Subrahmanya Ayyar 1944).

And what of the music played by the first Indian players of violin? The Western music to which Indians were exposed in South India was predominantly Irish and Scottish fiddling, rather than Western classical violin. Evidence for the idea that South Indians first heard reels and gigs rather than concertos and sonatas comes from what could be one of the first Indian violin experiments: Muthuswamy Dikshitar's compositions based on European melodies. In a volume of these "European Airs" culled from various sources, more than forty of Dikshitar's compositions are listed (and notated) with the names of the European songs—such as "Limerick," "Castilian Maid," "Lord MacDonald's Reel," "Voulez-vous Danser?," and "God Save the Queen"—on which they are based (Sankaramurthy 1990, xiv). It is probable that Muthuswamy Dikshitar heard many of these melodies played on the violin by his brother or other court violinists during his travels. What is remarkable about Dikshitar's compositions is that there is none of the melisma or *gamaka* (ornamentation) associated with Karnatic music, and the lyrics seem to be only a way of translating these Western tunes into a recognizable, palatable form.[6] Perhaps more important, the process of composition implied here was radically different from the Karnatic ideal of a singer-composer composing words and music simultaneously. Here the composer took melodies already formed, pure instrumental music, and added the words/voice as the music demanded. These compositions thus suggest two things: first, the original associations of the violin in South India were with fiddlers, not with European classical music; second, the violin was not only a physical sign of the colonial presence but also the vehicle for a kind of translation of Western music into Karnatic music.

Other Indian composers show the influence of European tunes in their work as well. Swati Tirunal (1813–1847), the patron and close friend of the violinist Vadivelu, also appointed Western musicians to his court. His *var-*

nam (a type of composition roughly equivalent to an etude) in the raga shankarabharanam, whose pitch intervals are equivalent to those of the Western major scale, includes a passage at the end that sounds distinctly like a European marching band. Unlike the other sections of the varnam, the last section breaks all the conventions of Karnatic music by employing large intervallic leaps and a minimum of gamaka. The principle of the varnam as a genre is to exhaust the possibilities of a raga with different permutations of phrases; it is clear from Swati Tirunal's varnam that in the early nineteenth century the possibilities of a raga included its transformation into a piece of semi-Western music. Along these lines, several compositions of Thyagaraja suggest strains of Scottish reels or waltzes, composed in unique ragas with suggestive names like "jingla." Pattnam Subramania Iyer (ca. 1840–1910), a disciple of Thyagaraja, composed his well-known "Raghuvamsa Sudha" in the raga kathanakuthuhoolam, which he had invented using a modified version of the Western major scale and that specifies large intervals and almost no gamaka. This composition and a variety of other "English notes" or "Western notes," as they are called, are staple fare at the end of any instrumental concert of Karnatic music to this day.

A Double to the Voice

In the mid-nineteenth century the violin came to be appreciated for its ability to mimic the singing voice. Toward the end of his hagiographical account of the life of the composer Thyagaraja, Wallajapet Ramaswamy Bhagavatar recalls a scene of "surprise" and "delight" from the mid-1840s. His grandfather, the composer Wallajapet Venkataramana Bhagavatar, and his father, Krishnaswamy, had been direct disciples of Thyagaraja. Krishnaswamy, who from childhood had always had less vocal facility (*cārīra cukam*), instead played the "kinnari-fiddle."[7] According to the account, Krishnaswamy played the kinnari "very skillfully" (*mikavum catūriyamāka*) while others—such as the *vidwans* (musicians) Govinda Marar, Tillaistanam Ramayyangar, Krishnaswamy's father, and even Thyagaraja himself—sang. Thyagaraja is reputed to have "attained bliss" on hearing the kinnari and to have said, by way of blessing, "Child! Krishnaswamy! If you keep on singing and playing the kinnari at my side, Sri Sita Ramacandra will give you a divine voice [*tivyamāṉa cārīram*]." Krishnaswamy immediately made a *namaskaram* (bow) at the feet of Thyagaraja and sang a *kriti* (composition) with him while playing the kinnari. "When the pallavi [first section] was over," recalls Ramaswamy, "the anupallavi [second section] began and the voice and kinnari met with a single sound [orē vitamāṉa nātattuṭaṉ kuṭi], so very pleasing that those in the audience were surprised and delighted. . . . When he was singing you couldn't tell whether it was the sound of the fiddle or the sound of the voice [ivar pāṭum samayattil piṭil nātamō cārīra nātamō eṉṟu kaṇṭaṟiya muṭiyātu]" (Ramaswamy Bhagavatar 1935, 53–54).

The idea of the violin as the perfect accompaniment to the voice became prevalent in the twentieth century, when the social context of Karnatic music shifted to the concert hall.[8] Without amplification, the volume of the voice was no longer adequate for audiences of more than a handful of people in the large, noisy spaces of Madras. Some kind of accompaniment was needed to make the voice audible above the din of the city without jeopardizing its delicacy; the violin, already widely in use in South India, seemed a natural solution. The musicologist S. K. Ramachandra Rao states that the first violinist to accompany vocalists in concerts was Tirukkodikaval Krishna Iyer (1857–1913), followed by a number of other violinists who lived into the first half of the twentieth century (1994, 5). Once it became necessary for vocalists to be accompanied, violinists were in demand and thus had more concert opportunities in what was fast becoming a lucrative business. A list of South Indian musicians, compiled in 1917, included more than 100 violinists, many of whom were described as accompanying artists (Pandithar 1917, 159).

The practice and aesthetic of the instrumentally accompanied voice is pervasive in South Asian musical traditions. The accompanying instrument, however, does more than simply repeat what the soloist sings; not only does it impart a particular sound quality, but the relationship, both musical and social, between soloist and accompanist stages the voice in a particular way. In much the same way as a quoted voice can potentially disrupt the authority or primacy of a quoting voice, as Mikhail Bakhtin suggests in relation to speech and literary genres, the violin, in accompanying, can influence the soloist's voice.[9] What, we may therefore ask, was the effect of putting an instrument with colonial origins in this role? How did the violin change and/or create the voice it was merely supposed to double?

Accompaniment in Karnatic music involves a mixture of support and competition, imitation and creativity, shape-giving and self-effacement.[10] P. Sambamoorthy, known as one of the great modernizers of Karnatic music,[11] described the violinist's duties at length in his 1952 article "Kacceri Dharma" (Concert etiquette): "It is his duty to *figurate* the music of principal performer . . . by giving judicious emphasis on sangatis and gamakas. . . . He should not be hasty in deciphering rare ragas and eduppus [*eṭuppu*]. He should remember that rare ragas and intricate eduppus are traps set for him by his (not very friendly) chief to catch him unawares. . . . His responses to his chief's alapana and kalpana swaras should . . . not run counter to the train of musical thoughts of his chief (1952, 269; italics in original).[12]

What is involved in the idea of "figuration"? It indicates precisely the tension between visibility and invisibility, audibility and inaudibility, sameness and difference.[13] At stake is not representation of the voice but a kind of partial repetition. The violinist plays something that is not identical to what the vocalist sings but is close enough to give the vocalist's sound a greater presence, a recognizable form. In contemporary musical practice, the role of the violinist as accompanist is to "double" whatever the vocalist sings, either in unison or, during improvisations, with a slight delay. Although Sambamoorthy insisted on the subordination of the violin to the vocal line, in reality an accompanying violinist has great power over a soloist. For instance, at any point in a section of raga alapana, a free-time improvised elaboration of the raga, the violinist can choose either to dwell on a single note, reproduce the entire phrase that the vocalist has sung, highlight only the end of the phrase, or play something that the vocalist has not sung at all. What the violinist chooses to play will often determine what the vocalist sings next. Indeed, the best accompanists, one vocalist told me in 1998, make the soloist sound better by covering up "imperfections" and by giving the vocalist ideas about what to sing next. Vocalists often talk of accompanists as inspiring, but also complain that they dominate soloists.

A skillful accompanist is an expert in mimesis and thus also in dissimulation. My violin teacher, who had worked for twenty-five years as a staff violinist for All India Radio, used English words relating to technological reproduction to describe her role as accompanist. One had to be ready for whatever the vocalist sang and get it "typed" in one's brain after the first line, like a "recording." Often one had to accompany compositions one had never heard before; in these cases, it was a matter of knowing the raga and its particular phrases, keeping track of the tala, and being on the ready—one had to "adjust" (the English term Indian musicians often use for faking or fudging something) so that one blended in but sounded confident at the same time. One did not have to know the words of the composition or even remember it afterward, as long as one could imitate realistically enough. Another violinist told me that a certain vocalist preferred her accompaniment because it blended so well that she forgot there was anybody accompanying her at all.

The delicacy and fragility of this accompanying operation stands in contrast to its importance; without proper accompaniment, even the best singer sounds incomplete. If the accompaniment is off-kilter, a concert listener once told me, the whole thing is ruined. We were at a violin concert in which the solo violinist was accompanied by his daughter and disciple. The daughter, instead of picking up a few phrases here and there, was repeating everything the father played in its entirety; the father would stop playing and wait for her to echo him. My neighbor seemed impatient and made no attempt to hide the fact that he was looking at my notes, looking for anything that would relieve his boredom. Although audiences sometimes talk during compositions, they are usually quiet during raga alapana, so I was surprised to find him telling me, in a stage whisper, how "childish" the performance sounded, as if it had all been staged beforehand. In accompaniment, one can't play too much, or the secret of what is going on becomes obvious and uninteresting. On the other hand, the violinist is there partly to provide intonation. Many vocalists, particularly when improvising at fast speed, lose their intonation and simply belt out the *swara* (musical note) names instead of singing them on pitch. The audience gets the impression that those pitches were sung partly because they hear the swara names, but also because the violinist plays the pitches the singer names.

The fine line between supporting and overshadowing suggests that accompaniment is a social as well as a musical matter. My violin teacher, who had accompanied the famous flautist Mahalingam many times, prized herself on the subtlety of her accompaniment. Once, Mahalingam, known for both his genius and for his drunkenness on stage, had had another violinist accompany him. On that occasion, Mali, as he was known, started a complicated rhythmic ending in the wrong place and had to abort it in the middle. The violinist, however, instead of covering up the mistake, proceeded to start the ending from the right place and finish the piece, which incensed Mali. Several months later, in order to get his revenge, Mali arranged a concert in which that violinist and my teacher both accompanied him. After a few warm-up pieces, the acid test came: an improvised *ragamalika* (combination of ragas) in which the violinists take turns accompanying. The first violinist played as usual, demonstrating her skill in that particular raga. But when, after Mali played some more, my teacher's turn came, she simply laid down her violin, turned her palms upward, and said into the microphone, "There is nothing I can play after such divine music," rousing the audience to cheers—and exemplifying how an accompanist can literally stage, in the sense of making or breaking, a soloist. It is perhaps for this reason that T. K. Jayarama Iyer wrote, "The Violin, as it is, is a wonderful instrument. If we call our Vina the queen of musical instruments, we can call the Violin the king of musical instruments. No other instrument is so powerful as the Violin" (1965, 28).

From "Fiddle" to "Violin"

When the violin began to appear regularly on the concert stage in the early twentieth century, its old "fiddle" image and sound were no longer adequate. The violinist had to be a classical musician in his own right, distinguished from those violinists who played dance music or *harikatha* (musical storytelling, usually on religious themes). For those who wrote about the violin in the early twentieth century, an overhaul of violin technique seemed necessary to rein in the wild gropings of Karnatic violinists on their fingerboards, to update their antiquated use of the bow. Hardly a century after the violin had come from Europe, these critics wrote, Karnatic violinists seemed to have forgotten that the West had a developed system of violin technique; violinists in India, ignoring this, seemed to be starting over again, literally, from scratch. While the ostensible subject of these writings was the violin, the reformation of violin technique was seen as the key to reforming and modernizing Karnatic music in general. Although the suggestions (especially those concerning posture) made by these writers were never implemented by Karnatic violinists, they illuminate the contours of debate about music in the early twentieth century, particularly the relationship between "Indian" and "Western" in these debates. The idea that emerges from these writings is that only Western violin technique can bring forth the true beauty and identity of Indian music.

In 1912 T. C. R. Johannes, a Christian violinist who had studied under the violinist "Photograph" Masilamani Mudaliyar (so named because he was the first musician in those days to have purchased a camera), published his Tamil treatise *Bhārata Sangīta Svāya Bōdhini* (*pārata caṅkīta svāya pōtiṉi*: Indian music self-instructor). Johannes devoted a large part of the treatise to violin technique. In his hortatory introduction of long-winded, sporadically Sanskritized Tamil, he railed against the tendencies of Indians (whom he addressed with biting sarcasm as "swadeshis"[14]) to adopt everything European, to speak in English, and to disdain Indian music for its lack of harmony (1912, xxii). These so-called swadeshis, he wrote, knew nothing about the European music they so blindly accepted other than the word *harmony* itself, which they repeated as if showing off a new and expensive possession ("Iṅta ārmoṉi eṉṉum vāḻttaiyai māttiram īs pīs piṭikkumpōtu vilaikkoṭuttu vāṅkiṉārkaḷ pōlum").[15] Even North Indians did not accept everything European as slavishly as did South Indians. Instruments like the guitar, banjo, mandolin, harmonium, and piano were "useless" and "without pride." For Johannes, it was precisely the visibility and rationality of the piano that rendered it unmusical and presumptuously vulgar: the piano's keys were laid out so that you could go up and down them in five minutes, he claimed, whereas in Karnatic music it ought to take three days and three nights to finish a raga (xxii).

Surprisingly, the violin escaped Johannes's wrath; in fact, he argued that while Indians should reject these other "foreign" instruments, they should accept the violin. "It is called the king of instruments; it accommodates itself naturally to the sound of any other instrument, to the human voice, to animals [yāvattu karuvikaliṉ nātattaiyum, maṉuṣa, miruka . . . mutaliya yāvattu iṉaṇkaḷiṉ tōṉikaḷaiyum itu iyalpilēyē aṉucāraṉai ceyyum]. To say it is a European instrument is an error. The Europeans did nothing other than civilize it a bit [koñcam nākarīkamāy ceytirukkiṟārkaḷ]; it was originally an Indian instrument brought to the West in Alexander's time" (xix).

In his first chapter, titled "Some Rare but Essential-to-know Things about Bharata Sangitam," Johannes devoted a large section to the proper way of playing the violin. First, he gave advice concerning posture: the usual Indian way of holding the violin with the scroll against the foot was wrong and an insult to Saraswati, and it had been condemned by Europeans; the violin should instead be held the European way (5). An illustration shows what seems to be an English violinist facing an Indian violinist, each one holding the violin in European fashion. In addition, Johannes wrote, it was a travesty that Indian violinists only used at best half the length of the bow. Johannes claimed that, if asked why they were playing that way, most violinists would say the audience liked it, that the sound was sweet. Furthermore, according to Johannes, their fingering was so unsystematic that they didn't even know what mistakes they were making (5). They simply played the same ten or fifteen ragas over and over again, without a clue as to the true notes of the raga or any theoretical knowledge of music.

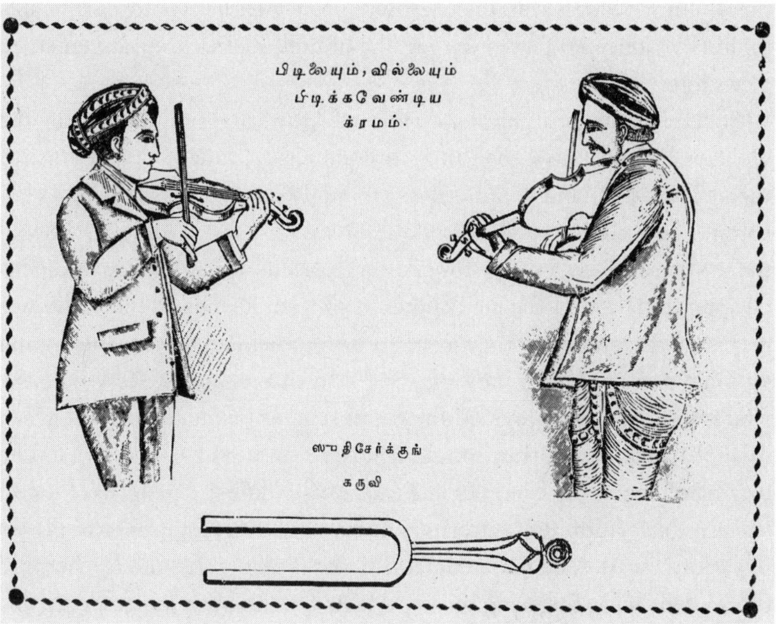

1 Method of holding the fiddle and bow (piṭilaiyum, villaiyum piṭikkavēṇṭiya kramam) and tuning fork (sruti cērkkuṅ karuvi). Drawing from T. C. R. Johannes, *Bhāratha Sangīta Svāya Bōdhini* (1912).

Johannes related an incident in which he heard another violinist playing a concert. The audience had been shaking their heads in appreciation like dolls ("talaiyāṭṭi patumaikaḷai pōl"). The man of the house where the concert was taking place asked Johannes how he liked the violinist. Johannes replied, "He is working very hard and so are his fingers. But he is playing in contradiction [nērvirōtamāy] to the sastras." The house owner was affronted and said, "Who are you to insult him like this?" Johannes said, "I will show you where he is wrong." He sidled up to the violinist afterward and made a comment about the violinist's rendition of a particular raga. The violinist replied, "Oh, but if I didn't play it that way, the audience wouldn't have appreciated it." "Very well," said Johannes. "Then can you play all the ragas this way?" The violinist said, stroking his mustache as if ready for a fight, "Of course! What objection could I have to that?" Immediately Johannes took a slate board and wrote out the *murchana* (ascending and descending pattern) of a raga. The violinist was dumbstruck. He asked Johannes if he could play it. So as to put to rest any suspicion that he might have already practiced that particular raga, Johannes asked the violinist to write another, knowing full well he would not be able to. Finally, Johannes played the raga he himself had written and emerged victorious (6).

So, besides an appalling lack of knowledge of theory and notation, the violinist had no knowledge of technique either; indeed, knowledge of theory, notation, and technique are tellingly conflated in Johannes's account. The violinist, resting his violin on his foot and holding the bow in the middle (already a recipe for disaster), placed his fingers in an accidental approximation of the raga's notes. A thorough study of the violin was necessary to counteract this. Johannes recommended that the beginning violinist paste paper on the fingerboard so that he might see where the swaras fell. He even provided the measurement of the distance between each of the fingers as they should be placed on the fingerboard (11). The playing of beginning exercises like *sarali varisai* (different patterns of notes) and *alankarams* (different patterns of notes set to different talas to be played in various ragas), Johannes maintained, was useless unless the teacher told the student what fingering to use (13). As for the bow, Johannes recommended practicing with the metronome, long bows 128 counts in duration, and he remarked gleefully on how amusing it would be to watch the violinists who held their bow in the middle trying to do this (13).

The Art and Technique of Violin Play, written by C. Subrahmanya Ayyar, appeared in 1941. Having studied the violin in Madras, Subrahmanya Ayyar gave his first public recital in 1922 at Presidency College, in conjunction with a lecture on the acoustics of the violin given by his brother, the physicist C. V. Raman (Subrahmanya Ayyar 1944, 1). Although Subrahmanya Ayyar remained an amateur, he devoted all his spare time to practicing and lecturing on the violin in various parts of India and worked intermittently on a project concerning the sound waves emitted by the violin. He took time off in 1933 to make a European tour on which he was primarily concerned with meeting European violinists, playing Karnatic violin for them ("I felt . . . [it] might serve as a harbinger of good-will and mutual understanding between the East and the West"), and buying violins (28).

The Art and Technique of Violin Play was originally given as a series of lectures for the students of the Indian music department at Madras University. As one gentleman remarked, "No violinist of South India today can satisfy by his technique even a trained European ear, nor make any deep impression on a Western violinist worth the name" (Subrahmanya Ayyar 1941, 2). Subrahmanya Ayyar's goal was to correct this state of affairs by helping the young generation of violinists improve their violin tone. His first recommendation was to get a European violin, for the Indian factory-made violins were of much inferior quality. Innovations such as Mysore Chowdiah's seven-stringed violin were to be abhorred for their "metallic screech" (4). The South Indians' preference for thin strings and their use of extra-heavy bows contributed to their poor tone (7). Like Johannes, Subrahmanya Ayyar criticized the posture of South Indian players, implying that squatting on the floor and playing was unnatural to the violin. "It is a pitiable sight to see the cotton towel of the South Indian artist, with such a mass of it touching the violin to avoid the sweat of his body wetting it, which further damps the tone. I wonder if even the next generation will give up this posture" (10). The "cramped posture" of South Indian violinists also prevented them from reaching the higher positions of the violin and thus from achieving the technological heights of perfection of Western violinists (10). Even the South Indian violinists' habit of using oil (continued to this day) did not escape Subrahmanya Ayyar's reforming scrutiny: "As if all his attempts to damp the full violin tone are not sufficient, the violinist occasionally rubs fine oil on his left finger tips while playing, to secure easy movement or slipping of fingers. What a mockery of violin play!" (11).

For vocalists, the aim was merely to get the right "effects." But for instrumentalists, there was a visible, and therefore systematic, technique (23). The veena, which served in Subramanya Ayyar's scheme as an *inspiration* to the voice, was different from the violin, which had succeeded almost entirely in *reproducing* the voice. But in their fascination with reproduction, South Indian violinists had forgotten the violin's original tone (15). Violinists must, he urged, strive for a continuity of sound, a technique of bowing which avoided the "belching sound" even advanced violinists made when changing the direction of their bow. Likewise, South Indian violinists must learn to conceptualize their fingering in terms of the positions in Western violin technique; only then would they get truly accurate intonation and be able to realize the "subtle microtonal changes" (19). His advice for young violinists was to play the sarali varisai and alankaram exercises stripped of all their gamakas and to effect the switch between positions, like a European violinist, as inaudibly as possible (15). Furthermore, they should play with all four fingers, avoiding the excessive sliding produced by the two-finger or single-finger techniques (31). And finally, once the young violinist had gotten all these elements under control, he had to work on his facial expression: "There is no need to look at the strings or the violin while playing as you become mature, but look at the audience.

The facial expression of the artist must be one of ease in bearing, with a graceful look. There should be a general relaxation of the limbs and an absence of stiffness . . . while there is perfect control over the facial muscles and a composure in the face of the artist" (34).

Getting a full tone out of the violin—putting South Indian violin on a par with the classical violin playing of the West—thus involved a new and rigorous discipline of the performer's body. Sliding and fingering entail different relationships to the violin as well as the music produced from it. Sliding along the fingerboard is conducive to understanding a melody as a continuous phrase, with no sharp distinction made between the notes and the space "between" the notes. Fingering entails recognizing individual pitches and their locations on the fingerboard; it means recognizing a standardized technical discourse on "positions" in Western violin technique. Knowledge of where to place one's fingers also includes the knowledge that the space between the notes is essentially forbidden. While the "excessive sliding" and "cramped posture" of Karnatic violinists was indicative of laziness, ignorance, and secrecy, the technique of discrete fingering identified with the West was associated with the advances of modernity: discipline, clarity, and theoretical knowledge of music.

In the 1940s the Madras Music Academy confirmed the classical status of the instrument by decreeing that its name be changed from "fiddle" to "violin" in all published programs. Others suggested further refining the name, replacing the Tamil pronunciation of fiddle, "piṭil," with lofty-sounding Sanskritized names like "bahuleen" (Bullard 1998, 255). An essay in the Madras-based magazine *Triveni*, self-proclaimed "Journal of the Indian Renaissance," suggested the name "vayuleena," to rhyme with "veena." The violin was, the essay claimed, even more suited to Karnatic music than it was to Western music, and its origin lay in the "genius of the Aryans" (Harinagabhushanam 1929, 202).

The Violin as a Sign of the Modern

In the early to mid-twentieth century the violin came to be explicitly associated with modernity. It was hailed as a necessary accompaniment to the voice, making it both clearer and more audible in the concert hall. There was something about the violin—its Westernness and newness but also its uncanny ability to imitate the Karnatic voice—that made it flexible and resilient enough to withstand various experiments. Like recording technology, the violin provided a way of reproducing the voice, a new way of representing Karnatic music. But the violin reproduced the voice with a difference, making the human ear into a more precise listening instrument. In 1944 C. Subrahmanya Ayyar wrote,

> The advent of the violin to South India from 1800 has made Carnatic music even more articulate than in the days of Tulajajee of Tanjore. . . . It has made the South Indian ear perceptive to microtones greater than twenty-two. . . . The sanity of Tamil genius is also seen in the fact that the violin was accepted as an accompaniment by the musical elite in South India . . . instead of the harmonium. The latter entered the portals of the All-India Radio of North India . . . and was later tabooed, as if by the command of a Dictator. (60)

The violin was thus associated not only with the progress of both music and its listeners but also with emotional maturity: "From this wonderful box we get a most ravishing sound, which affects most profoundly the emotions of the most civilized" (Subrahmanya Ayyar 1941, 3). Here the sign of a modern, "civilized" subject is precisely his or her ability to be moved by the sound of the violin, to recognize the connection between his or her voice and the sound emanating from that "wonderful box."

Between 1910 and 1930, several experiments were undertaken to increase the volume and improve the tone of the violin. Beginning in 1918, C. V. Raman, professor of physics and member of the Indian Association for the Advancement of Science, engaged in research on the acoustical principles of the violin family of instruments. His object in "Experiments with Mechanically Played Violins" was to "throw light on the modus operandi of the bow . . . [and] to furnish valuable information regarding the instrument itself, its characteristics as a resonator, and the emission of energy from it in various circumstances. . . . [It] could also be expected to furnish illustrations of the physical laws underlying the technique of the violinist and to put these laws on a precise quantitative basis" (1920, 20). The result of the experiment was a sixteen-page report detailing the construction of the mechanical player and graphs showing the interrelations between bowing speed, bowing pressure, pitch changes, and variations in the bowed region. Every care was taken to have the mechanical player, built out of used parts of other machineries, simulate the playing of a human violinist, even down to a leather-lined clamp to simulate the violinist's fingers (28).[16] The mechanical player radically changed the orientation of things by keeping the bow stationary and moving the violin back and forth, for the sake of more reliable data (21). What the experi-

2 Mechanical violin player designed by C. V. Raman. Photograph from *Proceedings of the Indian Association for the Cultivation of Science*, vol. 6, following p. 20. Calcutta, 1920. Courtesy of Widener Library, Harvard University.

ment provided was the chance for a repeatable, measurable motion to be observed, without the distraction, as it were, of music. In fact, the report never mentioned what kind of violinist's playing was being simulated, although from the horizontal position of the violin it would seem that Western technique (as in the writings of Johannes and Subrahmanya Ayyar) was taken as the model.

Pudukkottai Narayan Iyer and Marungapuri Gopalakrishna Iyer, violinists active in the first half of the twentieth century, both used horn violins so that the violin might be heard in the concert hall (Ramachandra Rao 1994, 23); in fact, one of the first violin recordings ever made in South India was Narayan Iyer on his horn violin, circa 1920.[17] The maharajas of Tanjavur, Mysore, Trivandrum, and Vizianagaram all purchased horn violins for their personal instrument collections. The famous Mysore violinist T. Chowdiah, meanwhile, was worried that his violin would not be audible over the strong voices of those whom he was accompanying. Adding a microphone for the violin alone didn't solve the problem, because it caused a slight delay; if the violin was amplified, then everything had to be amplified. Chowdiah instead decided to amplify his violin by making a nineteen-stringed version: seven playing strings, with the upper three reinforced by a string an octave lower in pitch, as well as twelve sympathetic strings (45–46). Although this perceptibly increased the violin's volume, some objected to the "metallic screech" of this souped-up violin and to the fact that gamakas were rendered more difficult and laborious by having to be played on two strings simultaneously. Chowdiah himself eventually gave up the sympathetic strings because of tuning problems but continued to play on seven strings until his death in 1967 (75).

Not only did the violin have the ability to produce loud and clear tones; it was also portable, simple, and flexible enough to meet the demands of accompaniment. In 1955, P. Sambamoorthy listed the advantages of the European violin.

1. Its sweet and loud tone.
2. Its handiness.
3. Its plain fingerboard enabling the performer to produce all the delicate gamakas (graces) and subtle srutis (quarter-tones) with ease and accuracy.
4. Its long bow helping the performer to produce a continuous tone and to play . . . with artistic finish.
5. Its wide compass of four octaves.
6. The ease with which the instrument could be used to accompany voices of different pitch, from the high-pitched voice of the lady singer to the deep voice of the male singer. (1955a, vol. 3, 271)

These characteristics were in contrast to those of the veena, which was too ungainly to be easily transported to concert halls, too soft to be audible from the concert stage, and, in Sambamoorthy's words, "too majestic and dignified to be used as an accompaniment in vocal concerts" (272). C. Subrahmanya Ayyar wrote that "fortunately for us, the veena is not a simple dead curio, but a living instrument, though a drawing room instrument relegated to our girls in South Indian homes, and veena play was all but dead but for the radio coming to save it from oblivion" (1944, 61). The veena might be the original model of Karnatic music, but it could not bring Karnatic music into the modern age.

Why was the violin, rather than the sarangi or harmonium, the chosen instrument in South India? The sarangi, an "indigenous" bowed fiddle, seemed to reproduce the voice just as accurately as the violin. It was (and is still) widely used in North India and seems to have been used in South India in the nineteenth century. But the sarangi—long associated in the North with *tawaifs* (courtesans) and Muslims, and in the South with *nautch* parties (performances by dancing girls) and musicians of non-Brahmin caste—did not have the social cachet of the violin.[18] As Regula Qureshi has noted, "instruments mean" (2000, 815); they literally embody meaning. What was important was not that the voice be "accurately" reproduced (although this was the rhetoric employed) but that it be reproduced in a certain way. The sarangi in North India, according to Qureshi, is associated with an "excess of meaning": its "embarrassingly human" sound and its associations with courtesans sets it apart from other concert instruments, making it never quite classical enough (815, 820). The violin, on the other hand, was in South India associated with the West and with modernity. In the context of South Indian musical politics in the late nineteenth and early twentieth centuries, it seemed more reasonable to adopt a fully foreign instrument than to bring the sarangi onto the classical stage.

But the instrument could not be too foreign; it could not, for instance, be the harmonium. Like the sarangi, the harmonium was edged out of South India by the middle of the twentieth century, although for different reasons. It was (and still is) used in music for dramas and for the musical storytelling known as katha kalakshepam but made only a brief appearance on the classical stage. The first to rail against it, perhaps not surprisingly, were English or highly Anglicized Indians. The art critic and essayist Ananda Coomaraswamy disparagingly called it a "blatant instrument" (Clements 1913, vii). The British musicologist A. Fox-Strangways urged Indian musicians to "prune away" such an "unnatural growth," testifying that it had already penetrated the remotest corners of India: "It dominates the theatre, and desolates the hearth; and before long it will . . . desecrate the temple. Besides its deadening effect on a living art, it falsifies it by being out of tune with itself. . . . A worse fault is that it is a borrowed instrument, constructed originally to minister to the less noble kind of music of other lands" (Fox-Strangways 1914, 164).

The Irish-born music enthusiast Margaret Cousins wrote that the harmonium had been a boon in some ways, helping to popularize classical music because it was cheap and easy to learn (1935, 185). But otherwise it was the bane of Indian music's existence.

> It is only the equipment of Central European beggars. It has no place as an Indian instrument. It is unworthy of both East and West. It is the most sinister influence in Eastern music today. It is tuned falsely and contrary to the natural tuning employed for countless centuries in India. Its harsh, over-loud tone is quite unsuitable for accompanying the human voice which is strained in trying to hold its own. . . . It is

> sapping all musical self-reliance in the voice so that even a good singer feels helpless unless he is propped up by the harmonium. It is no wonder it is called the harm-onium, for it works "harm" wherever it goes! (28)

In the same year, C. Subrahmanya Ayyar, lecturing before the seventh All-India Music Conference on the topic of "gamakas and srutis in South Indian music," concluded: "Burn all the harmoniums in the world and awake to the delicate intonations on the South Indian vina or the European violin, the queen and king of instruments" (Subrahmanya Ayyar 1944, 53).[19]

The harmonium was banned by All India Radio in the 1930s under the leadership of John Fouldes, an Englishman who was the head of the Delhi station's Western-music section in the 1930s (Neuman 1980, 184).[20] In 1938 a story entitled "Ārmoṉiya Pahiṣkāram" (Harmonium boycott) appeared in the Tamil journal *Bharata Mani* (*Pārata Maṇi*). In the story a conference of musical instruments (no humans allowed) is held on the beach at Madras to discuss the ban on harmonium. The tambura, opening the conference, states that the harmonium is a demon trying to disturb the peace of Karnatic music with a mixed-up mass of wrong notes ("ellai illāta pakaikkoṇṭa pēy iṉṉicai nāpraṉavattaik kulaikka apasvarakkalañciyamāṉa ārmoṉiyam") (Kalyanasundaram 1938, 210). The veena stands by impassively while the violin makes impassioned appeals to the other instruments: "Brothers and sisters! Even though I came from a foreign land, I immersed myself in the ocean of music and became Indian. The harmonium is also from a foreign land, but when it immersed itself in the ocean of music it polluted the whole thing!" (ibid., 229). The violin goes on to say that the harmonium has filled its stomach with Indian music and is letting out belches: it has cheated vocalists, who now sing in a shouting, bald voice ("kattaik kuraluṭaṉ moṭṭai moṭṭaiyāka apasvaraṇkaḷuṭaṉ pāṭuvārkaḷ") (ibid).[21]

To this day the violin retains a privileged status in comparison to other instruments in South India. Although the mandolin, saxophone, and guitar are now played as solo instruments, none of them has gained the status of accompanying instrument as the violin has. In accompanying these instruments on the concert stage, the violin stages them as "foreign" instruments while presenting itself as a native voice.

The popularity of the violin thus went beyond strictly musical elements; indeed, its sound and the way that sound was interpreted were inseparable from its extramusical associations, its social place. Whereas

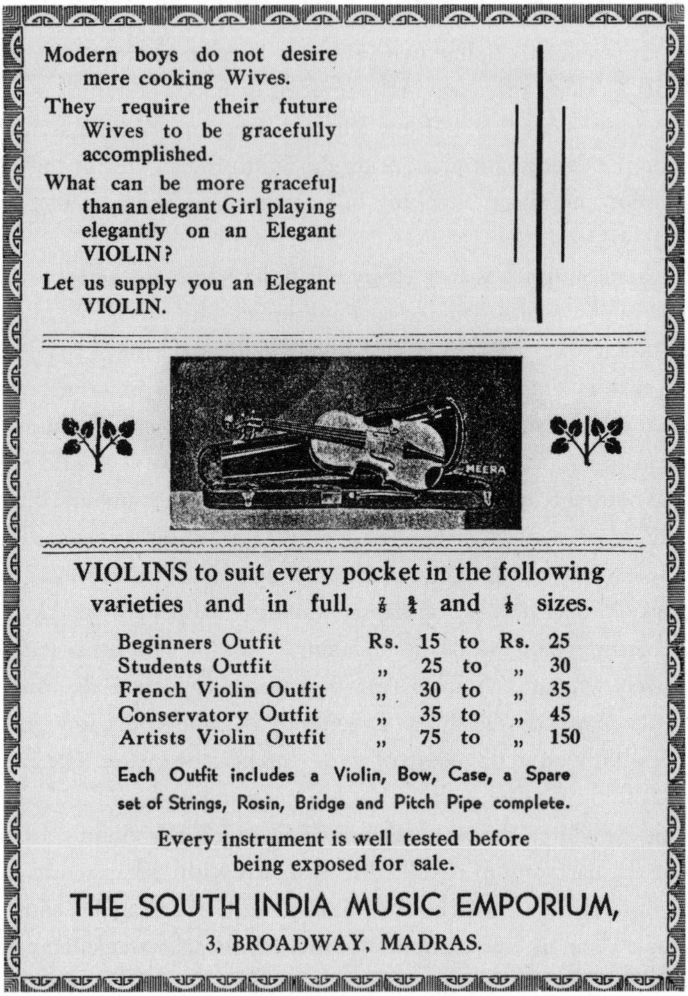

3 Violin advertisement. *Madras Music Academy Conference Souvenir* (ca. 1935–1940).

the harmonium was associated with the "beggars" of Central Europe, the violin was associated with Western classical music and with the emerging urban middle class that, in postcolonial India, were expected to be the custodians of a newly modernizing musical tradition. Unlike other instruments in the 1930s, the violin crossed caste lines; because it was a relatively new instrument, buying one was not mired in social or hereditary obligations, as acquiring a more traditional instrument like the veena might be. Between 1935 and 1940, violins of all sizes and qualities were imported to Madras from Europe and the factories of Calcutta. Advertisements for violins catered to a rising Brahmin middle class in Madras, featuring compact, portable outfits complete with case and bow, which, the ads suggested, would provide music for "modern" households; all one had to do was purchase a pre-tested outfit and present it to the woman of the house. Thus, the violin became both the sign of modernity and the ideal vehicle for bringing modernity into the middle-class home.

The Violin as Voice: Three Revolutions and a Change of Style

Perhaps no figure is more emblematic of Karnatic music's modernity than the famous violinist Dwaram Venkataswamy Naidu, who came from an unknown family in Andhra Pradesh to dominate the Madras music world from the 1930s to the 1960s.[22] In 1962 the musicologist B. V. K. Sastry wrote that Dwaram's "reverence for the classical tradition is tempered with the spirit of inquiry of the scientific age. . . . Unfettered by gurukula traditions, he is subject to few inhibitions and freely avails himself of the best ideas from everywhere, if these harmonise with classical Karnatic traditions" (33). Dwaram was hailed as "the best violinist of the day," universally praised for the imaginativeness and violinistic qualities of his music, called the "Dwaram touch." Coming not from a family of great musicians but one of military men and railroad officials, he was largely self-taught. He was greatly influenced by Western violin technique, especially with regard to the bow, which he used to give accents, emphasis, and dynamics. He listened to records of the European violinist Fritz Kreisler and is fabled to have charmed Yehudi Menuhin into letting him play his own violin after demonstrating the gentleness of his touch and respect for Western technique. At the height of his fame in the 1940s and 1950s, Dwaram was visited nightly by Indian ministers of parliament and other government officers, who would bring him records of Western classical music and commission him to incorporate them into his playing. If the record was brought in the evening, Dwaram sat until the wee hours playing the record a hundred times, counting each audition with the aid of tamarind seeds. By the next evening, he would have something new in store for the visitors.[23]

A man of eclectic tastes, Dwaram also listened to and incorporated many of the features of Hindustani music into his playing, commenting that what he appreciated about Hindustani music was the purity of tone and intonation, and the slow, meditative pace of much of it.[24] In the 1950s he stopped accompanying vocalists and played solo until his death in 1964. Dwaram was known for his treatment of rare ragas and his revival of many of Thyagaraja's and others' "Western notes." The characteristics of his playing were a judicious use of speed, a generally slower unfolding of elaboration in his alapanas, a sparse use of gamakas ("only where necessary"), and generally less *jāru* (sliding).[25] A student of Dwaram told me in 1998 that the violin "did not play in his hands—it spoke." When I asked how it spoke, she said that through the bowing and the trills and *piṭis* (from the Tamil verb *piṭi*, to catch or grab), he was able to pronounce the words of the song on his violin.

It is these very characteristics that made Dwaram's playing seem old-fashioned to many South Indian listeners at the end of the twentieth century. A young violinist told me in 1998 that the Dwaram style was no longer suitable to Karnatic music: it was too slow and plain and the bowing too rough, all right for solos but no good for accompanying vocalists. In the 1960s two more distinct styles had created revolutions in the Karnatic violin world. One was the Lalgudi style, so named after Lalgudi Jayaraman (b. 1930). Born to a family of violinists, Jayaraman moved with his family to Madras in the 1950s, accompanied many vocalists, and began playing solo from 1957 onward. A violin player in the Lalgudi style once demonstrated some of the features to me: there has to be a softness and sweetness about it, as if the voice is singing and pronouncing ("voicepāṭara mātiri, uccarika mātiri"); there should be no roughness (*karakkarappu*) in the bow but a continuity accomplished by keeping the bow on the string; the words are to be pronounced by means of fewer piṭis and trills and more jāru; the sweetness of the Lalgudi style is in the way it reproduces the singing voice without any of the roughness of a human voice.[26]

A third style, known as the Parur style, also became popular in the 1960s and remains the preferred style. Its most famous representative, and the one who popularized it, is M. S. Gopalakrishnan (b. ca. 1935; popularly known as "M.S.G."). His father, Parur Sundaram Iyer, though originally from Kerala, spent time in Bombay in the 1940s and there studied Hindustani music. M.S.G. himself later studied Hindustani music independently and has given Hindustani concerts. The hallmark of the Parur style is virtuosic speed and range. The technique is completely devoid of piṭis; instead, one or two fingers are used in a constant sliding motion along the fingerboard to produce a cascading effect. There is relatively little emphasis given with the bow. The result is a sound that is very vocal but with no vestige of speech—the kind of sound that is now recognizable to Western ears as "Indian music." M.S.G. gave several public demonstrations in which he showed off a special bowing technique he used—a kind of spiccato in which one long bow is divided into discrete, even units—playing in such a manner for twenty minutes straight. In this style, the use of technique to enunciate the words of compositions gives way to technique developed to exploit the possibilities of speed and virtuosity on the violin. A young violinist in Madras remarked to me in 1998 that the Parur style was the most suited to vocal accompaniment because it captured the speed and cascading effect of virtuosic vocal style.

These three revolutions in violin style reveal a more general change in Karnatic violin playing in the twentieth century: the switch from a piṭi style full of trills and catches, where the bow also gives emphasis, to a more florid style (often called "weepy" by its detractors) where the technique relies on sliding along the fingerboard with only one or two fingers and the bowing is constant.[27] Early recordings of violin playing, from before Dwaram Venkataswamy Naidu's time, reveal a general style that used fingered runs (rather than jāru) for speed, as well as numerous trills and catches;[28] the violinists of the 1990s, by contrast, sound much more florid. In the Madras of the 1960s, the question of which style to emulate was a pressing issue for violinists. That in the 1990s the florid style has become prevalent suggests that something in the notion of the voice has changed. The reproducible qualities are no longer words and phrases but a generalized, homogenized, virtuosic voice, a voice heavily influenced by the violin. Even in 1939, C. Subrahmanya Ayyar noted that vocalists in South India had already begun to increase their tempos in order to match the capabilities of the violin (115). Several vocalists remarked to me that much present-day vocal technique—not only the virtuosic speed which many vocalists command today but also the gamakas that define the sound of contemporary Karnatic music—are actually attempts to match the sound and capabilities of this virtuosic violin.

Magic Violin

In its short career in South India the violin has gone from being a colonial instrument to being, almost literally, the voice of Karnatic music. Throughout this career, the violin has also been at the center of musical experiments that articulate both its intimate relationship to colonialism and its seeming ability to reverse colonialism's effects. In these experiments the violin acts as a kind of translator or interpreter, a vehicle through which Karnatic music and Western music can communicate.

In the 1930s and 1940s, two violin-and-piano experiments were released in Madras. One was the brothers Muthu and Mani playing the Thyagaraja kriti "Nāgumōmu," for violin, piano, and *mridangam* (a double-headed drum). The other was Dwaram Venkataswamy Naidu playing a set of raga alapana improvisations with the American pianist and composer Alan Hovhaness on the piano. In both, the violin played in traditional Karnatic style, and the piano acted as an accompaniment in the Karnatic sense, trailing and highlighting the main melody. In Muthu and Mani's piece, released on record in the 1930s, the kriti, in the raga abheri, with its plain notes and fast-fingered passages, already suggested a Scottish flavor. The piano followed the violin, accompanying the same passage, when it was repeated, with different harmonies. In the alapana experiment, which was aired on All India Radio in the 1940s, the piano attempted to capture the violin's gamakas, particularly its slides and oscillations. The resulting impression, and perhaps desired effect, was that the violin seemed to be pulling the alapana in the direction of a traditional Karnatic elaboration, while the piano seemed to alight on various harmonies, longing for but never quite reaching resolution. The magic of the violin was its ability to lead the piano, without being dominated by the harmonic laws of Western music.

Since the 1980s these kinds of experiments, or "fusions," have become more self-conscious in the way they articulate Indian music with Western music. In his fusion album *How to Name It?* (1986) the film music director Illayaraja featured a piece entitled "I Met Bach in My House and We Had a Conversation," in which a Karnatic violin "accompanies" Bach's prelude to his third partita for violin. The piece starts with the solo violin's alapana, beginning in a typical Karnatic way but then building up to a virtuosic pitch, as if the violin is expecting a Western denouement. The Karnatic violin, amplified to a rich tone, contrasts with the orchestra of Western violins in the background, creating a sense of proximity for the listener.

This violin answers the orchestrated version of Bach's partita, while in the second half actual voices (those of the composer Illayaraja and the Karnatic violinist V. S. Narasimhan) articulate, or translate, parts of the melody using *sargam* syllables (syllables used to name the pitches in a scale, much like solfege in Western music). The effect is as if one is returning, via the wonders of multitrack recording, to a scene of first contact, perhaps the arrival of the European violin in India, but from the perspective of the Karnatic musician. Illayaraja describes the composition in the liner notes:

> "I Met Bach in My House" begins with an invocation that at first is contemplative, introspective, and becomes increasingly importunate; it comes to a climax, and is interrupted by the first notes of Bach's Prelude to his violin Partita III. The Prelude is soon played out in full brilliant dialogue with Indian instruments, a contrapuntal weaving that seems completely natural. Nor does it seem strange when voices break in spontaneously, in rapturous song, and we hear the Prelude articulated at speed in Indian solfeggio, so neatly, so fluently, that a great light dawns—the two musical cultures, Indian and Western—share a common ground, far more than is commonly perceived.

The Karnatic violin here literally articulates Karnatic music with Western music, providing a magical medium of sound through which the voice can enter and interpret Bach.

In Kunnakudi Vaidyanathan's *Magic Violin* (1998), belligerently subtitled "Everything Personal about It," the object seems to be not so much interpreting as outwitting. Kunnakudi had already used his violin to work other kinds of magic: in the 1970s he released the album *Cauvery* (after the river Kaveri, on whose banks Karnatic music is fabled to have been born) in which he, with only the aid of his violin, claimed to capture all the sounds of life along and in the river. Also in the 1970s he started playing with the thavil (the drum usually used to accompany the nagaswaram and therefore exclusively played by non-Brahmins) raising eyebrows in the classical world. This, along with his renditions of film songs on violin, contributed to his popular image as a violinist of the people. In "Magic Violin," Kunnakudi's violin, amplified with echo effects, "takes on" and "conquers" the computer, which is playing flattened, lifeless, synthetic versions of Western chords. The computer, equated with the West, in turn is equated with the world; on the cover of his cassette, Kunnakudi sits, larger than life, astride a cushion floating in space, with the planet earth in the background. The tracks have appropriately cosmic titles: "A Thing

4 "Magic violin" advertisement in *SRGMPDN* (10 April–10 May 1997).

of Beauty," "Full Moon," "Eclipse," "Creation." Kunnakudi's violin, with its bewildering rhythmic effects, dances above the computer, outwitting it every time.[29]

If the violin here acts as the instrument that helps Karnatic music outwit Western music and technology, elsewhere it helps constitute India's status as a nation by invoking Karnatic music's place in relation to the West. In August 1998 I was one of a group of violinists gathered by the violinist A. Kanyakumari for a musical celebration of the fiftieth anniversary of India's independence: a concert of fifty violins playing exactly in unison. In Madras concerts with multiple violins are common; concerts of two, three, and five violins happen frequently during the Madras music season. But whereas a concert of two, three, or even five violinists was manageable because the musicians could accompany one another, a concert of fifty violins was more difficult to coordinate. In the numerous rehearsals for the August 1998 event, Kanyakumari pared gamakas down to a bare minimum and revised the program so that it included more "English notes," which were deemed most suitable to group playing. No one commented on the irony of playing a concert of English notes at a celebration of India's independence. The concert was performed in a packed hall and got considerable coverage in the press, which described it as an "aural feast." After the event, Kanyakumari's success in having gotten fifty Karnatic violinists to play in unison was hailed as equivalent to the accomplishments of the great conductors of the West. What was significant was that no other group of fifty musicians, whether flutists, veena players, or mridangists, would have been conceivable. Here, perhaps enabled by its colonial origins, the violin itself became a figure of repetition. But, more important, the spectacle of unity created by fifty violins against green, orange, and white saris and *veshtis* was what people had come for. The violin thus became part of a visual and aural demonstration of national unity. "It could well be a one-time wonder," commented a reviewer, "but nevertheless a wonder."[30]

Voicing/Ventriloquizing

> A violin is an instrument, which is to say a tool. . . . The fact is that by using a mechanical contrivance, a violinist . . . can express something poignantly human that cannot be expressed without the mechanical contrivance. To achieve such expression of course the violinist . . . has to have interiorized the technology, made the tool or machine a second nature. . . . This calls for years of "practice."
>
> —Walter Ong, *Orality and Literacy*

The experiments that use the violin seem to have a common logic: through the violin they rearticulate the relationship between Karnatic music and the music of the West. But in so doing, they comment ironically on the desire—shared by an Indian middle class that looks to it as "tradition" and by Western consumers—for a pristine Indian music unaffected by colonialism. In fact, they present in each case a music profoundly affected by colonialism. It is due to the magic of the violin that Karnatic music is not weakened, but strengthened, by the encounter; each experiment reenacts and fulfills Karnatic music's stubborn insistence that it be considered on a par with Western classical music. If such a claim is the basis of the politics of classical music in South India, the violin is what makes it audible.

When the violin became the necessary accompaniment for the voice in Karnatic music, it displayed a seemingly natural ability to reproduce the voice. But what was elided in this transposition? The Karnatic voice, and the words it pronounced, were supplemented, or replaced, by the tone of the violin and piṭi and jāru and bowing techniques. Thus, the development of Karnatic violin technique over the last two centuries has been the development of a set of conventions by which the voice could be imitated and/or reproduced. That these conventions change (which demonstrates their conventional, rather than natural character) is apparent from the shifts in violin style in the twentieth century; as they change, so do notions of the voice.

In reproducing voice, the violin also becomes a ventriloquizer. The perfect violin accompanist is one whose playing is so self-effacing and unobtrusive that the vocalist forgets there is anything except her own voice. At the same time, the vocalist cannot be heard without the violin. The violin thus renders Karnatic music "more articulate." This same power of ventriloquism, which effects a separation between voice and subject, content and form, is perceived as the very magic that saved Karnatic music from destruction in the face of colonialism. "The emergence of the violin in Karnatic music," writes a violinist from Madras,

> is a very significant response—a response comprising co-option and adaptation of *just the musical means, not the content, thought, or style* of the colonial music system to the native/indigenous music system. This response, coupled with the high degree of sophistication and complexity that the indigenous musical system had already accomplished, was one of the ways by which the classical music system of South India was able to maintain itself, *quite intact*, in the face of the cultural onslaught. (Parasuram 1997, 40; emphasis added)

By the logic of ventriloquism, the site of deepest colonial impact is transformed into the very sign, and sound, of a pure Indian voice. The voice emerges as that which escapes the colonial impact precisely by allowing itself to flow through another medium, the hollow body of the violin. The authenticity of the Karnatic voice depends on articulating the relationship between violin and voice in terms of two oppositions crucial to modern thought: the separation between the real, or the original (the voice), and its representation (the violin, the "mere" accompaniment), and the separation between content (what the instrument represents, the true essence of Karnatic music, the voice) and form (in this case, the mere instrument).

Perhaps we are now in a position to answer the question posed in a lecture in 1935 by C. Subramanya Ayyar, who spent his life trying to fathom the peculiar power of the violin: "One may contend that in vocal music, the meaning of the words affects man. But why should music through stringed instruments, reproducing the nuances of the human voice, just like primeval speech akin to that before man ever learned or spoke any language, affect us? Can we offer any explanation?" (1941, 120). Here, the sound of the instrument is associated with a wordless, primeval voice, a pure voice that has the power to affect by transcending its colonial instrumental body and its ties to language. It is precisely the capacity of the instrument to be heard as a voice, to sound almost human while remaining nonhuman and to sound Indian while remaining foreign, which makes it powerful.[31] This ventriloquism works through a series of displacements which have occurred at particular historical moments. The voice is supplemented by the violin, whose sound then becomes a kind of super-voice; this virtuosic sound of a colonial instrument "gone native" is in turn imitated by vocalists. The change in violin styles in the twentieth century from a *piṭi* to a more florid sound is indicative not only of a change in vocal style but of a change in the concept of the voice itself. The history of voice in a particular time and place, then, is not simply the story of how people come to express themselves, but rather the story of how people come to let certain sounds speak and sing *for* them.[32] The late-twentieth-century preference for a virtuosic vocal sound and the claim that this is the natural and authentic sound of South Indian music mark a desire to create a distinctively Indian sound, a representative "voice" not in danger of being confused with anything remotely Western.

This is a distinctly modern and postcolonial desire. To say that the voice in Karnatic music is a modern construct is not to say that there was no vocal music in South India before the violin. Rather, the violin in Karnatic music stages the voice in a particular way so that it becomes available as a metaphor for a tradition and a self that have survived colonialism while remaining uncolonized. This staging is a repetitive act, borne through generations of musical practice that have made the violin in Karnatic music not an unnatural peculiarity but second nature. If one takes seriously Regula Qureshi's injunction that "musical meaning and affect need to be considered as . . . historically and socially situated," then one needs to consider how the habitual, repetitive patterns of musical practice—indeed, the very methods of fingering and bowing I have discussed above—articulate with the perhaps more academically accessible realm of history (2000, 812). One needs to consider musical practice or custom as "that obscure crossroads where the constructed and the habitual coalesce" (Taussig 1993, xv). At the heart of this inquiry is the question posed by Subrahmanya Ayyar of how sound acquires meaning, as well as the broader question of how things that are "social constructions" locatable in particular histories nevertheless come to be lived and deeply felt as truths (ibid.).

In this regard, one might say that the sound of the violin recalls, or reenacts, colonial first contact through what Michael Taussig has called "second contact": when the colonial power or personage is refracted in the images or sounds produced by the colonized. This often occurs through mimesis, an embodiment of power in which the terms of power are potentially redefined (Taussig 1993). Through mimesis, one is able to grasp and master that which is strange or other through resemblances or copies of it. Mimesis, like sympathetic magic, involves some kind of contact, often embodied in an object taken from its original context and reframed in a new one. Homi K. Bhabha describes mimicry in this sense as a "repetition of partial presence" that disrupts the authority of the original (1984, 129). For both Bhabha and Taussig, the force of mimicry/mimesis is in the power it gives the colonized to disrupt the supremacy of the colonizer. Indeed, the presence of the violin in Karnatic music, as a modernizing influence and above all as a classical instrument, was essential to placing Karnatic music on a par with Western art music and thus displacing the latter's supremacy as *the* classical music of the world.

But the fact that the violin is not native but *gone* native preserves its uncanniness, its potential to be disruptive to the postcolonial mythologies of Indian classical music as well.[33] The capacity of the violin to ventriloquize depends on its capacity to mimic, that is, not to *represent* the voice but to *repeat* it in such a way that the relations between original and copy, voice and accompaniment are destabilized.[34] In this sense, the Karnatic violin stands at the center of a complex set of mimetic relations between instrument and voice, India and the West, colonizer and colonized. The mimetic capacity of the violin guarantees the authenticity of the Karnatic voice, as a colonial instrument is used to ward off—and ultimately redeem Indian music from—the effects of colonialism.

2 From the Palace to the Street

STAGING "CLASSICAL" MUSIC

Not long after the advent of the Europeans, the Goddess of Indian Music had to jump from the palace into the open street.

—M. S. Ramaswamy Aiyar, *Lectures on Indian Music*

The staging of Karnatic music in public concerts beginning in the early twentieth century was not just a matter of shifting musical performances from one kind of venue to another. Rather, it involved a constellation of developments that profoundly affected the ways in which Karnatic music came to be performed and heard. In a concrete sense, the concert hall brought about a particular structure of presentation, one that was based on a clear separation between the musicians and the audience, and the idea of a "repertoire" of "timeless" compositions detachable both from their original context and the contexts of their repeated performances. It involved the microphone, necessary for making live music audible to large audiences in noisy urban settings but also a technology whose effects went far beyond mere amplification. In a less concrete but equally as real sense, the staging of "classical" music involved the creation of an audience, a group of concertgoers considerably more homogeneous in terms of caste and class than attendees at earlier temple or street performances.

One incident can serve as an entry point into the kinds of shifts entailed in this staging of classical music. In the late 1930s the maharaja of Mysore, Nalwadi Krishnaraja Wodeyar, installed microphones in his *durbar* (palace hall) and attached loudspeakers to the outside of the palace.[1] The purpose of these was to make the durbar concerts, which had long been reserved for an invited few, available to the general public. The implications of such an act were far-reaching: the private durbar concert was converted into a public broadcast; the palace became a site of entertainment for a newly imagined audience that listened from outside. The structure of the durbar hall, with its carefully arranged mirrors affording views of the maharaja from all angles while the concert was in progress and its essentially exclusive, private character, was considerably altered by the attachment of microphones; the microphones literally turned the palace inside out, converting the musical events there into concerts. If kingly authority in South India was built around the physical and geographical concentration of power in a single source, the microphones and loudspeakers introduced a very different order of power.[2] Theirs was the power not to concentrate but to disseminate. Their medium was not authority (in the sense of a single, authoritative source) but reproduction. Their power literally came from a reproducible source (electricity) and depended on the reproducibility of another source (music). If kingly authority radiated from a center, microphones worked by a different logic: that of the circuit. With the power of electricity, the king and his music literally became wired to the world outside the palace.

This moment highlights the difference and the conflict between two economies of music, a conflict that is at the heart of the discourse on classical music in South India. Musicians at the beginning of the twenty-first century routinely invoke images of a time before Karnatic music became a "business," before musicians were at the mercy of sabha organizers, before the noise, crowds, and "mechanical life"[3] of the city encroached on traditional methods of teaching and learning. The idea of a historical break, constructed both temporally (the nineteenth century vs. the twentieth) and spatially (royal courts and villages vs. the city of Madras), has been foundational to the politics of classical music in South India. The imagination of such a break provided the rationale for the "revival" of Karnatic music in the early twentieth century: the movement to "rescue" the arts of music and dance from their "degraded" status, which had been caused by the persistence of obsolete forms of patronage and performance in the twentieth century, and reframe them in new urban, bourgeois contexts. In this revivalist discourse Karnatic music was redefined as strictly devotional and invested with the peculiar power to exist outside politics, outside circuits of economic exchange or personal motivation.

The rise of public concerts and commercial music-making produced new standards of taste, articulated on the one hand in the emerging discipline of music criticism and on the other in the curricula of teaching institutions established to maintain those standards. At the same time, these standards were being amplified in a new set of conventions of voice brought about by the mechanism of the microphone and codified in the retrospective canonization of the composer Thyagaraja, whose devotional lyrics have come almost exclusively to represent the voice of Karnatic music.

The Sound of Royalty: Patronage of Music in Tanjavur and Travancore

At the beginning of the nineteenth century, the center of the Karnatic music world was the royal court of Tanjavur.[4] Before 1800, Tanjavur had had several rulers from the Nayak and Maratha dynasties who were interested in music. For instance, the first Maratha king Shahaji (r. 1684–1712) composed *padams* and *prabandhas* (types of composition characterized by their prosody and number of verses) as well as a classificatory work in Telugu entitled *Sahaji Rāgalakṣaṇamu* (*Shahaji's Raga Lakshanas*: Characteristics of ragas). King Tulaja I (r. 1728–1736) wrote a treatise in Sanskrit, *Saṅgīta Saramrita* (Garland of music) (Seetha 1981, 116). By the time of Tulaji II (r. 1739–1787), several musicians had been brought from neighboring villages and towns farther afield to be court musicians. King Amarasimha (r. 1787–1798) held a miniature court at the town of Tiruvitaimarutur, near Tanjavur, after he fell out of favor with the British East India company, which prohibited the composition of songs in his praise.

In the first few decades of the nineteenth century, under the rule of Serfoji II (1798–1832), Tanjavur reached its peak as a hub of musical and artistic activity. The young Serfoji received his training in English language, as well as other subjects, from the Protestant missionary Christian Friedrich Schwartz, who had been in Tanjavur since 1778. Through the intervention of Schwartz, who appealed to the British East India Company, Amarasimha, a temporary regent by an earlier agreement, was deposed and Serfoji was appointed king. During his reign, Serfoji maintained an interest in scholarly collecting and various projects of improvement.[5] He began the first printing press in South India (with Devanagari script), started a medical institution, collected European literature, and made preparations for the building of a port at Nagapattinam. He started the Saraswati Mahal Library in order to house his collections.

The Saraswati Mahal Modi manuscripts (records written in a version of Marathi on palm leaves) indicate that a separate division of the palace administration was given over to musicians patronized by Serfoji II (Venkataramiah 1984, 221). The position of overseer of these musicians was held by the violinist Varahappa Dikshitar (also known as Varahappayyar, mentioned in chapter 1), who also served a political post as one of Serfoji's ministers. The overseer was responsible for hiring musicians and seeing to their welfare. The most illustrious of the musicians patronized by Serfoji II were the Tanjore Quartette, four brothers: Ponniah (b. 1804), composer and vocalist; Vadivelu (b. 1810), composer and violinist (also mentioned in chapter 1); Chinniah (b. 1802), choreographer; and Sivanandam (b. 1808), mridangist and *nattuvanar* (*naṭṭuvaṇkam*: small cymbals used to keep tala in a dance performance) (Kittappa 1993, 6). These brothers were responsible for creating and standardizing a large dance repertoire and developing a teaching method. All four studied with the composer Muthuswamy Dikshitar, and Serfoji's court provided them with a forum for their own and their students' performances. As court musicians, the brothers were required to sing for Serfoji each morning and regularly composed kritis and varnams in his name (ibid., 7, 9). Serfoji presented Ponniah with a gift of 5000 rupees on his first performance in the court (ibid., 6). In addition to attracting Tamil and Telugu musicians from the immediate region, Serfoji's court drew Hindustani musicians from more distant places like Cuddapah and Gwalior (Venkataramiah 1984, 230); many also came to Tanjavur to learn music.

In addition to his interests in European art and literature, Serfoji was drawn to European music. The Modi manuscripts record the purchases of instruments like "fiddle," "Irish pipes," harp, French horn, flute, trumpet, and piano in the 1820s. Serfoji himself studied Western music, and it was from a European priest employed in Serfoji's court who played violin that Vadivelu is said to have learned Western violin (Kittappa 1993, 10). Serfoji also founded the Tanjavur palace band, with forty-two musicians playing both Indian and Western instruments, and maintained a separate dance orchestra (Seetha 1981, 116). The band apparently played not only Western music but also Indian music that had been arranged in staff notation. Several books in Serfoji's library contain staff notation under which he had written the names of the swaras in Devanagari script. Books filled with staff notation suggest that he employed people to write out tunes, probably for the band's use; he himself also composed tunes for the band. Serfoji's collections contain a wide variety of printed Western music (at least twenty volumes), from chamber music for pianoforte and string instruments by Haydn and Muzio Clemente to ballads from English comic operas and handwritten books of reels, strathspeys, and waltzes. Serfoji's successor, Shivaji II, also arranged Western music concerts and was a patron of musicians (ibid., 120). After Shivaji's death, however, in the absence of an heir, the Madras government took over the reign of Tanjavur. The British, who considered the Tanjavur kings' expenditures on music and dance extravagant, discontinued the traditions of patronage that had developed in Tanjavur. Musicians migrated to the other princely states of Trivandrum (Travancore), Mysore, Pudukkottai, and Ramanathapuram in the 1830s (ibid., 22–23).

Among those musicians who migrated was Vadivelu of the Tanjore Quartette. Because of a disagreement over the nature of their services in the Tanjavur temple, Serfoji II had removed the brothers from his court. Although he invited them back shortly afterward, Vadivelu refused the offer, instead accepting one from the king of Travancore, Swati Tirunal, in whose court he remained for the rest of his life (Kittappa 1993, 9). Swati Tirunal (b. 1813) assumed the rule of Travancore state in 1829, at the age of sixteen. At the suggestion of Colonel John Munro, the British resident of Travancore state, Swati Tirunal had been tutored in English, Sanskrit, Marathi, political science, and Karnatic music by Subba Rao from Tanjavur, also known as "English" Subba Rao for his skill in the English language (Venkitasubramonia Iyer 1975, 4–6). In 1830 Swati Tirunal appointed Subba Rao as Dewan. Together, they attempted to make the kingship an example of enlightened leadership and Travancore a center of learning.

The most important elements in this improvement were the English language and Karnatic music. An English school was started in Trivandrum as early as 1834, earlier than English education was imparted in the areas of the Madras Presidency directly under British rule (Venkitasubramonia Iyer 1975, 12–13). With the help of Tanjore Subba Rao's contacts and superb negotiating ability, Swati Tirunal sought to make Travancore as much a center of Karnatic music as Tanjavur was. Subba Rao personally negotiated with the durbars of Tanjavur and Pudukkottai to bring many of Serfoji II's court musicians to Travancore, including the Tanjore Quartette and the vocalist Meruswami, who became Swati Tirunal's music teacher (156). Under Swati Tirunal's rule, the forms of music and dance peculiar to Travancore—the *sopana sangitam* (literally, "step music") sung on the steps of temples and the dance form *mōhini aṭṭam*—were significantly altered, brought closer to the forms of music and dance practiced at Tanjavur. Sopana sangitam, known for its slow renditions and limited improvisation, was altered not only by the influx of a new style of composing and singing represented by Vadivelu and other Tanjavur musicians but also by the very structure of music making that Swati Tirunal's court suggested.[6] Instead of taking place on the temple steps, music making took place in Swati Tirunal's durbar hall as a recital, with the king himself as the audience; musicians were invited to his court because of their skill. Swati Tirunal himself is said to have kept a small room in his palace with a view of Padmanabhaswamy Temple as his composing room. The palace structure thus introduced the idea of a space for music that was separate from the temple and from other living spaces. Meanwhile, the economic structure in which musicians were supported out of the palace budget, with some holding official positions like chief palace musician, created the atmosphere in which music became a profession.[7]

Not content with having musicians from Tanjavur and several disciples of the composer Thyagaraja, Swati Tirunal desired to have Thyagaraja himself in his court (Venkitasubramonia Iyer 1975, 161). In 1838 he sent a party of his court musicians—including Vadivelu and Govinda Marar, as well as the superintendent of stables who knew the composer personally—to Thyagaraja's house in the town of Tiruvaiyaru, near Tanjavur. Thyagaraja, who had already refused the patronage of Serfoji II, conveyed his respects to Swati Tirunal but refused to come to Travancore. Otherwise, however, Swati Tirunal's handsome payments attracted musicians from far and wide. He invited Hindustani musicians from Gwalior, Benares, Pune, and Hyderabad, in addition to maintaining on a permanent basis a Hindustani dance troupe and several musicians who had learned Hindustani music in Tanjavur at Serfoji's court. He also employed an Anglo-Indian to play Western music and purchased Western instruments (165).

What Swati Tirunal's court introduced, as had Serfoji's before and the Mysore and Vizianagaram courts later, was the idea of the court as a showpiece of culture, a collection of the best musicians from around the world. The better the musicians were, the more the power that accrued to the king's name.[8] Swati Tirunal's desire to patronize the worthy appeared to be a selfless act of generosity and devotion to the art of music at the same time as it was also a desire for power, a political act, part of the logic of the gift that characterized kingship in South India. Swati Tirunal's liberal patronage of music was eventually curtailed by the administration of the Madras Presidency. In 1840 a new resident of Travancore state who aspired to be Dewan reported to Madras that Swati Tirunal's spending on his court musicians was extravagant and unnecessary. The resident's continuous complaints effectively undermined Swati Tirunal's authority several years before his death in 1846 (Venkitasubramonia Iyer 1975, 155). Under his successors Vishakam Tirunal and Ayilyam Tirunal, the Travancore court continued to attract musicians but was no longer at its peak.

Institutionalizing Music at Mysore and Vizianagaram

Between 1850 and 1950, the largest and most renowned court for music was that of Mysore. Under four rulers—Mummadi Krishnaraja Wodeyar (r. 1799–1868), Chamaraja Wodeyar IX (r. 1868–1894), Nalvadi Krishnaraja Wodeyar (r. 1895–1940), and Jayachamaraja Wodeyar (r. 1940–1950)—the Mysore court was contemporaneous with the rise of Madras as the center of the Karnatic music world. The combination of royal patronage of individual musicians and the founding of institutions to teach music, a connection with European music publishers and record producers, and an articulated concern for the musical education of the public made Mysore's court, especially after 1900, significantly different from the earlier courts at Tanjavur and Travancore. But like these other courts, the Mysore court laid heavy emphasis on preservation. Chamaraja Wodeyar collected books on music and founded the Oriental Library in 1891 to house them. Also, in the 1890s, he made phonograph recordings of several musicians and kept them in a library at the palace (Vedavalli 1992, 29). Under Nalvadi Krishnaraja Wodeyar, the concept of preservation came to include the printing of kritis composed by his court musicians and the writing of Karnatic music in European staff notation.[9] Two court musicians—Veena Venkatagiriappa and Veena Sivaramiah—were employed to write notation for songs on gramophone records in the collection of the royal family (36).

Nalvadi Krishnaraja Wodeyar also put a premium on teaching. In 1915 he founded the Royal School of Music at the palace; each court musician was assigned to teach a certain number of students, meeting with them daily from five to six in the evening.[10] Although most of the teaching at the school was on a one-on-one basis and many court vidwans had been teachers before becoming affiliated with the court, Krishnaraja Wodeyar felt it necessary to institutionalize the teaching of music. In 1928 the school had twenty-five students, most whom were probably hereditary musicians; nevertheless, the idea of such a school may have opened the way for nonhereditary musicians to learn music. Krishnaraja Wodeyar also supported the study of European music. In 1913 he paid 1000 rupees—a hefty sum even now—for an institution in Mysore run by an English woman to prepare students to appear for the examination of the Trinity College of Music, London. The Chamarajendra Ursu Boarding School, which had been under the administration of the Mysore Palace since 1892, employed several teachers "to teach the boys to play drums and pipes and to read Western music."[11]

Although the maharajas of Tanjavur and Travancore were interested in Western music, the Mysore court seems to have become most involved with it. In 1920 Krishnaraja Wodeyar arranged for a celebration of Beethoven's centenary in Bangalore, at which Margaret Cousins played a Beethoven piano concerto with the Palace Orchestra. In her account of the event she seemed astonished by the good order and tune the piano was in, as well as the respectfulness of the audience (Cousins 1940, 142). Nalvadi Krishnaraja Wodeyar, who had himself received training in Western music, employed the German Otto Schmidt to conduct the Palace Orchestra and to teach Western staff notation and harmonic theory. Jayachamaraja Wodeyar extended his patronage to the Russian composer Nikolas Medtner, sponsoring a series of recordings of his works in the late 1940s. A series of correspondences between Jayachamaraja Wodeyar and the American record producer Walter Legge demonstrates the maharaja's interest in recording "neglected" European music (Legge 1998, 187–92).

The Mysore maharajas' interest in Western music was deep enough to have produced several varieties of Western ensembles, including a reed band, a full orchestra, and a small orchestra, whose members, although conducted by Otto Schmidt, were all Indian. The Palace Orchestra and Reed Band gave performances for visiting maharajas and British officials, for the opening ceremonies of medical and industrial conferences, and for other notable occasions.[12] Perhaps even more important, these ensembles served as the model for the Palace Karnatic Band (also called the Indian Orchestra), which played Karnatic repertoire on an ensemble of instruments containing violins, veenas, flutes, clarinets, sitars, dilrubas, harmoniums, mridangam, tabla, and dholak. Part of the function of the maharaja's durbar was to display the harmonious interweaving of India and Europe, and the Palace Karnatic Band suggested an ensemble comparable to those of the West.

The Mysore maharajas were interested in seeing this accomplished on an even more musicologically minute level, sponsoring various experiments combining Indian and Western music. A clerk named Pattabhirammaya was appointed to the palace controller's office in the late nineteenth century by Chamaraja Wodeyar because of his "note swarams," compositions with English words (Krishna Rao 1917). In Krishnaraja Wodeyar's

5 *Mysore Yuvaraja's Indian and European Musical Series* cover page (1940).

time the purpose of having Karnatic melodies written down in European notation was not only to preserve them but also to render them suitable for harmonization. These "harmonized Indian airs" were performed by the Palace Western Band, under the direction of Veena Venkatagiriappa and Otto Schmidt. A series of airs were composed by Yuvaraja Narasimharaja Wodeyar (Krishnaraja's younger brother) and published in London as a series in 1940. The title page of these airs, most of which are scored for small ensembles with tempos like "fox-trot" and "waltz," bears the motto "To popularise Eastern music harmonised in Western style."

The Mysore maharajas' orientation to "tradition" seems to have been different from the orientation prevalent later in the twentieth century: instead of dwelling on a golden past, they concentrated on the future of Karnatic music, which for them involved the successful wedding of Karnatic music not only with Western music but also with technology. Between 1920 and 1930 the bands of Mysore Palace made gramophone recordings that were sold commercially and competed with the Madras-based Nadamuni Band, which was then popular at the weddings of the Madras bourgeoisie. Some of the Mysore palace's most lavish expenditures were on acquiring pianos, harmoniums, and organs, as well as more unconventional instruments like the horn violin, theremin, and calliaphone, a mechanical music player (Vedavalli 1992, 34, 36).

The maharajas of Mysore were also interested in the technology of the concert and concert hall itself, from the loudspeakers attached to the palace to the staging of durbar concerts. The Trivandrum journalist A. Padmanabha Iyer offered the following description of the European durbar in his 1936 account, *Modern Mysore: Impressions of a Visitor.*

> The taking of his seat on the Throne is signalised by the blaze of electric lights in multi-coloured forms and shape. The huge crowds of spectators in front . . . are naturally surprised at the magnificent sight so suddenly sprung on them. . . . The set of Indian Bhagavathars come and go like angels, so suggestive their movements and so magnificent their surroundings, because the Durbar Hall is Heaven itself on this earth. These entertainers who are Palace employees are to sit on a seat in the Electric Lift after tuning their instruments. . . . The Lift goes up and stops just in front of His Highness. The signal is then given for them to begin their entertainment. After their allotted time the bell rings when they bring their entertainment to a close. Immediately, these performers disappear like celestial beings of Puranic fame, as the Lift goes down. (60–61)

Note here the exquisite staging of the music: if a regular concert stage has the effect of physically separating the musicians from the audience and thus presenting the musical performance as detached from the ordinary activities of tuning or practicing, the electric lift accomplishes this even more so. A perfectly choreographed performance also requires a certain kind of audience, one that will sit attentively listening and watching. From Padmanabha Iyer's description one can almost feel the discipline that the electric lights and the sudden appearance of the musicians exerted on the spectators.

In the princely state of Vizianagaram, at the northern extremity of the Madras Presidency, similar activities were going on, if on a smaller scale than those in Mysore. Ananda Gajapathi, who ruled Vizianagaram from 1879 to 1897, had interests in history, philology, literature, and music. He commissioned translations of Sanskrit treatises into Telugu, patronized Telugu poets and writers, oversaw the founding of Telugu literary journals, and founded the Maharaja's Dramatic Society, which staged new plays

(Rama Rao 1985, 12–17). In 1894, at the request of the Madras government, he himself wrote a historiographic treatise on the Vizianagaram treaty of 1758, in which he detailed his family's involvement in aiding the British in their war with the French over the Vizianagaram territory (appendix). An accomplished veena player himself, Ananda Gajapathi patronized both Karnatic and Hindustani musicians in his court and maintained several performing ensembles to play Western music (15). These included an Italian string band (consisting of twelve violins, two violas, and one cello) and a brass-and-woodwind band.[13] Like other maharajas, he purchased a horn violin for the use of his court violinists.

Most important, Ananda Gajapathi imagined a music college that would carry on the long-developing artistic traditions of Vizianagaram in a more modern form.[14] The Maharaja's Music College, however, was not founded until 1919, and then by Ananda Gajapathi successor, Vijayarama Gajapathi. The college's first principal was Adhipatla Narayana Das, a harikatha artist from Vizianagaram who first received royal patronage from Ananda Gajapathi in the 1890s after returning from successful performances at the Mysore court. As Narayana Das went from his post as court artist to music college principal, the Vizianagaram Maharaja's Music College became the first of its kind in the Madras Presidency. Some elements of the college, like free boarding for all students, remained similar to the structure of royal patronage. However, the relatively unstructured flow of musical knowledge between musicians in the court was transformed into a six-year syllabus, drawn up in 1919.[15] For each year, the syllabus was divided into a "theory" and a "practical" section, and included lessons on the life and work of famous composers and the writing of notation. The six-year course was carefully graded, officially introducing students to the concept of raga only in the third year and to improvisatory techniques only in the fifth. The students were expected to learn a specific number of compositions. Stories of court composers and musicians, instead of being handed down through generations of court musicians, were relegated to lessons on "music history."[16] At the end of their studies, the students were tested by six examiners who had been elected with the sanction of the estate collector. An introduction in the college's silver jubilee souvenir from 1944 notes ironically that though Vizianagaram had always been a center for music, there had never been as much interest in music there as there was after 1919.[17]

Narrating the Nineteenth Century

Adhipatla Narayana Das's transformation from court musician to music-college principal was repeated by many other musicians in the 1940s.[18] As royal patronage of music began increasingly to be replaced by state patronage in the form of government music colleges, a new genre began to appear: anecdotes and biographical sketches of nineteenth-century musicians in the royal courts. Prominent among these were U. V. Swaminathayyar's *Caṅkīta Mummaṇikaḷ* (published serially before being collected in book form in 1936); V. S. Gomathi Shankara Ayyar's *Icai Vallunarkaḷ* (1970), a collection of anecdotes related by his father in the 1930s; numerous anecdotes written by the critic Ellarvi, all in Tamil, throughout the 1940s and 50s; Mysore Vasudevachar's memoir in Kannada, *Na Kaṇḍa Kalavidāru* (1955); and P. Sambamoorthy's *Great Musicians* (1959). These writings were directed at a new audience of music students and concert-going music lovers: those who had no direct contact with the royal courts. For music students at the universities, many of whom did not grow up in musical families, the stories of these musicians of the nineteenth century were available only through such books.

Some of the writings seemed to be aimed at a more casual audience of middle-class Madras music lovers, who might read these stories in their leisure hours. Ellarvi's writings appeared in the popular Tamil newspaper *Svadēṣa Mitran* before they were collected and published in several volumes in the 1950s. In these writings the generous patronage of kings and the escapades of musicians in royal courts were remembered as elements of a disappearing past. Mysore Vasudevachar, for instance, dedicated his memoir to Chamaraja Wodeyar, the king who had patronized him, but he wrote it only after the Mysore court had lost its ability to patronize musicians and he had moved to Madras to become the vice president of the music-and-dance school Kalakshetra (Vedavalli 1992, 26, 87).

The subject of these writings is a prior time, when music was patronized by kings and wealthy citizens who themselves took an interest in music, and before the city of Madras became the center of Karnatic music. The picture that emerges is of a musical world that thrived on competition and in which audiences routinely were thrilled to the point of ecstasy by the performances. In *Caṅkīta Mummaṇikaḷ* (Three gems of music), Swaminathayyar (1855–1942) offers biographies of three nineteenth-century musicians, portraying this world most vividly. (Swaminathayyar is best known for his editing and publishing of Tamil Sangam literature in the 1930s; he also wrote a number of biographies and memoirs pertaining to the late nineteenth and early twentieth centuries.) In *Caṅkīta Mummaṇikaḷ* Swaminathayyar uses a florid style to capture the glory of the music of that period. In his portrait of Ganam Krishnayyar, he describes the atmosphere of competition and the culture of challenges that thrived in the royal court of Amarasimha, the Tanjavur king who preceded Serfoji II. When Krishnayyar was a young boy, a famous vidwan named Bobbili Kesavayyar came from Andhra Pradesh to visit the court. Kesavayyar was famous not only for his *ganam* (*kaṉam*: heavy, grand) style of singing but also for his flamboyant manner: he adorned his tambura with a flag and required that any musician who lost to him in a musical contest surrender his tambura, shawls, and other gifts from his patron; Kesavayyar would then visit other courts on horseback, followed by a cartload of these surrendered items (Sambamoorthy 1939, 429). Swaminathayyar relates that after Kesavayyar's performance at the court was over, King Amarasimha asked if any of his court musicians could equal so difficult a style, with a voice "like a lion's roar" (*ciṅkakarjanai pōl*). The court vidwans answered, one by one, that such a task was beyond them. Finally, the young Krishnayyar stood up and said, "If he teaches me the grammar [*lakṣaṉam*] of it, I will be able to sing like that." The king then arranged for the visiting musician to teach Krishnayyar, who became so famous for that style that the title "Ganam" was attached to his name (Swaminathayyar 1936, 8–10).

Similarly, Swaminathayyar relates that the career of Maha Vaidyanathayyar (1844–1893) began with a challenge and a competition. Vaidyanathayyar was patronized by Subramania Desikar, who held a government post in Tiruvavaturai, a place noted as a gathering spot for musicians as well as for experts in Tamil and Sanskrit. Desikar had various designs for boosting the reputation of his young musician. One day, two elder vidwans, Periya Vaidyanathayyar and Chinna Vaidyanathayyar, came to Tiruvavaturai. Since some people had expressed doubt about Maha Vaidyanathayyar on account of his young age, Desikar arranged for a contest between him and the two older musicians, complete with a referee (*mattiyastar*). After showing his mettle by correcting the two elder musicians' rendition of one raga, picking out a single mistake of a single note, Maha Vaidyanathayyar himself sang. He chose a common raga but sang so fast that the two elder musicians could not identify it and guessed that it was some rare raga. When Maha Vaidyanathayyar emerged victorious, a long deliberation ensued over what title he should be given; finally, they came up with the title "Mahā" (great). Swaminathayyar implies that such titles bestowed on musicians were not mere honorifics but equivalent to costly presents, because such a title would forever call up the memory of, in this instance, Maha Vaidyanathayyar's victory. Indeed, a song by Tandavarayya Tambiran in praise of Maha Vaidyanathayyar described Saraswati herself as "white with the agony of having lost" to him (197).

There was competition among patrons for musicians as well. Ganam Krishnayyar eventually left Amarasimha's court to be patronized by the merchant Ramabhadra Mupanar, and then by the zamindar of Udayarpalayam, Kacci Kalyanarangadurai. To attract such a well-known vidwan to a small court was not easy: Kalyanarangadurai had to impress Krishnayyar with a fancy palanquin and a handsome monthly salary (31). If a vidwan employed by a patron showed himself to be poor, it was a loss of face for the patron. For example, one time Krishnayyar had gotten low on money and decided to sell a precious belt that Ramabhadra Mupanar had presented to him. When Mupanar heard of this, he became angry and exclaimed, "If they tell us they need money, will we not give it?!" (38). Krishnayyar tried to reconcile with Mupanar but could not soften the other's anger. Finally, he began to sing a song, addressing his patron informally.

> Eṉṉaṭā colluṭā eṉ cāmi nīyē
> Eṉṉaṭā eṉ mītu kōpam
> [Hey you, tell me, you are my lord
> What for this anger at me?] (38–39)

Hearing his musician's voice Mupanar's heart melted. He found it impossible to remain angry and explained that it was "only a test" to see how Krishnayyar would respond.

In "Tōṭi Aṭaku" (Pawning todi raga), a whimsical story told by Ellarvi, there is a similar theme of the royal patron having to compete with a local merchant. In the story, which Ellarvi dates around 1860, a local merchant decided to cash in on royal patronage when the vidwan Sitaramayyar, famous for his renditions of todi raga, confided that he was out of cash and needed a loan. The merchant, who knew how much people would pay to hear Sitaramayyar sing todi, asked him to mortgage it, so that until the loan was repaid, he was not allowed to sing todi. Embarrassed by this last resort, Sitaramayyar did not tell anyone about the deal but secretly went along with it. The king of Tanjavur was first bewildered, then finally exasperated when Sitaramayyar sang every raga except todi. At last, when cornered, Sitaramayyar explained his deal with the merchant and said he would only be able to sing it again if the merchant was paid off. The exasperated king exclaimed, "If you told me you needed money do you really think you wouldn't get it?" and immediately sent the money off to the merchant so that he could hear todi raga again (Ellarvi 1963, 1–3). In this story the tension between two economies of music, one based on royal patronage and the other on market value, is thematized.

The loving but testy relationship between musicians and their patrons was another element of this nineteenth-century musical scene. U. V. Swaminathayyar shows the power of words, when sung, to create and undo anger (1936, 37–39). One day, while under the patronage of Kacci Kalyanarangadurai, Krishnayyar met his patron for one of their habitual talks (*callāpam*). Kalyanarangadurai, however, was preoccupied with matters relating to his lands and failed to give Krishnayyar his full attention. Noticing this, Krishnayyar became angry and sang,

> Pattuppai muttuppai vacra paṭakkaḻam
> paipaiyāp paṇattaik koṭuttavar pōlap
> pāṭina pāṭṭukkum āṭṭukkum nīreṉṉaip
> pacappinatē pōtum palaṉaṟivēn kāṇum.
> [You're just like one who gives money and pearls and
> diamond pendants for the songs I sing; enough of your
> ingratiating me; I can't see what the benefit is.] (38)

Krishnayyar turned the system of patronage against his patron, implying that his gifts were a kind of bribe, crass and material, and that the patron knew and cared nothing about the music he was getting in return. Kalyanarangar, on hearing this, realized his neglect, especially toward a vidwan who could, had he wanted to, found a place in a much larger and more prestigious court. He apologized profusely, and Krishnayyar continued the song, deftly changing the words of the pallavi to those a female bhakta would sing to her lord.

> Pattuppai muttuppai vacrap patakkamum
> parintu koṭuttu mikac cukan tantupin
> pañcaṇai mītiṉiṟ koñci viḷaiyāṭi
> rañcitamum aṟrinta makarājanē.
> [Maharaja! You know what is good, who gave me
> money and pearls and diamond pendants, and played
> gently on a mattress.] (39)

The same material gifts that were crass before are now transformed into the signs of a good patron. As Krishnayyar's sentiments change from anger to love, the zamindar referred to coldly and without a name as "nīr" in the first pallavi becomes "makarāja" (maharaja) in the second. The system of patronage is thematized as the songs themselves become part of the exchange of material and immaterial goods.

The value of words implied the valuing of adeptness with language. A sign of this adeptness was a musician's ability to hear a song with a particular tune and to make up new words to the same tune (Swaminathayyar 1936, 17). This went along with the ability to make whatever one sang pertinent to the situation at hand. For instance, at a banquet given by Governor Thomas Munro in Madras, Ganam Krishnayyar sang a song in which the name "Munro Sahib" appeared, much to the governor's delight (24). In an incident related by Mysore Vasudevachar, two brothers named Kuppiah and Appiah, although they were already accomplished musicians, could not get into the Tanjore court. In order to get in, they disguised themselves and enrolled as students of two court musicians. The king came to know who they really were and accepted them as court vidwans. But several senior musicians were envious and composed a new varnam they planned to challenge Kuppiah and Appiah with when the king held a ceremony to honor them. Having caught wind of this, the two brothers engaged a spy to secretly notate the varnam for them. When, at the ceremony, the elder musicians played the varnam and then challenged the brothers to play it in three tempos, Kuppiah and Appiah played the varnam not only correctly but at triple the speed, vanquishing the elder musicians. The king, utterly impressed, presented Kuppiah with a gold-threaded turban, and Kuppiah spontaneously sang a pallavi in Telugu in which the syllables of the notes also meant, "Is it right that the ruler should present such a turban?" ("Pāga iccara sarigā?"). Using the same virtuosic technique of *swarakshara* (in which the note names and the syllables of the words coincide), the king spontaneously sang back, "It is only an ordinary turban" ("Sadā pāga iccanē") (Vasudevachar 1955, 13–14). The feat of singing a pallavi was brought to even greater heights by making the pallavi punningly appropriate to the situation at hand in both music and words, allowing both musician and king, without missing a beat, to show off their ability and their modesty at the same time.[19]

Such contests happened even without the presence of kings in Madras. For instance, the absence of a royal figure did not prevent the vocalist Venugopaldas Naidu from pulling out all the stops to try to defeat Maha

Vaidyanathayyar before the eyes of the public. V. S. Gomathi Shankara Ayyar related the story, elaborately and suspensefully, as it was told to him by his father, Pallavi Subbiah Bhagavatar, who was a student of Maha Vaidyanathayyar from 1876–1882 (1970, foreword). In the late 1880s Maha Vaidyanathayyar was on an extended stay in Madras, enjoying popularity with audiences and the governor of Madras. In a special feast given for the governor, he gave a concert in which he sang English notes for the governor's sake. In the midst of such gracious society, however, envy was brewing. A vidwan so popular that "if he merely moved his mouth, thousands would gather," Venugopaldas Naidu, known as Venu, was living in Madras at that time. Shankara Ayyar describes at length Venu's kinglike appearance, his penchant for riding around Madras on horseback, and the fear he inspired in people. Venu was angry that he himself hadn't been asked to sing for the governor, so to get even, he began grumbling that Vaidyanathayyar's "Maha" was a fake degree and that by calling himself that he was cheating the public. Venu confided with his close friend, the violinist "Photograph" Masilamani Mudaliyar, and the two decided that there should be a contest if Vaidyanathayyar wanted to keep his title "Maha." Informing a group of their allies, the two collected a sum of 2000 rupees and bought a huge silver salver, shawls, and ear-studs, which would be the prize for the winner. They used the remaining money to print notices to the public describing the time, location, and condition of the concert: it would take place at the house of "Fiddle" Ramayya Pillai, a wealthy musician, in George Town, Madras. Vaidyanathayyar would have the opportunity to sing first, choosing the raga. Venu would then sing a pallavi in that raga, and Vaidyanathayyar would be challenged to elaborate it. If he could not, he would have to give up his title.

Hearing of the challenge, Vaidyanathayyar and his brother, Ramaswamy Ayyar, became nervous. But their friends goaded them on, saying they couldn't let a threat like this scare them. As soon as they sent back their reply, the date was set and Venu began preparing intricate pallavis in all the major ragas in which pallavis are usually sung. On the appointed day, a large crowd gathered, including all the musicians then in Madras, expecting that Vaidyanathayyar would be defeated. When the stage was set, with Masilamani Mudaliyar as the referee, Vaidyanathayyar asked Venu which raga he would like. "Any one you want," replied Venu. Vaidyanathayyar decided to sing the raga shankarabharanam. But at that very moment, his brother Ramaswamy whispered to him in their special, secret language, which they called Pandava Basha, to sing the raga narayanagowla. Unlike shankarabharanam, narayanagowla does not have a straight ascending and descending order but prescribes a certain *vakra*, or turn of notes, in its ascent and descent, making it difficult for manipulation in a pallavi. The crowd, stunned to hear such an unusual raga chosen for a pallavi, listened as Vaidyanathayyar sang an elaborate alapana for forty-five minutes. Venu sat frozen, mentally trying to fit his pre-arranged pallavi into the raga, then went off to find a quiet place where he could work it out. When Vaidyanathayyar was finished, however, Venu was nowhere to be seen. Masilamani Mudaliyar, chagrinned, asked Vaidyanathayyar to sing his own pallavi, as Venu, in hiding, listened angrily. In the end Vaidyanathayyar left with the presents, a thousand rupees, and his title intact, and the vanquished Venu never was able to regain his status (Shankara Ayyar 1970, 125–45).

Finding the Past in Madras

In the 1930s and 1940s two scholarly articles suggested that, like Tanjavur, Mysore, and other places, Madras too had a musical past. Unlike Swaminathayyar's or Shankara Ayyar's anecdotes, these articles were in English and clearly had a pretension toward history, supplying the reader with dates and exact locations. If the anecdotes by Swaminathayyar and others discussed above reflect a kind of nostalgia for an unrecoverable musical past, these articles reflect a desire to connect the music world of Madras in the 1930s and 1940s to that past.

In "Madras as a Seat of Musical Learning" (1939), P. Sambamoorthy detailed the lives of several musician/composers who had settled in Madras in the nineteenth century, including Veena Kuppier, Tiruvottriyur Thyagaiyar, Pattnam Subramania Iyer, and Taccur Singaracaryulu. The musical activity of Madras was centered largely in the George Town area, the oldest section of the city adjoining the upscale European area of Mount Road.[20] Musicians from Tanjavur, Bobilli, Mysore, and Trivandrum often stopped in Madras and stayed in the residences of these musicians. Concerts were arranged in conjunction with festivals at the major temples in the George Town area as well as the temples in Triplicane and Mylapore, and at the houses of various musicians. The patrons in Madras were wealthy merchants who seem to have combined the model of royal patronage and another kind of patronage suggested by city life. For instance, the composer Veena Kuppier was appointed to be the samasthana vidwan of the village of Kovur, near Madras, by the patron Sundaresa Mudaliar. But Sundaresa Mudaliar also kept a residence on Bunder Street in George Town, where he was able to host traveling musicians, including Thyagaraja himself on one occasion. The Manali Mudaliars, from the nearby village of Manali, were responsible for placing Baluswamy Dikshitar under the tutelage of a European violinist in Madras and later for encouraging Subbarama Dikshitar to write the monumental book of notations *Sangīta Sampradāya Pradārṣini* in 1904.

According to Sambamoorthy, some of the first institutions of music in Madras were festivals: the Vinayaka Chaturti celebrated in Veena Kuppier's house and the Ramanavami festival concerts arranged by Taccur Singaracaryulu (1834–1892) near his house in George Town. The Singaracaryulu brothers themselves became something of an institution, training a large number of students and writing a series of graded music textbooks. Indeed, it is said that every musician who wanted to make a name in Madras had first to pay respects to and perform before the Singaracaryulu brothers.[21] Juttur Subrahmanya Chetty, a wealthy George Town merchant, created an endowment for nagaswaram players to perform at the Periyalwar festival at the Chenna Kesava Perumal Temple in George Town and for a different player to be honored each year. Other smaller bhajan and concert parties were maintained on Mint Street, in George Town, and near the temples in Mylapore and Triplicane. The Nadamuni Band, a non-Brahmin organization that performed commercially for weddings and dance music, employing wind players and nagaswaram artists, was also established in Madras in the late nineteenth century (Sambamoorthy 1939, 430–35).

The second article, "Some Musicians and Their Patrons about 1800 AD in Madras City," by the musicologist and Sanskrit scholar V. Raghavan, appeared in the *Journal of the Madras Music Academy* in 1944. The article summarized allusions to musicians and patrons in a very peculiar document: a Sanskrit manuscript entitled *Sārvadēvavilāsa*, apparently written by two Tamil Brahmins about the cultural life of Madras, which had been preserved in the Adyar Library in Madras. The manuscript possessed no date, but by a series of complicated correlations with Madras district records, Raghavan placed it at around 1800. He followed the two "scholars" as they traveled around Madras, conversing with each other about what they saw. In one scene they met the patron Vedachala, the dharmakarta of a temple, as he was traveling to the temple with all his retinue, with two musicians at his side. That evening, Vedachala arranged a gathering (*sādas*) with other patrons of equal status (that is, dharmakartas in charge of other temples), in which three courtesans, attached to various patrons, provided dance and music. Another chapter provided a lengthy description of patrons and musicians present at another gathering, but the document broke off in the middle of it. Raghavan suggested that musical life in Madras around this time was centered in temples and that musicians were employed by the dharmakartas, or caretaker/patrons of those temples (1944, 128–31).

The work *Sārvadēvavilāsa*, Raghavan argued, was probably written by these two scholars at the request of the patrons. But what could have been Raghavan's motivation, in 1944, for "discovering" and translating a manuscript which had been left untouched, presumably for almost 150 years? Raghavan's idea seems to have been to show the long continuity of musical tradition in Madras. The present-day importance of Madras in music motivated his search for its past.

> Madras City occupies today a very important and influential place in the field of Carnatic music, a position which had steadily grown during the last one hundred years, and had built itself on the foundation of musical associations whose antiquity can be traced up to the latter part of the 18th century. The discovery of the *Sarvadevavilasa* throws more light on the history of these associations and reveals to us the personalities of some hitherto unknown patrons of our musicians. (130)

Sambamoorthy similarly finished his article in the present tense, ending his narrative of nineteenth-century musical life in Madras with a description of the way such activities are now overseen by the University of Madras: "The facilities given for the advanced study and practice of music by samasthanas [royal courts] in former times are now given by Madras University which has recently established a permanent Department of Music and instituted a Diploma Course in Music" (1939, 437).

The Music Business and Its Institutions

Such anecdotes and scholarly articles were responses to a growing anxiety about the burgeoning music "business" in Madras. Starting in the 1930s, music critics regularly decried the "commercialization" of music through the sabhas, organizations that arranged concerts. They lamented the time limits put on concerts, the new musicians' lack of spontaneity and real musicality, and their penchant for mere show. Yet mixed with this anxiety were a kind of pride and fascination at how music sabhas and institutions in Madras were multiplying, at how there were more and more notated compositions, more musicians to sing them, and more concerts every day. The music business seemed to be running on its own, open to entrepreneurship, no longer dependent on a few wealthy patrons. The key elements in this boom were the rise of concerts with tickets, the establishment of music sabhas, and the founding of teaching institutions.

According to Sambamoorthy, the practice of remunerative concerts was beginning to be established by the late nineteenth century. The musician Maha Vaidyanathayyar regularly sang for money in the 1870s and 1880s, but he never took the money himself, asking his brother Ramaswamy to take it (1959, 5–6). The flutist Sarabha Sastri (1872–1904) is supposed to have practiced rarely but kept in shape by playing frequent concerts, for which he appeared punctually. He had set graded rates for different areas of Madras Presidency and refused to accept a penny more or a penny less (72). Indeed, the very word used for *concert*—*kaccēri*—suggests the presence of money. Unlike the rarely used Tamil word *viṉikai*, which refers to the action of hearing or listening, kaccēri, an Arabic loan word, means both an "assembly for vocal and dramatic entertainments" and "a revenue or police office, court of justice, or place of business" (Winslow 1862).

Hints from E. Krishna Iyer's *Personalities in Present Day Music*, a collection of biographical and critical sketches of performing musicians published in 1933, indicate that by then the concept of the public concert was well enough entrenched for the author to compare different types of performances. Krishna Iyer wrote frequently of "catchy" and "popular styles," of musicians whose voices were suited to the microphone, and of musicians "playing to the gallery," suggesting that public concerts had been happening long enough for these concepts to become thinkable (28, 77). In describing the vocalist "Tiger" Varadachariar, he quipped, "The stylish or catchy music of the popular musician is like the light tea which refreshes you after a day's toil. 'Tiger's' performance is a full meal, provided you have got the stomach to digest it. The former is beach oratory of a popular demagogue and the latter [the] University lecture of a learned professor" (7). The comparison of musical performance to different kinds of public speaking here is telling, for music concerts were beginning to constitute a part of the public sphere alongside such events. Krishna Iyer's clear preference for the university lecture over political beach oratory shows that he, like others, thought that Karnatic music should take pains to distance itself from politics as it entered the same urban public space.

Music sabhas, organizations of city residents that arranged concerts, were responsible for increasing numbers of concerts by the 1930s. Sambamoorthy states that the first sabha in Madras was started in 1895 (1959, 14).

The earliest sabhas in Madras were in the George Town area: the Krishna Gana Sabha, the Bhagavath Katha Prasanga Sabha, the Bhakti Marga Prasanga Sabha, the Punarvarasu Sabha on Mint Street (Sambamoorthy 1939, 435; 1959, 76). Several sabhas, including the Indian Fine Arts Society and the Katchaleeswarar Gana Sabha, held their events in Gokhale Hall, a social and political center in George Town, the site of many speeches by political leaders.[22] Outside of George Town, in neighborhoods to the south, the Parthasarathy Swamy Sabha was founded in Triplicane in 1901, followed by the Rasika Ranjani Sabha in Mylapore. Among other early sabhas were the Thyagaraja Sangeetha Vidwat Samajam, founded in Mylapore in 1929; Kalakshetra, founded in Tiruvanmiyur in 1935; Thyaga Brahma Gana Sabha, founded in Thyagaraja Nagar in 1944; and Krishna Gana Sabha, founded in Thyagaraja Nagar in 1954. Since then, the number of sabhas in Madras has increased astronomically, particularly in the last thirty years.[23]

Sabhas were crucial to making music a remunerative business and at the same time to communalizing it. Most of them started as community organizations, established by groups of concerned citizens, usually Brahmins, with the idea of providing music to the neighborhood. V. Raghavan likened sabhas to "earlier gatherings of old Madras, called *sadas*, convened by rich patrons at fixed intervals or whenever there was a happy event" (1958, 89). The sabhas "patronized" musicians on the model of the royal courts and these sādas, but with a crucial difference: they were entirely dependent on the audience for support. This audience had to be of a certain economic class, one that not only had the concept of music as a leisure-time activity (that is, as part of "culture" and "tradition," not as a money making career) but could also afford to pay for it. Even the term *sabha*, with meanings like "congregation, company, society, assembly of literati, select society of believers" has connotations of exclusivity (Winslow 1862, 401). The sabhas maintained their concert halls and paid musicians by charging membership fees and/or charging money for concert tickets; they therefore depended on sizeable audiences. The more popular artists who drew larger audiences naturally were more profitable for the sabhas; holding concerts more frequently also increased profits. Because of the sale of tickets and the location of performances inside concert halls, sabha concerts were different in character from earlier temple or street concerts, which were free and not necessarily attended from beginning to end. A new kind of concert culture came into being, with audiences becoming conscious of themselves as a self-selected group, defined in opposition to other groups whose tastes might differ.[24] At the beginning of the twenty-first century, this idea has been carried to such an extreme that many concert-goers identify the type of music lover they are by the sabhas whose concerts they attend; even though for the most part all the sabhas feature the same musicians, one makes a social statement by choosing where one goes to hear them.

The life of the Indian Fine Arts Society, established in 1932, reflects the fact that sabhas are differentiated by caste and socioeconomic status. Located in George Town for the first thirty years of its existence, the Indian Fine Arts Society catered to the residential population of North Madras, consisting largely of Telugu Chettys (traditionally a mercantile caste) and some Brahmins. By the 1960s the Telugu Chettys had mostly moved out of George Town and the location could not accommodate wealthier audiences from Triplicane and Mylapore, who arrived by car. Since Mylapore had already been staked out as a Brahmin area, the sabha, with its non-Brahmin founders, moved to the newer Thyagaraja Nagar, whose nouveau-riche residents were distinguished more by their wealth than their caste.[25] In its early days the sabha arranged two concerts every month and, during the ten-day festival in December, one concert per day. At the beginning of the twenty-first century, the number of concerts it arranges, during the festival period alone, has quadrupled, because, according to the sabha secretary, "There are so many musicians today, and we have to make room for all of them."

Concurrent with the growth of music sabhas and concert halls in the early twentieth century was the founding of institutions to teach music. The sabha system, which profited from greater numbers of concerts, created a greater demand for musicians than there had ever been before. The requirement that these musicians be paid according to some fair scale was very different from the economy of royal patronage, in which the king or patron supported musicians by giving them food and shelter, and in addition honored them publicly with gifts. This new system of "fair" payment required that musicians all be somehow equally qualified; it implied that the audience was paying to hear musicians of a certain standard.

The idea that such standards were detachable from individual musicians themselves brought with it a mixture of fascination and concern. It was in such an atmosphere that, in 1928, the Madras Music Academy was founded. The previous year, the All-India Music Conference, held in Madras, had expressed among its aims and objects the following: "to correctly understand, improve and standardize [the theory and practice of Indian Music]; to provide facilities for widespread instruction in music on correct and up-to-date lines; to open a separate faculty of music in universities" (Report of the All-India Music Conference, Madras, 1927, 1). Foremost among the priorities of the conference secretaries, P. Sambamoorthy and E. Krishna Iyer, was the opening of a music academy at Madras that would provide music instruction and concerts, thus acting as a model for other sabhas. The academy was, according to an appeal to the public for support in 1935,

> not a mere music sabha of the sort with which we are familiar. Its aims are far higher. In addition to arranging musical performances, it is making every attempt to purify Indian Music and to set definite standards. Even the performances are so programmed as to educate the audience. . . . We run a Teacher's College of Music to train teachers who would maintain a pure standard in the art and who would provide the kind of tuition required by our younger generation, particularly the girls of our families. (Madras Music Academy 1935, 2)

The academy proposed itself as the ultimate standard in everything from holding concerts to publishing music manuscripts, to administering a college for music teachers and placing them in model schools, to sending out a committee to tour South India and record, on gramophone, "authentic versions of compositions" (ibid., 2–4).[26] Shortly after the academy opened, other music institutions were established: a music department at Madras University in 1932, music classes for the female students of Queen Mary's College in 1933, and Kalakshetra in 1935.

Playing to the Gallery

The need for standardized syllabi in music instruction and for a standard concert format were felt in the 1930s with unprecedented intensity. In Vizianagaram in 1945 the Maharaja's Music College was seen as ill-equipped to maintain musical standards in the face of the monstrous development of the music business, and to that end the Vizianagaram Music Academy was opened. T. V. Subba Rao, who had traveled from Madras to give the opening speech, admonished its founders: "Do not confuse its function with that of the common sabhas. . . . It is a well-known fact that the conditions of life for the musicians are now very prosperous. They will spring up in thousands. This is a state of affairs which may be deemed satisfactory enough, yet there is a subtle danger lurking in it." Those institutions whose eyes were fixed on the box office were among "other forces of destruction. . . . Their craze for novelty and uncouth experimentation has succeeded in developing only the monstrous or the obscene in music" (*Maharaja's Music College Silver Jubilee Souvenir* 1945, 20).

In order to ward off these "forces of destruction," the concert form itself had to be honed to perfect balance. P. Sambamoorthy, in his 1944 essay, "Our Concert Programme: Some Underlying Principles," wrote that the concert format was "based on certain aesthetic principles" that were derived from centuries of musical practice in royal courts (39). But "the vidwan who formerly delighted in expounding a raga for hours together and earned the encomiums of even his jealous colleagues, had to remodel his programme to suit the new type of audience" (ibid.). In effect, more time had to be given to compositions and less to creative improvisation. For this new audience, the performer could afford to waste no time. In a later elaboration of this essay, entitled "Kacceri Dharma" (Concert etiquette), Sambamoorthy advised against preceding every composition with raga alapana, which would result in "monotony" (1955, 267). The fabled hours of leisurely elaboration of ragas by nineteenth-century artists suddenly, it seemed, held a threat of boredom; modern ears could not tolerate anything too unrecognizable. The performer should also, wrote Sambamoorthy, make sure that the concert included a good variety of languages, ragas, and talas, so as to keep the interest of the audience. Above all, complete professionalism should be maintained. The main performer should not let any of his weaknesses show, take any unnecessary risks, or draw any attention to the lapses of his accompanists. This kind of professionalism was called for on the part of the audience also: Sambamoorthy advised that "members of the audience should particularly take care that they do not talk with each other or become restless, when the tambura or some other instrument is being tuned. Nor should a member of an audience make an entry or exit during the middle of an item." In effect, Sambamoorthy was calling for the perfect choreography of performers and audience to enact the rules of concert behavior. If both performers and audience followed these rules, the concert itself would act like a well-oiled, self-running machine. "An appreciative audience is like a catalytic agent and draws the best out of the performer. Audiences should remember that an encouraging applause from them produces very good results" (ibid., 268–71).

If Sambamoorthy seemed to put all his faith in the concert form itself as a kind of technology for producing good music, others seemed to feel somewhat uneasy about it. To simply "let loose" all this music on inexperienced or ignorant audiences was to invite disaster. In the 1930s and 1940s a new discourse about the role of the music critic arose. In his foreword to E. Krishna Iyer's *Personalities in Present-Day Music* (1933), S. Doraiswamy Iyer asked, "Are we not today on the verge of almost forgetting the high state and royalty of Carnatic music, its true origin and true nature? Are we not too thinking, too intellectual in our appreciation of it?" (ix). It was the responsibility of the music critic—and the goal of Krishna Iyer's book—to help ignorant audiences develop their "taste" in music. Krishna Iyer began by remarking on the unprecedented enthusiasm for music, the increasing numbers of concertgoers, and the growth in general knowledge of music. Yet amid this explosion was a deterioration in standards. In effect, Krishna Iyer blamed this on the arrogance of audiences, suggesting that the complete "ignorance" of country bumpkins was better than the "nibbling acquaintance" that so many urban concertgoers had developed.

> The effect of the change of patronage from discerning princes and patricians to the mixed crowd of the streets is indelibly marked in the present-day growth and development of the art. The demand of the populace of varying tastes and degrees of understanding has brought in a corresponding supply. . . . A wholly ignorant audience would ordinarily enjoy the pleasing aspect of sweet sounds and might be content to take the lead of the initiated on the scientific and higher features of the art. But considerable sections of the present day music hall audiences with their nibbling acquaintance with a good number of catchy songs are not seldom found to crave more. . . . With them, the man who sings a large number of pieces—preferably short ones—has . . . a surer chance of wide popularity than others who may be able to expound their ragas, pallavi, and other scholarly features of the art in a profound or elaborate manner. (xii)

The desire to know music and the sudden availability of music had enthralled audiences to the degree that they had lost their reverence for true musical values. The ears of concert audiences in 1933 could respond to more than mere sweet sounds, but therein lay the danger: they had lost the music for the tunes. The craze for catchy songs was part of the jangle of city life, as reflected in Krishna Iyer's cityscape metaphors: "As a result of the excessive development of tala accompaniments music has been driven to attune itself to the steel-frame jathis of the rhythmic variety" (xiii). An obsession with "technique" had overshadowed "natural" music (65). Of the vocalist Naina Pillai he wrote, "His voice and training with obsession in tala have on the whole contributed to make his mastermind delight in building up amazingly wonderful steel-frame structures and spectacular skyscrapers, rather than enchanting villas and breezy mansions in the midst of broad open grounds of undulating green" (62). Not only the architecture of the city but also its low-class entertainments had encroached on the concert. As for showiness on stage, "The cheers of the audience are ready and vociferous in proportion to the . . . length and noisiness of the display. One mridangam is a sufficient tala accompaniment for any concert. Add to this . . . kanjeera, dolak, a morsing and konnakole, and you have a regular circus performance of the lion, tiger, bear, wolf and all other wild animals vociferously brawling and fighting with each other and the poor lamb of a vocalist quivering in their midst and the heart and soul of Indian music—melody and raga bhava—dished up beyond redemption" (53).

The music critic's role was to redeem Karnatic music from its surroundings, from the circus it had become, by serving as a link to the past. The music critic had "onerous responsibilities," M. Ramachandra Rao stated in his paper "Music Criticism," which he read in Vizianagaram in 1945 (*Maharaja's Music College Silver Jubilee Souvenir* 1945, 48). With the growth of English education, university departments, and cinema, he claimed, audiences were being bombarded with music of varying standards. "The music critic has therefore the obligation of correlating the present-day endeavours in the realm of music with old standards in order to polish the public taste for genuine music." But the critic could not simply rely on his gut impressions; he had to have a knowledge of the sastras and the entire history of music in order to respond in detail to questions his readers might ask him about his judgments. The critic had to take the place of the discerning patron, but his orientation toward music was different from that of the patron's. Instead of being able to choose his music, the critic had to wade through whatever there was, with his memories of the past, now endowed with the authority of "history," as the basis for his judgments. Public tastes could not be dictated but had to be gently trained into the correct "grooves of discipline"; the critic's job was to teach the audience how to listen from within these grooves (48–51).

It is no coincidence that recording—recovering music from the past for the present—provided Ramachandra Rao's metaphor. As I will discuss in chapter 6, during this period sound reproduction came to be a central metaphor for authenticity and fidelity to tradition. The music critic emerged as the one who could manage the profusion of music available on record and in concerts. By the 1930s and 1940s, Tamil journals like *Ananda Vikatan*, *Kalki*, *Bharata Mani*, and *Kaveri* had started regular columns of music criticism.

Music-Hall Silence, or the Greatness of the Mic

In his study of the rise of the idea of musical "classics" in eighteenth-century England, William Weber points out that the establishment of the European art-music canon "involved a set of notions or ideas, a moral ideology, that propounded the value and the authority of the classics in reference to issues within the society at large" (1992, 22). This "moral ideology of taste" connected the idea of a musical canon with the sense of an elite of educated listeners, a hierarchy of genres, and the demand that audiences be serious and quiet (21). In South India, as in England, music concerts constituted a "peculiarly modern musical institution: upper-class people displaying their social status and their musical sophistication while revering great music from the past" (1).[27] The concert hall and its trappings played a significant role in this development, for canons, although perhaps originating in moral ideologies of taste, are maintained and cultivated by physical staging and modes of listening; their authority lies in their power to insinuate themselves into everyday habit and the rituals of public life.

In 1938 an advertisement for a water-pumping system in the *Madras Music Academy Souvenir* used the phrase "Music Hall Silence" to sell its product. The automatic water system was so silent, it said, that even in a music hall it would not disturb the pin-drop silence of an audience listening to music from the best masters. "Music Hall Silence," the ad explained, had "become a standard expression to describe silence." The association between the new middle-class home, with its technologies that obviate the need for servants, and the concert hall, which should attract only refined listeners, is clear: the newly imagined concert hall is the public counterpart to the private middle-class home. The self-oiling automatic water system is reminiscent of Sambamoorthy's image of concert hall dynamics, another smoothly working system. Silence here is associated with technology and automaticity: the absence of human intervention. Yet the fact that the advertiser felt the need to explain the origins of the term *music-hall silence*—even to the audience of concertgoers at whom the ad was directed—suggests that it was far from standard. A cartoon from 1940 provides an ironic commentary on the state of music-hall silence in Madras, showing a sabha secretary removing all sources of noise until the audience is entirely de-

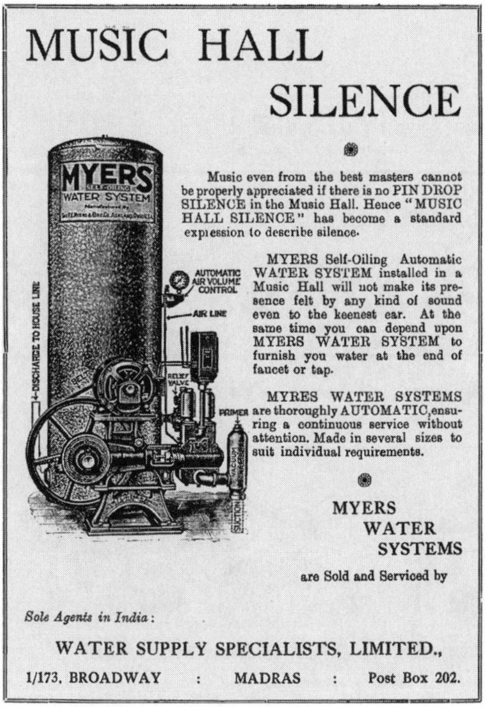

6 Advertisement in *Madras Music Academy Souvenir* (1938).

pleted. Sources such as these suggest that in the Madras of the 1940s the concert hall was still an awkward concept, provoking a mixture of awe and uneasiness, a sense that music and audiences did not quite fit into it yet.

If music-hall silence was daunting, however, so was the prospect of filling a hall with music. The microphone had by the 1940s become necessary in sabha halls, many of which were large enough to seat 500 people but had no acoustic structuring, or even walls, and were often situated alongside railroad tracks or major roads. The first instance of microphone use was in 1931 at the religious festival of Mahamaham at Kumbakonam. In the 1930s microphones were purchased from Europe by radio dealers; the microphone was first used in a concert setting in 1933 for the singer K. B. Sundarambal. By the 1950s almost every sabha in Madras had a microphone for the singer, although it was not until the 1970s that microphones began to be provided for accompanying artists as well.[28] By the end of the twentieth century, microphones had become required for all the performers in a concert.

The microphone warranted its own chapter in Deivasikamani Achariyar's 1949 treatise on public speaking.[29] Achariyar noted that although

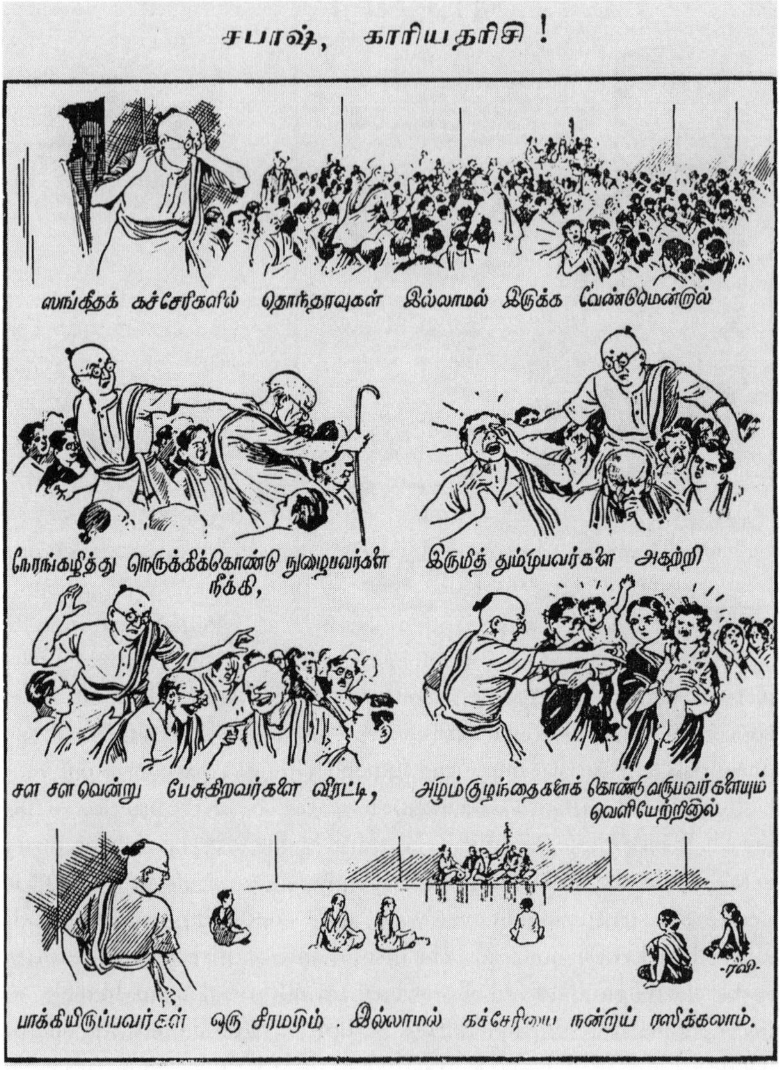

7 "Well done, sabha secretary!" (Capaṣ, kāriyadarici!): "If you want the music concert to be without interruptions, remove those who come late and try to squeeze in, remove those who are coughing and sneezing, drive out those who are talking noisily, throw out those who bring crying children, and the rest can enjoy the concert without difficulty." Cartoon in *Ananta Vikatan* (27 October 1940).

speaking in one's natural voice (*iyarkai kuralil*) was preferable, it was increasingly common to have gatherings of several thousand people on the beach or in open fields, and that in such situations a microphone and loudspeaker system (*oliperukki*) were absolutely necessary. If an orator were to raise his voice to accommodate these kinds of crowds, he would end up with a permanent case of laryngitis and there would be nothing but confusion in the audience. Electric microphones and loudspeakers allowed one to speak with one's natural sound, and even those in the women's section would be able to hear it (251).[30]

Achariyar suggested that learning to use a microphone was not a simple matter. It did not just mean speaking as one normally would and turning up the volume; rather, it required a more complex shift in one's bodily attitude and way of speaking, a new set of practices. Achariyar instructed the speaker to stand approximately one arm-length from the mic and, without moving his body, adjust the height and diaphragm of the mic to the level of his mouth. Strong speakers (*nāvaṉmai koṇṭa nāvalarkaḷ*) would have to be aware that certain oratorical aspects (*pēccilakkaṇaṅkaḷ*), such as speaking posture (*pēccattōraṇai*), gesture (*kai mēy kāṭṭal*), and "savoring of the words" (*cōṟccuvai*), would be lost before the mic. Nor would a speaker be able to switch voice qualities (*kuralōcai*) in a single speech. Instead of preparing his voice with reference to the crowd, the speaker had to prepare with reference to the mic. Here, Achariyar found that an older mode of speaking was the most appropriate parallel: that of a schoolboy reciting his lessons by rote, focusing so hard on not forgetting his lines that he neither moves his body nor modulates his voice. While speaking like this in a normal setting would be disastrous, Achariyar suggested that if "injected" through the mic (*oliperukki mītum celuttappaṭuvatāl*), it would have a great effect (1949, 253). In essence, the ideal was to focus one's attention entirely on one's voice, almost forgetting one's body. One can get a sense of the very basic kinds of adjustments the mic demanded from another piece of advice Achariyar gave. The first-time mic user, he wrote, ought not to be disconcerted by the visual "deformation" of his body, the way the long neck of the mic, once he was standing behind it and had adjusted it, appeared to cut his body in two (253).

The microphone had wonderful potential, but Achariyar also warned his readers to be prepared for its uncanny effects. Sometimes, seemingly for no reason, the mic could "vomit out" harsh sounds, breaking the continuity of one's speech (1949, 255). One had to be very conscious, as well, of the volume of one's natural voice. Just as in sculpture or painting in which artists portrayed forms slightly larger than life size to increase their effect, the mic could have a positive effect on a voice if used properly. But if turned up beyond a reasonable setting, the mic would create sounds that were monstrous. Unlike a veena or tambura, which had no settings for volume, a microphone had to be set to the correct level, Achariyar wrote. If a speaker listened to his voice amplified from an incorrectly set mic, he might mistakenly assume that such an awful sound was the real sound of his own voice and would artificially change his voice to compensate (253).

In 1947 the microphone was the subject of a satiric article, "Maikiṉ Ṃakātmiyam" (The greatness of the mic), published in *Kalki* magazine. The author, Subbashri, marveled at the gradual but steady rise of the microphone, that "modern excellent creation" (*navīna arputa ṣriṣti*), pondering how he might describe its myriad uses. The microphone, he noted, made possible both the political rally—the "heartwarming speeches of the Mahatma, Rajaji's scholarly discourses, and the brave lion-roar of Nehru"—and the sabha concert. No matter what the occasion, the mic, with its thin, awkward body, could gauge the success of the event "like a thermometer." And just as the notice on a flyer that a special section would be reserved for women could draw greater crowds, the promise of microphone arrangements would make people imagine that a great crowd would show up and therefore that the event couldn't be missed ("'Olippaṟappu ēṟpāṭukaḷ uṇṭu' eṉṟu oru noticil piracurittāltāṉ atu 'ohō' eṉṟu collumpaṭiyāṉa avvaḷavu periya kūṭṭam eṉṟu tōṉṟum, pōtu janaṅkaḷukku!") (41).

But the microphone was not just a simple tool for amplification; speaking with one was a skill that had to be practiced to avoid public embarrassment, as Achariyar, too, had noted. Subbashri related how one day he had a burning desire to become a well-known man among the people but did not know how to go about it. His friend, "Sethu," suggested that there was no other way but to go give speeches with a microphone. But he had to practice before going out in public, didn't he? So he devised a practice mic out of a long stick with a tumbler (drinking glass) placed on top. Within a month, he had become so proficient at speaking into the mic that he hardly noticed what he was saying, until one day he discovered to his horror that Sethu had been cueing him to campaign for contributions to Sethu's own home-building fund (1947, 42). The mic was so seductive one might find oneself saying anything into it.

But the microphone also conferred unexpected benefits. After his brief campaigning career, Subbashri wrote, he decided to become a "mic operator"—"the one, who, just before the concert, goes up to the stage and says 'Sivan'[31] into the mic, turning it a little this way and that, and flashes a little smile to the audience as he walks to the back." "Do you know how wonderful it feels?" he asked. "No one captures the attention of the audience as these mic operators do" ("Adanāl ēṟpaṭum perumaiyum evvaḷavu pirammāntamāṉatu eṉṟu niṉaikkiṟīrkaḷā? Inta 'maik āperētar'kaḷ capaiyōriṉ kavaṉattaik kavaruvatu pōl vēru yār kavarukiṟārkaḷ?"). With peculiar power, the microphone held its sway over audiences. It could strike "with the force of an atom-bomb" ("aṉukkuṇṭu pōl avarkaḷai aṭiyoṭu āḻntakkuṭiya caktiyum uṇṭu") if the amplifier malfunctioned, causing a terrible lions' roar of a sound and sending stunned men running as if they themselves had been hit or knuckled on the head (1947, 42). That same mic that could convert a lion's roar into a sweet lamb's voice reserved, mysteriously, the power to convert it back, with a difference, at any moment. The same mic that could make its operator feel so grand could also make a fool of a man or a musician.

The microphone also had another kind of power. It was beginning to control Karnatic vocalists. The phrase "maikukku ēṟṟa toṇṭai" (a voice suited to the mic) was being used more and more frequently by music critics on the radio. It was a miracle to hear: this tiny mic controlling the power of a man, changing the harsh, heavy voice of a vidwan into a shining, soft melodic one ("karṉa katūramāna cārīram paṭaitta vitvāṅkaḷin kuralaikkūṭa māṟṟi, vēku nāyamākac cōpikkac ceyyum amanuṣya cakti intac cinnañciru maikkiniṭam aṭaṅki kiṭakiṟatu") (Subbashri 1947, 42). In 1949 Achariyar differentiated between the *uccakural* orators of the pre-microphone period—literally those who spoke at the top of their voices or lungs—and microphone-using orators, who were able to speak with a "natural sound" (*iyaṟkai oli*) (1949, 251). He gave examples of uccakural orators, like the young Tiru V. Kalyanasundaram and T. P. Meenakshisundaram, who were able to make themselves heard to crowds of thousands. "If these people were to stand before a mic and speak, the instrument would be ruined and cease to function. [The sound] would pierce the ears of the audience [*tuḷai*: bore into]" (ibid., 252).

Most interesting here is Achariyar's discussion of how a microphone, properly used, can actually produce a new and aesthetically pleasing effect of its own. According to Achariyar, among orators and singers, the one who most successfully used the mic was M. K. Thyagaraja Bhagavatar, for only he knew how to "unite" his voice with the mic so that the two "blended harmoniously," "suffusing" the sound with "sweetness" ("iṉimai kāmala oliperukkiyuṭan iraṇṭara kalantu ilaintu") (1949, 255). This unity of voice with microphone, however, was not to be confused with the dangerous intimacy with and reliance on the mic that some singers had developed. Achariyar mentioned a young *sangita* vidwan (singer) who, despite the natural wealth of his voice (*cārīrac celvam*), had come to rely on the help of the mic, sitting before it with his head bowed as if he were about to give it a kiss ("talaikuṉintu ataṉai muttamiṭupavar pōl") (254).

In contemporary Karnatic musical practice, the microphone has to a great extent become naturalized, but not in exactly the same ways as in the West. According to many present-day musicians, the microphone has produced a general change in the vocal and instrumental aesthetics of Karnatic music. They have noted that the microphone has obviated the need for singers to project their voices, so that an earlier "shouting," open-mouthed style has been replaced by a "crooning" style which involves singing with a closed mouth, almost like humming.[32] Vocalists have accordingly lowered their pitch; whereas the typical tonic pitch for male vocalists was E or F before the use of microphones, it has now dropped to somewhere around B-flat. As vocalists have lowered their pitch, so have accompanying violinists. South Indian musicians are intimate with their mics; vocalists tend to be only a few inches from the mic, and violinists so close to it that lifting the bow off the string would mean hitting it. The mic is also essential to projecting a certain intimacy in highly public spaces. When singers in a concert hall embody or portray the soft-spoken, meek Saint Thyagaraja beseeching his lord Rama, the mic is absolutely essential.[33]

For the most part, South Indian musicians and audiences prefer to have amplification systems turned up to a level much beyond what Western audiences would consider "tasteful." There is little pretense of "realistic" amplification; instead, there is a sense that if one possesses the power of amplification, one should use it. For the mic is not only a technological mechanism but also a social mechanism. Both having a mic and knowing how to use one convey social status. I have attended house concerts where audibility was clearly no concern, yet a full complement of microphones was provided. During a Madras music festival in the late 1990s, several nagaswaram players who had been invited to perform at the opening of one sabha's festival program refused to play until they were given microphones. The sabha head had figured that the nagaswaram, a famously loud instrument traditionally played outdoors, hardly needed amplification, while the nagaswaram players, already sensitized to their marginal status in the festival and in the larger Madras music world, had interpreted

நாதசுரக்காரர் தடுமாறுகிருர்!

8 "The naga-
swaram player
gets flustered"
(Nātasurakkārar
taṭumārukiṟār).
Cartoon in *Kalki*
(28 September
1947).

the absence of microphones as a slight. Indeed, a 1947 cartoon that shows a nagaswaram player accidentally preparing to play the mic instead of his instrument suggests that nagaswaram players lack the sophistication to know how to deal with a microphone; at the same time, it pokes fun at the ubiquity of microphones.

The microphone, as Subbashri's satire revealed, gave music concerts a peculiar kinship with political speeches. Indeed, Deivasikamani Achariyar's book included another section that explicitly recommended that those interested in public speaking and rhetoric look toward sangita vidwans as models of how to cultivate voice and breathing. He included the familiar diagram of the midsagittal view of the upper vocal tract, but his diagram additionally showed the position of the tongue, lips, and larynx as the sounds *sa, ri, ga, ma, pa, da,* and *ni* are pronounced (1949, 204–11). In a lengthy digression that included anecdotes about the singers M. K. Thyagaraja Bhagavatar and Birsahib, Achariyar suggested that for speakers and singers alike, certain sounds were more difficult to produce than others. He also suggested that, like singers, aspiring orators give attention to breathing practice. "For public speaking, words and their pronunciation are basic; for music, the basis is raga and tala. For both, a sweet voice without defects is indispensable. A person's throat alone does not account for vocal quality; how he draws in and lets out his breath is also very important" (204). The desired result of this breathing practice was to develop what Achariyar called *ōcaiyuṇarvu*, a term which does not translate easily into English. Literally translatable as "sound-feeling" or "sound-sense," *ōcaiyuṇarvu* conveys a sense of the knowledge of sound that comes from producing it oneself, the hearing or awareness of sound from within one's own body (209).[34]

In addition to sharing these concerns about vocal technique, music concerts and political speeches also shared public space. In fact, another aspect of the uneasiness with the concert form in the 1940s seems to have stemmed from the fact that its closest analogues were either to speeches given during political campaigns or to variety entertainments such as films or the circus. Music concerts, with their star systems, behind-the-scenes agents, tickets, and mass audiences, were disturbingly close to the political maneuverings of the post–World War II years; in many respects, they shared the same public space. In his study of the rise of the notion of musical "classics" in England, William Weber articulates a useful formulation of this particular relation between music and politics.

> This is not to say that what happened in musical life "mirrored" English politics, or that the upper classes were interested in performing old music strictly for political reasons. In is instead to suggest that musical culture was closely bound up with public affairs on a broad plane, both socially and politically, and that, to understand what was going on in concerts or the opera, we have to see how it related to that world. Music did not simply serve political purposes; it contributed to the ritual of public life. . . . When we speak of "politics" we mean something broader than parties and Parliament; we mean a broad compass of authority as it was exerted in different areas of society. For that reason musical life both had its own politics and was part of that larger world. (1992, 15)

The humor of several cartoons published in Tamil weekly magazines from the late 1940s and early 1950s hinged on the way the concert party and the idea of the concert can be easily used to express opinions about politics. A 1941 issue of *Kalki* included a cartoon that showed the governor of Chennai, satirically referred to as the "Bhavanagar Maharaja," engaging in so many different sports that "if he were to show up at the Thyagaraja Festival in Tiruvaiyaru and sing and play all the accompaniments himself, no one would be surprised." The cartoon's comment is twofold: it shocks first by showing a political figure on the concert stage, and second by sug-

9 "The everyday excesses of the Bhavnagar Maharaja" (Pavanakar catāvatānam): "We know that the governor of Chennai, the Bhavnagar maharaja, plays cricket, that he mounts a horse and plays polo, that he plays hockey and is skilled at shooting arrows. Therefore, if he were to appear at the upcoming Thyagaraja festival in Tiruvaiyaru and sing and play all the accompaniments himself, no one would be surprised." Cartoon in *Kalki* (7 February 1941).

10 "Music vidwans on the world stage" (Ulaka mēṭaiyil caṅkīta vitvāṅkaḷ): "Lion of vocal music Stalin sings a sarvasamhara pallavi in eka tala. The audience must listen happily and be satisfied. To open one's mouth to express an opinion is forbidden!" Cartoon depicting Stalin as a singer in *Kalki* (20 March 1949).

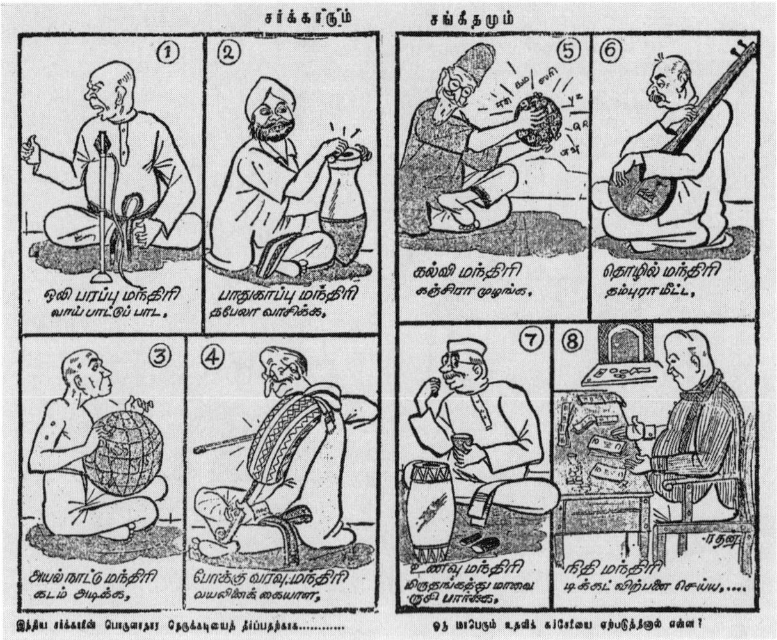

11 "Politics and Music" (Carkkārum caṅkītamum): "(1) The minister of broadcasting can sing, (2) the defense minister can play the tabla, (3) the foreign minister can play the ghatam, (4) the transportation minister can play the violin, (5) the education minister can play the kanjira, (6) the labor minister can strum the tambura, (7) the food minister can taste the mridangam paste, (8) the finance minister can sell the tickets." The text at the bottom says, "To solve India's economic crisis . . . why not hold a great big benefit concert?" Cartoon in *Kalki* (25 December 1949).

gesting that music on the concert stage has descended to mere sport. A 1949 issue of *Kalki* included a cartoon that showed the tactics of world leaders through the medium of the concert form: Stalin sings a complicated pallavi while the East European countries in the audience, gagged, are forced to applaud; Truman sings an "atom-bomb raga" while throwing money to countries in the audience so that they will not notice what he is singing; Churchill keeps on singing long after the entire audience has left; the prime minister of Holland sings while his foreign accompanists shoot into the audience. The cartoon thus shows the concert as an oppressive tool of propaganda, a forum wherein leaders can control or deceive their followers. Another 1949 cartoon in *Kalki* commented on the money-making aspect of concerts. "To solve India's economic crisis," the cartoon asks, "why not hold a great big benefit concert?" The cartoon shows a different political minister on each instrument, with the broadcasting minister as vocalist and the finance minister selling tickets. Here it is the surprising congruity of the members of a concert party with the political cabinet that is shocking. The cartoon is critical of the use of music to further political ends and make money, and is thus critical of the whole sabha system; at the same time, it mocks audiences who will pay money for a concert without even knowing who the musicians are.

From these cartoons it is clear that the worldly aspects of the concert and the music sabha—their politics and economics—were by the 1940s and 50s considered threatening to the "real" values of music. Even as stories of royal patrons paying musicians and kings using musicians to further their own political power were part of the "music history" curriculum, such politics and economics, when they appeared in a different form in the present, were seen as dangerous. The political and economic aspects of music concerts came to be seen as twentieth-century aberrations from a timeless ideal: a classical music that was purely devotional.

Enter Saint Thyagaraja

As the concert became the predominant forum for hearing Karnatic music in Madras, certain hierarchies emerged within the concert format itself, with composition placed over improvisation, certain composers over others, and melody over rhythm. Audiences could no longer be expected to come ready to listen to a complicated pallavi improvisation for hours. Instead, they had to be coaxed into a musical mood with shorter compositions that they might recognize and presented with a variety of ragas to avoid "monotony." In a two-hour concert (just the amount of leisure time a working man could afford), the first hour would be given over to kritis of fair to middling weight and difficulty. The centerpiece of the concert would be the "main item": either a much-shortened pallavi or a lengthy kriti with improvisation. Following the main item would be "lighter" pieces, called *thukkada* (a Marathi word meaning "miscellaneous"), to send the audience off on a cheerful note. These thukkada pieces could be *javalis* or *padams* from the dance repertoire (both noted for their love lyrics), Hindustani pieces, Western notes, or, depending on the artist, film tunes: in short, anything that fell outside the boundaries of strict "classical" music. By including such pieces but relegating them to a position that lessened their status, the new concert format was set up to repeatedly perform, and thus maintain, the boundary between "classical" music and thukkada pieces.

Maintaining this strict boundary depended as well on defining the music in terms of compositions. By the 1950s concerts had become composition oriented. The time limit of two to two-and-a-half hours, in combination with the ever-looming threat of boredom on the part of the audience, made singing a number of compositions (or "items," as they are called) in different ragas with limited improvisation the most favored way of presenting the variety audiences were thought to crave. Since the medium of the concert was largely compositions, the division between serious or classical music and light music was based on compositions, rather than on types of improvisation. More important, classical music was now an entity definable by genre and composition, existing independently of individual musicians and their styles of improvisation. Accordingly, most conventional explanations of Karnatic music at the end of the twentieth century distinguish between the composed parts of the music and the improvised. In reality, the boundaries between composition and improvisation are quite fluid. A "composition" in Karnatic music is hardly the same as a composed piece of music in the Western tradition; it is a certain number of lines, each of which are played or sung with a number of variations. While the lyrics of most compositions are fairly standardized, there is no standard notation for compositions, and different versions of the "same" composition vary widely. Even within compositions, musicians often add improvised flourishes that eventually become part of the composition.

Coexisting uneasily with the ambiguities of musical practice is the notion of "masterworks"—entirely composed pieces that are sufficient in themselves without any improvisation. Having masterworks is a late-twentieth-century idea in South India. It is now common to hear one of the composer Thyagaraja's five *pancharatna* (five gems) kritis played as an item in itself at a Karnatic concert. Whereas thirty or forty years ago, according to many musicians, these kritis would be improvised upon in a concert, the pancharatna kritis are now seen as so complete and well composed that improvising anything before or after them would be an insult to the audience and the composer.[35] Playing or singing a masterwork, in this sense, makes the musician's relationship to the composition very different. Playing or singing a composition in which one improvises makes it necessary to be aware of where one is in the composition and to remain on the ready to jump in. Playing or singing a straight composition—a masterwork—on the other hand affords musicians a sort of relief, an opportunity for detachment, a sure thing, as if by playing something standard that everybody knows, they can tune out for ten minutes without having to be responsible for the quality of the music.

It is no coincidence that most of the compositions treated as masterworks are by Thyagaraja, whose music came to be seen in the twentieth century as the embodiment of a devotional or spiritual quality considered essential to all classical music. In the 1930s a new term appeared in writing on Karnatic music: "the trinity." It referred to the three nineteenth-century singer-saints who were becoming canonized as the great composers of Karnatic music. Out of hundreds of composers, these three—Thyagaraja, Muthuswamy Dikshitar, and Syama Sastri—were considered to have caused a revolution in Karnatic music. Thyagaraja, in particular, ascended to saintly status and came to dominate the concert platform, eclipsing not only the other two but many other composers who had thrived in the royal courts in the nineteenth century.

In the first half of the twentieth century, a flood of life stories of Thyagaraja were published. They included *Tyākarāja Carittiram*, a historical novel by Panju Bhagavatar (ca. 1910); *Tyagayyar: The Greatest Musical Composer of South India*, by C. Tirumalayya Naidu (1919); *Thiagaraja: A Great Musician Saint*, by M. S. Ramaswamy Aiyar (1927); *Thyāgabramopaniṣad*, by Wallajapet Ramaswamy Bhagavatar (1935); and *The Songs of Thyagaraja: English Translation with Originals*, by C. Narayana Rao (1939). In 1942 a popular film about the life of Thyagaraja, *Tyāgayyar*, was made in Telugu. Following this were A. V. S. Sharma's *Lines of Devotion* (1954), C. Ramanujachari's *The Spiritual Heritage of Thyagaraja* (1957), and Suddhananda Bharathi's *Saint Thyagaraja: The Divine Singer* (1968).

The titles alone are indicative of the way Thyagaraja's life was used to produce a message for the twentieth century. Most of these life stories cover the same events. Thyagaraja, a devotee of Rama, spends his time singing and is scorned and tormented by his materialistic elder brothers; he attracts a crowd of disciples and scolds them when they reveal that they have gone to enjoy music in a devadasi's house; he reforms thieves by telling them they can take the money given to him by the king since it was given to him against his will.[36] The story told most often describes how Thyagaraja refused the patronage of the kings Serfoji and Swati Tirunal, preferring instead to sing in the streets of Tiruvaiyaru and to subsist on donations (Ramaswamy Aiyar 1927, 46). The more the music business flourished, the more the figure of Thyagaraja as a musician existing outside of (and even resisting) the money economy was celebrated. Compositions by others extolling the glories of royal patrons could not, in comparison, be considered fully classical.

English translations of Thyagaraja's lyrics that appeared in the mid-twentieth century stressed the importance of grasping Thyagaraja's spiritual message. C. Narayana Rao's English translations were aimed at those who didn't know Telugu as well as at Telugus who "through the influence of English education have forgotten to appreciate the treasures of their own language except when they are in English" (1939, xi). For mid-twentieth century translators, the actual language Thyagaraja used was less important than the spiritual message that could be distilled from it. In *Lines of Devotion* A. V. S. Sharma excluded the originals entirely, "translating" them into a Shakespearean iambic pentameter that an English-educated leisure reader might enjoy. He appended a short conclusion directed to the reader: "My purpose is achieved if you have developed a desire to appreciate the spiritual bearing of the devotional lines written above" (Sharma 1954, 34).[37] Having read such translations and been inculcated with the desire for spirituality, a concertgoer would not need to understand the words of Thyagaraja's songs as long as he could sense this spiritual undercurrent.

In representing Thyagaraja as a saint, these hagiographic accounts endow him with an almost miraculous ability to rise above his circumstances, a representation which is echoed in more recent accounts of Thyagaraja's life as well. In his book on Thyagaraja, Bill Jackson suggests that Thyagaraja's uniqueness is due to the fact that although he lived in a time of great upheaval, he managed to filter out all political and social influences from his music, leaving behind a pure "intangible" residue of devotion

(1991, 61). Not only his ideas but his music, too, possessed this spirituality, which made it peculiarly suitable to nationalist imaginations of music as a universal language. In 1941 S. V. Ramamurthi wrote in *The Hindu*,

> [Thyagaraja's] music is a synthesis of South Indian culture and is as great as any form of Indian culture. Its Telugu is as simple almost as the Telugu of the girl that goes home in the evening, singing, with her bundle of fresh cut grass. But from such slim footing Tyagaraja's music rises tall as the world. Its tradition is Tamil, the tradition of Alwars and Nayanmars. Its grammar is Carnatic, that is to say, South Indian. Its spirit is human, the spirit of man, the top of creation, communing with his creator. Everyone in South India can understand it, can feel its rhythm, can follow its spirit and feel at home in it. Tyagaraja, more perhaps than any other single musician, has preserved for us our one great live art with an appeal both far and wide. (quoted in Jackson 1991, 60)

As the nationalist gaze makes its sweep from the country girl to the "spirit of man," the simplicity of Thyagaraja's language gives way to a universal "human" spirit, which "everyone . . . can understand."

Such "simplicity" and universal appeal indicated that Thyagaraja belonged in the modern world, the world of the concert hall and the music sabha. In an essay entitled "The Modernity of Thyagaraja," T. V. Subba Rao cited songs "ultra-modern in tone and sentiment," whose lyrics denounced expensive rituals and cruelty to animals (1962, 145). "What language is more simple and thoroughly modern," he wondered, than Thyagaraja's, which was "suggestive of infinite meaning and yet most familiar like the simple dialect of the common man"? (ibid., 146). Tirumalayya Naidu contrasted Thyagaraja's songs, which "please the moment they are heard," with Dikshitar's, which, set in difficult and "unpronounceable" Sanskrit, "have to be studied over and over again" (1919, 22). More remarkable, for Subba Rao, was the way Thyagaraja seemed to have anticipated the future: "He knew that ages to come would expect a variety of new scales and ragas with compositions in them . . . [while] he anticipated the musical expressions which were likely to go out of use and avoided them" (1962, 146). Thyagaraja seemed to have anticipated that his songs would one day become the staple fare of the concert hall, and thus he left clearly defined areas for improvisation in his compositions, for "modern taste cannot be gratified by mere recitative type of music" (ibid., 147). Moreover, Thyagaraja seemed to have known that modern ears preferred a catchy melody to rhythm. "Thyagaraja has so refined, softened and subdued his rhythms that they lose all their grossness and become spiritualized," remarked K. Suryanarayanamurthy Naidu (*Maharaja's Music College Silver Jubilee Souvenir* 1945, 14). "Primitive music," wrote Subba Rao, "had more tala and less raga. Thyagaraja subdues rhythm and enriches the melody. . . . His marked preference of melody to tala . . . shows how modern he is" (1962, 148–49).

The privileging of melody over rhythm, here defined as a modern attribute, is a pervasive element of contemporary discourse about Karnatic music and is one of the more prominent aspects of the canonization process. The rhythmic accompaniment in Karnatic music consists most commonly of a mridangam (double-headed drum), *ghatam* (clay pot), and/or *kanjira* (single-headed hand-held drum). Less commonly seen are the *morsing*, a kind of jew's-harp, and *konnakkol*, the art of saying/singing the rhythm syllables; indeed, konnakkol is usually now found only in lecture-demonstrations, and rarely as part of a concert performance. The dwindling of konnakkol is emblematic of the broader way in which percussion has come to be seen as secondary to the melody in Karnatic music. Whereas, according to older musicians, it was customary in the early twentieth century for a concert party to have a full percussion section led by the konnakkol artist, the presence of four or five percussion artists now renders a performance less than classical. The privileging of melody over rhythm is apparent in the comment of an elderly musicologist on why konnakkol was discontinued: "It was interfering with the music."[38] This is not, of course, a purely musical decision. The rhythmic intricacies of Karnatic music are strongly associated with the non-Brahmin traditions of *periya mēḷam* (music that accompanies Hindu rituals and festive occasions) and *cinna mēḷam* (music that accompanies *Bharata Natyam*). The instruments one sees on the Karnatic stage and the music one hears are thus the result of a discourse about what constitutes music and who can be called a musician. The canonization of Thyagaraja as the voice of Karnatic music involved more than selecting a composer; it also determined what that voice was supposed to sound like and who would be allowed to play along with it.

Lip Service

With the shift from royal patronage to the urban music business in the twentieth century, Karnatic musicians and audiences found themselves in the new contexts of the concert hall or university classroom. The disorientation caused by the silence of the music hall or by hearing one's own voice through the microphone was amplified by music's uncanny power to move money, to become a business. In 1951 the music reviewer Kalki Krishnamoorthy wondered whether to call his meditations on the music business "music makes money" or "money makes music," noting that the meaning would be essentially the same (14). Money and music seemed to be interchangeable, throwing certainties of origin and agency into question. The resulting uneasiness prompted several responses. Anecdotes about the period of royal patronage, for instance, seem written to preserve memories of a world that was perceived to be passing. Authors of more scholarly articles sought instead to connect their present—1930s and 1940s Madras—to the period of royal patronage. A third response, which became stronger as the concert format became more entrenched and as concerts and audiences became more numerous, was to delve into the past for a different history, one that could locate the origins of Karnatic music in a pre-economic world, even if that world was purely imaginary. The definition of Karnatic music as spiritual or devotional and the preoccupation with the figure of Thyagaraja as a saint who refused royal patronage were responses to anxiety about the commercialization of music.[39] Finding a usable past now meant finding one in which Karnatic music was dissociated from politics and money, from the whims of Westernized maharajas. As the songs of composers celebrating their patrons disappeared from the concert stage, the songs of Thyagaraja, the saint with peculiarly modern qualities, came to dominate.[40]

In a very real sense, this meant a shift from compositions tied to the context of their performance toward compositions that stood free of such social contexts and instead had their origins in a personalized, timeless devotion. Thyagaraja's lyrics became appealing precisely because, being addressed primarily to the god Rama, they obscured the relation between the composer and his social milieu. Like the singers at the Mysore palace who appear and disappear before the audience like "celestial beings," Thyagaraja seems to float, detached, above the world of the social and the political, the means (and history) of his entry into the scene hidden from view.

The persona of the individualized saint-singer-composer is tied to the notion of the expressive individual, an idea central to modernity. Tracing the history of this idea in Western thought, Charles Taylor has noted that it was closely bound to a view of art as expression rather than mimesis (1989, 368–90). This in turn depends on the notion of an interior self that is known primarily from inward sources rather than from its relation to others.[41] Undoubtedly Thyagaraja himself sang in and in relation to a particular social context. The way that context became obscured as he came to be celebrated, indeed deified, in the twentieth century is indicative of a peculiarly modern way of thinking about art in general and the musician in particular. The distinction between art as expression and art as mimesis sets up, in the most literal sense, a distinction between what is supposedly authentic (that which comes from within) and what is simply paying lip service (an imitation, an effect without substance, a voice which is made to appear as though it comes from within when it actually comes from an external source).

The celebration of Thyagaraja as a modern composer is thus ironically apt, for the label unwittingly acknowledges the modern institutions and modern ideas about individuality and authenticity—collectively embodied in the figure of the saint-composer—that have made Thyagaraja what he is today. The music festival is one such institution, and no festival reflects the tensions inherent in the modern desire for a music free of politics and commercialism better than the annual Thyagaraja Aradhana (memorial) held at Tiruvaiyaru. Each year, in homage to Thyagaraja, thousands of these aradhanas are held around the world. But the original is held annually in Tiruvaiyaru, a small town on the banks of the Kaveri River where Thyagaraja lived and died. The aradhana, attended by thousands of "pilgrims" from Madras and other places in South India, takes place next to a shrine built for Thyagaraja in 1925. From its inception, the administration of this particular aradhana has been in the hands of Madras musicians and has been riven by politics. The aradhana was established in 1905 by a group of musicians from Madras; a separate group of musicians who had not been invited to the meeting took offense and decided to start their own aradhana. These two groups operated under the names *periya kaṭci* (big party) and *cinna kaṭci* (little party)—*kaṭci* is the term used for political parties—along with a third group, started by the female musician Bangalore Nagaratnammal, for women only (Srinivas Iyer 1991). These three "parties" conducted aradhanas on different days until 1940, when they joined together and the Thyagabrahma Mahotsava Sabha was formed (G. Srinivasan 1991).[42] Since then, however, splinter groups have formed continuously, depending on who is appointed as sabha secretary. In 1998, for instance, a separate aradhana was held several miles away at Tiruvarur for those who refused to participate in an aradhana run by the controversial violinist Kunnakudi Vaidyanathan, who was secretary of the Tiruvaiyaru Sabha at the time.

It is ironic that although Tiruvaiyaru represents a kind of origin, the village world of Karnatic music before Madras became its center, almost everything and everyone who participates in the Tiruvaiyaru aradhana is imported from Madras. The sabha secretaries who run the aradhana are now appointed by the Tamil Nadu state government and have no personal connection to the descendants of Thyagaraja still living in Tiruvaiyaru. In January 1998, during the three days of the aradhana, I stayed with some of Thyagaraja's descendants who are the year-round caretakers of Thyagaraja's shrine. During the festival, their house, about 500 feet from the shrine, was suddenly engulfed by a maze of concessions selling cassettes and food, a makeshift stage and backstage area, a large tent, giant electrically lit outlines of Thyagaraja in his usual pose with tambura, and thousands of performers and tourists. Elaborate security arrangements were made and fees collected to insure that no disruptive people could enter.[43]

Every five minutes throughout the day new performers mounted the stage to sing or play a Thyagaraja kriti, regardless of their skill; this was obviously a place to see and be seen. In the evening an All India Radio broadcasting crew was brought in to record the concerts given by famous artists. The major event of the three days was the group singing of Thyagaraja's masterworks, his pancharatna kritis, by all the All India Radio–qualified "vidwans" present. The festival tent was carefully divided into spaces for vidwans and places for spectators, who were not meant to participate in the singing. Meanwhile, merchants distributed flyers with the lyrics of the songs on one side and advertisements for their products on the back. A disgruntled pilgrim wrote in to *The Hindu* afterward that the singing of the pancharatnas, in which the aradhana was supposed to reach its devotional peak, was treated by the performing musicians more like an opportunity to show off on a concert stage. "Breaking into alap and swaras at will," he wrote,

> many of them in the choir sang with total lack of involvement, bordering on irreverence. . . . It was a show of one-upmanship of the worst kind as one of them in the choir went into briga pyrotechnics at every conceivable moment, unmindful of the comical effect it had on the solemn occasion. Some of them resorted to "lip-service," looking for dubbing artists to provide them voice support, as they had not read the script. . . . Chaos of this magnitude is never witnessed in other music festivals. . . . Why then make it a mockery at Tiruvaiyaru?[44]

Amid this chaos a small bhajan group composed of local musicians made its rounds. On the Monday morning after the last day of the festival, the place was suddenly deserted, with only the remains of the concessions and

12 Idol of Thyagaraja being carried to his house in Tiruvaiyaru at the close of the Thyagaraja Aradhana (January 1998). Photograph by Amanda Weidman.

the tent littering the ground near the shrine. The musicians and "pilgrims" from Madras had left during the night, leaving the locals to carry out one of the purportedly most sacred duties: the procession of Thyagaraja's idol from the shrine to Thyagaraja's house.

At Tiruvaiyaru, where the present world of Karnatic music confronts its imagined past, one senses several anxieties. Celebrating Thyagaraja's life and work is supposed to be a gesture of remembering what Karnatic music was before it was a business. Yet the county fair atmosphere of the 1998 aradhana shows that worshipping at Thyagaraja's shrine and doing business at it are dependent on each other. Moreover, if the aradhana at Tiruvaiyaru is supposed to celebrate this place of origins, it is ironic that Madras politics control it, that so much of the event is imported from Madras, and that such a careful separation is maintained between Madras musicians and local musicians. Tiruvaiyaru, the place, serves only as a kind of sacred backdrop; traveling to it in space gives the impression of having traveled to some originary point in the history of Karnatic music, but when one arrives one is confronted—as though looking in a mirror—with the present. As the show of devotion through singing in front of Thyagaraja's shrine proceeds, the possibility that it is precisely a show can never be ruled out. Once the idea of the concert becomes entrenched, it is impossible to tell, as the disgruntled pilgrim points out, whether professional musicians singing on the stage are showing their devotion or simply taking the opportunity to be in the limelight; it is impossible to tell where their voices end and their lip service begins.

The anxiety that music, like money, could simply be exchanged without embodying any real value is reflected in comments about the tendency of concerts toward show without substance, the loss of value of once prestigious awards, and the endless proliferation of concerts. In an interview in 1989 the vocalist C. S. Sankarasiva Bhagavatar, formerly chief samasthana vidwan in the court of Ramanathapuram and later principal of the Sathguru Sangeeta Samajam, a music college in Madurai, spoke of the changes he perceived in the world of Karnatic music. After an involved description of the strenuous swarakshara pallavis that his guru, Harikesanallur Muthiah Bhagavatar, would sing for the king of Ramanathapuram, he made an eloquent and alliterative statement about the present day: "Ippa cumma utaṭṭaiviṭṭu niraval paṇṇamāṭṭā oṉṉum paṇṇamāṭṭā. Cumma pallaviṅkiṟatu pallai kāṭṭiṭṭu viṭṭiṭuva!" (Now they won't even open their lips and do *niraval* [improvisation on a single melodic line of a composition]. They won't do anything. If they just show their teeth, they call it a pallavi!).[45] Punning on the word for *teeth* (*pal*) and the word *pallavi*, Sankarasiva Bhagavatar's comment suggests that audiences are gullible enough to be cheated by lip service or, in this case, a mere show of teeth and that the present day has retained only the appearance, not the substance, of music.

A similar anxiety about the loss of value for the sake of show appears in comments about awards given by the government to musicians and other artists. The Kalaimamani awards, for instance, given by the chief minister of Tamil Nadu, seem to be based on the model of a royal patron honoring distinguished members of his court. But where the honor ends and farce begins is hard to tell; in 1998 an unprecedented seventy-five Kalaimamani awards were presented by Chief Minister Karunanidhi, prompting many of those awarded the honor in previous years to return it in indignation, saying that the award had lost all value. Karunanidhi's action also prompted a front-page cartoon in the Tamil daily *Tiṉa Maṇi*, which suggested that the Kalaimamani award had been given out as liberally as daily rations. The seemingly uncontrollable proliferation of concerts also provokes anxieties about the loss of music's value, the fear that music will cease to have an effect when heard. The disorientation caused by endless repetition and abundance is the theme of the cartoon "Chennai Winter Season." The traditional expression of reverence, "Music is an ocean," suddenly

becomes a cause for worry when the flood of concerts in the December season threatens to swamp even Thyagaraja himself.

Backstage and Outside

In October 1998 my violin teacher was embroiled in a bitter family dispute over what should be done with the valuable medals and gems that had been presented to her father, a famous violinist, by various maharajas in the 1920s, 1930s, and 1940s. Some in the family wanted to sell the medals for money. My teacher, who was in favor of keeping the medals as they were or making a "museum," as she put it, to preserve them, was plunged into a state of anxiety. The medals were a present-day relic of a past that only she, as a musician, cared about but had never directly experienced. What would happen to the family name if the medals were sold off? Would anyone remember her father? Would her father, who had earned these medals by sheer talent and merit, have understood selling them for money?

In the midst of the dispute, I took a trip to Mysore with my teacher, and her cook, Chinnamma.[46] The Mysore palace is no longer inhabited now that the members of the royal family have become politicians in Bangalore; it became the property of the Indian government and is now open to the public as a museum. Neither my teacher nor Chinnamma had seen the palace before. We took a tour of the interior, gazing at portraits of British and Indian royalty. By the time we got to the durbar hall, it was almost closing time, but my teacher was too absorbed to notice: here was the hall in which her father had played before the king of Mysore and received one of his many medals. Other tourists had long since left, herded out by the palace guards, but she wandered around at length in the silent hall, placing herself first where the maharaja would have sat, then where her father would have sat, then imagining herself in the audience. Seeing the durbar hall, she was inspired to "remember" an event she herself had not experi-

13 The excesses of Chief Minister Karunanidhi caricatured. A man with a turban and mustache tells a decidedly Brahmin-looking man, "You, too?! This isn't a rations line. Everyone here is waiting to get their 'kalaimamani award.'" Cartoon in *Tiṉa Maṇi* (19 June 1998).

enced, an era she was too young to have known. The preserved palace seemed to represent for her a haven from the nagging possibility that anything, against all propriety, even her father's talent and music, could be converted into money.

Chinnamma and I left her and exited the palace, joining a crowd of tourists outside waiting for the weekly light-and-music show. The lights on the outside of the palace were turned on exactly at 7 PM, and a marching band (formerly owned by the maharaja, now run by the police department) played for one hour, until the lights were shut off. The show, carefully planned for tourists, is supposed to recreate the atmosphere of the early twentieth century. But Chinnamma was not interested in authenticity in the way the tourist industry imagined. At one moment during the show, she turned to me, struck by a sudden epiphany: she had finally realized where an expression she had been using all these years came from. The expression—"Eṉṉa? Periya rāja familyā? Icai muḻaṅkutā?" (What are you, from a big royal family? Is the music roaring?)—was used when you wanted to mock somebody for acting pretentiously. It could be shortened into a sarcastic half-question: "Icai muḻaṅkutā?" (meaning something like "I can hear the band rumbling"). Chinnamma, an illiterate cook who, unlike my teacher, could have had no personal connection to the palace, had found one embedded in the language she used every day: an expression that reflected her own sense of social propriety and her own location (her authenticity, as it were) within a politics of music from which she, through caste and economic class, had been excluded.

Many of the concertgoers and musicians with whom I spoke in the course of my research lamented that Karnatic music is much more exclusive now than it used to be; they remembered temple concerts, free and open to all, where the audience poured out onto the streets. But if the atmosphere of Karnatic music concerts has become much more exclusive, the music is, ironically, more available to the general public now than ever

14 The music season threatens to swamp even Thyagaraja himself. Cartoon in *The Hindu* (17 December 1997).

before through other mediums: cassettes, radio, Tamil cinema. However, it is now framed within a thoroughly culturalist discourse where it operates as a sign of culture, tradition, refinement, and Brahmin middle-class identity. Chinnamma's epiphany in a sense talks back to these exclusions, just as the expression itself talks back to an imagined interlocutor. Unlike the ideal audience imagined by Sambamoorthy, she does not sit quietly, and if she applauds at the end, it is because she has appreciated the music in a different manner than he would have prescribed. She finds in the palace band's performance not an occasion for nostalgic recollection of a golden age, but rather the origins of a class system that justifies itself by distinctions of taste. Here I have shown how, through the rise of the concert as the dominant mode of performing and listening, these distinctions were established, made to seem logical and natural. In doing so, I hope to have hinted—as Chinnamma does—at how the ritual of the concert might, quite literally, be disconcerted.

3 Gender and the Politics of Voice

It is always the body social that is enunciated in and through the voice.
—Steven Feld, Aaron Fox, Thomas Porcello, and David Samuels,
"Vocal Anthropology," in *A Companion to Linguistic Anthropology*

As a music student in Madras, I spent the better part of every day engaged in music lessons at my teacher's house. Since she, having never married, had few conventional household obligations, these music lessons, liberally interspersed with periods of conversation, usually lasted the whole afternoon. The conversations often moved from music to marriage, and she was decidedly ambivalent on this point. At times, she attributed her failure to live up to her potential to the fact that she was a non-Brahmin woman without even a husband to help her. Every now and then a visitor would stop by, perhaps someone who had been a fan of her father's. On one such occasion, the visitor was a lawyer who lived on the next block, who happened to be passing by as I approached the gate of the house. My teacher came out to greet me, and the lawyer stopped to introduce himself to her, to say how much he had enjoyed her father's music. After a few words about the greatness of her father, she turned to her own story, speaking in English, as she felt the presence of a lawyer called for. "I sacrificed everything—marriage, children, money—for the sake of music. I am a helpless lady," she told the lawyer, a perfect stranger, who was listening seriously and compassionately. The idea of an unmarried woman who has "devoted" herself to music has great appeal in South Indian classical music circles, and my teacher was convinced that her "sacrifice" had brought her closer to the divine. Telling of her sacrifices often brought tears to her eyes. However, although she spoke wistfully about how other female musicians got chances to perform because their husbands acted as managers, she believed that music and marriage were basically incompatible.

She herself cultivated disorder both in her personal appearance and in her household. The house—a large old-style building with front arches, verandahs, and a courtyard—had fallen into a state of decay in the years since her mother's death in the mid-1980s, but signs of its former illustriousness were everywhere, piled in corners and festooned with cobwebs. Most fellow musicians thought my teacher highly eccentric, and a few speculated to me that she might have psychological problems. She, meanwhile, admitted that her life and personality were out of the ordinary but attributed this to the effects of "Madras politics," which had forced her to the margins of the music world. For others—friends and family members—her eccentricity was thought to be explainable by the fact that she was a musician, a true artist. Her cook, who had worked in the house for more than forty years, would roll her eyes at my teacher's perversities but, when pressed, would claim, "Avakiṭṭe kalai irukke" (There is art in her).

A Music Lesson

One day in June 1998 my teacher had decided to teach me the well-known kriti "Rāma nannu brōva rā" (Rama, come save me). Fingering through a crumbling book of compositions her father had kept, she commented on the aptness of the words to her own life, offering me a colloquial translation of the Telugu lyrics in mixed Tamil and English: Thyagaraja asks Rama, "Rāma! Enakku show, fraud, gossip, putting soap, wrong ways-um teriyātu. Eṉkiṭṭe nī vara kūṭātā?" (Rama, I don't know show, fraud, gossip, putting soap, or wrong ways. Why do you not come to me?) Perhaps it was the quietness of the mid-afternoon lull, or the physical act of going through one of her father's old books that brought out a flood of associations; in the words of the kriti lurked voices other than her own. The first was that of an American student who had come to learn Karnatic music from her father perhaps thirty-five years before. She remembered sitting in the corner of the room while her father sang the words and the student repeated them in flat, operatic syllables: RAA-MA-NAA-NU-BRO-VA-RAA. In stark contrast was the second voice, that of the celebrated vocalist M. S. Subbulakshmi (often referred to simply as "M.S."), who had made this composition famous. My teacher recalled that M.S. used to sing this song with so much emotion that there would be tears rolling down her cheeks. That, my teacher said, was because the song related to a period of unhappiness in M.S.'s life.

It was astonishing to hear something unharmonious about the life of

M.S., who has been celebrated almost universally as the "greatest female vocalist of India," as the woman who broke the male stronghold of Karnatic music, as the "only Karnatic musician with a national image" (Indira Menon 1999, 134). At one point, T. T. Krishnamachari, one of the founders of the Madras Music Academy, called M.S.'s voice "the voice of the century" (quoted in ibid., 132). A Tamil biography of M.S. entitled *Icai Ulakiṉ Imayam* (The Himalaya of the music world), speaks of M.S.'s voice as the voice of god, claiming that "if music can be said to have a form it is M.S. herself. . . . Her life *is* the history of music" (Sarathy 1997, 5). Born into the community of devadasis, lower-caste women who performed music and dance in Hindu temples and by the late nineteenth century were branded as prostitutes, Subbulakshmi married a prominent Brahmin man of letters, T. Sadasivam, who brought her talents out into the middle-class Brahmin music world of Madras. Her life seems to represent the success story that everyone wants to hear about. What discordant note was there in the life of a woman who, coming from a devadasi background at a time when devadasis were being disenfranchised, was able, by sheer force of talent, to become universally accepted in the Karnatic music world?

My teacher's answer to that question can be understood less as a truth about M.S.'s circumstances and more as a sample of discourse about her life, which has been the subject of much speculation both inside and outside the Karnatic music world. My teacher claimed that M.S. sang the song with such emotion because of the difficulties of her marriage, that she was mistrusted by her husband, that he accused her of infidelity. While the present generation may be unaware of such speculations, at that time—my teacher was referring to the late 1950s—it was the talk of musicians and *rasikas* (connoisseurs). Sadasivam had fallen in love with the idea of a woman vocalist, and he made M.S. into the first really celebrated vocalist the Karnatic music world had known. However, he became envious of her popularity and, paranoid that her admirers might be lovers, began to fear that she was a "characterless lady" (my teacher's expression). After all, he was a Brahmin, and she was from the caste of devadasis. But, my teacher wondered, how could he fear such a thing about M.S.? *He* was the characterless one to even think such things. He controlled M.S. so absolutely that if she sang something he did not like he would call out to chide her in public. How could an artist flourish with this kind of husband? "I would rather stay in a hostel than be at the mercy of a husband like that," she concluded.

This led her off into a more general discussion of the difference between men and women. It was okay for a man to "wander" with ten women, but a woman could not do likewise, she said, as if to criticize the unfairness of society. Sensing a familiar sentiment, I was about to join the critique when it took a sharp turn toward something else. That double standard, she continued, was as it should be, because there was an essential difference between men and women. Women were a special birth (*vastiyāna ja<u>n</u>mam*); there was so much power, honor, and dignity (*kauravam*) in a woman's body that it was important to control it; otherwise it would be too dangerous.[1] "Men?" My teacher spat out the word, as if the very idea was a joke. "Who cares? Let them go have ten wives; it doesn't make a difference."

This music lesson was, in fact, a lesson in the complex ways that classical music is implicated in present-day discourses about marriage and womanhood.[2] Most striking here is the way a remembrance of M. S. Subbulakshmi provided the occasion for reasserting a particular notion of womanly virtue. My teacher had used Thyagaraja's lyrics, presumably composed in an attitude of humble devotion to Rama, to signify a specifically gendered position: that of a virtuous woman rebuking society. Sung in her own voice, the lyrics outlined the ambiguity of my teacher's position. As a woman who had remained unmarried and "devoted herself to music," thereby embodying the nationalist ideal of a woman who devotes herself to the preservation of Indian tradition, she invited admiration; at the same time, her unmarried state, her lack of domesticity, aroused accusations of eccentricity and suspicions of abnormality. Sung in M.S.'s voice, the lyrics outlined the contradictions of M.S.'s position: as an internationally known artist, she belonged to her public, to her audiences. Her appearance in public, however, depended on her enactment of virtuous womanhood during performances and on having a husband who acted as her manager.

Also striking is the way the story about M.S. juxtaposes several conflicting ideals of marriage. My teacher was convinced that a traditional arranged marriage had been impossible in her case because a traditional husband would have expected a wife who would bear children and do housework and not pursue a career as a professional violinist. In M.S.'s case a traditional marriage would not have worked either; it was her "love marriage" (and all the implications of social mobility, companionship, and modernity that such a term carries) that had enabled her to pursue a performing career by allowing her to appear in public as a traditional Brahmin woman. Finally, the shadow of the devadasi, a woman outside the bonds of conventional marriage, hung over the conversation, not as an indigenous version of liberated womanhood but as an almost unspeakable contrast against which any female musician had to place herself. The sense of outrage that my teacher expressed, that Sadasivam could suspect M.S. of infidelity, indicates the distance she placed between herself and those "characterless ladies."

That afternoon we eventually got back to the music "itself." But I was astonished at the distance we had managed to cover, moving from music to ideas of womanhood, to marriage, and finally to a discourse on the essential difference between men and women. What history made possible such a chain of associations?

A Politics of Voice

Toward the end of the nineteenth century, when older temple- and court-based forms of patronage ceased to be viable in the late colonial economy of South India, musicians moved in large numbers to the colonial city of Madras; there, music organizations, concert halls, and academies were established by an upper-caste, largely Brahmin elite interested in what they called the "revival" of Karnatic music and its transformation into the classical music of South India. At the heart of the revival of Karnatic music was the notion that it could serve as a sign of tradition and Indianness, as one of the trappings of an emergent middle-class modernity. Just as particular notions of female respectability and ideal womanhood played a crucial role in defining the aims of anticolonial nationalism, they were also central to the project of defining middle-class modernity.[3] While devadasis came to be regarded as prostitutes and their opportunities to perform gradually diminished, upper-caste women were encouraged to learn, and eventually perform, music and dance. Indeed, for many Brahmin elites, the sign of the successful classicization of music and dance from the 1920s to 1940s was the transformation of these forms into "arts" fit for upper-caste, middle-class "family women."

My teacher's comments fit into this larger story of how music became available to "respectable" women as a vocation and sometimes a career, and the particular kinds of performance practice, discourse about music, and notions of ideal womanhood engendered by this newfound respectability. Classical music in twentieth-century South India helped constitute a private or domestic sphere at the same time as it participated in the production of a new urban, modern public sphere through the establishment of institutions for teaching and disseminating music. Beginning in the 1930s, the classical concert stage provided a public arena in which the sound and image of Indian womanhood could be constructed and displayed.[4] Connections emerged between the way music was placed and discursively imagined by the newly developing middle-class and what was happening in terms of actual performance practice onstage. The literal *domestication* of music as a sign of bourgeois respectability—its connection to a discourse about family values—parallels music's progressive *interiorization* within the body in terms of performance practice. The notion of the artist that underlay the revival of Karnatic music as the classical music of South India depended on this new sense of interiority.

A certain politics of voice emerged in the moment that upper-caste women began to sing in public, a politics that involved both privileging the voice itself as Karnatic music's locus of authenticity and valuing a certain kind of voice. By midcentury, the ideal of a voice that came naturally from within, unmediated by performance of any kind, a voice that seemed to transcend its body, came to be valued as the true voice of Karnatic classical music. A number of circumstances enabled the emergence of this politics of voice: a social reform movement that stressed the virtues of domesticity and female chastity; the rise of an urban middle class, defined in part by an ideal of traditional Indian womanhood; and, crucially, the development of technologies of recording and amplifying the voice, such as the gramophone and microphone. This politics or ideology of voice emerged, then, not only in live performance but also in moments of sonic communication mediated by technologies of sound reproduction and the cultures of listening associated with them.

Social Reform and the Emergence of "Art"

Comparing M.S.'s life to the history of music is quite apt, since her conversion from devadasi to married Brahmin woman mirrors the reforms that were effected on music and dance in the late nineteenth century and early twentieth. At the end of the nineteenth century, the devadasi "system"—a generalized term referring to a variety of economic, religious, and political practices through which women of the devadasi community were employed by temples—became the object of social reform. The campaign to end the practice of dedicating girls to a life of service in temples as dancers and musicians attained success in 1947, when the practice was legally abolished.[5] The debates surrounding the issues of how devadasis were to be defined and whether or not their activities in the temples constituted prostitution, and the controversy over the bill to outlaw their practices, had crucial effects on the idea of "art" and conceptions of women's relationship to it.

Kalpana Kannabiran traces the origins of the devadasi abolition movement in the Madras Presidency to the social-reform movement started by Kandukuri Veeresalingam in what would later become Andhra Pradesh, in the 1830s. Focusing on women's emancipation, Veeresalingam was concerned with social hygiene: conjugality and sexual relationships, education, religious practices, as well as government corruption. By the last decades of the nineteenth century, not only such social reform movements but also colonial ideas about prostitution combined to make the devadasi issue prominent in the agenda for social reform. The Social Purity movement, begun in 1880 in Madras by Raghupati Venkataratnam Naidu, was influenced by the Purity Crusade in England and America. As Kannabiran writes, one of the crucial elements of the crusade was the broadening of the term "prostitution" to refer not only to sexual intercourse for monetary gain, but also as a metaphor for social depravity and moral corruption in general (1995, 63).[6]

The development of a discourse about prostitution determined the way family women were differentiated from devadasis. In a detailed article on Anglo-Indian legal conceptions of dancing girls between 1800 and 1914, Kunal Parker traces the process by which dancing girls came to be criminalized as prostitutes. Crucial in this process was the representation of dancing girls as a professional group rather than as a caste, which might have its own laws concerning marriage and property inheritance. The representation of dancing girls as a professional group characterized by the activities of dancing and prostitution brought them under the purview of Hindu law and led to a public perception that they had fallen from caste because of their practice of prostitution (Parker 1998, 566). Ruling that their singing and dancing were merely "vestigial" and that their true source of income was from prostitution, the Madras High Court denied dancing girls status as artists (607). Placing prostitution in opposition to legal Hindu marriage, Parker states, the legislation was "directed explicitly towards the valorization of marriage, the construction of a Hindu community organized around marriage, and the sanitization of Hindu religious practice" (632).

The devadasi abolition movement came to a head under the leadership of Dr. Muthulakshmi Reddy, a medical doctor, legislator, and member of the Women's India Association, who was herself born to a devadasi mother. Beginning in the 1920s, Reddy launched a campaign against the practice of dedicating minor girls to temple deities. "I want the Honorable members of the House to understand that these [devadasis] are neither descended from heaven nor imported from foreign countries," Reddy began a speech to the Madras legislative assembly in 1927. "They . . . are our kith and kin." "At an age when they cannot think and act for themselves," she continued, these girls were "sacrificed to a most blind and degrading custom." The crime of it was that the innocent girls, if only left alone, would become "virtuous and loyal wives, affectionate mothers, and useful citizens" (1928–1931, 3). Reddy implied that girls who became devadasis were lost to society, that they were useless; their "sacrifice" made them undependable subjects. In a series of appeals, each with affecting signatures like "By a Woman" or "From One that Loves the Children," Reddy drummed up support for her bill. "The dedication of a girl to a life of vice is a heinous crime—is it not a worse form of Sati? A hygienic mistake? A moral monstrosity?" (5).

Reddy was helped in her efforts by caste associations of Icai Vel̤l̤ālars and Sengundars, castes from which devadasis generally came; male members of these castes saw the abolition of the devadasi system as a matter of retrieving the honor and dignity of their caste (Anandi 1991, 741). In 1936 Ramamirtham Ammaiyar, a devadasi from the Icai Vel̤l̤ālar caste who had rebelled against the system, married a music teacher, became a political activist, and published a novel in Tamil, *Tācikaḷ Mocāvalai Allatu Mati Pe<u>r</u><u>r</u>a Mainar* (The treacherous net of the devadasis, or a minor grown wise).[7] The novel, a mixture of autobiography and propaganda, follows the lives of several devadasis who come to the realization that the system is exploiting them and mobilize to effect legislation.[8]

Many devadasis opposed abolition, claiming that they were being unfairly grouped together with common prostitutes. Others claimed that the men of the Icai Vel̤l̤ālar caste were supporting the abolition because of ulterior motives; they were jealous of the wealth and status that some devadasis had obtained (Kannabiran 1995, 67). The Madras Presidency Devadasi Association and the Madras Rudrakannikai Sangam issued statements to counter the abolitionists in the late 1920s. Bangalore Nagaratnammal, a prominent devadasi who led the protest against male and Brahmin domination of the Thyagaraja festival at Tiruvaiyaru (and later commissioned the building of the shrine where the festival now takes place), spoke out against the legislation, claiming that it denied devadasis not only their right to own and inherit property but also their status as artists (67).

Indeed, and perhaps most crucially, the campaign against the devadasi system helped redefine the status of art, particularly music and dance. If the official debate about devadasis came, by the early decades of the twentieth century, to center on devadasis' property rights and alleged prostitution, it is because the matter of their music and dance had been effectively removed from the discourse on devadasis and relocated to a realm now self-consciously referred to as "art." Separating the woman question from the question of what constituted art enabled art to have a trajectory apart from its practitioners' lives. It was precisely because revivalists like E. Krishna Iyer and Rukmini Devi considered the music and dance of the devadasis to be part of an ancient tradition that extended far beyond the lives of specific devadasis that these practices could assume the status of art. In the 1920s and 1930s, at the height of the campaign to end the devadasi system, both Brahmins and non-Brahmins involved with the Tamil renaissance began to speak about the revival of India's classical arts. They used the English word *art* or the Tamil term *kalai* to signify a generalized concept of art, rather than a particular practice like music or painting. In this discourse, the distinction between art and craft was essential. Where craft implied hereditary practitioners who worked repetitively and unthinkingly, art implied an individual artist, a subject who made choices, was original, and somehow expressed herself through her art.[9]

In the early 1930s a number of prominent members of the Congress Party in Madras, including E. Krishna Iyer, Tirumalayya Naidu, and T. Prakasam defined their position bluntly as "pro-art," maintaining that the extremity of Muthulakshmi Reddy's anti-nautch movement was killing the art of the devadasis.[10] In a pamphlet entitled "Music and the Anti-Nautch Movement," written circa 1912, Tirumalayya Naidu, an advocate by profession, stated that the anti-nautch movement had been negative in character, set up to demolish the "long-standing institution" of the art of the devadasis (6). E. Krishna Iyer represented the pro-art position most vociferously. He was born in 1897 in Kallidaikuricci, known then for its lavish musical and dance events in connection with weddings. While completing his law degree at Madras Law College, Krishna Iyer acted female roles in dramas and studied Karnatic music on the violin. He later joined the Suguna Vilas Sabha, a prominent theatrical group in Madras, and received formal training in *sadir*, the dance form of the devadasis. Committed to reviving the dance, he was instrumental in starting the Madras Music Academy and in bringing dancers, first devadasis and then Brahmins, to its stage. In a series of letters against Muthulakshmi Reddy's condemnation of all public performance of nautch published in the *Madras Mail* in 1932, Krishna Iyer mobilized public support for his pro-art position. In addition, he was behind the Music Academy's 1932 resolution to rename the dance "Bharata Natyam," or "Indian dance." The word *Bharata* gave the dance an image of national importance; at the same time the use of the Sanskrit word *natya* suggested its origin in the Sanskrit treatises on dance.

The idea was not necessarily to help the devadasis continue to practice their arts; it was rather to rid music and dance of their impure associations. Music and dance had to be rescued from the hands of degenerate devadasis and taken up by women from respectable (that is, Brahmin) families. The most prominent upholder of this idea was Rukmini Devi, one of the first Brahmin women in the twentieth century to perform South Indian dance and the founder of Kalakshetra, one of the first institutions to teach dance and music in Madras. Devi stated that her goal was to prove that "girls from good families" could dance and that they no longer had to depend on traditional dance teachers (Allen 1997, 64). Influenced by Theosophy and the idea of the original devadasis as a "band of pure virgin devotees," Devi reconceptualized the dance to stress its religious and spiritual aspects, presenting the dancer as a chaste and holy woman.[11] Importantly, the shift from devadasis to Brahmins involved not only a new kind of woman but also a new kind of artist, one who was an individual interpreter, rather than merely a hereditary practitioner of the art. In a pamphlet entitled "The Creative Spirit" written in the early 1940s, Devi described the shift as an awakening from the merely physical level of the "acrobat" to the "meaning" and "expression" conveyed by the slightest movements of the dancer.[12] "A tiny finger lifted with meaning," she concluded, "is far more thrilling than all the turns and gyrations and tricks of the circus performer."[13] Notions of chaste womanly behavior here converge with the idea of an art whose basic currencies are "meaning" and "expression."

Amrit Srinivasan notes that although the devadasi abolition legislation was not officially passed until 1947, the combination of social reform and purification involved in transforming music and dance into classical arts in the first three decades of the twentieth century had already effectively prevented devadasis from continuing their traditions. The bill, she writes, "seemed to have been pushed through not so much to deal the death of the Tamil caste of professional dancers as to approve and permit the birth of a new elite class of amateur performers" (1985, 1875). Matthew Allen has noted that "in the face of overwhelming social pressures, a significant number of women from the traditional dancing community [stopped dancing but] nevertheless continued in the profession of musical (most often vocal) performance," but that since the 1990s very few of the female descendants of this community have chosen to go into musical performance (1997, 68). Many Brahmin women did not perform onstage in the 1920s and 1930s for fear of being mistaken as devadasis (Bullard 1998, 128). By the 1950s, after the passage of the Devadasi Dedication Abolition Act, more and more Brahmins were taking up music and dance; both arts became desirable talents for women of marriageable age. The entry of Brahmin women as singers onto the concert stage solidified the developing caste rift: many felt that female Brahmin singers in particular could not sit next to Icai Veḷḷāḷar accompanists on stage (ibid., 128, 263). The rise of Brahmin women as performing musicians thus served as a catalyst to the Brahminizing of music as a profession. Since the 1980s, Karnatic music and Bharata Natyam have become almost exclusive markers of middle-class English-educated Brahmin identity.

The Voice of the Century

In 1933 E. Krishna Iyer wrote of the "sweetness of natural music, as found in the voices of women, young boys, and singing birds" (xvi). If the listening public, or the "democracy," as he called them, seemed to be taking a new interest in such sweet sounds, it was because Karnatic music had lost its sweetness. "It is but natural," he wrote, "in the general dearth of good and well-trained voices, and scared away by the excesses of dry acrobatics of the musical experts," that the public should desire music that was pleasurable to listen to (xvi). Women inherently possessed the raw material of music. In a sketch of Saraswati Bai (1894–1974), the first Brahmin woman to sing on the concert stage, he wrote that "women vocalists are found to possess certain desirable advantages over men. They have pleasant voices to begin with and none of the contortions of the struggling male musicians. They do not fight with their accompanists, who usually follow them closely. They are free from acrobatics of any kind and they seldom overdo anything" (46). Krishna Iyer wrote of the discrimination Saraswati Bai faced from a Madras sabha where she had been scheduled to give a kalakshepam performance: "The music world then [around 1910] was not as liberal as it is now," he remarked (49). The boycott of Saraswati Bai's performance by her male accompanist at the Madras sabha stands in contrast to the enthusiastic reception she had at a wedding performance several years later, where the audience was attracted by the novelty of hearing a "lady bhagavatar."

> It was one of the marriage seasons at Kallidaikurichi—the Brahmin Chettinad of the Tinnevelly District as it then was—notorious for the lavish expenditure of its fortunes on spectacular marriages and choice musicians. A huge concourse of people were hovering in and about a pandal [enclosure with a makeshift stage] to hear the beginning of a Kalakshepam—the daring feat of a new fledged lady bhagavatar—and then to decide whether to remain or disperse. . . . Scarcely did the frail form of a young girl of fifteen or sixteen years of age sound her jalar [small metal cymbals] and go through her opening song when the scattered crowds closed into the pandal to its full with barely standing space for the musician herself. The organisers had no small difficulty in accommodating the vast crowds that sat through the performance with eager interest. . . . Her performances invariably draw crowded houses and the ladies' section of the audience is generally overfull. (47)

What accounted for such excitement about a female musician? While Krishna Iyer suggested that women's music, without the competition and "acrobatics," had a more "natural" feel, he also implied that the rising popularity of female vocalists was in part due to the explosion of gramophone recordings. In the early years of recording in South India, more records were made of female vocalists than male vocalists (Indira Menon 1999, 74). Gramophone records, made to be played in the home, needed a different kind of appeal than concerts; the competition and the acrobatics that might make a concert exciting would be lost on a gramophone record, where anything that did not go as planned might later simply sound like a recording glitch.

Gramophone records also provided a solution to the problems faced by female musicians, whether from the devadasi community or the Brahmin community: recording presented a way for women from both communities to be heard without being seen, to escape association with their bodies. A social reform movement that stressed the virtues of marriage and domesticity and referred to the activities of devadasis as "debauchery" and "prostitution" left female musicians of the devadasi community with few traditional performance venues and almost no opportunities to perform in the newly built concert halls of Madras. Gramophone companies, however, initially run not by Brahmins but by Americans and Europeans, actively recruited devadasi women for their first recordings.[14] Unlike All India Radio, which was founded in the 1930s as a vehicle for the nationalist project of making music respectable (thus denying broadcasting opportunities to devadasi women), the gramophone companies were purely capitalist enterprises. Between 1910 and 1930, their best-selling recordings in South India were of Dhanakoti Ammal, Bangalore Nagaratnammal, Bangalore Thayi, Coimbatore Thayi, M. Shanmughavadivu, Veena Dhanammal, and Madras Lalithangi, all women from the devadasi community (Indira Menon 1999, 74–75; Kinnear 1994).

Meanwhile, for Brahmin women, recording provided a way to sing for the public without appearing in public and jeopardizing their respectability. In the early 1930s Columbia Records "discovered" a girl genius, the thirteen-year-old D. K. Pattammal (b. 1919). Many years later, in a speech given at the Madras Music Academy, Pattammal stated that her success, in the absence of a family connection to music, was due to the gramophone. As a Brahmin girl growing up in an orthodox family, she was unable to undergo the traditional gurukulavasam, which would require leaving home to live with a male, non-Brahmin teacher. Instead, she supplemented her brief periods of learning from various teachers with listening to gramophone records. When she was ready to perform, the gramophone, as an interface between private and public, provided her with a way to sing without being seen. The radio, similarly, provided Brahmin women an opportunity to perform without emerging in public; a woman described to me how in the 1930s, as a girl in her late teens and twenties, she was forbidden to sing concerts, but her father would chaperone her to the Madras All India Radio station each week for a broadcast.[15]

The gramophone companies sought out novelty and found a ready source of it in girl singers. By the 1920s, recordings of them were so common that G. Venkatachalam, a patron of many artists and musicians at that time, referred to them with distaste as "baby stunts." Of his first meeting with M. S. Subbulakshmi in 1929, he wrote, "She was 13 when I met her. Subbulakshmi came to Bangalore to record her songs by His Master's Voice (HMV) Company. 'We are recording an extraordinarily talented girl from Madras. Would you care to listen to her and tell us what you think of her?' was the cordial invitation from my friend, the manager. My first reactions were: 'Ah! Another of those baby stunts!' I went, however, and met not a fake, but a real girl genius" (1966, 65).

The idea of novelty, so crucial to the gramophone companies' success, was intimately tied up with notions of the child prodigy.[16] If earlier discourse on Karnatic musicians stressed the importance of seasoned experience and long years of discipleship, the figure of the prodigy stood in stark contrast. The prodigy was independent of the traditional gurukula system in which the student lived in the guru's household. The figure of the prodigy suggests a preternatural ability or gift, an element that goes beyond nature into the realm of the supernatural. It implies a certain isolation or protection from the world, an incompleteness compensated for by a larger-than-life voice and a selfless devotion to music. The notion of the prodigy complicates classic formulations of agency: the prodigy does not sing because she desires to, but because a voice sings through her—her body is merely a vessel. As Felicia Miller Frank has pointed out, the association between women, the voice, and the artificial or technological has a long history in European discourse on the arts. Female prodigies, in this discourse, are represented as sexless or artificial angels, emblematic of the sublime and of artistic modernity (Frank 1995, 2). Among the elite of twentieth-century South India, who borrowed much of this European discourse about art, it is no coincidence that the word *prodigy* was first used with regard to female musicians and that the prodigy's first vehicle was the gramophone. In South India the female voice, disassociated from its body, came to be thought of as the essence of music itself.

Of the female musicians that the gramophone companies popularized, M. S. Subbulakshmi became by far the most famous. What made hers "the voice of the century"? M.S. was born in 1916 in Madurai to a veena player from the devadasi community named Madurai Shanmughavadivu.[17] In her memoir of a childhood steeped in music M.S. recalled, "I was fascinated by records—gramophone plates, we called them. Inspired by the gramophone company's logo of the dog listening to his master's voice, I would pick up a sheet of paper, roll it into a long cone, and sing into it for hours" (Ramnarayan 1997, 10). Shanmughavadivu was ambitious for her daughter and brought her to her own recording sessions in Madras, where she persuaded the HMV company to record the thirteen-year-old Subbulakshmi. The records sold well and M.S. began to get concert opportunities in Madras. In the early 1930s she and her mother moved from Madurai to Madras for the sake of M.S.'s career. Her concerts attracted the elite of Madras at that time, a group of Brahmin or other high-caste men who considered themselves aestheticians, journalists, and freedom fighters. Among them were Kalki Krishnamoorthy, journalist for the Tamil weekly *Ananda Vikatan*, who later started his own magazine called *Kalki*, in which he wrote a weekly column on music and dance; "Rasi-

15 M. S. Subbalakshmi record jacket (1945).

kamani" (Gem among connoisseurs) T. K. Chidambaranatha Mudaliar, aesthetician and man of letters; the director K. Subramaniam, who became known for his patriotic films; and the journalist and freedom fighter T. Sadasivam.

Sadasivam, a widower with two daughters and ten years older than M.S., married her in 1940. He became not only her husband but also the manager of her career, overseeing her acting in films such as *Shakuntala* (1940) and *Meera* (1945), and coaching her in what to sing on the concert stage.[18] It is said that he would sit in the front row of the audience during her concerts and plan every detail of her concert programs (Sarathy 1997, 169). As her public-relations man, Sadasivam introduced her to Gandhi and Nehru and a host of other political figures. M.S. became a larger-than-life presence not simply by her musical talent but also by Sadasivam's careful cultivation of her persona as a singer of pan-Indian and international appeal. If the nation had a voice, Sadasivam at least thought he knew what it sounded like.

Not only the gramophone but also the microphone shaped M.S.'s voice. The beginning of her public singing career coincided with the establishment of large concert halls in Madras. Essential to these halls was the microphone, which began to be used in South India in the 1930s. The microphone allowed Karnatic vocalists and instrumentalists to concentrate less on projecting volume and more on shifts in dynamics and speed. It also allowed those with softer voices (including many women) to sing to large audiences. As noted in chapter 2, many musicians attribute changes in vocal style in Karnatic music in the twentieth century to the use of the microphone, particularly the shift from an earlier, higher-pitched style of singing accompanied by more gesturing—often referred to today as "shouting"—to a lower-pitched, more introspective style. The microphone also narrows the physical range of a performer, serving as a kind of ballast for a singer or violinist, limiting the distance he or she can move. At the same time, one of the microphone's most prominent effects is the projection of intimacy to vast audiences.[19] As one listener said of hearing M.S. in a concert hall, "It seemed like we were overhearing a conversation in which a devotee spoke intimately to her God."[20] M.S.'s voice and career, notes Indira Menon, were products of the microphone: "The greatest gift to the world of this little instrument of the technological revolution is M.S. Subbulakshmi. The innumerable nuances of her multi-faceted voice can be captured by it. . . . She is truly the product of the modern age—of the sabha culture, teeming audiences, and large halls where her voice can soar—thanks to the mike" (1999, 89). It is crucial to note that the voice with "innumerable nuances" is itself a product of the microphone; as the microphone makes these nuances audible in a physical sense, it also makes them available to an aesthetic discourse about music.

By the 1940s, M.S. and D. K. Pattammal had come to dominate the market for female voices and would do so until the 1970s. Both sang in films as well as recordings and classical stage performances, but their personae were quite different. The two singers had essentially different audiences, as one older concertgoer told me. Pattammal was "dependable, intellectual," her voice had a "weight" to it, and audiences who prized these characteristics would attend her concerts. After M.S.'s concerts, however, audiences came away ecstatic, raving about the fine qualities of her voice and her expression. According to her fans, M.S. concentrated on conveying bhakti (devotion) and *bhāvam* (emotion) through her singing, always paying great attention to the pronunciation of lyrics and singing not only Karnatic compositions but also Hindi bhajans and Sanskrit chants. Only after Pattammal released a record with a pallavi did M.S. begin to include more "intellectual" items in her concerts. "Natural" music was considered the opposite of intellectual feats. It is worth noting Venkatachalam's description of M.S.:

> Her voice has the rich cadence of a mountain stream and the purity of a veena-note. . . . She takes the highest notes with the effortlessness of a nightingale's flight to its mate. This is an art by itself. And when you consider how even some of the great *vidwans* and *ustads* [the Hindu and Muslim terms for "artist," respectively] contort their faces and make ridiculous caricatures of themselves in such attempts, it is some consolation to see a natural face for once. Women (because of their innate vanity, I suppose!) avoid that exhibition of agonized looks and tortured faces! Her recitals have not the long drawn out boredom of the ordinary South Indian cutcheries [Tamil *kaccēri*]. . . . It is the art of music she wishes to display and not its mathematics." (1966, 66–67)

What emerges in writing and talk about M.S.'s voice is a new discourse about the natural voice; constantly remarked on are her genuineness on stage, her complete emotional involvement as she sings. Recent biographies play up M.S.'s personal humility and innocence, opposing it to the "grandeur" and "majesty" of her voice, noting that she "knows nothing but music" and when offstage is a simple housewife like any other (Indira Menon 1999, 141).[21]

Many descriptions of her voice use the metaphor of flight, implying at once an escape from the body and an association with nature: "the effortlessness of a nightingale's flight to its mate." Reviews of M.S.'s records are replete with metaphors of bodilessness or dissolution of the body. Good music should "melt" (*kēṭṭavarkaḷai urukki*) the listener, make the mind "swoon" (*uḷḷam māyaṅkum*), or the listener "forget himself" (*mey marantu*: literally, "forget the body"). In a 1942 review, after remarking that the gramophone record "captures" the range of M.S.'s voice from its lowest to highest notes, Kalki Krishnamurthy comments, with regard to a particular line of a song, "If you hear it once, you'll have the desire to hear it again and again, a thousand times. Good thing this is a music record and there is no problem hearing it again and again!" (75). It is as if the ideal listening experience had come to be identified with listening to gramophone records; the recognition of the perfection of M.S.'s voice is linked to its disembodiment and mechanical repetition on the record.[22]

Comments on the naturalness of M.S.'s voice found their way into a discourse about art as well; reviewers slipped easily from descriptions of her performances or recordings to ideas about what art should be. The letters of Rasikamani T. K. Chidambaranatha Mudaliar from the 1940s are laden with references to M.S.'s performances. After hearing one of her radio concerts, he wrote that her rendition of a song had "melted the listeners. That is art, is it not? It must make our feelings mingle with Truth [*tattuvam*], and make us into different beings [*vēṟu vastuvāka akkiviṭavēṇṭum*]" (Maharajan 1979, 136). However, as Venkatachalam noted, art was also for more mundane purposes.

> "What six singers would you select from India to represent this country in a World Music Festival?" asked a well-known European impresario not long ago, and I had no hesitation in suggesting Roshanara and Kesarbai for Hindustani music; M.S. Subbulakshmi and D.K. Pattammal for the Carnatic; Kamala Jharia and Kananbala for popular songs [all women artists].
>
> This list would, of course, amuse the orthodox and the music pundits. "What about Faiyaz Khan and Omkarnath?" I can hear the Hindustaniwalas shout. "Why not Aryakudi and Musiri?" will be the Tamils' cry. The film fans will plead for Saigal and Kurshid [all male artists].
>
> I am not unmindful of the merits of the above. . . . But I wouldn't risk them in a World Jamboree. They will simply not be understood. Terrible is the ignorance of the world to things Indian, and unbridgeable as yet is the gulf between the music of the East and the West. . . . People of the world understand art and appreciate artistes. . . . And I claim, my six are *artistes*! (1966, 68)

Two points warrant attention here. First, it is female vocalists, not male, who are thought to represent not only India but also art itself in the new global market; Venkatachalam implies that although the male vocalists had a local following, they would not be able to travel as representatives of India. Second, art—here, the art of music—is identified with a naturalness that is gendered as female.[23]

By the 1940s, the connection between women and music had ascended to the level of an assumption. In a series of essays written in English and published by the Theosophical Society, Rukmini Devi elaborated on the special connection that she felt existed between women and the fine arts. "The spirit of womanhood," she wrote, "is the spirit of the artist."[24] Women possessed an "innate refinement" which made it incumbent on them to take up the revival of Indian art: "Innate as this refinement is, the study and practice of such arts as dancing, music, and painting can distinctly help in its development. . . . Without the expression of the arts in life, in the very home itself, there can be no real refinement and of course no real civilization."[25] To be an artist meant not necessarily *producing* music or art but *being* art itself: "It is necessary that in her walk, in her speech and her actions she should be the very embodiment of beauty and grace."[26] In learning the arts, what was necessary was "rigorous work, the complete subjugation of all other personal desires and pleasures, the abandonment of one's being to the Cause."[27] The success of the Indian nation, as well as the Indian arts, depended on restoring woman from her degraded position to that of "a divine influence rising above the material aspect of things."[28]

Devi imagined the relationship between voice and body to be analogous to the relationship between music and dance. Although she could not completely efface the physicality or eroticism of dance, her writings point to the necessity, in her view, of putting its physicality to some higher use. Music was, for her, the divine influence that would insure this. In her essay "Dance and Music" she wrote that music, "the basic language of Gods," was what saved dance from being "mere physical acrobatics."[29] It was the "universal language of the soul," the "saving grace of humanity."[30] In such a conception the materiality of music is effaced. Instead of being seen as social, something which comes into being through performance and the mediation of human actors, it is seen as a kind of pure voice from within, a voice deeply contained *within* the body, but neither connected to nor manifested on its surface.

The Limits of Performance

In her article on the agenda of the Madras Music Academy between 1930 and 1947, Lakshmi Subramanian states that the reorientation of music and dance—performance style, repertoire, and the performers themselves—toward an urban, largely Brahmin, middle class was part of a "sanitizing" mission that emphasized the spirituality of Karnatic music and Bharata Natyam over their sensual aspects (1999a). On the dance stage, this meant that "spiritual love" and "restrained devotion," rather than "sensual experience" and "raw passion," had to be projected (82).[31] On the music stage, the sanitizing project produced a distinction between "classical" and "light classical" music; the compositions of the trinity of composer-saints came to be considered the central repertoire of Karnatic music, while padams and javalis (associated with the devadasi tradition) were considered "light classical" (83).[32] The compositions of the trinity, which expressed spiritual devotion to Rama, were seen as the appropriate subject matter for classical music. This reorientation of Karnatic music toward the spiritual realm was accompanied by the changes in infrastructure discussed in chapter 2—the establishment of concert halls, music sabhas, and music-teaching institutions—that created a public sphere distinctly different from the temple and courtly milieus in which Karnatic music had flourished in the nineteenth century.

A central effect of the shift from these settings to the public concert hall was that music and dance were separated from each other, physically and conceptually.[33] Under the reforming eye of Rukmini Devi, musicians—who had previously accompanied dancers by moving with or behind them on stage—were seated at the left end of the stage, presumably to give them more respect. However, musicians who performed for dance never got as much respect as concert musicians; their music was seen as somehow not pure or classical enough (Allen 1997, 66). E. Krishna Iyer, in his 1933 sketch on the dancer Balasaraswati, wrote that the art of Bharata Natyam needed to be "overhauled if it should have any real appeal in these days" (98). Changing the character of the accompanying music could, he suggested, bring about the desired change in atmosphere. "If possible the vociferous clarionet will have to be substituted by the flute or other more agreeable and indigenous instruments. The noise of the jalar [small metal cymbals used to beat the tala] in the hands of the nattuvans [musicians who keep the tala with these cymbals] will have to be controlled and reduced considerably so as to allow the beautiful sound of the ankle bells to be heard" (98). "Noise" implied a spectacle, an excess of performance and an unruly audience, while "beautiful sound" evoked the image of a silent audience appreciating an aesthetic production.

Perhaps more important, dancers stopped singing. Unlike traditional devadasis, who sang as they danced, the Bharata Natyam dancers trained at Rukmini Devi's Kalakshetra not only did not sing but did a minimum of *abhinaya* (facial gestures and/or mime, often contrasted with "pure dance"). Krishna Iyer suggested that the "low atmosphere" of nautch performances was due to a kind of overperformance of abhinaya: "The over-developed technique of the art, admirable as it is in much of the details of abhinaya . . .

has to be kept within limits and desirable proportions so as not to obscure or interfere with the natural grace of movements and poses" (1933, 98). If respectable dancers no longer sang, it was perhaps because the sound of their voice would add a kind of unseemly interiority to the performance. On the music stage, the reverse was true: respectable musicians did not dance when they sang, for this would interfere with the singer's projection of interiority. The association of dance with something improper in music can be seen in a 1941 article in *Nāṭṭiyam* entitled "Apiṉayam Vēṇṭām" (We do not want abhinaya). The author, Gottuvadyam Durayappa Bhagavatar, turned the meaning of the verb *apiṉayi* from the rather neutral idea of miming or "showing in gestures" to the negative connotation of "imitation," suggesting that many young musicians, instead of developing their own original style, were simply imitating others. A term from dance became a metaphor for imitation, a kind of excess of performance that would be unseemly on the music stage.

What were the implications of this separation for the performing subject? For female musicians in particular, a convention of music performance developed in which the body was effaced; too much physical movement or "show" on the stage was seen not only as extraneous to the music but as unseemly. In 1939 the violinist C. Subrahmanya Ayyar wrote that excessive gesturing by singers had become so prevalent that there were special Tamil terms coined to describe them: *iyantiram araikkiṟatu* (a phrase suggesting the motions of a machine hulling paddy) and *mallayuttam* (wrestling). "Sometime back," he noted disapprovingly, "the Tamil weekly *Ananta Vikatan* published photos of such ugly poses of several vocalists, but the satire was lost on them; for they deemed the photos as a matter of advertisement for their renown in music" (1939, 45).

The ideal became a kind of performance of nonperformance: nothing visible was supposed to happen on the music stage. Until D. K. Pattammal began singing *ragam-tanam-pallavi* (a highly intellectual type of improvisation) onstage in the 1940s, and even after that, women musicians had confined themselves to performing only compositions; their only improvisation was a small raga alapana.[34] Singing compositions was not really considered to be performance. Women's voices, it was said, were not suited to the competitive type of music that men sang, where they tried to upstage each other in improvisatory virtuosity. In the late 1930s a reviewer in the Tamil magazine *Bharata Mani* wrote that "women's music needs to have its own character; women's concerts should not just be a copy of men's concerts. We do not need pallavis and elaborate raga alapana from women.

Padams and javalis are being forgotten as we speak. It would be good for women to give importance to them" ("Ceṉṉai caṅkīta vitvat capai: 12-āvatu mēlam" 1938, 372). Women's activity on the stage, suggested R. Rangaramanuja Ayyangar, a prominent male musician from the 1940s to the 1970s, should be akin to housekeeping. "The craze for *sahitya neeraval* and *swara prastara* [two types of improvisation] as a prestige symbol detracts from the inherent charm of a lady's voice. Lady musicians can resuscitate values . . . if they concentrate on repertoire. Hundreds of classical compositions need to be revived. The Hindu housewife has a reputation for keeping alive religious traditions" (quoted in Indira Menon 1999, 102–3). By such logic, family values are indistinguishable from the values of classical music.

The effacement of the female musician's body on the concert stage is accomplished not only by a lack of gesture but also by an implicit dress code that ensures that all female musicians look the same. Unlike Western concert black, which is supposed to make the musician's body symbolically invisible, Karnatic concert attire makes female musician's bodies visible as a certain type: a respectable family woman.[35] Whereas men's appearances on the Karnatic concert stage vary—pants, *veshtis* (cloth worn by men over the legs as a long skirt), silk *jibbahs* (tunics), Western-style button-down shirts, hairstyles from topknots to short haircuts—women's appearances have changed little over the years. All female musicians wear a fairly lavish (but not too lavish) silk sari and have their hair pulled back in a neat, tight plait or bun. Whereas male musicians who present an eccentric appearance are often thought to be geniuses, female musicians whose appearance differs from the norm provoke negative comments; their appearance is considered extramusical excess, an unseemly element. My violin teacher, whose unkempt appearance was a source of anxiety to her family members, often received advice about how she might improve her appearance so that she might be called for concerts more often. She compared her own "fate" to that of a male flutist she had accompanied many times when he was drunk and disheveled on stage; his eccentricities, however, were universally hailed as a sign of his genius. Eccentric women, my teacher pointed out, were not likely to be taken as geniuses.

The association between female respectability and classical music is so strong that metaphors of dress often motivate conversations about music. For several months in 1998 I took lessons with a female vocalist in her fifties. Her persona in the Karnatic music world was one of intellectual musicianship, a rigor devoid of the show or gimmicks often associated

16 Women's clothing and classical music as interchangeable signs of tradition. Binny Silks advertisement (1994). Photograph by Amanda Weidman.

with younger male performers. In a sense, this "intellectual" image was the only one available for a female musician of her age, neither old enough to be a pioneer nor young enough to be a rising star. On one occasion she remarked to me that if she had been born some twenty years earlier, she would have been M. S. Subbulakshmi, as if M.S. had simply occupied a slot that had become available in the public world of Karnatic music in the 1930s. Although she did indeed put emphasis on elements usually described as intellectual, such as pallavi and a ganam style of singing alapana, more important was the way *intellectual*, in critics' and audience members' descriptions of her music, serves as a code word for a female musician whose music is without "feminine" charm. The opposition between showiness and intellect is much less stark for male musicians, if it operates at all.

After our strictly timed one-hour lesson, she would, depending on her mood, ask me personal questions. One day she asked me why I always showed up in a sari, while other young women my age were wearing *salwar kameez* or even "jeans" (the summary term for all Western dress). I replied that by wearing the sari I got more respect and was even, on some occasions, able to pass as some kind of Indian. The conversation then turned to music. She expressed her distaste for many current trends in Karnatic

17 Sari advertisement in *Sruti* (January 2003).

music performance, its so-called innovations. Traditional music and traditional dress were unassailable signs of Indianness; despite the fact that one was intangible and the other quite literally material, they were often used as signs for and of each other. "You tie a sari and you get respect," she told me. "That is sangitam." Advertisements for saris often play on the same slippage between music and clothing as symbols of tradition. In an advertisement for Binny Silks, shown on a billboard in Madras in 1994, a woman dressed in a lavish, decorously draped silk sari sits with a veena, with the caption "Traditional beauty made to grace any occasion." In 2003 a newspaper advertisement played on the word *sari* and the musical syllables *sa* and *ri* to suggest that the vendor's saris were the most traditional ones available.

The metaphoric opposition between prostitution and chastity, between uncontrolled female sexuality and domestic womanhood, continues to determine the definition and limits of performance in Karnatic music.[36] During the period in 1998 when I had daily violin lessons with my teacher in Madras, I was always impatient to do swara kalpana, a type of improvisation that takes place within the tala cycle after a composition. My teacher was generally uninterested in it. "It is not really music," she would say. "Just calculations." Raga alapana (also called *ragam*) was the most important thing. She remembered as a young woman also having had a "craze" for swara kalpana. She asked a male musician she accompanied at the time to teach her some of his kalpana tricks. He had berated her: "Paittiyam poṇṇu! [Crazy girl!] You play such beautiful ragam. Why do you want to ruin it with this cheap stuff?" She had come to agree with him. "All this is just kavarcci [attraction; also, sexual attraction], just feats with the tala, like a characterless woman. But ragam—that is like your mother." Ragam, she explained, should be born within: first you enjoy it inside yourself, and then it comes out for others. Swara kalpana, for her, could not claim the same purity of origin; calculation [*kaṇakku*: the same word as that used for accounting, giving it a businesslike connotation] gave it a kind of external, unseemly quality.[37] To imitate certain vocalists doing swara kalpana, she began to slap her leg loudly in mock tala-keeping and barked out an unmelodic string of swaras. Then, to demonstrate raga alapana, she assumed a posture of utter stillness, turned her palms upward, closed her eyes, and began to hum.[38]

Such restrictions might seem antiquated, yet they continue, perhaps in subtler form, in present-day conventions of Karnatic music performance. In 1998 I attended a concert by the immensely popular young vocalist Sowmya, who was accompanied by M. Narmada on the violin. Both women were dressed, as usual, in appropriately lavish silk saris. The concert was uneventful. However, it is precisely the uneventfulness that is part of the aesthetic production: nothing out of the ordinary is supposed to happen. During her raga alapana, Narmada played with closed eyes, face screwed up perhaps in concentration, perhaps to avoid the gaze of the audience. Meanwhile, during the tradeoffs in swara kalpana, when the concert would presumably reach a fever pitch of excitement, Sowmya, waiting for her turn to come around, adjusted her sari, refolded the handkerchief in her lap, and checked her watch, as if nothing exciting were happening. The more classical the music, the less there is to watch on stage; if anything, musicians perform a kind of interiority through bodily posture.[39]

Family Values . . .

Notions of classical music and musicianship became conflated with notions of ideal womanhood in twentieth-century South India through a particular model of domesticity. The Tamil nationalist poet and essayist Subramania Bharatiyar wrote in 1909 of the need for *kuṭumpa strīkaḷ* (family women) to take up music. His essay "Caṅkīta Viṣayam" was concerned with the problem of what he conceived of as a loss of musical sensibility among Tamils. The best way of stemming this loss, he suggested, was to improve women's music in the home—a kind of trickle-up approach that tapped the natural musicality of women. If family women could be given a proper grasp and appreciation of music, the rest of society would improve. For women, he stated, "have an especial connection to music" (1909, 222); if one prohibited women from singing, one would find that one had not only no music but no life at all (221). If women could just be taught to sing correctly what they were already singing in the home as folk ditties and lullabies, the connection would be realized. Bharatiyar offered several practical suggestions. First, women must acquire *tāla ñāṉam* (a rhythmic sense, literally, knowledge of tala). Some said that women innately lacked tala sense, but Bharatiyar maintained that it was a matter of practice. To those who objected on the grounds that family women were not *tācis* (devadasis) and did not need to sing concerts, he responded that singing incorrectly, without regard for the tala, sounded *virācam* (vulgar) (221). For those women who wanted to sing, Bharatiyar recommended that they hire a teacher to teach them proper voice culture and that they stay away from *nāṭaka meṭṭu* (drama tunes), cheap songs with *koccai moḻi* (slang), and, most of all, English and Parsi songs (227–28). For family women interested in learning an instrument, Bharatiyar recommended the veena, with its calm, soft sound, as being particularly appropriate. "If more women played on the veena, there would be a greater appreciation of aesthetic beauty and the niceties of life [rācapayircci, vāḻkkai nayam]" (224).

Through its literal domestication, then, music would produce domesticity; classical music was seen as the soundtrack for the modern marriage and the modern home. In 1894 a letter in the *Mysore Herald* declared that the publication of Karnatic music compositions in European notation, released a year earlier, "must be introduced to our girls." The writer remarked excitedly that, with such a system of notation, "songs could be mastered from mere books" (Chinnaswamy Mudaliar 1892, 208–9). The effect would be a double solution to the "anti-nautch-girl question": it would spare girls from respectable families from having to go to less respectable types to learn music and would provide "respectable musicians who could socially mix and move with us, on social occasions like marriages and similar gatherings where we have been [hearing] the prostitute's music" (208–9). Meanwhile, music would become the agent, or vehicle, of the kind of noncorporeal, spiritual love that should exist between a husband and wife: "There must be a unity of feeling in all pursuits, . . . emphatically so in a Hindu home where the tie is not of the senses but of

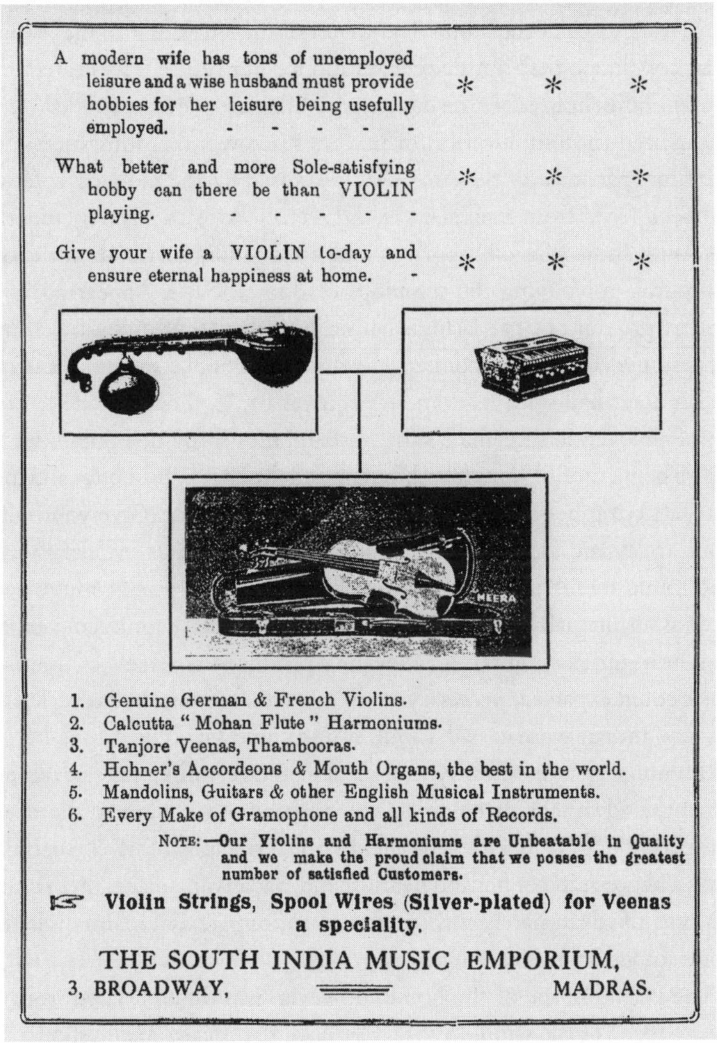

18 South India Music Emporium advertisement in *Madras Music Academy Souvenir* (ca. 1935–1940).

a sacred character, emblematical of the eternal wedding of souls together in harmonious fusion" (209). The lofty musical metaphor of harmony was thus used to characterize marriage. At the same time, music domesticated the private space of the home. The writer of the letter, as if to make things clear, concluded that "music preparation for our future wives is to secure pleasant households after the day's weary life-struggle is suspended" (209).

Essential to domestication of private space was the domestication of free time, particularly the time now possessed by the modern wife who had been freed from menial tasks and chores. A 1930s advertisement for the South India Music Emporium addressed young husbands as the ones responsible for buying the trappings of domestic life. Appearing in the concert program of the Madras Music Academy, the ad counseled male concertgoers on how to connect the bourgeois public sphere of the classical concert hall with its domestic equivalent. "A modern wife has tons of unemployed leisure and a wise husband must provide hobbies for her leisure being usefully employed," suggested the ad. "What better and more soul-satisfying hobby can there be than violin playing. Give your wife a violin today and ensure eternal happiness at home." For "modern wives" who found themselves with too much time on their hands, music could serve as a spiritually uplifting domestic activity that would convert free time into spiritual capital. If modernity produced an excess of free time, music could expand as necessary to fill it; if this free time had revealed that the new Indian woman had a soul, music could satisfy it. Music became the bonding agent in a new type of ideal marriage; unlike caste or religion, it had the advantage of being able to appear both voluntary and deeply traditional, private as well as public. In one biography of M. S. Subbulakshmi, a photograph of her and her husband, Sadasivam, places them within this type of ideal marriage through its caption: "Icaiyil iṉainta uḻḻaṅkaḷ" (Souls joined in music) (Sarathy 1997, 43).

The private space of the home, however, was differentiated from the private space of the salon. In 1932 a letter to the *Madras Mail* responded to the anti-nautch movement, particularly its opposition to public performances of nautch, with this bit of reasoning: "If the dance is to be free from its less respectable associations, the encouragement of public display appears to be the best way to do it. Private parties tend to encourage the notion of lack of respectability. Public functions, on the other hand, show the dance for what it is" (*Sruti* 1997, 5). The private space of the salon was considered unseemly and deceptive, while the concert hall allowed room only for clear observation and not for illusion; any identification with the performer would not be felt as personal attraction but would be mediated by the language of art. The concert hall, unlike a private salon, ensured a respectable distance between the performer and the audience, not only physically but also psychologically; in public, the performer performed for no one in particular. Such a shift was accomplished not only by the rise of concert halls but through the music itself. The repertoire of public concert-hall music featured the devotional compositions of the "trinity" (the composers Thyagaraja, Muthuswamy Dikshitar, and Syama Sastri), which eschewed all reference to human patrons. This form of spiritual devotion came to be thought of not as an extramusical element, as was thought of the human love expressed in padams and javalis (musical compositions for dance conveying the meanings of sensuous love), but as the essence of music itself.[40]

How did such notions affect conventions of music performance and the way music was thought of? Music's relationship to notions of public and private space was determined by the kind of ideological and practical domestication of music that was taking place. By "domestication" I do not mean just that music was brought into the home but also that its relationship to notions of public and private changed. The "respectability" that music gained in the 1930s and 1940s was in part due to its peculiar ability to mediate between public and private. Music brought women into the public sphere in a particular way, as the voice of tradition. They were not perceived as innovators, much less as performers; rather, a woman was to sing as though music were a natural property of her voice. To ease the problem of women appearing on the concert stage, they often appeared (and continue to appear) in duos; sisters performing together imparted a very different aura from a woman performing solo. Many women who played accompanying instruments like the violin were allowed to accompany only their brothers or other family members onstage, as if their entry into public could be thus controlled.

Meanwhile, in many upper-caste families, women became musicians because it was something they could do without formal school education and because it did not necessarily require them to leave the house; it was a vocation that could be learned and practiced in the home.[41] Indeed, many of the interviews with female musicians in a volume entitled *The Singer and the Song* (Lakshmi 2000) convey a sense of how music has been practiced as a means of compensation for the frustration of other social, familial, and professional desires.[42] Some of the women interviewed speak of their devotion to music in particular as a kind of strategy for coping with the oppression of family obligations. On the other hand, careers as professional musicians have allowed many women to escape marriage entirely. In a society where remaining unmarried is, for a woman, practically unheard of, there is a disproportionately large number of unmarried female musicians who are "devoted to music." If my teacher spoke wistfully about female musicians who had husbands to help them, other female musicians often remarked to me that they didn't understand why my teacher was unhappy and why she moped around and refused to practice. "She has no obligations to a husband," said one. "She could be devoting herself to her music."

. . . *And Their Limits*

The public face of such "devotion" may be very different from its private motivations, however. One afternoon, my teacher, whose stories usually managed to disrupt the platitudes of the Karnatic music world, launched into a telling of how she became devoted to music. She was about seventeen years old, her sister thirteen or so. There were brothers older and younger. She had been playing the violin for years, sitting in the corner of the room and listening while her father's students came to learn. Her sister had not shown as much interest but was more studious in school, so their parents decided to send the sister to a boarding school to prepare her for college. My teacher, who had had only a tenth-standard education, felt slighted.

She got to thinking: why should only her sister have the opportunity to become educated, go to college, and eventually work outside the home? How could they have been born of the same parents and be treated so unequally, one kept at home in the bonds of hereditary musicianship, while the other was sent away to get a college education? She began to doubt she was her father's child after all. In anger and protest, she retreated to the upper verandah of the house, refusing to eat, talk, or play the violin for two weeks. Her father, who was almost blind, and absorbed in his music anyway, did not notice until her mother said something. Then he came up the stairs to where she was sitting. She had expected harsh words, but instead, as if reading her mind, her father had gently said, "So, you are doubting whether you are really my child or not?" But rather than simply laying her doubt to rest, he had said, "You play your violin. Listen to that sound. And you will know." From that moment, she said, her resentments had melted away, and she became aware that musical ties were as strong as ties of blood.

In this scenario music again restores domestic tranquility, but in the interest of a very different set of family values: one based on hereditary musicianship rather than bourgeois middle-class family arrangements. As classical music came to be a respectable art for upper-caste women, it took its part in a larger imagination of ideal womanhood that included ideas of the artist (as opposed to the hereditary musician) and the natural voice, on one hand, and companionate marriage and domesticity, on the other. But for female musicians from non-Brahmin families these ideals seem to be much more difficult to achieve. These women must negotiate the contradiction between the modern notion of Karnatic music as a secular art music, presumably without specified gender roles, and the nonbourgeois contexts in which they have become musicians.

In 1996 I sought out M. S. Ponnuthai, one of the first women to become a professional nagaswaram player. Nagaswaram (also called nadaswaram), a double-reed instrument, is associated almost exclusively with musicians from the Icai Veḷḷālar caste. Until the 1940s, when Ponnuthai began to play in public, the instrument was played exclusively by men, as it was believed to be too strenuous for women. Although much of its musical tradition is shared with Karnatic music, it remains to this day on the fringes of what is approved as classical, having only marginal status as a concert-hall instrument. Its traditional role has been to provide music for auspicious occasions, such as temple rituals and weddings.[43]

Ponnuthai, who was in her mid-sixties at the time I met her in Madurai, had had an illustrious career as a nagaswaram player for temple and political processions, as well as on the concert stage; one of her distinctions was that she had made concert audiences appreciate the nagaswaram. As I made repeated visits to her house, however, it became clear that she was uninterested in talking about her life. My attempts to steer the conversation in that direction on several occasions ended in our watching televised cricket games. On other occasions, instead of talking, she would play at great length, taking obvious delight in my inability to keep up with her virtuosic raga alapana as I struggled to accompany her on the violin. I thought that these sessions would eventually soften her resistance, but on my last visit to her house I found that she had invited her grown son to answer my questions instead. While this was an ironic comment on the ethnographic project of finding authentic voices, it also revealed much about the politics of representation regarding the life of a woman who had led a very public life and then retreated.

From Ponnuthai's son I learned that her father, a government servant with progressive ideas, was inspired by the essays of Subramania Bharathiyar. Having decided that his daughter should take up the nagaswaram, Ponnuthai's father apparently groomed her for a public life. After her debut at age thirteen, he resigned from his job in order to escort her to performances and also began collecting concert reviews and other press releases about her. Indeed, among the many clippings her son showed me were reviews of her performances in Ceylon, Singapore, and elsewhere, which her father had neatly preserved by mounting on paper. Ponnuthai married a prominent citizen of Madurai who served as a representative for the Congress Party, and she herself served as the head of the Madurai Icai Veḷḷālar Sangam, an organization that served the welfare of nagaswaram musicians, from 1953 to 1963. In 1972, after her husband died, she stopped playing in temples and gradually retreated from public view. Among the clippings were several magazine articles written about her in the early 1990s. I asked her which she thought was the best, and she pointed to the cover story in *Ananta Vikatan*, "Maturai Poṉṉutāy: Oru Kaṇṇīr Katai" (Madurai Ponnuthai: A sad story) (Saupa 1990).

The article begins with an imagined scene of Ponnuthai's *araṅkēṟṟam* (debut), panning through the astonished crowd listening on the banks of the Vaigai River. After describing Ponnuthai's fame and success in hyperbolic terms, it notes her "sudden" disappearance from public life in 1972. "We wondered what had happened to her, and searched for her. . . . Some people told us that she had passed away. We were surprised by that, since just last month the Tamil Nadu government had announced that it was going to award her the title of 'Kalaimamani' [Great Jewel of the Arts]. We resumed our search with more urgency . . . and finally found her living a life of misery in a small house in an out-of-the-way part of Madurai." The narrative then cuts, cinematically, to the scene at the house, where Ponnuthai's "still majestic" look contrasts with the poverty of her circumstances. She goes next door to fetch the nagaswaram, the only place it can be kept safe from rats, and returns wearing earrings. "I had more than a hundred pounds of jewelry and gold medals," she laments. "Now it is all lost." Presumably prompted by the writer, she describes her meteoric rise, against the odds, and her ability to play for all-night temple functions even while pregnant. She describes how, after her marriage, her husband "never interfered" with her career, and how their large house, in the center of town, was always full of distinguished guests. Then, comments the reporter, "for a few moments, the great nagaswaram artist was silent. Her eyes welled up with tears." Ponnuthai goes on to say, "My husband died in 1972. With that, my musical life was finished." The reporter feigns an innocent question: "Why? Couldn't you continue playing?" And the article moves to what is obviously the clincher. "Nagaswaram," Ponnuthai explains, "is an auspicious instrument. After my husband's death I became an inauspicious woman [*amaṅkala peṇ*] and could no longer play in temples. People talked behind my back. I stopped playing for radio, too. There was no income, and I was too proud to ask for any help." The reporter comes in for the fadeout: "Wiping the dust from the nagaswaram, she raised it to her lips. What dignity! What majesty! From her unhesitating fingers a shower of music poured forth" (Saupa 1990, 10–14).

What politics of representation are at work here? The article is meant to evoke sympathy, even outrage that society has allowed so distinguished a musician to sink into poverty and oblivion.[44] It invites the reader—given this journal's readership, most likely a housewife reading in her leisure time—to witness the conflict between modernity, signified by Ponnuthai's emergence into the public sphere, and the views of a tradition-bound society that still believes that women become inauspicious when they are widowed. Modernity, here, is articulated in the voice of the narrator, whose reportage is mixed with exclamations—"What dignity! What majesty!"—that indicate a subject able to appreciate good music no matter who or where it is coming from. By melodramatically staging Ponnuthai's problem as a secret that must be revealed, the article assumes a "modern" reader innocent of such antiquated conflicts; the unspoken comparison is to the middle-class, Brahmin music world of Madras in which it is a modern discourse on family values, not traditional religious values, that both makes possible and sets limits for women's professional musicianship.

What is striking, then, is the discontinuity between Ponnuthai's career as a professional musician and the careers of women in the middle-class music world of Madras. In a conversation in 1997 Bhairavi, a professional musician from an Icai Veḷḷāḷar family, then in her early thirties, spoke of a similar discontinuity.[45] Although her great-grandparents had been musicians, neither her grandparents nor her parents had continued the tradition; she herself had made a conscious decision to become a professional flutist. She had recently been married, but the match had taken a long time to make, since she was in an anomalous category: not only was she a professional musician, but she played the flute, an instrument that has not been taken up by non-Brahmin women since the beginning of the twentieth century.[46] It was rare for women of her caste to take up music at all, much less as a profession. She remarked to me that young musicians from

Brahmin families were increasingly engaging in love marriages but that this was not possible for her; for someone of her caste, music did not provide the same kind of avenue toward bourgeois, middle-class sensibility. For a husband and wife of her caste to have their "souls joined in music" was not an option. At the time of our conversation, Bhairavi's husband, who was not a musician, was having trouble finding employment, so Bhairavi was supporting the family by giving music lessons and had applied for teaching positions in schools. I asked if such an arrangement would be acceptable. "That's how it used to be in our caste anyway," she replied. "The ladies were all dancers and musicians and they supported the men." For her, the irony was that the very transformations in the music world that had in the name of respectability taken professionalism away from female musicians of her caste in the early twentieth century now made it possible for her to earn a living as a professional musician.[47]

Stage Goddesses and Studio Divas

I have dwelled on the lives and commentary of these two women because they occupy the fringes of a dominant discourse that links classical music, ideal womanhood, and domesticity in a particular way. In doing so, they clarify the contours of this discourse and the kinds of exclusions on which it is built. For both Ponnuthai and Bhairavi, the dilemma has been how to create a life for themselves as women musicians who are neither from the Brahmin, middle-class music world of Madras nor from conventional hereditary musical families. For both, much of the discourse linking classical music, ideal womanhood, and the nationalist aspirations of an urban middle class had been enabling: it had enabled Ponnuthai (through her father's desires) to take up the nagaswaram and to travel widely, setting an example for many younger female musicians aspiring to become professional; it had enabled Bhairavi to pursue music as a career, something that the women in generations preceding hers could not have respectably done. At the same time, Ponnuthai and Bhairavi were also alienated, as was my violin teacher, from the subjects of this discourse. Much of the irony of Bhairavi's comment comes from the realization that the profound discontinuity effected by the emergence of classical music in the twentieth century made possible a strange kind of continuity.

In the century or so that separated Bhairavi's life from the lives of her female ancestors, tremendous changes had taken place in the way music was conceptualized and practiced—including infrastructure changes like the building of concert halls and music schools, and technological changes like the emergence of gramophone recording and radio—which engendered a new kind of discourse about music. Not only did music become available to "respectable" women as a vocation and sometimes a career but it became available in particular ways. If my teacher found the transition from music to the topic of marriage to the essential difference between women and men "quite natural," it is because twentieth-century discourse about music was connected, metaphorically and quite literally, to a discourse about family values.[48]

In the 1930s and 1940s ideals of chaste womanly behavior—not drawing attention to one's body or relying on physical charms—became a metaphor for a new kind of art that privileged meaning and naturalness over cleverness and acrobatics. In that sense, classical singing was refigured as a natural expression of devotion. A woman was expected to sing music as though it were a natural property of her voice. The natural voice and the chaste female body were thus linked. By the 1950s, the adjectives *natural* and *artificial* had come to be used to contrast female voices singing classical music and film songs, respectively. Kalki Krishnamoorthy, the same reviewer who had raved about M.S.'s voice, wrote disparagingly of the "insipid" and "artificial" sweetness of the renowned film singer Lata Mangeshkar's voice. Kalki used the Tamil word *vacīkara*, meaning attractive or alluring, with distinct sexual connotations, to describe the film voice, warning readers not to get infatuated with film music and forget the natural beauty of classical singing (Kalki 1951).

In this discourse on classical music, performance that drew attention to the body came to be associated with the artificial; good music was not something to be performed but rather was simply "expressed." The "voice of the century" referred not only to M. S. Subbulakshmi's sound but to a particular kind of voice that was imagined to come naturally from within, unmediated by performance of any kind, a voice embodied in a distinct way. The notion of "expression," as Webb Keane has written, is predicated on a particular linguistic ideology that separates form from content and in which the voice merely "refers to" other sites of action or "reflects" a prior, interior self but is not considered to have a role in *creating* that self (1997, 684). In tracing the development of the modern notion of self in European thought Charles Taylor suggests that the notion of expression is itself a modern idea very much linked to the imagination of the self's interiority; the concept of art, as he notes, relies on both the rejection of an outwardly oriented mimesis and the embrace of an inwardly oriented expression (1989).[49]

Indian nationalist discourse linked the notion of an "inner voice" with the "inner sphere" of the Indian nation, imagined to be India's uncolonized interior and often equated metaphorically and literally with the domestic sphere.[50] Indeed, Mahatma Gandhi linked "good music," "harmony," and the concept of an "inner voice" in a series of nationalist writings from the mid-1940s. For Gandhi, who was a great admirer of M.S., singing classical music was a metaphor for leading a moral life.[51] "As I am nearing the end of my earthly life," he wrote, "I can say that producing good music from a cultivated voice can be achieved by many, but the art of producing that music from the harmony of a pure life is achieved only rarely" (Gandhi 1958, 132).

The "voice of the century" was as much a product of the technologies that mediated it as it was a product of individual ability or genius. In a very real sense, the gramophone and the microphone created the "perfection" and "nuance" of M. S. Subbulakshmi's voice for the listeners who heard her through these media. The idea of perfection is only possible when a piece of music becomes an object to be contemplated over and over again rather than heard in a single live performance. Nuances become audible and locatable in a voice only when the voice is amplified—separated, in a sense—from the body that produces it. In twentieth-century South India, the female voice, disassociated from its body through these technologies and through a particular way of performing interiority, came to have a certain ideological significance.

The purity of this voice was maintained by a careful maintenance of its boundaries; it was not a "disembodied" voice that could travel freely but a voice that was embodied in a particular way. By midcentury, Tamil films began to feature female dancing bodies that were, by the standards of the time, decidedly immodest; the voices with which those actresses sang onscreen became another foil for the respectability of classical music and its prodigies. Although many successful classical musicians, including M. S. Subbulakshmi and D. K. Pattammal, gained considerable fame through their acting and singing for films, the limits of their participation in the cinema world were carefully defined. M.S. stopped acting in films after 1945 in order to devote herself to classical performances; apparently, it was not possible for her to do both. D. K. Pattammal, on the other hand, remained active in the Tamil cinema world as a playback singer on the carefully observed condition that she sing only patriotic songs, never love songs, as if she could ensure the authority, and fidelity, of her voice by making sure its referent was Mother India and not her own or any other actress's body.

M.S. and D. K. Pattammal were an inspiration to numerous playback singers, women who recorded their voices for actresses' characters. Three playback singers I spoke with—women in their sixties and seventies in the early 2000s—all spoke of wanting to be "just like M.S." when they were young but being forced by economic necessity to sing for films. Interestingly, while the *younger* female playback singers I spoke with talked about changing their voices depending on the character they were portraying, the *older* singers insisted that they did not change their voices for different characters. In the words of one, "God has given you one voice. If you start changing it around, it stops being singing and turns into mimicry."[52] Value and authenticity were thus attached to singing, in contrast to mimicry. Indeed, maintaining one's status as a playback "artiste" required an insistence on having "one's own voice," which remained constant. Another playback singer described how in order to sing playback for films one had to learn to "give expression just in the voice, not in the face," in order to channel all of one's expressive power into the voice, leaving the face and body neutral.[53] To demonstrate this, she sang in a range of voices, from little boy to young woman to old lady, while keeping her face and body utterly immobile.

Female playback singers, much more than actresses, often become celebrities in their own right; many make frequent stage appearances in which they sing their hit songs with a backup orchestra for audiences of dedicated fans. For older female playback singers, their stage personae often contrast greatly with the lyrics they are singing; in these stage appearances, it often seems like they make a particular effort *not* to embody their voices, as if in doing so they might maintain greater control over them. I attended a wedding concert by the renowned playback singer P. Susheela in 2002, during which she sang a number of romantic duet songs. Throughout the performance, she stood close to the microphone, with one hand at her ear and the other carefully keeping the end of her sari draped over her shoulder in the style of a chaste classical singer. This purposeful dissociation of body from voice is, I would argue, part of the politics of voice inaugurated by earlier female classical singers, and further enabled by the technology of playback singing.

For the "voice of the century," then, the kinds of bodies with which it could associate constituted one limit; the ways in which it could be heard constituted another. Although M.S. and D. K. Pattammal *sang* in public, they never *spoke* in public, an act more conventionally associated with agency and "having a voice." Whereas Bangalore Nagaratnammal and Vai. Mu. Kothainayaki, part of the previous generation of female singers, spoke in public on issues such as Indian independence and the betterment of Indian women, Subbulakshmi and Pattammal assiduously avoided public speaking.[54] Indeed, it seems as though the "naturalness" and "purity" of their voices could only be guaranteed by maintaining the idea that those voices expressed an interior self, an innocent self detached from the world at large, who knew "nothing but music"—except, perhaps, a little housekeeping. In this sense, the very *audibility* of their singing voices depended on the silence of their speaking voices in the public sphere.

Gender and the Politics of Voice

Agency, in Western philosophy, is linked to the speaking voice, a link that is embedded in the classic methodology of ethnography as well (in which the ethnographer seeks verbal explanations or "meanings" for nonverbal forms in order to fill them with referential content). The dichotomy often drawn between "having a voice" and being silent or silenced, however, leaves us with little way to interpret voices that are highly audible and public yet not agentive in a classic sense, such as voices that have musical instead of referential content or voices that circulate through technologies of sound reproduction.

M.S.'s voice, as revealed by the various discourses *about* her voice and persona, is as much a product of a particular historical and social moment as it is a vehicle of her individual expression. This is not to deny her status as a creative artist and a powerful persona on stage, but rather to suggest, as does Mrinhalini Sinha, that "a focus on the voice or agency of women themselves does not have to be opposed to an examination of the ideological structures from which they emerged" (1996, 483). In exploring the creation of a voice in which women could speak as the "Indian woman" in the 1930s, Sinha moves beyond notions of pure feminist consciousness to show how the creation of a voice is always a strategic maneuver within certain ideological structures.

The creation of *musical* voices by women in the 1930s and 1940s was equally strategic, even though these voices emerged in a part of the public sphere seemingly far removed from political or even social discourse. Indeed, it is useful to ask how the speaking voices of women who emerged in the 1930s as public speakers on nationalist causes and the subject of women's rights, on the one hand, and the singing voices of M. S. Subbulakshmi and D. K. Pattammal, on the other, may have worked to shape each other. The nationalist and poet Sarojini Naidu's onscreen introduction to the Hindi version of M.S.'s film *Meera*, in which she introduces M.S. as "the nightingale of India," is a literal example of this. The fact that Vai. Mu. Kothainayaki was partly responsible for bringing D. K. Pattammal onto the concert stage is another.[55] But beyond such literal connections, the fact that these voices were heard side by side is important; their juxtaposition defined the possibilities for "respectable" women's participation in the public sphere, even as they defined the content of that respectability.

Once the voice becomes recognizable as culturally and historically constructed, it is possible to ask what new forms of subjectivity are enabled by changing ideologies of voice. The politics of voice that came to operate in the 1930s imagined the voice in a particular relation to the body, as something that transcended the body. This relationship was articulated by Rukmini Devi, among others, as the relationship between music and dance, where music was supposed to raise dance above the physical, to make it more than the sum of its gestures. In the process, music itself had to be purified; in order to be truly classical, the voice of Karnatic music had to be reconceived as an "inner voice."

By a synecdochic chain of associations, this newly conceived domain of interiority became connected with another domain newly conceived as an essential part of bourgeois modernity: the middle-class home. The female musical voice and the middle-class home together constituted and stood for the inner sphere of the nation, a construct central to middle-class nationalism. The interiorized conception of voice made possible the subject positions of both the "classical artist" and the "respectable woman"; the natural voice of the artist was—and still is—identified with the chaste body of the respectable woman. Thus, even now, when it is no longer a novelty for upper-caste women to perform publicly, singing on the classical stage involves engaging not just the conventions of musical art but also the conventions of female respectability.

4 Can the Subaltern Sing?

MUSIC, LANGUAGE, AND THE POLITICS OF VOICE

[The Tamil music movement] gives sight to the blind, hearing to the deaf, a voice to the mute, a wake-up call to those who are sleeping.
—Editorial in *The Liberator* (1943)

In 1943 T. V. Subba Rao opened the annual Madras Music Conference at the makeshift quarters of the Madras Music Academy in the neighborhood of Mylapore. "What matters in music is not the letter but the tone," he stated. "We have no politics. Our sphere is only aesthetics wherein we stand for all that is noblest and best" (Proceedings of the 17th Madras Music Conference, 1944, 1). The guest speaker of the conference, Dr. S. Radhakrishnan, a philosopher and, later, president of India, went on to speak of music as a "great reconciler," not only of India but of the whole world; music was an instrument of reconciliation, unlike politics and economics. To a cheering audience, Radhakrishnan continued, "You know we are fighting today against the Axis powers. Why? Not because of their art and literature . . . but because of their politics and economics. . . . But think of the metaphysics and music of Germany. . . . From a thousand different orchestras and records, Beethoven and Mozart are pouring out their songs, pleading for reconciliation." Music, in Radhakrishnan's view, had a certain kind of universality that enabled it to reach people regardless of language, religion, caste, or nationality. But this very universality also rendered it liable to certain misuses. "It is essential that so far as music is concerned, it should know no politics. It stands for certain permanent values of life. When it is prostituted for ephemeral and irrelevant ends, it is not music. It is propaganda, narrow, arid and hypocritical" (3–4).

Such strong statements were a direct argument against the Tamil music movement, which had reached a peak in the mid-1940s and whose message was that the letter was indeed as important as the tone. A year after

Radhakrishnan's speech to the music academy, R. K. Shanmugham Chettiar roused the audience to cheers with his speech at the first Tamil Music Conference, held at Saint Mary's Hall in the George Town area of Madras. During a visit to America, he said, he had been explaining the Tamil music movement to an American friend. The friend was flabbergasted that such a movement was necessary: wasn't it a given that people needed to have music with words in their own mother tongue (*tāypaṣai*)? Apparently, in the rest of the world this was not even an issue. But in Tamil Nadu, a strange aberration had taken hold.

> I did research to find out whether there was any other place, other than this Tamil Nadu, where the music was in a language other than the mother tongue of the people. There was no other place. . . . As far as I know, even in other Indian states the mother tongues are not in such danger. If you want to know what the state of Tamil is, listen: In order to get a job, you need to study English. If you want to get married, you have to do it in Sanskrit. If you are going to make a name as a patriot, you must use Hindi. If you learn music, it is all Telugu. And if you are just talking ordinarily, you use a strange conglomerate [*maṇipiravāḷam*]: "*Nēṟṟu uṅkaḷai* meet *paṇṇumpōtu oru* matter *colluvatarku* complete-*ā marantu pōyviṭṭēn sār*." This is the place we have reserved for Tamil! (*Tamiḻ Icai Makānāṭu Ceṉṉai Nikaḻcci Mālar* 1944, 40; italics in original)

Emphasizing the naturalness of wanting music with words in Tamil, Shanmugham Chettiar proclaimed, "I don't care if the tradition of Tamil music has been around for the last two thousand years or not, whether it is special or not. I was born a Tamilian and I need Tamil music" (40). He was describing a society that had in effect lost its senses; for him, as for the author of the editorial in *The Liberator*, Tamil music would, in restoring a person's voice, quite literally restore all of his senses.

The Tamil music movement (*Tamiḻ icai iyakkam*) brought to the fore the issue of how the relationship between music and language should be defined. As the problem of language *in* music became the subject of debate in the 1930s and 1940s, a series of new questions assumed urgency. Why, asked members of the Tamil music movement, was Karnatic music confined to such a small group of people? What was the relationship of words to music? How was a Tamil to make sense of the fact that although the majority of Karnatic musicians were Tamil vocalists singing in Tamil Nadu, the lyrics they sang—and the songs that were considered the heart of Karnatic classical repertoire—were almost entirely in Telugu?

The Tamil music movement was more than a demand that the classical music repertoire include more songs in Tamil; it was part of a new set of discourses about the singing subject and the relationship between music and language. I present here not simply a history of the Tamil Music movement, but an inquiry into the kinds of discourses that made such a movement possible. I speculate here on the process by which "music" and "literature" began to emerge as two separate, mutually exclusive fields in late-nineteenth-century South India, preparing the way for a new kind of relationship between music and language to be imagined: a relationship of analogy.[1] As music became a distinct field separated from literary practices, it was increasingly imagined as a language. Such a notion marks a departure from an earlier idea, prominent in Tamil literature, of the musicality *of* language, where the relationship between music and language is one of contiguity, cooperation, or commingling, and it is the poetic and sonic aspects of language that are emphasized. The twentieth-century idea that music "is a language" or is "like language" entails a very different set of premises, applying to music the concepts of meaning, intentionality, and understanding that are commonly applied to language in modernist thought.

By the 1930s, the analogy of music to language had become an especially useful way for both Indian and Tamil nationalists to imagine the place of music in a new nation. Once this analogy had taken hold, colonial classifications like "classical language" and "mother tongue" increasingly came into play in competing ideas about how music should be defined and experienced, as did ideas about the "meaning" of music and where it was to be found. Those who identified with the Tamil music movement assumed that definable performing and listening subjects could be located through the use of the mother tongue, the language with which people identified and that thus identified them as authentic subjects. But then, the Brahmin music establishment asked, would such music still live up to the standards of a classical art? Was music akin to a mother tongue or a universal, aesthetically motivated language?[2]

The debates surrounding the issue of language in music were essentially debates about what a singer should feel when singing and what a listener should feel when listening. The issue of precisely what kind of language music was to be compared to—a universal language or a mother tongue—was in a sense also a question about the singing subject's relation to his or her voice. Was the voice best conceived of as an aestheticized instrument, as the Brahmin musical establishment thought, or as a transparent representation of one's self, as the Tamil music movement suggested? The fact that these two choices were seen not only as logical or natural but also as exhaustive of the possibilities for a subject's relation to his or her voice suggests that a particular politics of voice was emerging at the time. Within this politics of voice, music could be an expressive language or an aesthetic language, but in either case language was the central metaphor for articulating the relationship between voice and singing or listening subject.

Sacrificing for Mother Tamil

Such ideas are not natural or inevitable; rather, they are the results of shifts in musicolinguistic practices that occurred during the nineteenth century and early twentieth. One may be used to thinking of music and language as two separate entities or systems, whose main possibility for connection is through a one-way analogy: music, one may say, is "a language" or is "like language." In nineteenth-century South India, however, music and language did not necessarily exist as mutually discrete categories available for this particular metaphoric relationship. Instead, what did exist were a multitude of genres—poems, plays, epics—and practices for performing them musically or with musical accompaniment. The ideal inseparability of music and language is suggested by the term *muttamiḻ* (literally, "triple Tamil"), used in Tamil literature from the Sangam era (second century BC) to the present to refer to the interlinked arts of *iyal* (word), *icai* (sound or musical rendering), and *nāṭakam* (mimetic rendering, dance, or drama).[3]

U. V. Swaminathayyar's *Caṅkīta Mummaṇikaḷ* (Three gems of music) offers some insight into a series of shifts that were occurring in the late nineteenth century. His reason for publishing the book, Swaminathayyar wrote in his foreword, was that "friends tell me that in Tamil Nadu, no one sings in Tamil anymore." "At that time," presumably in the 1870s and 1880s, there was great *matippu* (respect, value) for the compositions of Ganam Krishnayyar and Gopalakrishna Bharatiyar, which were in Tamil; after that, it became popular—a matter of *perumai* (pride)—even for Tamil-speaking musicians to sing in Telugu (1936, 2–3). What had happened to "music" and "Tamil" between the 1870s and the 1920s, when Swaminathayyar wrote his biographical sketches?

Swaminathayyar's biographical sketches include numerous descriptions of "vidwans adept in both music and Tamil" (1936, 2). For the nineteenth-century musicians he described, in keeping with the ideal of muttamiḻ, it was not only possible but necessary to combine virtuosity in music *and* language. The title "vidwan" (literally, "the one who knows") was used for poets, musicians, and scholars alike; what united them was their prowess in verbal-musical performance and their ability to provide exegeses of the texts they sang or recited.[4] But the fact that Swaminathayyar consistently referred to music *and* Tamil points to a shift that had occurred by the time he was writing his account; music and Tamil (specifically, Tamil literature) were coming to be recognized, and canonized, as two distinct fields with their own experts, a process that had been going on since the late nineteenth century. Swaminathayyar, best known as the editor and publisher of many of the Tamil literary works now considered classics, was a key figure in this canonization process, responsible for rediscovering and publishing numerous palm leaf manuscripts.[5]

Along with the institution of Tamil literature came an increased specialization of roles. Whereas poetic and musical composition were often combined in the creation of dramatic and poetic works, the dual role of *kirtana* composer and erudite poet was becoming increasingly unusual in the nineteenth century (Peterson 2004, 33). In his autobiography Swaminathayyar reports the contempt of his teacher, the noted Tamil scholar Meenakshisundaram Pillai, for poets who composed musical works; music was thought to be a distraction from the more important aspects of grammar, poetics, and mastery of traditional commentaries (Zvelebil 1992, 132–33). Thus, although becoming a Tamil vidwan involved being able to recite and perform Tamil texts musically, the study of music per se was considered a separate pursuit.

In *Caṅkīta Mummaṇikaḷ* Swaminathayyar himself recalled having to make a choice between music and Tamil in his youth. He described meeting as a young boy with the composer Gopalakrishna Bharatiyar, noted for his musical compositions in Tamil, in 1871, when his father had brought him to Mayuram to study Tamil with Meenakshisundaram Pillai. Bharatiyar asked Swaminathayyar's father, who had himself trained with the Tamil composer Ganam Krishnayyar, why the boy was not studying music and agreed to teach him as long as he was in Mayuram. Unbeknown to his Tamil master, Swaminathayyar happily took up music lessons, seeing Bharatiyar in the morning and Meenakshisundaram Pillai in the evening. All went well until one day the two teachers happened to meet, and Meenakshisundaram Pillai boasted about his pupil to Bharatiyar: "A very talented young boy is learning with me; he sings poems with music—it is sweet to the ears. If you heard it you would have satisfaction." Bharatiyar replied, "I know that boy and his father. He has been coming to me every day for music training. He said he had come here to study with you." Meenakshisundaram Pillai immediately left and went to Swaminathayyar's house, where he confronted the boy: "If you spend all this training and effort on music, you will not gain wisdom from the Tamil literature and grammatical treatises [*ilakkiya ilakkaṉa nūlkaḷ*]. That music will be a barrier to the careful study and reading of the texts." The next day, Swaminathayyar wrote, he stopped attending music lessons. "It was true that, as Bharatiyar had said, Meenakshisundaram Pillai was an enemy of music [*caṅkīta virōti*]. But I didn't resent him at all for that. Even though I had developed an affection for music naturally at a young age, my most important subject was Tamil, so naturally I made the sacrifice. If I hadn't, the opportunity to . . . do sacred service to Tamiḻttāy [Mother Tamil] would have been lost" (136–41).

What is striking here is the "naturalness" of this sacrifice for Swaminathayyar; it indicates the degree to which Karnatic music and Tamil literature had become separate and mutually exclusive fields. The proof of Tamil's status as a classical language in the twentieth century depended on having a body of written, published texts that could exist apart from individual recitations or performances. Meanwhile, the classicization of Karnatic music depended on considering the lyrics less important than "the music itself." Classical music was redefined as that in which language was secondary to music, indeed, as that which was distanced from the mother tongue and required special knowledge.

This redefinition was part and parcel of the way caste communities came to be differentiated through their relation to the Tamil language in the twentieth century. As musical standard-setting was increasingly dominated by Brahmins, Telugu and Sanskrit repertoires were privileged, and Karnatic music was disconnected from Tamil both as a literary language and as a mother tongue. This is because in the twentieth century Tamil Brahmins were progressively distanced—and distanced themselves—from the Tamil language in Dravidianist discourse; those Brahmins who did continue to profess their love for and devotion to Tamil in the 1930s and 1940s were accused of secretly wanting to Sanskritize it.[6] In the wake of the Dravidian renaissance and the non-Brahmin movement, many Tamil Brahmins came to identify themselves as belonging to a separate "race" from other Tamils, studying Sanskrit or English but rarely learning to read or write Tamil.[7] For the Brahmin community, which saw itself as the primary guardian of South India's classical music, the mother tongue was devalued instead of glorified.

Thus, both the canonization of Tamil literature and the canonization of Karnatic music were deeply intertwined with the way the category of language was becoming differentiated and given new meaning in early-twentieth-century India. Ideas of music as a means of communication and the concern that emerged in the 1940s with the meaning of music and how it was to be enjoyed and understood operated by treating music analogously to language. Yet the analogy did not stop—or could not stop—at the undifferentiated category of "language." By the 1930s a complicated hierarchy of languages had developed in India, which rendered any unitary notion of language too simple. Bernard Cohn has argued that the British production of translations, grammars, dictionaries, and treatises concerning Indian languages (as well as the publishing of palm-leaf manuscripts as literary texts) was part of a project of "converting Indian forms of knowledge into European objects"; it produced a "discourse of differentiations which came to mark the social and political map of nineteenth-century India" (1987, 283–84). These differentiations were the basis of a hierarchy that included so-called classical languages as well as "vulgar" or "vernacular" languages or mother tongues. While Sanskrit was considered a classical language, Tamil was, like other spoken languages, considered a vernacular. Tamil nationalists protested the inferior status given to Tamil, arguing that the unbroken continuity of Tamil from ancient times to the present made it a classical language (Arooran 1980, 109).[8] The figure of Tamiḻttāy, or Mother Tamil, found in earlier Tamil literature, was elaborated as a central trope encompassing pride in Tamil as both classical language and mother tongue.[9]

The "naturalness" of Swaminathayyar's sacrifice was thus made possible not only by the construction of Karnatic classical music and Tamil literature as separate and mutually exclusive fields but also by the emergence and naturalization of the category "mother tongue" beginning in the last decades of the nineteenth century. The concept of the mother tongue (Tamil, *tāymoḻi* or *tāypaṣai*), far from reflecting a natural or necessary relation between a subject or community and "their" language, has a particular history. Indeed, it was partially colonial discourse about Indian languages that made the concept of the mother tongue available as a marker of identity in twentieth-century India.[10] In tracing the emergence of this category in Telugu-speaking South India, Lisa Mitchell has argued that its naturalization required a new understanding of both language itself and a subject's relation to language: in effect, a "different sense of selfhood" (2004, 39). Before the nineteenth century, as Mitchell and others suggest, discourses on and practices of language depended on a multilingual sensibility in which the ability to move fluidly *between* languages and registers was prized; court poets would not have "devoted" themselves to a single language.[11] Swaminathayyar, by contrast, was by his own admittance profoundly uninterested in other languages, especially Telugu and Sanskrit. Consider this passage from his autobiography, written in 1940–42:

> Father worried himself constantly about my education. He had set his heart on making me too a musician. All musicians of the day were well acquainted with Telugu. They used to sing compositions in all three languages—Tamil, Telugu, and Sanskrit. Father felt that a knowledge of Telugu would be helpful to a student of music. . . . I had, I should admit, a bias towards music and Tamil—none at all towards Telugu. . . . Music and Tamil gave me joy. I didn't find such joy in Telugu. Even at the outset, I realized that Telugu and I were poles apart. The dislike was natural, not deliberate. (Swaminathayyar 1940–1942, 27–28)

Swaminathayyar is at pains to say that his dislike of Telugu is "natural," the implication being that his love of Tamil and his willingness to cease his study of music and other languages to concentrate on Tamil are just as natural. While such single-minded devotion to *a* language, rather than to language in a more general, less differentiated sense, would hardly have allowed Swaminathayyar to become a scholar (much less a vidwan) at the beginning of the nineteenth century, it made him an ideal scholar at the end of the nineteenth century.

The idea of having a single language with which one identifies depends on the notion of language as an object, as "something to be loved, admired, protected, and patronized, and something which one can have affection for and pride in" (Lisa Mitchell 2004, 37).[12] Just as it motivated Swaminathayyar's sacrifice, the threatened figure of Tamiḻttāy was used by politicians and university professors to gain popular support for anti-Hindi protests in the 1930s and for causes such as the Tamil music movement (Ramaswamy 1993, 704). On the role of the metaphor "mother tongue" in shaping Tamil identity and rallying people around the cause of "saving" the Tamil language, Sumathi Ramaswamy writes,

> It familiarized and familialized the relationship between the Tamilians and their community by couching it in the comfortable everyday terms of the home and family. The metaphor also naturalized this relationship by constituting a sense of primordial and selfless devotion that the Tamilians as children naturally owed to their language as mother. It dehistoricized the bonds between the language and the people by presenting them as timeless, essential, and beyond the vagaries of history. Above all, it depoliticized the relationship by enabling the abstraction of the community from politics and by resignifying that community as a family whose members were united as harmonious siblings (Ibid., 719)[13]

The representation of the Tamil language as Mother Tamil, Ramaswamy states, came about "in a late colonial situation in which motherhood came to be privileged, not only as the sine qua non of women's identity, but also as the foundational site on which pure and true subjectivities and communities could be imagined and reproduced" (1997, 125). The mother tongue created bonds between subjects and between a subject and his or her language which were seen to be pure and true because they were cast as being as natural as a child's bond to its mother. As far as those in the Tamil music movement were concerned, if music could operate on analogy with and *in* the mother tongue, it could create a pure and true community of singers and listeners.

"The Power of Music"

Music, however, was threatening because of its potential to move in ways that language did not, to create bonds or associations that were not as pure or as true as Tamil or other nationalists desired. In this respect, Swaminathayyar's *Caṅkīta Mummaṇikaḷ* provides another point of contrast. When Swaminathayyar, looking back to the nineteenth century, wrote his biographies of famous musicians, he was perhaps inspired by ideas about music in the abstract. Yet his writings do not concern the power of music in any general sense; they instead attest to the power of individual musicians in particular contexts. For example, Maha Vaidyanathayyar's power as a musician lay in his ability to rise to a particular situation, to sing something appropriate to the context, something that bore the mark of his own creation. In the nineteenth-century world of royal patronage that Swaminathayyar described, the "power of music," as an abstract concept, separable from the musician and the context of performance, did not exist. By the 1930s and 1940s, however, it was precisely the separation of music from its performers and contexts of performance that gave rise to a new discourse about the power of music, a power that lay in its capacity as a medium for communicating with or reaching large numbers of people.

In South India in the first few decades of the twentieth century, what made this possible was sound reproduction: the technologies of recording, film, radio, and loudspeakers, which brought music into homes and villages. The possibility of hearing music that one was not producing oneself, that was coming from some other undefined place, and that was being sung in some other language was radically new. The artist and writer Manohar Devadoss describes in *Green Well Years*, a memoir of his boyhood in Madurai in the 1940s, the kind of power music attained through these technologies.[14]

> Radios were rare then but the citizens of Madurai had ample opportunity to listen to cinema music. Indeed, they could hardly have escaped listening to it. Let a girl come of age, let there be a wedding, a pregnancy, or a birth, let there be an ear-piercing ceremony, and let any little wayside temple celebrate an obscure festival—people at once thought of gramophone records of film music. Low-quality, high decibel, metal loudspeaker horns sprouted here, there, everywhere, spewing out 78 rpm music in harsh metallic tones, along with a continuous loud drone caused by the scratches on the records, and the music reached every nook and corner of the city. (1997, 156)

Music literally became part of the atmosphere, its new power apparent in the seemingly spontaneous "sprouting" of metal loudspeaker horns. Divorced from its original context and separated from the musicians who created it, cinema music plunged itself into new contexts, attaching itself to the lives of those who overheard it. Overhearing became a new type of listening, thereby enabling music to work by a kind of metonymic, accidental power of association.[15] As described in *Green Well Years*, Sundar and his friends discovered the power of music by overhearing. Music's power to evoke memories, the boys discovered, did not depend on the pertinence of the lyrics. Rather, it derived its power from being inescapable, from attaching itself accidentally, acting not as a language but as a kind of mnemonic device. "When he heard Wagner's 'fest march' from 'Tannhäuser,' he was transported to a winter in the late sixties in South India and he saw green paddy fields, coconut and betel nut groves, thatched huts and bullock carts. But if he listened to 'Meera Bhajans' by M.S. Subbulakshmi, he was flooded with memories of a summer in the early seventies in the USA and images of the Grand Canyon, Mesa Verde, and the Grand Tetons and Yellowstone filled his mind" (159). The new power of music was exhilarating and disorienting at the same time. One could find oneself humming a song and suddenly be transported back to another time and place. "This new awareness of the 'power of music' excited the boys greatly. They kept talking about 'remembrance of songs' again and again. They realised that if a particular song was heard frequently over a certain period, then memories of that period would come rushing to the mind when the song was sung or heard after a reasonably long time. The break was essential" (157). The radically new power that music had gained derived from its ability to be free from its original context, enabling it to dis-orient and re-orient at the same time. The "power of music" in an abstract sense became thinkable because the technologies of recording and amplification made music incorporeal, invisible yet ubiquitous, part of the air itself. In the world Devadoss describes, one became connected to particular songs not by understanding them or grasping their meaning but simply by virtue of hearing them again and again. One's connection to the songs was not through the metaphor of language but through a more metonymical operation: one found oneself humming almost involuntarily, like a sympathetic string vibrating. Music, transmitted through the ear and the voice, operated unpredictably and irrationally, with a power that was, literally, unspeakable.[16]

Making Sense of Music

Such power was at odds with nationalist thought on the place of music in India, according to which music should be able to give voice to people, but not the kind of irrational, unpredictable voice described above. The idea of music as a language turned out to be a particularly useful way for those with nationalist ideas to figure the place of music in newly independent India. A potentially bewildering and recalcitrant domain could, by analogy to language, be used to classify and communicate with the people; music could be turned into something as rational as language. At the same time, music was imagined as a universal, truly national language, able to overcome barriers that would have interfered with any merely verbal language.

The problem of how to make sense of music was a pervasive theme of the All-India Music Conferences convened between 1916 and 1926 by the Marathi musicologist V. N. Bhatkhande, who is now recognized as a major figure in the twentieth-century redefinition of North Indian music.[17] These conferences, modeled on the Indian National Congress, were meant to bring together musicians, musicologists, scientists, connoisseurs, and critics from all over India to determine the standards and boundaries of a national music for India (Bakhle 2005, 180–181). Bhatkhande himself believed passionately in two projects that he hoped would culminate in the establishment of a national academy of music: the rationalizing and standardizing of musical training, and the construction of a "connected" history of music that would encompass both the North and South Indian systems (ibid., 104–6). In 1916, at the first All-India Music Conference in Baroda, Bhatkhande expressed his excitement at the thrilling potential of music as a medium to unify the people of India (ibid., 107). But his vision was utterly different from the power of music described by Devadoss. Whereas for Devadoss music worked by a kind of accidental association, evoking memories without regard for national boundaries, for Bhatkhande the desired end was a state of musical unification that could only come about after diligent training. Music instruction should become "common and universal," he stated at the first All-India Music Conference. "And if it please Providence to so dispense that there is a fusion between the North and the South, then there will be a National music for the whole country and the last of our ambitions will be reached, for then the great Nation will sing *one* song" (Bhatkhande 1919, 42–43). For Bhatkhande the mysteries of how music worked needed to be separated from musicians—whom he saw as ignorant, illiterate, and secretive—and studied rationally and scientifically by musicologists. The juxtaposition of the nation's crying need for a standardized and accessible music with the purported narrow-mindedness, ignorance, and secrecy of musicians themselves became a dominant theme at the All-India Music Conferences (Bakhle 2005, 195).

Among the invited lecturers at the first All-India Music Conference was H. P. Krishna Rao, subregistrar of Mysore and headmaster of a music school there, who had come to present his research into what he called the "psychology of music." Krishna Rao stated at the outset of his lectures that "music is but the language of the emotions" (1917, 1). The lectures, later published as a book, began with a chapter titled "Definition and Nature of Music," which considered the problem of language. Language could be divided into three classes: "sound-language," "sign-language,"

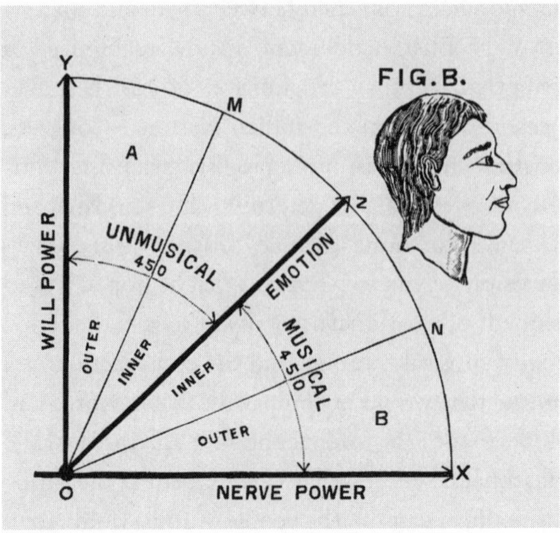

19 "Musical angles." In H. P. Krishna Rao, *The Psychology of Music* (1916).

and "word-language" (1).[18] Music, as sound-language, was privileged over word-language and sign-language because it was "natural": "A word has only a conventional meaning, while a sound has a natural meaning" (2). Music, he implied, had greater potential to express and control the emotions of human beings because its sounds were motivated by nature, not by mere convention: "The sound language originates from instinct, and develops into music as cultivated by different nations" (2). Krishna Rao thus articulated a theory of the relation between music and the subject. According to his theory, music had to be meaningful; it had to express one's own unique emotions but at the same time be understandable to other Indians. "Meaning," in this case, meant that music was recognizably anchored to the nation. Music, as both a national art and the privileged language of the emotions, could be used to define the subject's relation to the nation.

But how, precisely, did this relation work? Krishna Rao imagined the production of emotion by music through an analogy with the technological amplification of sound: music acted as a stimulus to produce emotion, "a form of energy . . . like heat or electricity," which would be carried and "amplified" by the "conductor," the human subject (1917, 13). Music was powerful in this way only when the "nerve-substance" of the subject was a good conductor: that is, when the subject was "musical" (ibid.). A sure way to determine the musicality of any person, Krishna Rao suggested, was to determine their place on the diagram of musicality that he had developed.

The diagram showed an O-origin and an Y-axis and X-axis representing will power and nerve power, respectively. The line representing the progression of emotion could fall anywhere between the two axes. If it fell in the quadrant closer to the nerve-power axis, the subject was musical, that is, able to be moved by music. The closer one's "musical angle" moved to the will-power axis, the less musical one became. When the diagram was applied to the subjects of a nation, the musical angle had direct ramifications for society. For instance, "an unmusical person near A is, as a member of society, a mechanical being. . . . He does everything as a duty, . . . reserved and strategic" (ibid.). On the other hand, "A musical person with a sound general education is an ornament to society. Stationed on the line OZ, he can oscillate like a pendulum to OX or OY, according to circumstances. He it is that knows the right and the wrong. . . . The motive for doing good proceeds in him instinctively, while that of the unmusical person is based on reason. The musical person is a friend, . . . a dear partner, a loving parent and a loyal subject" (14). For the good of society and the nation, then, music education should be made compulsory. In fact, the unity of the nation worked on the analogy of the resonating body: "The state is a body politic. The governing power represents the brain, and the subjects so many nerve centres. The sovereign of the State can exercise a powerful influence on them. . . . They resonate to the vibrations transmitted to them from the brain" (17).

If it was possible to produce a diagram to measure musicality, it was also possible, according to Krishna Rao, to show exactly what kinds of emotions music was capable of producing. He claimed that each note of the scale or raga produced a different kind of mood when heard against the background of the note *sa*: "Sa and pa are tranquil notes; ri 1 and da 1 indicate disturbance; ri 2 and da 2 are perceptions; ga 1 and ni 1 indicate disagreeableness; ga 2 and ni 2 indicate enquiry; ma 1 denotes optimism or egoism; ma 2 denotes degradation" (1917, 23).[19] Bearing this general set of rules in mind, Krishna Rao transcribed a section of alapana in the raga sankarabharanam and "translated" it into "word-language."

S a a a a a a a a a a a
I am Menaka.
G R S a a a a a a a a a a
I am your Menaka.
M G R S a a a a a a a a a a
I am your beloved Menaka.

M G M P D N S a a a a a a a a
Look at me; surely I am your love.
S N D P M G R S a a a a a a a a
I, your love, have come to you again.
R i i i i i i i i
This is your baby, is it not?
P M G M G R i i i i i i i
Do you see how beautiful it is?
G M D P M G R i i i i i i i
How nice are its limbs?
G a a a a a a a a a a a
Imagine how matters stand now.
G M P D P M G a a a a a a a a a a
Is it proper that you should thus neglect us? (35)[20]

If this musical language was taught, Krishna Rao maintained, people would learn how to express their emotions and to hear the emotions of others; this was tantamount to being a decent citizen. But only Indian music, because of its melodic nature, was suited to expressing these "inner emotions." Meanwhile, the harmony of the West was suited only to expressing "external emotions" and "effects of grandeur" (41–42). While Western harmony was basically an artificial innovation, melody was an uncorrupted, natural language.

Central to Krishna Rao's theories was the idea of the universal applicability of music, expressed in his notion that music provided more reliable and direct access to the mind of the common man than language. His ideas about the relation between music, the nation, and its subjects were taken up in the late 1940s in "Music and Healing," a lecture delivered at the Madras Music Academy by Rao Bahadur N. M. Adyanthaya, former director of Industries and Commerce, Madras. Noting the desperate situation of India's people, Adyanthaya said, "It is being increasingly recognised that the psychology of the average man in the street is fast deteriorating and that of the masses is dangerously on the verge of collapse. There is therefore need for an effective antidote for the ever increasing tendency for revolt" (1949, i). Since the problem was at heart a psychological one, Adyanthaya recommended a medium he thought would provide access to the masses: music. "Perhaps a judicious treatment with mass music of the right kind may offer a remedy as music has been proved to soothe strained nerves" (i). Adyanthaya suggested that using music in this scientific way would not kill the art but rejuvenate it, make it even more powerful. If the already immense scholarship on classifying ragas could be put to use for a social cause, he suggested, more people would be able to enjoy Karnatic music. Not only that, but patient reactions to different types of music might provide a scientific basis for distinguishing classical and nonclassical music (6). The answers to both musical questions and social problems lay in the auditory capacities of the nation's subjects. "Important musical associations may take up the matter and with the cooperation of the Universities & Government may institute scholarships for the study of [these] problems," he recommended. "These scholars may be attached to hospitals equipped with all the requisite instruments for measurements of the reactions of patients to music of different kinds. There should be a separate ward and an auditorium for the treatment of patients." Such a scientific and psychological approach could also address the "much discussed subject of language in music" (10).

For Krishna Rao and Adyanthaya after him, the meaning of music was a function of human psychology, a matter of stimuli and response. For others on the quest for meaning in Karnatic music, it seemed more logical to look for meaning in a more conventional linguistic sense. In 1929 the new magazine *Triveni*, self-characterized as "A Journal of the Indian Renaissance," published a series of articles on Karnatic music written by the well-known Telugu violinist Harinagabhushanam. Music, he stated, was of two kinds: conventional music, which dealt with the things of this world, and transcendental music, which was a tool for attaining eternal bliss (1929, 50). Appealing to an imaginary, ideal nation of Aryans, he maintained that transcendental music was the unique heritage of the Aryan system of music and that this heritage was best preserved in the Karnatic music of South India (50). The transcendental aspect of the music took place in the wordless parts of the music. But present-day musicians partook of it unknowingly, for they did not know that even those parts had a meaning, or referent. "Musicians say only swara names: Ri Ri Ri Ni Ni Ni AAA, etcetera, which ejaculations have no sense whatsoever," he complained. "I used to hear great musicians of old sing ragam saying 'Tha Da Ri Na Tom' and I was all the time thinking that it must be some expression with a great meaning. . . . Sometime back the real expression dawned on me with its import, to my great relief. [It was] a mutilated form of 'Thath Are Anamtham Aum,' [which] means 'Brahman is Infinite and he is Aumkara.' Alas, our present day musicians have incurred the bane of meaninglessness on our sacred music" (54). To Harinagabhushanam's great relief, the apparently meaningless syllables musicians were singing could actually be traced back to the sounds of language, thus revealing the motivation for using those sounds and at the same time restoring the true purpose of music. Against the threat of senseless sounds stood the assurance of an ancient language—Sanskrit—and the assurance that the music "meant" something appropriately elevated.

The quest for meaning in music that motivates the writing of Krishna Rao, Adyanthaya, and Harinagabhushanam reveals an underlying discourse about music which emerged only in the first decades of the twentieth century. What these thinkers proposed was, in effect, a certain relationship between music and subjectivity that was based on language. For Krishna Rao and Adyanthaya, music communicated with listeners on the model of language. For Harinagabhushanam, to sing was to already be speaking, if only unconsciously, language itself; the perception of a language standing behind music assuaged the fear that music might be "senseless." Through this metaphor of language, the ideal of finding meaning in and understanding the meaning of music became central. Through the metaphor of language, Karnatic music could be related to specifically Indian subjects. Krishna Rao and Adyanthaya made sense of music by positing that music was a language in itself that could be used by sufficiently musical—and therefore sufficiently Indian—subjects. Harinagabhushanam made sense of music by discovering that a language, Sanskrit, was submerged within its sounds, making it quite literally *speak for* Aryan India. It was precisely because it became impossible, by the 1940s, to speak of music without speaking of language that the issue of language *in* music assumed such importance.

The Tamil Music Movement

The Tamil music movement took place in the wake of the anti-Hindi agitations and the formation of the Self-Respect Party, and amid debates about where the boundaries between the linguistic provinces Andhra Pradesh and Tamil Nadu should be drawn.[21] The Self-Respect (*cuya mariyātai*) movement was begun in 1927 to protest the oppressions of the caste system and the dominance of Brahmins in fields such as law, journalism, medicine, government, and music. The movement's main leader, E. V. Ramasami, had broken off from the Congress Party in 1927 and joined the Justice Party, which ran on a platform that advocated rationalism, as opposed to religion, and mobilized followers on the basis of a Dravidian identity that was specifically Tamil. The notion of a Dravidian linguistic and racial group distinct from Aryan languages and races was based on the philological project of Robert Caldwell and formed the basis of the twentieth-century Dravidian renaissance, an efflorescence of scholarship on the literature, history, and culture of the ancient Tamils.[22]

E. V. Ramasami made a point of recognizing the contribution of non-Brahmin musicians to Karnatic music, to compensate for their being edged out of the music scene in Madras. In 1937 the Congress Party called for Hindi to become the national language of India and suggested compulsory Hindi education, sparking violent protests in Tamil-speaking areas, where such a proposal exemplified Aryan domination of the Dravidians. Whereas the Tamil language was considered, by Dravidian nationalists, to be an original language unsullied by Aryan influences, Telugu, with considerably more borrowings from Sanskrit, was considered to be a corrupted "daughter" of Tamil, whose loyalties were ambiguous.

Talk of Tamil songs as part of the Karnatic music tradition was sporadic until the late 1930s (Arooran 1980, 254). In 1929 the philanthropist Raja Sir Annamalai Chettiar founded the Raja Annamalai Music College at Chidambaram, which became affiliated with Annamalai University in 1932. But although it was later to become the bastion of the Tamil music movement, in the early 1930s its purpose was simply to develop the musical talent of South India (ibid., 255). It was not until the 1940s that the demand for Tamil songs began to be justified by the claim that it was necessary to hear songs in one's mother tongue. At the convocation of Annamalai University in 1940, Raja Sir Annamalai, as he was known, announced a fund of ten thousand rupees, to be awarded in prizes to those who composed new songs with Tamil lyrics. The first conference for the development of Tamil Icai was held at that university in August 1941. About a month later another conference was held under the auspices of E. V. Ramasami in Tiruchirappalli; roughly two weeks after that, a group of musicians in Madras came forward to sign a statement avowing their support of the movement (Ramanathan Chettiar 1993, 4–6).

In 1941 Raja Sir Annamalai made another donation, this time of fifteen thousand rupees, to be given as prizes for those who sang and composed Tamil songs. Many professional musicians, such as Papanasam Sivan, Dhandapani Desikar, and Mariappa Swamy, participated in these competitions. The winning songs were collected and published, with notation, by the university, for dissemination throughout Tamil Nadu. In order to create public awareness about the cause of Tamil music, a series of conferences were held between 1941 and 1945 in Devakottai, Madurai, Pudukkottai, Kumbakonam, Valampuri, and Ayampettai. The Tamil Icai Sangaṃ was established in Madras in 1943, as a parent to other Tamil Icai Sangams founded in 1944 in Vellore, Erode, Tirunelveli, Kanchipuram, and Coimbatore (Ramanathan Chettiar 1993, 7–11).

In December 1943 the first Tamil Icai Conference was held in Madras, at the same time as the Madras Music Academy Conference. During the conference several resolutions were passed to insure that Tamil songs would be in majority in radio broadcasts, concerts, and university curriculums, as Tamils were in majority in Tamil Nadu. Accordingly, it was resolved that at the Madras radio station, 40 percent of broadcasted songs had to be in Tamil, 40 percent in Telugu, and the remaining 20 percent in other languages like Kannada or Sanskrit. However, in Tiruchirappalli, which was more solidly Tamil, 80 percent of the songs broadcasted had to be in Tamil, with the remaining 20 percent reserved for songs in Telugu and other languages. In addition, the conference resolved that in concerts the opening and closing songs—so often in Telugu, Sanskrit, or Hindustani—had to be in Tamil. Music sabhas were called on to enforce this resolution. Members of the conference asked that the Madras University music-department syllabus reserve a solid 40 percent of required repertoire for Tamil songs (*Tamiḻ icai makānāṭu ceṉṉai nikaḻcci mālar* 1944, 61). It is not clear if these resolutions were ever followed. For its own part, the Madras Tamil Icai Sangam resolved to be a bastion of Tamil music in a city where the music scene was dominated by Telugus and Tamil Brahmins. In 1948, after Raja Sir Annamalai's death, Dr. R. K. Shanmugham Chettiar was elected president. Under his leadership a hall, the Raja Annamalai Manram, was built in 1950 in the Esplanade area of George Town in Madras (Ramanathan Chettiar 1993, 28).[23] That building, at a meaningful remove from the Madras Music Academy in Mylapore, continues to house the annual Tamil Icai Sangam conference and the Tamil Icai Sangam College of Music.

From the Shores of Lemuria

Members of the Tamil music movement traced the history of their demand for Tamil songs back to Abraham Pandithar, medical doctor and author of the monumental *Karunamirtha Sagaram* (*Karuṇamirtacākaram*), which extolled the refinement and musicality of the Tamil language and also included a section of Pandithar's own Tamil compositions for Tamil children. Pandithar began his treatise on music with an account of the deluge that destroyed Lemuria, a continent of Tamil speakers which had supposedly existed to the south of India before it was subsumed by the ocean.[24] The imagination of an antique land was crucial to Pandithar's theory of music and its origins.

Always interested in music, Pandithar devoted himself to it in the last ten tears of his life, having retired from his medical career.[25] Raised in a family who had converted to Christianity two generations before, Pandithar had learned violin as a boy and it was thought that his interest in church music would blossom. However, under the influence of the Tamil renaissance, he became more interested in Karnatic music and particularly in the idea of Tamil music. Bothered by the claim that Telugu was more suitable than Tamil for music, he wrote Tamil lyrics for the tunes of Telugu compositions and published these (Nadar 1954, 113). Yet this was, Pandithar felt, merely an imitation. Only when he or any other student of music was able to compose a completely new song with Tamil words could the music really be called Tamil music. He was certain that music was not only an artistic but also a scientific matter. By 1910 he had come up with a method for composing new kritis, but his pursuits had led him to an interest in the "theory" of Karnatic music: how many srutis were in an octave? How were ragas constructed? What was the basic principle that differentiated one raga from another? (114). In order to publicize his research on these topics, Pandithar founded the Tanjore Sangita Vidya Maha Sabha in 1912, and in the five following years convened seven conferences for the purposes of debating these questions (115). He came into conflict with the musical authorities of the time at the First All-India Music Conference in Baroda in 1916, when he demonstrated his theory of twenty-four srutis to the octave, rather than the twenty-two mentioned in the Sanskrit treatises.[26] The conflict concerned much more than the probably inaudible difference of two srutis; on one side was the authority of the Sanskrit treatises, and on the other was the ancient Tamil theory of music, bolstered by Western rationality. At stake was the origin of Karnatic music itself.

Indeed, the question of origins dominated Pandithar's monumental work *Karunamirtha Sagaram: A Treatise on Music, or Isai-Tamil, which Is One of the Main Divisions of Muttamil or Language, Music, and Drama*, published in 1917, two years before his death. Quoting liberally from the Bible, the recently published editions of the Tamil "classics" *Tolkappiam* and *Cilapatikaram*, and Caldwell's grammar of Dravidian languages, he gave a detailed account of how the ancient land of Lemuria was the cradle of Tamil civilization and Tamil music, and of how Tamil civilization had given rise to the rest of the world. Using passages from the Bible, Pandithar demonstrated the antiquity of music, in particular, the existence of instruments such as the nagaswaram before the deluge (9). By corroborating biblical accounts of the deluge with Tamil accounts produced by the new generation of Dravidianists, Pandithar showed that the deluge had been universal. From this assumption it was logical to hypothesize that "the ancient continent of Lemuria, which was to the south of India in the Indian Ocean, was the original habitation of man, that it was the cradle of all nations, and that after the destruction of the continent, the various races occupied the shores which were against them" (23).

The original inhabitants of Lemuria spoke a primordial language, which must have been Tamil. For Pandithar, one proof of Tamil's primordial origin was its sound: "The softness of the words, the fewness of the letters and the comparative ease with which the words are pronounced warrant us to infer that Tamil must have been the language of early mankind" (1917, 47). Another proof was the evidence that Tamil was independent, that it "[stood] by itself without being affected by other languages, in spite of other languages borrowing from it" (47). To demonstrate this point, Pandithar included long lists of "original" Tamil words that had been borrowed by Sanskrit, Hebrew, and other languages (43–47). The priority of languages was thus reversed; Tamil was now the ancient original, and Sanskrit the corrupt imitation.[27]

But the most important proof of the primordiality of the Tamil language was, for Pandithar, its proximity to music, which implied that the perfect language was one that was united with music. Muttamiḻ, in which grammar and music were two equal branches of a larger entity called language, was, for twentieth-century Dravidianists like Pandithar, the epitome of the perfect language, a language that was literally enchanted. "Noble readers!" he urged,

> If we want to understand clearly the subtlety and antiquity of Indian music we would do well to make a few observations on the Tamil language which includes within itself . . . music. The period of the origin of Indian Music is as ancient as the . . . Tamil language, and the sweetness of Indian Music is the sweetness of the language itself. Just as the language stands unmixed and unaffected by other languages, so also the Music of South India is perfect in itself having special rules of its own without seeking the aid of other music. (30)

But just as the Tamil language had undergone admixture with Sanskrit and other languages over the centuries, Tamil music had also fallen from its state of original, Sangam-era purity. This had happened through translation. In a section titled "The Influence of the Aryans on the Music of South India," Pandithar stated that the Aryans ("Brahmins") had learned music from Tamils but then had written their music treatises in Sanskrit. It was thus that South Indian music had become corrupted. By Pandithar's calculation, South Indian music had been "in the hands of foreigners for the last seven or eight hundred years," ever since Aryans had come to the South (1917, 120). "[The Aryans] have completely changed the names of some of the most ancient ragams and technical terms, giving Sanskrit names. . . . So we must understand that the ancient Tevarams are now found as ragas in a new Sanskrit garb" (111–112). At stake for Pandithar was not only the past but also the future of Indian music. In an essay on Indian music which he sent to several English music journals, Pandithar decried the fact that no one seemed to be interested in uncovering the "one theory and one law of constructing melody for all people from the Himalayas to Cape Comorin and from the Indus to the Bay of Bengal" (217).[28] To discover such a law would, he implied, enable a return to the ancient past, that glorious period when all Indian music—indeed, the music of the entire world—was Tamil music. Pandithar's vision is reminiscent of Bhatkhande's vision of music as a universal language uniting India; the difference was that for Pandithar the universal language would have distinctly Tamil inflections.

Like those in the Tamil music movement, Pandithar was concerned with determining the precise relationship of music and language. The milieu in which Pandithar worked in the first decades of the twentieth century, however, was very different from that of the 1940s, when the movement for Tamil music arose. Working at the margins of Dravidian studies, Pandithar was primarily concerned with the reconstruction of ancient Tamil music. The projects of reconstructing ancient Tamil music and creating modern music in Tamil were based on a common set of concerns, especially the desire to find a motivating relationship between music and language. But the more immediate political purposes of each project differed; while the reconstruction of ancient Tamil music, beginning in the 1910s, sought to find a prior musical system distinct from (although perhaps the basis of) modern Karnatic music, the Tamil music movement of the 1940s called on Tamils to seize the contemporary practice of Karnatic music and make it their own.

Iron Ears

Music is well said to be the speech of angels; in fact, nothing among the utterances allowed to man is felt to be so divine. . . . Serious nations . . . have prized song and music as the highest. . . . [But] what a road men have travelled! The waste that is made in music is probably among the saddest of all our squanderings of God's gifts. Music has, for a long time past, been avowedly mad, divorced from sense and the reality of things; and runs about now as an open Bedlamite. . . . bragging that she has nothing to do with sense and reality, but with fiction and delirium only.
—Thomas Carlyle, *The Opera* (1852)

T. K. Chidambaranatha Mudaliar (hereafter T.K.C.), aesthetician and man of letters, began his essay "Caṅkītamum Cakityamum" (Music and lyrics) with a Tamil paraphrase of these words from the Scottish essayist Thomas Carlyle. Such comments, he marveled, sounded as if they could be from "somebody speaking about our present-day music" (Chidambaranatha Mudaliar 1941, 140). How angry Carlyle would have been, T.K.C. wrote, if he had known of the worth of Karnatic music in former days and how it was being wasted in the present. Echoing the distinction drawn by H. P. Krishna Rao, T.K.C. stated that whereas Western music was based on the ascent and descent of scales and artful combinations of notes, or "calculations," Karnatic music was, as Westerners themselves pointed out, "intimately connected to feelings" ("Kaṇakkiliruntu pirantatu mēlnāṭṭu caṅkītam. Uṇarcciyiliruntu pirantatu nammuṭaiya caṅkītam"). Western music, being based on calculations, could only be appreciated by those who had studied it. But Karnatic music, being born from feeling (*uṇarcci*), was based on a natural philosophy, so anyone ought to be able to enjoy it (142). However, the concept of high art didn't accommodate such a natural relationship to music: pandits and vidwans made pronouncements that such music as could be enjoyed by everybody was of a low standard. Musicians, T.K.C. claimed, sang supposedly high-class music with such closed-up, artificial voices so lacking in emotion that the common people had come to believe that in high-class music there was not supposed to be any emotion, or bhāvam (*pāvam*). They had become so accustomed to understanding and feeling nothing when they listened to Karnatic music that they assumed the music was devoid of emotion (143).

T.K.C. went on to address the problem of meaning in music and the precise role of the *sahityam*, or lyrics. To those who had complained that Karnatic music was not understandable to Tamilians because the lyrics were in Telugu, the pandits had answered that they should learn Telugu in order to fully enjoy the music. T.K.C. commented sarcastically on the absurdity of this simplistic, utilitarian view of language: "If that is so, then they need to put up a notice outside the concert hall saying 'today there will be a three-hour concert. All the songs will be in Telugu. Only those who know Telugu should come. We are not responsible for those who do not know Telugu. If they come, we cannot refund their tickets'" (1941, 14). Following this logic, those who came to only one or two concerts a year would have to learn Telugu just for that, while those who knew Tamil only should choose to go to dramas instead. But why should the audience be bothered to learn Telugu, T.K.C. asked, when most of the singers themselves hadn't learned it? In any case, learning a language in order to speak it was one matter, but singing in another language could hardly be learned. It was a matter not of merely understanding the language but of enjoying it in all the senses of the Tamil word *anubhavam* (*aṉupavam*: experience). For how could one really understand a song in Telugu merely by being told the meaning of the words? While Tamil translations of Telugu lyrics for the benefit of Tamil musicians abounded, T.K.C. doubted that they would help matters. The problem, as he saw it, was that there was a difference between learning something and feeling it in one's heart ("itaya pāvam uṇarvatu"). To be a poet required years of training in one's own language, much less in a foreign one; given this, how could any singer with a superficial knowledge of the meaning of the Telugu lyrics be expected to sing them with feeling? (146).

Moreover, T.K.C. added, if any Tamilian said at that point that he enjoyed the song, it was a lie, a self-deception (*ēmāḷittaṉam*). There could be no true meaning without an enjoyment of sound, a subjective sense of the motivation of language. To what authentically Tamil ears could those Telugu words sound good, like drops of nectar ("kātukku amirtam vārttār pōl")? (1941, 148). Any Tamilian who doubted the law of the untranslatability of language should try explaining a Tamil song word by word to any Telugu-speaking person and see if they enjoyed it. They certainly would not, T.K.C. said, and they would think one crazy for expecting them to. To prove his point about the futility of translating songs from other languages, T.K.C. related a story about a Karnatic vocalist who went to Calcutta and gave a concert of Telugu and Sanskrit songs. The Tamilians in the audience did not complain but sat docilely and acted as though they were enjoying the concert. The Bengalis in the audience assumed from the Tamilians' attitude that the songs were in Tamil, and exclaimed to the singer, "Because the songs were all in Tamil we could not enjoy/understand them. Could you sing some Bengali songs?" (149). The Bengalis, T.K.C. concluded, had real respect for their mother tongue and were not afraid to ask for songs in it. Tamilians, on the other hand, would be willing to say they enjoyed any song, even a Bengali one, because they did not have the courage to say otherwise. This "disease" of self-hatred, born of being made to study English, to repeat words without knowing their meaning (*ārttam*), had "entered the bones" of Tamilians more than it had for other Indians (149–50). As long as Tamilians were afraid to demand music in their mother tongue, they would be deprived of the true pleasures of music. "Singing and singing in Telugu, our bhāvam, our feeling has gone. The songs do not stick in our minds; when the musician sings the song, the audience sits like stone statues" (156).

For T.K.C. meaning in music was located not only in the lyrics or words but in the ways those words resonated in the ears and hearts of listeners. His struggle to explain the importance of hearing music with words in one's mother tongue reveals a quest for pure and true singing and listening subjects, musicians and audiences who showed their identity as Tamilians. The specter of audiences sitting still as stone statues was particularly disturbing because it threatened to make a charade of classical music, a show based on such ingrained pretense that it took a foreigner—a Bengali—to point out that something was wrong. The Tamil poet and essayist Bharathiyar had struck a similar note in his 1916 essay "Caṅkīta Viṣayam" (The issue of music), claiming that the Tamil people had lost their feeling for music (*caṅkīta ñānam*) from years of hearing the same Telugu and Sanskrit songs over and over again. They sang them gulping and murdering the words, imparting no feeling to them at all (216). In the name of a ghost called the "vocal concert," the musicians murdered the sweetness of the music by slapping out the tala ("'Pāṭṭu kaccēri' eṉṟu pēy vaittukkoṇṭu aṅkē icaiyiṉpaṅkaḷai koṉṟu tāla muḻakkattai pirataṉamākkutal takātu") (217). "Go to any district, any village," Bharathiyar wrote. "Whichever vidwan comes, it will be this same story. Because Tamilians have iron ears, they can stand to listen to the same seven or eight songs over and over and over and over again. In places where people have ears of flesh they would not endure such a thing ("Enta jillāvukku pō, enta kirāmattiṟku pō enta 'vitvāṉ' vantālum, itē katai tāṉ. Tamiḻnāṭṭu jaṉaṅkaḷukku irumpukātāka iruppatāl varuhak kaṇakkākak kēṭṭuk koṇṭirukkiṟārkaḷ. Tōṟ kātu uḷḷe tēcaṅkalilē intat tuṉpattaip poṟuttuk koṇṭirukka māṭṭārkal) (213).

The Sound of the Heart

Have you heard the voice of a newborn infant calling its mother? There is a special kind of music in it.

—C. N. Annadurai, "Tamiḻariṉ Maṟumalarcci"

For those who had lost their feeling for music, the way to regain it was to nurture their mother tongue, Tamil.[29] In much of the discourse of *tamiḻpaṟṟu* (Tamil devotion) in the 1930s and 1940s, music—not the high art of Karnatic classical music but a generalized power of music, or musicality—was repeatedly invoked to explain the untranslatability and special power of the mother tongue. Essays on the concept of the mother tongue in the 1930s and following decades frequently invoked music to illustrate the subject's special relation to his or her mother tongue. "Itaya Oli" (The sound of the heart), an essay by T.K.C., and "Olic Celvam" (The treasure of sound), written by his student the Justice S. Maharajan, both center on the idea of there being a kind of music *in* language that makes it unique and untranslatable. The music of Tamil, both argued, was only audible to those who had Tamil as their mother tongue.

To experience this music within language, T.K.C. suggested in "Itaya Oli," one should go to any small Tamil village and walk the streets with a keen ear. From sunrise to sunset, on any verandah, one might listen to "concerts of talk" ("arattaik kaccērikaḷ"), the speed and nuance of which one could never find in the so-called civilized speech of the city ("aṅkē pēcum irukkiṟa vēkamum nāyamum, nākarattil pēcum nākarika pēccil illai") (1936, 34). In these concerts of talk, whatever was in the speaker's mind would come out directly in the act of speaking ("uḷḷattil uḷḷe viṣayam appaṭiyē vākkil varum") (34). One person might be speaking, but the bond of understanding created by their common mother tongue would make those listening feel that they themselves were speaking ("Kēṭkiṟa ovvoruvarum tāṅkaḷētāṉ pēcikoṇṭirukkiṟōm eṉṟa niṉaippil iruppārkaḷ") (34). Music, here, was imagined as a vehicle of immediate and uninterrupted communication.

These village concerts of talk stood in sharp contrast to the music concerts in the city, T.K.C. wrote. Although the audiences for these concerts were Tamils, they did not express their approval or enjoyment in Tamil as they listened. It was all in Hindustani: "Bale Bale! Besh! Savash!" An Englishman who only knew a little Hindustani, a word here and there, might think that all the Telugu songs the singer was singing were Hindustani, and therefore the audience was speaking to him in Hindustani. After all, after the Telugu songs, singers would often end with a few Hindustani songs. Was it any wonder that a crowd of hundreds of Tamilians would use Hindustani rather than Tamil? It would hardly be surprising if they used English expressions like "Capital!" or "Excellent!" An observer might mistakenly conclude from this that Tamils had no feeling for music (caṅkīta uṇarcci). But how could this be true, when even foreigners were commenting on the remarkable musical feeling of the Tamils? Rabindranath Tagore himself had written that Tamil Nadu was a land of music. Go to any village, and you would find temples with endowments for nadaswaram players and dance musicians. You couldn't find anything like it in the world. Such a tradition must have taken thousands of years to develop, T.K.C. speculated. During all those years, would Tamilians have sat like stone statues, unable to express their appreciation? No. They would have at least said, "Rompa naṉṟāy irukkiratu" (It is very good) or roared "Aha! Aha!" or trilled "Aṭaṭā! Aṭaṭā!" or have drunk it in, saying it was like "honey, milk, or nectar" ("tēnō, pālō, amirtamō"). These ancient Tamils would have said such things whole-heartedly (1936, 35–36).

For T.K.C., then, the question of how one's response to music should be registered *in* language came to the forefront. For a musical subject, music should provoke an involuntary vocal response. The fact that Tamils, to express their feelings about music, had words only in other languages was a problem. Language that came naturally, for T.K.C., was "the sound of the heart," a language that existed outside of and before translation. The real character of a language had to be felt precisely through what was untranslatable into any other language: its sound. T.K.C.'s student Justice S. Maharajan (later president of the Madras Tamil Icai Sangam) continued this obsession with the sound of language in his 1962 essay "Olic Celvam." To an ear accustomed to the sounds of Tamil, he wrote, the sound of the language (*tamiḻ oli*) gives pleasure (*cukam*) (Maharajan 1962, 1). Like T.K.C., Maharajan suggested that to rediscover this pleasure in the Tamil sound, one should listen to the speech of common people, especially street hawkers, whose cries rang with alliteration and onomotopoeia and the *nāyam* (melody, nuance) of the Tamil language. For Maharajan, street hawkers' cries illustrated what amounted to the motivation of language. In these unpretentiously poetic calls, every choice of word, every repetition, seemed necessary; the street hawker obeyed the rules of meaning and the conventions of sound as if they were one. "In this way, Tamil speech and poetry sound to our ears and minds as one" ("Ippaṭiyāka tamiḻ pēccum, kaviyum nam kātukkum, karuttukkum icaintu olikkiṉṟaṉa") (2). Interestingly, Maharajan used a verb whose referent was music (icai) to express the unity between sound and idea. Ideal music, he suggested, was the most free of all the arts because it did not have the problem of a split between sound and idea. Poetry, because of its proximity to music through sound, could come close to music if Tamilians recognized and enjoyed the music in the sounds of the language they spoke and read. Words did for speech and poetry what swaras did for music. In recognizing this, Tamilians would see that they were heirs to an abundant treasure of sound ("Icaiyil svaram ceykiṟa vēlaiyai, colliṉ oli ceytu kāṭṭukiṟatu kavitaiyil. Ippaṭi valamāna oliccelvattukkellām varicāka irrukiṟāṉ tamiḻaṉ") (7).

The Tamil poet Namakkal Ramalingam Pillai, in the midst of his treatise on Tamil music (*Icaittamiḻ*), written in 1942, included a page-long chapter entitled "Tāy Moḻi" (Mother tongue) that makes similar points. "The mother tongue," he wrote, "is the language the mother feeds to us" (Tāy moḻi eṉṟāl tāyār pukuṭṭiya moḻi). "Our knowledge begins with the words she says. Afterwards no matter how many languages we study, we understand them only through our mother tongue" (1942, 92). The power of the mother tongue was such that it held the key to a person's identity. If you were to take a Tamil child away from his mother before he could speak and give him to a Telugu mother to raise, the child would become Telugu (92). The mother tongue, once instilled in a person, was irreversible; it was the language closest to one's subjectivity, the place where the work of translation ended. Music, suggested Ramalingam Pillai, occupied this special territory of the mother tongue; it should not require translation but should be immediately understandable, a natural expression. But this required the aid of the mother tongue; otherwise, it was merely clever combinations of notes, spectacular acrobatics, meaningless sounds that stuck in the ears but did not get to the mind or heart (88, 90). "However cleverly ragam, talam, and swaram are mixed together, they are still only sound. . . . The forms of that sound can produce amazement in us. But everything that thus falls on the ear will stop at the ear. It will not penetrate the mind. It will not melt the soul. It will not kindle the emotions" (88). By way of analogy, Ramalingam Pillai included a lengthy description of an acrobat balancing on a wire and the thrilling effect it would have on an audience. "But even a feat which requires so much practice, we will forget even before we reach home. That is because it is mere entertainment" (vēṭikkai) (90). Similarly, music with lyrics in another language, like Telugu, was "useless" for Tamils (93). Many Tamil vidwans and audiences had the uncanny experience of singing or hearing Telugu lyrics so often that the sound of the lyrics became intensely familiar but the meaning was unknown. The natural thing for listeners and singers to do was to Tamilize the lyrics by singing/hearing them as the Tamil words they sounded like, completely changing the meaning of the song and depriving them of its bhāvam (6–7).

The problem, as T.K.C. saw it, was that Tamils were too accepting of music in other languages, ignoring the imperative to hear music in their mother tongue. Tamils' feeling for art (*kalai uṇarcci*) was dwindling, so much so that Madras had earned the epithet "iruḻ māṭiya ceṉṉai" (Madras covered in darkness) (Chidambaranatha Mudaliar 1936, 153–54). Tamil musicians and composers were blindly following the example of Thyagaraja by composing, like him, in Telugu. This had succeeded in producing a lot of "fake Thyagarajas" (*poli tyākayyarkaḷ*). It was as if a peacock had happened to dance, and all over Tamil Nadu, from Tirupati to Kanyakumari, a breed of turkeys had arisen. To Tamil eyes, they all seemed like peacocks. What would poor Thyagaraja have thought? Instead of blindly copying Thyagaraja, suggested T.K.C., musicians should follow his example as one who had composed heartfelt lyrics in his own mother tongue (153–54). Tamils should use Thyagaraja's lyrics as an inspiration to compose in Tamil, their own mother tongue. For "music in Tamil Nadu should be the property of Tamils. Someone coming from the North or a Western country could not enjoy it in the same way as a Tamil could. If they said they did, it would be mere preaching" (153–54). Art and music could not be transported and translated from place to place. "Just as we don't understand their music, they don't understand ours. That is art. To take it from one place to another is futile," concluded T.K.C. (153–54). He used the idea that Karnatic music was more intimately related to feelings than Western music not to argue that it therefore could be universally understood but to impress on his readers how far astray music had gone in Tamil Nadu.

C. ("Rajaji") Rajagopalachari was considered inimical to the Tamil cause because, as chief minister of Tamil Nadu, he advocated compulsory Hindi education in the late 1930s. Interestingly, however, when it came to music, Rajaji's respect for the "mother tongue" was unquestionable. It was true, he said at the Tamil Icai Conference in Madras in 1943, that music was really composed of sounds. But if that was so, why wasn't instrumental music sufficient? If music was just sounds, what could explain its special power? Such power, Rajaji argued, came especially from vocal music; when music was joined with language, it produced a special kind of happiness ("Mol̲ikal̲utan̲ cērttuk kēṭkumpōtu oru tan̲i cantōṣam uṇṭākir̲atu"). As soon as one heard the music, one understood the words ("Caṅkītam man̲atil er̲uvatuṭan̲, en̲n̲a collukir̲ār en̲r̲um kūṭa er̲ukir̲atu") (Muthiah 1996, 25). It was as if words and music were united in this seamless kind of listening, this immediate understanding. One needed to understand the words when somebody spoke, Rajaji wrote, so why did some think it not necessary to understand the words when somebody sang? (27). "Meaningless" music might produce a vague sort of blissful feeling, but besides that it had no value ("Poruḷar̲r̲a icai, ētōmātiri ān̲antamē tavira vēr̲u pirayōjan̲am illai") (27). For Rajaji, listening to music ideally had to approximate the supposedly immediate, unselfconscious understanding produced between two native speakers of Tamil. Music was valuable not as an external collection of beautiful sounds—Rajaji compared this to the folly of a Tamilian writing a love letter in English—but as the sound of one's own subjectivity, a sonic reflection of one's self. More to the point, this would be a self, and a subject, only imaginable within the new kind of discourse about music that was developing. Just as music, for Rajaji, produced a kind of immediate understanding, which required no work of interpretation for the listener, this new type of subject was one whose outer self and speech transparently reflected his thoughts and emotions.

The movement for music in Tamil did not entail a mere switching of languages from Telugu to Tamil, but rather a new concept of the role of language in music. The Telugu of most Karnatic compositions was hard to understand even for a Telugu-speaking audience; it was quasi-formulaic, specialized, half-literary, "colloquial" only in the sense that it was not classical Telugu. A Telugu listener might hear a familiar word here and there, but this was not the same kind of "understanding" that proponents of the Tamil music movement called for. For them, as Rajaji's essay suggests, music was to be communicative, and the presence of foreign-sounding words had the potential to lead such communication astray. The idea of musicality emerged in this discourse as a metaphor for such communication, a communication so direct that the medium almost effaced itself. The threat of Telugu words was the threat that their very foreignness would make them musical, but in a negative sense: they would cease to have meaning and would become mere sounds.

"To praise and love one's mother, mother land, and mother tongue is natural to humans. In Tamil Nadu this love has been raised to an uncommon pitch, as we attribute divine qualities to Tamil," wrote Kalki Krishnamoorthy in his regular column on music and dance, "Āṭal Pāṭal," in 1943. "But in this era there have been born some peculiar beings who seem to have a hatred for Tamil. Without flinching, they say there are no good songs in Tamil, and that Tamil is not a suitable language for music, and that ṣinging in Tamil will bring the decline of Karnatic music" (1943b, 13). He went on to contrast the concerts in the Madras Music Academy with those held under the auspices of the Indian Fine Arts Society. The music academy concerts, he wrote, had been going on for the last sixteen years, organized by Tamilians, but no Tamil songs were ever sung there; it seemed as if they had taken a vow to dismiss them. The academy administration actively enforced its judgment about the inferiority of Tamil songs by changing the programs of performers. M. S. Subbulakshmi, for example, was forced in 1943 to add a Telugu kriti to her program so that the majority of her songs would not be in Tamil (14). In the case of Madurai Mani Iyer, Kalki wrote, the academy administration eliminated three out of the four Tamil songs he wanted to sing when they printed the program for his concert. Mani Iyer, in reply, sang a sarcastic impromptu lyric addressing the academy administration: "Mahā Mahā akatemikkārarkaḷē! Uṅkaḷukku tamiḻ eṉṟāl avvaḷavu veruppā? Pōkaṭṭum, iṉṉoru teluṅku kirttaṉattai kēḷuṅkaḷ" (Great, great academy men! Do you hate Tamil so much? Well, so be it. Hear another Telugu song) (15). By contrast, the concerts held under the auspices of the Indian Fine Arts Society, wrote Kalki, were much more relaxed in atmosphere; the musicians sang whatever they wished, which was mostly Tamil (15).

During the years of his column "Āṭal Pāṭal," Kalki wrote regularly on the topic of the Tamil music movement. What was most at stake for him in these debates was a certain politics of identity they seemed to assume: that Karnatic music was primarily the property of Brahmins, while Tamil was primarily the mother tongue of Tamilians, who were by definition not Brahmins. Anti-Brahmin rhetoric was employed most forcefully by E. V. Ramasami (E.V.R.), particularly during protests held in the 1930s against making Hindi a compulsory language in schools (Ramaswamy 1997, 194–204). The domination of Karnatic music by Brahmins was, for E.V.R., another example of the way Brahmins had taken over what was essentially Tamil culture and disguised it in Sanskritized terms in order to call it their own. In an editorial in the newspaper *Kuṭi Aracu* in 1930, he criticized the Brahmins for monopolizing Karnatic music and claimed that non-Brahmin artists were being mistreated. He arranged a music section at the second Self-Respect Conference at Erode in 1930, calling on non-Brahmins to patronize non-Brahmin artists and to make sure that non-Brahmin children had musical education (Arooran 1980, 255). In a pamphlet published in 1944, entitled *Tamiḻ Icai, Naṭippu Kalaikaḷ: Iṉi Eṉṉa Ceyya Vēṇṭum?* (Tamil music and drama: What still needs to be done?), E.V.R. wrote that Brahmins (whom he glossed as "Aryans") were dominating all the fields of cultural production. "We need to enter those fields, find out the secrets, and make them public," he urged (Ramasami 1944, 7). The purpose of music, he claimed, was primarily to communicate, and only secondarily to give pleasure. The *ceyti* (message) had to be more important than the *cuvai* (pleasure, taste) (ibid., 3). Accordingly, he urged that songs on Puranic or bhakti themes be dismissed in favor of songs with useful social messages (ibid., 16).

An editorial in *Kuṭi Aracu* from 1943 had already suggested that Tamils needed to hear songs in "good, natural Tamil" about the courage of the Tamils and their love for the Tamil language, songs that would undo the bad deeds of the Brahmins (*Tamiḻ icai makānāṭu ceṉṉai nikaḻcci malar* 1944, 113). This editorial took for granted the opposition between Brahmins and Tamilians. Who was opposing the Tamil Icai movement? The Brahmins, came the blunt answer. It was the Brahmins who were eating the Tamils' salt, coming to live in Tamil Nadu, building up their strength by Tamils' hard work, making Tamils into slaves, smearing an Aryan coating onto Tamil arts ("tamiḻ kalaikku ārya mēṟpucciṭṭu"), mixing up Sanskrit words with Tamil to make a maṇipiravāḷam (110–11). Brahmins, the editorial stated, could not be Tamilian because their mother tongue was not really Tamil but some mixture of Sanskrit and English.

It was in the midst of such discourse that Kalki Krishnamoorthy, a Brahmin himself, wrote his "Tamiḻicaiyum Pirāmaṇarkaḷum" (Tamil music and Brahmins). For more than a thousand years, music in Tamil Nadu had developed without regard for differences in *jati* (caste), he wrote. How, then, could music suddenly become the rightful property of only non-Brahmins? "There must be some sort of curse on our country," he wrote. "Take any perfectly good thing and sooner or later, in some form, the jati problem will enter into it" (Kalki 1943a, 12). Those in the Self-Respect Movement wanted to make the Tamil music movement a non-

Brahmin movement, and Brahmins were agreeing with them, saying that they were not Tamilians. But, Kalki asked, did not Brahmins speak Tamil? A Tamilian was anyone whose mother tongue was Tamil. Brahmins in Andhra Pradesh and Bengal considered themselves Andhras and Bengalis, so why did Brahmins in Tamil Nadu insist on their own foreignness? The Tamil music movement was a movement of the Tamil people (*tamil̲ makkal*), not a non-Brahmin movement. Many Brahmins had served the cause of Tamil music, like the composers Gopalakrishna Bharati, Maha Vaidyanathayyar, and Papanasam Sivan. Brahmins, just like other Tamilians—like all humans, in fact—needed songs in their own mother tongue; even Rajagopalachari, the Brahmin chief minister of Tamil Nadu who supported compulsory Hindi education, was in favor of the Tamil music movement, Kalki stated (12–13). Whereas language issues still divided Brahmins from non-Brahmins and provoked arguments about who was really Tamil, the music issue, he argued, should be able to bring all Tamilians together.

C. N. Annadurai, script and story writer, founder of a branch of the Tirāvita Munēr̲r̲a Kal̲akam (Dravidian Advancement Party) and later chief minister of Tamil Nadu, presented the music issue as a cause for Tamils against Aryan domination. Although he did not use the language of caste, in his lengthy piece entitled "Tamil̲arin̲ Mar̲umalarcci" (The renaissance of the Tamils), he presumed to speak for non-Brahmins, who, he assumed, were the "real" Tamils. The reasons that some opposed the Tamil music movement were not aesthetic, as they claimed, but political: they were afraid that if Tamilians pushed for music in Tamil, they would soon demand a separate Tamil nation. Being afraid to say this, the small opposition group instead claimed that there were no classical songs in Tamil or that they were of inferior standard. Why should this be? Were Tamils vagabonds, wanderers (*nāṭōṭik kūṭṭamā*)? No they were indigenous people, the owners of this land ("Illai! Pal̲aṅkuṭi makkaḷ! Inta nāṭṭukku contakkārarkaḷ!") (Muthiah 1996, 43). Tamils, he maintained, had a long musical history. After all, what did Tamils sing before the 1800s, when Thyagaraja and Dikshitar composed in Telugu and Sanskrit? There must have been Tamil music. In the time of the Tamil kings, he wrote, Tamil music and arts had spread all over the world. Where was that music today? When the British came, Aryans had "enchanted" them with "propaganda" ("āriyarin̲ piracyāram āṅkila nāṭṭavariayum māyakir̲r̲u"), saying that they had taught the Tamils everything about art and music (49). Thus had developed a mistaken idea that Karnatic music did not really belong to Tamils, that it was different from the original Tamil music. In fact, underneath the show of technique that alienated many listeners uneducated in Karnatic music was a kind of music that was completely understandable to Tamilians. The Tamil people were not interested in feats of musicianship but in songs that they could understand. Thus, if M. S. Subbulakshmi sang Telugu kritis, as she did with beautiful correctness, it might move the other musicians but not the *nāṭṭu makkal* (common people, people of the land). Other than knowing that she sang beautifully, they would not enjoy/understand the meaning, or mood (*cuvai*: literally, "taste") (53). But if M.S. happened to sing a Tamil song, immediately the ears and hearts of the Tamilians would be thrilled ("Tamiḻariṉ maṉamellām kulirntatu"); the music's sweetness (*iṉpam*) would truly reach everybody (53).

A Language of Aesthetics?

Those who argued against the Tamil music movement did so in the name of "classical music," fearing that if Tamil songs became a priority, the standards of Karnatic music would drop. At the heart of the debate was the question of just what kind of language music was to be imagined as: a mother tongue or an aesthetically motivated language of art? Was the listener to find meaning in the words of the songs or in the melodies, the sound itself? Was the listener's appreciation grounded in a sense of identity based on his mother tongue or a sense of awe inspired by his awareness of a great classical tradition? This dichotomy between the mother tongue and a classical language of art and aesthetics was imagined to be at work in music precisely because it had, as Bernard Cohn's work suggests, already become part of the assumed hierarchy of languages in India. If music was imagined through the analogy of language, it had to belong in one category or the other. Thus, in 1941, in response to the growing activity of the Tamil music movement, the Vellore Sangita Sabha went so far as to pass a resolution saying that "the essential thing about music was its melody, and its appeal to the inner emotions of the listeners did not matter" (Arooran 1980, 259). In the same year, the Madras Music Academy passed a similar resolution: "It should be the aim of all musicians and lovers of music to preserve and maintain the highest standard of classical Carnatic music and no consideration of language should be imported so as to lower or impair that standard" (260).

In the same year, T. T. Krishnamachari, one of the founders of the Madras Music Academy, published an essay entitled "Karnāṭaka Caṅkītamum Tamiḻ Icai Iyakkamum" (Karnatic music and the Tamil music movement) in the Tamil weekly *Ananta Vikatan*. He argued that the Tamil Music movement (which he referred to as *pāṣai piraccinai*, the "language problem") was concerned less with music than it was with politics and that those who argued for Tamil songs knew nothing about the art and aesthetics of music. There was a difference, he maintained, between a pure music concert (*cuttamāṉa caṅkītak kaccēri*) and bhajans or katha kalakshepam. For the latter, he implied, it would be justified to demand that the songs be in an understandable language. But those who demanded that pure Karnatic music be in a language they could understand were missing this crucial distinction (Krishnamachari 1941, 38). "In order to enjoy a music concert," he wrote, "you need to have some knowledge" (*ñāṉam*). You might ask, couldn't someone with no knowledge at all enjoy a concert if the singing were interesting enough? Yes, it would give them peace of mind, perhaps. But this is not experiencing music (*caṅkīta aṉupavamakātu*). Now that it had suddenly become imperative for everyone to enjoy music, there was a real threat to the standard of Karnatic music. For "the tendency of the common man is to destroy anything that he cannot understand" (38–40). One might condone Tamil songs, wrote Krishnamachari, if they followed the restrictions and conventions of Karnatic music. "Everyone knows that the way most Tamil songs are 'composed' nowadays is by taking songs in other languages and putting Tamil words to them. . . . A Tamil hearing these might get a lot of pleasure from understanding the words. But that is not what it means to experience music" (40). For Krishnamachari, Karnatic music followed certain conventions quite apart from the concerns of everyday language; it was an independent musical language. People did not attend music concerts to hear the words of songs as though they were some kind of religious discourse; for that, one could go to a temple. The music concert was for a different kind of aesthetic enjoyment.

Like Krishnamachari, other opponents of the Tamil music movement argued that it was a political, not a musical, movement, identifying their own cause, the cause of classical music, as purely aesthetic and thus above politics. An editorial in *The Hindu* in 1943 claimed that R. K. Shanmugham Chettiar's demand for Tamil songs was a kind of "extremism" (*Tamiḻ icai makānāṭu ceṉṉai nikaḻcci mālar* 1944, 91). "Raja Sir Annamalai Chettiar has said that the Tamil Music movement is not a political movement. . . . But the resolutions they passed concerning percentages of Tamil songs to be sung on the radio and in concerts seem like an effort to control the propagation of art" (91). The language problem had only recently become an issue in music. "Until now, Tamil Nadu has never seen such exclusiveness/provincialism [*taniyuṭaimai*], and such parochialism will not go on in the future," the editorial continued. For in India there was a long tradition of musicians composing in languages other than their mother tongues and other than those of the place they were living. In the days when Thyagaraja was singing his Telugu songs in Tamil Nadu, when Purandara Dasa, though he was from Maharastra, sang in Kannada, no one complained; when Mirabai and Kabir sang, thousands of people who did not know the language flocked to hear them (92). The editorialist suggested that a classical tradition of music comparable to that of the West had existed in India for countless generations and that the "language problem" should be too provincial and trivial to affect it. In the West, the great composers like Bach and Beethoven were universally recognized, even though they were, technically, German. There might be some in the West who, out of a misguided affection for their own mother tongue, refused to listen to these great composers, but the Western music establishment would never allow such people to dominate (92).

Opponents of the Tamil music movement also made their case on aesthetic grounds, claiming that Tamil was simply not suited to the aesthetics of Karnatic music. The reason that Tamil songs were only sung at the end of concert programs, stated the 1943 editorial, was that Tamil songs didn't provide enough opportunity for vidwans to show their prowess at raga elaboration; they didn't provide enough inspiration for *manōdharma* (improvisation) (*Tamil̲ icai makānāṭu cen̲n̲ai nikal̲cci māḷar* 1944, 95). Moreover, Telugu was thought of by many as "the Italian of the East" (a phrase that dates from nineteenth-century philology), a mellifluous language that was particularly suited to Karnatic music. Krishnamachari, among others, argued that Tamil, with its hard consonant sounds and consonantal endings, was not suited for Karnatic music, that such sounds would ruin the melody. "The words *kuṭṭi*, *kāṭṭi*, and *kātti* may have special meanings. But when the tongue is flowing [*pural̲um*: literally, "wallowing"] in the sound of music, to have to pronounce such sounds as 'iṭ,' 'ip,' and 'it' would interfere with the tempo of the music [Ān̲āl caṅkīta kān̲attil nākku pural̲umpōtu 'ṭ,' 'p,' 't' en̲patellām uccarikka vēṇṭumān̲āl kālap piramān̲am tallip pōyviṭum]" (93). The wallowing tongue produces no articulation; it enables a voice to emerge with a minimum of interference from the tongue—a voice that comes from within the body without being in contact with it. For Krishnamachari and others, what distinguished music from speech and what made a voice musical, was this very bodiless character.

Here, then, was a discourse about musicality being located not in a human subject but in language itself. Musicality was something inherent in language, rather than a property of a subject's relation to the language she spoke; thus, Telugu could be claimed as a more musical language. Thyagaraja himself, argued the opponents of the Tamil music movement, had made the choice to compose in Telugu a hundred years earlier because he had realized it was a more musical language than Tamil; those in the 1940s should follow his example. In arguing that Telugu was better suited to music than Tamil, Krishnamachari and others were suggesting that the proper way to appreciate music was through an ostensibly objective, aesthetic contemplation, to hear it as a musical language that crossed over the boundaries of one's subjective attachment to any mother tongue. T. V. Subba Rao's comment at the 1943 conference of the Madras Music Academy summed it up: "To fix a percentage of songs with reference to any particular language is to make a woeful confusion between literature and music. Sangita is solely the art of expressing beauty in sound; and to require the aid of language is to reduce its power. The grandest achievement of Karnatic music is Raga, which knows no bounds. To insist on language in musical composition is to be deaf to the highest beauty of music. There is none so deaf as those who will not hear good music in whatever language it may be" (Proceedings of the 17th Madras Music Conference, 1943, 12).

Genre and Voice

In the decades after the 1940s, the language issue in Karnatic music was not resolved in the domain of classical music itself but in the proliferation of other categories of music alongside the classical. Thus, beginning in the 1940s, "devotional music" and "film music" came into being as categories distinct from classical music. What distinguished them was the importance given to the words and the audience's understanding of them: devotional music and film songs were in Tamil and appealed to audiences on the basis of their words as well as—or perhaps more than—their music. Since the 1940s, these categories have become increasingly distinct from Karnatic classical music in regard to musical style, the musicians who perform them, and their audiences. They have become industries in their own right, and part of their appeal is their distinctness from Karnatic music.

At the time of the Tamil music movement, however, the same musicians sang all of these genres: D. K. Pattammal and M. S. Subbulakshmi sang on the classical stage many Tamil songs that they also sang in Tamil films of the time; the vocalist Madurai Somasundaram sang Tamil songs on the classical stage in the 1940s that would later be considered devotional rather than classical. A vocalist in Madras who was actively concertizing in the late 1990s pointed out that in principle there was really no difference between classical and devotional music.[30] Thyagaraja, the great classical composer himself, had sung his songs in devotion to the deity Rama; he would have concentrated on the words, not obscured them with elaborate variations and improvisations. In classical music, singers routinely swallowed words but were not criticized for it. But in singing devotional music, the vocalist pointed out, one could not afford to garble any of the words because devotional music uses music as a "communicative medium." The devotional singer has to convey not only a message but an emotional involvement with that message. Thus there is a drastic difference in the ambience of a classical concert and that of a devotional concert; in performing devotional concerts, this vocalist said, he and his accompanists felt much more relaxed and in communication with the audience. Another vocalist who until recently sang both devotional and classical concerts said that any song could be sung in either style; it was a matter of changing one's "technique." One could give a "classical touch" to a song by singing raga alapana, sangatis, and swaras with it or give it "devotional fervor" by singing it plain but with attention to the words.

But as the idea of classical music as a kind of pure, absolute music became the dominant frame for assessing Karnatic music, it became increasingly difficult for musicians who sang in Tamil and paid attention to the enunciation and meaning of words to be considered classical singers. Musicians active in the 1950s, like Sirkali Govindarajan, Dhandapani Desikar, M. K. Thyagaraja Bhagavatar, and K. B. Sundarambal, who sang devotional and film songs as well as classical music, were never fully accepted into the Madras Music Academy's canon of classical musicians; they were instead labeled as "devotional" or "film" singers. Even the vocalist who stated that there was no difference, in principle, between classical and devotional songs revealed that in the 1990s it was not possible to make a name by doing both because you got "labeled" as one or the other; he had decided to sing only classical concerts in an attempt to shed his "devotional" label.

The 1940s debates about the importance of language in music and about what kind of language music was were thus in one way resolved by the partitioning of music into the categories "classical" and "devotional"; "devotional" became the category in which many of the heroes of the Tamil music movement found their place in the 1950s and 1960s. Devotional music became the realm in which expressing oneself in Tamil was privileged. Meanwhile, on the classical stage, after the initial furor of the Tamil music movement, Tamil songs continued to be sung for the most part only in the thukkada section of "lighter" songs at the end of concerts; to this day, only six or seven Tamil songs are generally accepted and sung as classical compositions.

Yet the ramifications of the language debates also play themselves out in perhaps more subtle distinctions of voice. In January 1998 a disciple of the late vocalist Madurai ("Somu") Somasundaram spent the better part of an afternoon explaining to me what was special about his teacher's style. For most of his career, which spanned the period from 1930 to the 1970s, Somu, who belonged to the Icai Veḷḷālar community, refused to sing in any language but Tamil. He carried this to such an extent that he even refused to sing kalpana swaras using the note names *sa*, *ri*, *ga*, *ma*, *pa*, *da*, and *ni*, which he presumed to be Sanskrit. Instead, he sang Tamil words. His concerts always included a long *viruttam*, a type of recitative genre in which the singer elaborates a raga in alapana style while singing lines of Tamil poetry. In demonstrating the style of these viruttams for me, Somu's disciple hit on the most distinctive characteristic of Somu's singing: the passion that was not just in the words he sang but that carried through to his voice. Somu's was a strong voice, with tremendous range, a voice that was not afraid to strain, crack, or leap under the burden of words and their emotion. It was, the disciple explained, distinctly unlike the "Karnatic" style of voice, which was nasal and small, and which proceeded hesitantly and tremulously from note to note. Somu's voice was a truly "Tamil" voice; in singing, his vocal gestures were large, impassioned, and daring. By comparison, the Karnatic style that now predominates emanates hesitation and control. To demonstrate this, the disciple imitated a Karnatic singer trying to find his pitch, starting and restarting, covering one ear, covering both ears. Somu, by contrast, would begin with a large, unhesitating flourish. Another singer who had been trained in singing Tevaram (Tamil religious poetry from the twelfth century) as well as in Karnatic music drew a similar contrast.[31] Karnatic vocalists, he said, sing blandly, without taste (*uppucappu illāmal*: literally, "without salt"), whereas truly Tamil singers like Somu had a *curucuruppu*, a *viruviruppu* (both onomatopoeic Tamil words indicating briskness, crispness). The relation between the singing subject and his/her voice was entirely different in each of these, Somu's disciple implied. In the Tamil style the voice was the unguarded expression of emotion, while in the Karnatic style the voice was controlled as though it were an external instrument. In presenting a voice connected to its mother tongue, Somu's disciple critiqued the Karnatic voice and the Brahmin, middle-class music establishment it had come to represent.

Can the Subaltern Sing?

At one level, the debates concerning the Tamil music movement can be seen as debates about what exactly constitutes classical music. The movement gained prominence at a key moment in the canonization of Karnatic music as the classical music of South India. The role of language in music became a central issue in deciding what repertoire and which musicians would be admitted to the canon. At stake in the debates concerning the Tamil music movement was not just the issue of words but the problem of voice: who could have a voice in Karnatic music, and what kind of voice was it to be?

In discourse concerning the Tamil music movement the specter of an unruly voice figured prominently: as a voice that swallowed, gulped, or "murdered" words; as a voice that sang without emotion, without connection to its owner, and might therefore be coming from anywhere; or as a voice that got carried away with the emotional effect of its mother tongue and forgot the conventions of music. The metaphor of music as a language emerged as an effort to control this potentially unruly voice by once and for all specifying the nature of the relationship between music and words, and therefore the "meaning" of music. But even as the analogy of music to language was used by those engaged in these debates to argue that their cause was "purely artistic" or "natural" and not political, it was appropriated and interpreted in various ways to serve different agendas. For nationalists, considering music as a language was a way of rationalizing music, a way of universalizing it so that it could reach, and subject, in every sense of that word, all the inhabitants of India. For the proponents of the Tamil music movement, the analogy between music and language went both ways, for just as language in music could make a listening subject musical again, music could be invoked to explain a subject's special relationship to his mother tongue; music represented an ideal to which language should aspire. For the opponents of the Tamil music movement, the analogy of music to language meant that music could be conceived as an aesthetically motivated language in itself, which had to be divorced as much as possible from actual language in order to be appreciated.

In chapter 3, I showed how the concept of the voice as issuing from an inner domain and as transcending the body led to a discourse that opposed true or real music against "mere acrobatics." For Rukmini Devi, acrobatics represented the threat of purely physical, automatic action, spectacle without content, exteriority without interiority. Likewise, for the Tamil poet Ramalingam Pillai, writing around the same time as Rukmini Devi, acrobatics represented the polar opposite of what he thought music should be. Watching it was mere *vēṭikkai*, amusement derived from being an onlooker who is not really involved, and not anubhavam, experience derived from direct involvement. According to Ramalingam Pillai, only through language—the Tamil language—could one achieve *anubhavam*. For those holding the opposite point of view, like T. T. Krishnamachari, Tamil songs might provide a pleasant experience for audiences, but they could not provide the experience—and here he used the same word, *anubhavam*—of music, which relied on recognizing music as a language of its own and training oneself to hear it. Significantly, for those on both sides of the debate, the only way one's encounter with music could rise from vēṭikkai to anubhavam was by conceiving music through an analogy with language.

The analogy between music and language depended on the erasure of earlier practices in which music and language stood in other relations to each other. This erasure was partly accomplished by the canonization of Tamil literature and Karnatic classical music as categories mutually opposed in their orientation to the mother tongue. The subsequent debates about language in music reflect a politics of voice that is shot through with the notions of meaning, comprehension, and sincerity demanded of modern musical and linguistic subjects. By insisting on language as a metaphor and model for articulating the relationship between voice and singing or listening subject, this politics of voice engenders the poles of the debate I have analyzed here. What makes this politics of voice a particularly modern approach to music is the way it conceives musical meaning. "Meaning," the key term here, relies on two parallel oppositions. One is the split between linguistic or sonic form and referential content, also conceived as the split between exterior and interior (and the notion, in both cases, that meaning is located in the latter). The other is the split between a speaker's voice or speech and his self, where the (external) voice is assumed to be a reflection of the (internal) self. Indeed, it is this split between exteriority and interiority that is articulated in the contrast between vēṭikkai and anubhavam.

Motivating the debates surrounding the Tamil music movement was the figure of a subaltern, voiceless, still, unresponsive as a statue, deaf by virtue of his "iron ears," and, above all, unable to appreciate music—a figure profoundly disturbing because he seemed to possess no interiority. Members of the Tamil music movement argued their cause in the name of bringing music back to this imagined subaltern in the name of making him sing, of restoring his voice and thus his senses. Yet humming beneath this project was the possibility that the subaltern might already be singing, but with a voice that could be neither domesticated into Karnatic classical music nor assimilated to the desires of the Tamil music movement. Manohar Devadoss's memoir suggests an alternative to the politics of voice, and the insistence on meaning, that came to dominate discussions of music in the mid-twentieth century. For just as nationalists, Tamil and otherwise, rushed to pin down the meaning of music, it had gained a new kind of power. This, as Devadoss eloquently describes, was precisely the power to move, and to affect, without being dependent on the logic of language, and thus to circulate outside the bounds of modernity's claims to its meaning.

5 ⊛ A Writing Lesson

MUSICOLOGY AND THE BIRTH OF THE COMPOSER

The scriptural operation which produces, preserves, and cultivates imperishable "truths" is connected to a rumor of words that vanish no sooner than they are uttered, and are therefore lost forever. An irreparable loss is the trace of these spoken words in the texts whose object they have become. Hence through writing is formed our relation with the other, the past.
—Michel de Certeau, *The Writing of History*

The birth of writing (in the colloquial sense) was nearly everywhere and most often linked to genealogical anxiety. The memory and oral tradition of generations, which sometimes goes back very far for peoples supposedly "without writing," are often cited in this connection.
—Jacques Derrida, *Of Grammatology*

In the mid-1980s a scandal swept through the Karnatic music world. S. Balachander, the flamboyant, self-proclaimed "veena virtuoso," published a booklet entitled *Eḻutiṉār Puttakattai! Kiḻappiṉār Pūtattai!* (He wrote a book . . . and . . . kindled the genie!), in which he argued that the nineteenth-century composer-king of Travancore, Swati Tirunal, never existed and that the compositions attributed to him were really composed by others.[1] Through the 1980s Balachander elaborated his arguments in various publications and open letters, spinning a lurid tale of fake notations, lost books, sequestered palm-leaf manuscripts, and mistaken identity. The arguments that swirled around the case went far beyond the figure of Swati Tirunal himself, bringing into question not only the reliability of notation but the very notion of the composer and the way modern musicology should be conceived.

The debates quieted down with Balachander's unexpected death in 1992. Swati Tirunal was reclaimed as a true composer, and those who doubted him were deemed to be part of an unruly faction with ulterior motives. Yet the Swati Tirunal issue had inserted a kernel of doubt into the firmament of Karnatic classical music. For at the very scene of composing, the original moment of authenticity that made Karnatic music classical, Balachander had posited a scandal. If one composer could be discredited by the historical probing Balachander suggested, couldn't any composer presumably be shown to be a fake by similar methods? What constituted authorship, and what guaranteed authenticity? What order of things made the assertion that Swati Tirunal was a fake appear scandalous?[2]

Issues of authorship and authenticity that reemerged in the Swati Tirunal debate bring into focus the shifts in musical institutions and ideas about music that occurred in the twentieth century. At stake in the Swati Tirunal debate was the boundary between the written and the oral—which had greater authority, and exactly how should the boundary be crossed? The vexed nature of these questions is apparent in the conflicting ideas about the role of notation. Notation was seen both as a site of resistance to the encroachment of Western classical music and as a space of progress. It was imagined both as a guarantor of literacy (and therefore classical status) *and* as a transparent and legible representation of essential orality (and therefore Indianness).[3] In spite of its promises, however, notation was also viewed with ambivalence. The desire to capture the voice in writing was bound up with the fear that the voice could be lost precisely by being completely captured by writing.

At another level, the Swati Tirunal debate brought into question the relationship between theory and practice, text and performance. If theory was meant to provide a structure, or system, underlying the music, how did one determine where basic structure ended and embellishments began? How much of a musical work was original, and how much was added on? Where did one draw the line between composition and improvisation? Such questions point to the intimate connection between the notion of the authorship of the composer and the authority of a system of rules about structure.

A Composer Is Born

Balachander began an open letter to the musicologists of Madras in 1989 with the statement that the Swati Tirunal question was not just a musical issue but also a musicological one.[4] His letter, which summarized what he had already presented in a fifty-page thesis at a press conference in Madras in April 1989, emphasized not merely musical knowledge but the production of that knowledge. First and foremost, Balachander's letter was a statement about the necessity of doing music history, of consulting written sources. In the proceedings for the 1887 jubilee of the Madras Gayan Samaj, a musical organization with branches in both Pune and Madras, he had found the first reference to the musical activities of a certain Kulasekhara Perumal, a musical king of Travancore (r. 1829–1847) who would later be known as Swati Tirunal. This original mention of Kulasekhara Perumal provided the source for all later references used by the Swati Tirunal scholars but had been completely unacknowledged. The reason for this, Balachander stated, was that the reference contained "incriminating evidence" showing not only that the *name* "Swati Tirunal" did not exist in 1882 but also that the composer-king to whom that name was later assigned may also never have existed.[5]

Balachander demonstrated the truth of his assertion using the *Madras Jubilee Gayan Samaj Proceedings*. He began by situating the proceedings historically, amid the late-nineteenth-century revival of interest in Indian music, a revival that focused on standardizing and preserving Indian music. At the center of this revival was the Gayan Samaj, established in Pune in 1874 with the decidedly nationalist purpose of training young boys and girls in their "national" music. In 1883 a branch of the organization was established in Madras. Balachander noted that between 1880 and 1915 the publication of music books with notation was gaining "special attention and momentum."[6] Several musicologists, in fact, had made use of the print media to publish music books with notation. The late nineteenth century, Balachander maintained, was a "transition period" in which the old guru-sisya *parampara* (lineage, tradition) was dying out and being replaced by books with notation and institutionalized teaching methods. In capital letters Balachander trumpeted the first bit of his damning "evidence": "AND, HERE CAME THE IMMEDIATE NECESSITY FOR MUSIC BOOKS WITH 'NOTATION,' FOR USE EVERYWHERE, FOR SALES EVERYWHERE, FOR HOMES AND INSTITUTIONS EVERYWHERE, FOR DOMESTIC USE AND ABROAD."[7]

Balachander proceeded with a close reading of the Gayan Samaj proceedings' account of the 1882 visit to Pune of the then maharaja of Travancore. His analysis hinged on the maharaja's lack of voice in the text. For surely any maharaja—especially one whose close ancestor was a composer-king—who visited a newly established music institution would surely speak a few words of appreciation and encouragement. Yet this maharaja, Balachander commented, merely had his Dewan read a short reply, which perhaps implied that the maharaja had not been so musically minded after all or that he had not even been there. Such speculations were only confirmed by the maharaja's replies to a series of questions asked by the members of the Pune Gayan Samaj. For Balachander, the very fact that these questions and the answers to them were written (not spoken) implied that the maharaja himself could not answer them or was not present to answer them. The questions, submitted as a written memorandum, received a written reply only three years later. The content of the answers, Balachander argued, showed that there was little musical life in Travancore during the so-called composer-king's reign.[8] In answer to the question of whether Hindustani music was practiced in Travancore, for example, the maharaja appeared to reply that primarily Karnatic music was practiced and that, too, "at an indifferent level." To a question regarding whether a particular song had been composed by Kulasekhara Maharaja (presumably Swati Tirunal), the reply should have been a "plain and simple" yes or no, Balachander asserted; a composition (and this shows the late-twentieth-century assumptions under which Balachander was operating) should have had a single, unambiguous author and date. Yet the reply instead obfuscated the matter, saying that it was impossible to date the composition, "as every year His Highness produced lots of them."[9] The last answer, as far as Balachander was concerned, was an "open confession." In answer to a question about music schools in Travancore, the reply stated that there were none and that music was not taught under any system of notation.[10] With this evidence, Balachander proceeded to flesh out his account of the twentieth-century invention of Swati Tirunal.

According to Balachander, the reference to the composer-king Kulasekhara Perumal in the Gayan Samaj publication triggered the imaginations of those in Travancore in the 1920s and 1930s who were interested in positing a Kerala school of Karnatic music that would equal the Tanjore tradition. The compositions that were eventually attributed to Swati Tirunal were actually composed, he maintained, by the musicians employed in the Travancore court. For example, the composer Irayaman Thampi, who had been employed in Swati Tirunal's court, had apparently published a book of the lyrics of his compositions as early as 1854, but this book had been conveniently "lost," Balachander suggested, and many of Irayaman Thampi's compositions had ended up being ascribed to Swati Tirunal. Furthermore, Balachander continued, the royal family of Travancore had appointed musicians to supply notations for compositions by the court musician Tanjore Vadivelu as well, then printed them in their own printing press.[11] These compositions were published in 1916 as having been composed under the royal command of "H. H. the Maharaja of Travancore." Yet several years later, Balachander wrote, these same compositions were claimed as the sole work of "Kulasekhara Perumal."[12] Such a name, which referred more to a lineage than to a particular person, could not satisfy the modern demand that a composer be a single distinctive individual. How could one Kulasekhara Perumal be distinguished from the next? And so, Balachander wrote, the "perpetrators" of the hoax decided to invent a new name: "Yes! They decided to create a new person with the novel star name" of Swati Tirunal, and then claimed this form of naming was a centuries-old ritual convention.[13]

In 1939 a music college by that name opened in Trivandrum, and Harikesanallur Muthiah Bhagavatar, who had been responsible for "rediscovering" and notating Swati Tirunal's compositions, was appointed principal; in the same year, under the direction of Muthiah Bhagavatar, a comprehensive collection of Swati Tirunal compositions was published under the auspices of the Swati Tirunal Academy of Music (K. V. Ramanathan 1996, 18). Balachander stated that as it was the custom for the court musicians to compose in the name of Padmanabha, the tutelary deity of Trivandrum, the perpetrators of the Swati Tirunal hoax conveniently decided to make "Padmanabha" Swati Tirunal's *mudra*, or composing signature.[14] Thus, the newfound composer appeared to have an enormous number of works to his name. In 1940 a portrait of Swati Tirunal was hung in the Madras Music Academy next to the portraits of the trinity to signify his status as a great composer (K. V. Ramanathan 1996, 20). Balachander closed his letter by claiming that the Swati Tirunal question was a problem of naming, of writing—in short, a historiographical issue—and expressed the hope that his own publications and letters would see the fake composer to his rightful end.

Balachander's assertions challenge certain common assumptions about authorship and authority, suggesting that in the twentieth century, older practices in which different principles of authority operated were overlaid by the modern institution of authorship. Publishing compositions "under the command of" the maharaja of Travancore evokes an older form of patronage in which authority lay with the patron, not necessarily with the "original author" of a particular work. The fact that the same compositions were published several years later as the songs of Swati Tirunal suggests an entirely different set of values, one in which authority and authorship are tightly linked; publishing demands a single author who can be named and distinguished from his ancestors. In a similar vein, the idea of a mudra in the lyrics of a composition, now taken as evidence of authorship, may have originated as a very different concept. Mudras, formulaic phrases generally incorporated into the last line of a composition, are now commonly thought of as the composer's "signature" (Peterson 1984, 167–68). The term *mudra* itself has a range of meanings: distinguishing mark, stamp, brand, impress, royal seal, emblem, badge, and mark on a ballot paper (Winslow 1862, 881; Subramaniam 1992, 844). While we might think of such things as signifying an "author" just as a signature does, there is an important difference. Royal seals, emblems, and badges are not just identifying marks but material objects which are themselves endowed with authority precisely because they are standardized and alienable from the figure of authority. Someone who wears a royal badge or stamps a royal seal thus does not *claim authorship* or originality for himself but *invokes the authority* of a king or deity through a standardized or formulaic sign.

Certain composers, such as Thyagaraja, seem to have used their own name, so that many of Thyagaraja's mudras, in the context of compositions addressed directly to the god Rama, translate as "Thyagaraja entreats you" or "May Thyagaraja be your servant"; the author's name is itself incorporated into the lyrics. Other composers' mudras, however, were not their own names but those of the deities in whose name they composed, suggesting a different locus of authority and a different set of ideas *about* authority as well. In his examination of the colonial encounter of Dutch Calvinist missionaries with Sumbanese ritual speech in Indonesia, Webb Keane has suggested that one of the problems that ritual speech posed for the missionaries was that its authority was based on the idea that the words did not originate with the speaker. Contrary to the notion of the sincere speaking subject, the power of ritual speech lay in its capacity to portray the speaker as "someone who is *not* their author or the agent of the actions they perform. . . . The signs of power are conceived to be generated by a source that remains distinct from the bodily individuals who wield them" (Keane 1997, 680). In using the name of a deity, then, a "composer" might be not so much "signing" his work as using the name to invoke or call the deity or king. Instead of referring to the authorship of an absent composer, "Padmanabha" might be a sign that effectively makes the authority of the deity, or the king who worshipped him, present. Indeed, Balachander suggested that it was precisely this latter strategy that nineteenth-century court musicians employed when they composed "in the name of" the tutelary deity of Trivandrum.

In 1982, just before Balachander had come out with his case against Swati Tirunal, K. P. Sivanandam and K. P. Kittappa, descendants of Tanjore Vadivelu, wrote an article for the popular Tamil journal *Kumutam*, in which they argued that Vadivelu and his brothers had merely translated the Telugu songs they had composed for King Serfoji of Tanjore into Sanskrit and inserted the name Padmanabha to make the songs suitable for Swati Tirunal's court.[15] The article brought issues about originality and composers' integrity to the forefront, suggesting that ideas about these subjects in the late twentieth century were different from the logics of authenticity that operated in the royal courts of the nineteenth century. Whereas composing in the late twentieth century carried connotations of originality and individual work, such ideas could hardly have existed in the milieu of the royal courts, where musicians were commissioned to produce songs for their kings and regularly moved between courts. Indeed, when I discussed the Swati Tirunal issue with a musician in Madurai in 1998, he asserted that in those days musicians couldn't have had the same concerns about originality and authorship.[16] They circulated around the courts of South India, composing in the name of whoever happened to be their patron; it didn't matter who composed the pieces as long as they were attributed to the person in power. The life of Harikesanallur Muthiah Bhagavatar was a good example, he argued. Living at the time of the transition from royal courts to music institutions, Muthiah Bhagavatar, like many other musicians who were samasthana vidwans in courts, got an academic position in a music college when those courts folded. While at Mysore, he composed in the name of Mysore's tutelary deity, Chamundiswari. As head of the Swati Tirunal Academy of Music in Travancore, however, he took on the job of notating many of the "neglected" or "lost" Swati Tirunal kritis. The situation of the nineteenth-century musician situation, my informant declared, could be compared to that of a man with a double-bordered veshti: if he wore it on one side, the border would be red, but the next day he could wear it on the other side and have a purple border.

Such speculations about the nature of composing in the nineteenth century seem logical enough. But taking them to the extreme by asserting that *all* the songs attributed to Swati Tirunal were really composed by his court musicians would "lead to chaos in South Indian Karnatic music," declared the violinist V. V. Subrahmanyam. In a small book entitled *Satyameva Jeyate* (Let Truth Reign), Subrahmanyam offered an impassioned refutation of Balachander's allegations. Yet although he was arguing against Balachander, both were waging their battles in a field determined by similar assumptions: art for its own sake, originality, and the sole authorship of the composer. In response to the allegation that Swati Tirunal's songs were really composed by Vadivelu of the Tanjore Quartette, Subrahmanyam noted a story about how Swati Tirunal would not allow his court musicians to compose in his name, insisting that music should be only for god and therefore in the name of the deity. "While the Maharaja has prohibited his courtiers to sing in praise of him will he allow other kritis to be published in his name?" Subrahmanyam asked (1986, 6). Here, he equates Swati Tirunal's prohibition of songs in praise of the king with the idea of art for its own sake, free of political motivation, putting a decidedly twentieth-century spin on a nineteenth-century practice.

Yet there are many ways in which even the twentieth-century practice of Karnatic music militates against such notions of authorship and the composer. The same composition sung by two different people might be almost unrecognizable when sung with different *sangatis* (variations) or elaborated in different spots. The twentieth-century composer Papanasam Sivan, it is said, could hardly recognize his own compositions when they were sung by other musicians (K. V. Ramanathan 1996, 20). The possibility of change to the point of unrecognizability seems to threaten the very idea of original compositions and the authorship of the composer. Subrahmanyam conceded that it was possible that many of Swati Tirunal's compositions would have been greatly embellished by his court musicians when they were sung. But the "framework," he insisted, would remain the same (Subrahmanyam 1986, 8). At stake in the idea of an "essential structure" or "framework" of a composition were the agency and originality of the composer, indeed, the very notion of the composer. The definition of a composition depended on the idea that any song had an essential structure which was laid down by the composer and subsequently varied by other musicians who sang it. Structure implied the use of notation, a method by which the basic structure could be laid out and made permanent. As Balachander alleged that Harikesanallur Muthiah Bhagavatar and his successor at the Swati Tirunal Academy of Music, Semmangudi Srinivas Iyer, had composed the tunes for found lyrics and then attributed them to Swati Tirunal, the controversy moved from discussions of composers' motivations to the definition of composition itself and the proper way to do musicology.

In a response to Balachander, Brig. R. B. Nayar, a musicologist from Kerala, claimed that it was wrong to say that Muthiah Bhagavatar and Semmangudi Srinivas Iyer (popularly referred to as Semmangudi) had dug up lyrics and composed new tunes for them, thus inventing Swati Tirunal's repertoire. Rather, they collected what were already complete compositions with specified ragas and talas, "not just a bunch of lyrics found on palm leaves" (Nayar 1997, 24). The absence of exact notation, in Nayar's view, pointed to another, perhaps even more authoritative oral tradition by which the kritis had been preserved in their "pristine form": the court musicians known as Mullamoodu Bhagavatars. In the court of Swati Tirunal they had sung in a style known as *Sopanam*, a style peculiar to Kerala, characterized by a slower pace and less ornamentation and improvisation.[17] "Unadulterated" versions of these kritis could have been collected with the help of the last generation of Mullamoodu Bhagavatars, claimed Nayar. Through an oral tradition preserved by court musicians native to Kerala, who had no ulterior motives and were permanently bound to Swati Tirunal's court, the original compositions could have emerged into notation. Proper musicology, in Nayar's 1990s vision, would have required listening to the aging Mullamoodu Bhagavatars and painstakingly recording, through notation, exactly what they sang, no more and no less.

The Muthiah Bhagavatar-Semmangudi team, however, worked with a decidedly different notion of what it meant to do musicology. The Dewan of Travancore state, C. P. Ramaswami Iyer, had proposed in 1937 that the musical compositions of Swati Tirunal were a great contribution of the state to culture and should therefore be revived (K. V. Ramanathan 1996, 18). At the request of the royal family, Muthiah Bhagavatar, newly appointed as the principal of the Swati Tirunal Music Academy in 1939, began the task of collecting and notating Swati Tirunal's compositions. His son, H. M. Vaidyalingam, who assisted him, recalled the process: he and his father went to different places in search of elderly people who might remember songs. Muthiah Bhagavatar "reduced" the songs to notation and then "polished" them (*a̲lakupaṭuttu*: literally, "to make beautiful") (ibid., 19). What was involved in this polishing? Apparently it was a process of making the kritis conform to the sound of Karnatic music, rather than to the "original" Sopanam style. Brigadier Nayar states that instead of preserving the songs as they had been sung by the court musicians, Muthiah Bhagavatar and Semmangudi reinvented them, increasing the tempo and adding sangatis that were reminiscent of other Karnatic composers, so that the songs would sound like Karnatic music and please audiences in Madras (1997, 25–26). In the case of compositions where only lyrics were available, Muthiah Bhagavatar and Semmangudi "retuned" the lyrics. Their object seemed to be not recovering an original sound, but instead creating music that was plausible, and pleasurable, to their own ears.

> Muthiah Bhagavatar would identify the raga and tala which seemed appropriate to him vis-à-vis the lyrics and sketch the music for them. Semmangudi would then work on them further. When [Muthiah Bhagavatar] felt satisfied with the outcome, both would go to Maharani Sethu Parvathi Bayi who was highly knowledgable in music. She would listen to the song as . . . reset to tune and rendered by the young research assistant. She might suggest a change here or there but, once she gave her seal of approval, the composition would be considered ready to be released. (K. V. Ramanathan 1996, 18)

Thus, the process of recovering lost music in the 1940s seemed to involve retuning lyrics to the preferences of one's own ear. The newly composed music, when approved by the requisite number of ears, would then be agreed on as the true composition. In this process, the notation was the origin of the composition, the act that brought it into being. By the 1980s and 1990s, however, such a process could not have passed for true musicology.[18] As Balachander's allegations and the refutations of V. V. Subrahmanyam and R. B. Nayar show, musicology at the beginning of the twenty-first century has a decidedly different set of assumptions. Notation, in this new order, refers back to an authoritative act of composition by a single composer: an original act occurring prior to the composition being recorded in written form. Thus it is only through the positing of a voice *before* writing, an authoritative oral tradition, that the notion of the composer becomes possible. Looking at this shift in the order of things between the 1940s and the 1980s, one can see that the notion of an authentic "oral tradition" and the authority of writing to represent it emerged simultaneously.

Nation and Notation

> We fear we must defer the prospect of a universal language of music till the millennium arrives.
>
> —Sourindro Mohun Tagore, "Hindu Music" (1874)

In 1874 the newly founded Pune Gayan Samaj put out a statement of its rationale, which included, among other things, providing an arena in which Indian music would be respected and preserved.[19] After detailing the numerous activities that had been planned in this regard, the statement read, "Lastly, the Samaj will be instrumental in preserving our nationality in the sense of our possessing an indigenous art of singing, which, unlike English music, has challenged all its attempts at being reduced to writing" (Gayan Samaj 1887, 34). A sense of pride in Indian music, according to this statement, followed from the fact that it could *not* be written in notation; this recalcitrance, in fact, was precisely what made it Indian and kept other music from influencing it. Music, in India, was to be kept Indian by being kept away from writing. The Gayan Samaj, in keeping with its spirit of good relations with the British, invited Lord Mark Kerr, whose "vocal powers were of the real indigenous type," to become a member. But Kerr, apparently troubled by the attitude toward notation, replied with a piece of advice.

> You imply, I think, although all possible musical instruments are to be welcomed to perform at the Gayan Samaj, that science can have no place there, for the music to be performed has hitherto challenged [it]. I presume you will continue to defy all attempts to put [your music] in writing. Now without a science, that is to say, knowledge without the power of writing your music, so as it can be made a study of . . . , you can have no art. . . . I, very seriously, invite you to do what, against your opinion, I maintain is very possible, namely—put on paper—put into writing all the quaint and melodious airs that I have heard sung by your children, Mhotvallas, and others. Let this be arranged with care and good taste, and, I repeat, put into writing what has hitherto defied you (35).

Kerr's admonition apparently had its effect. By 1879 the Gayan Samaj was singing a different tune entirely. Its main object had become to convince the Indian intelligentsia and the West that Indian music was an object worthy of study, possessed of "a science . . . such as will vie in its nicety with the Sanskrit grammar, which is recognised as almost the perfection of deductive logic" (Gayan Samaj 1887, 20). The problem, however, was that there was no way to represent this logic. "It is musical notation which we want. . . . It is true we have a musical notation we can claim as our own, but we think it is not sufficient nor elegant enough to mark the various graces of Hindu music with the rapidity of a phonographer" (20). The idea of preserving the Indianness of music by not writing it down had given way to the fear that a lack of notation was causing Indian music to "fade away." The Gayan Samaj announced its plan: "We think the English system of music [notation], such as it is, cannot be adopted by us without making necessary changes; this we mean to do ere long" (20).

Accordingly, during the fateful visit of the Travancore maharaja to Pune in 1882, the members of the Gayan Samaj, headed by Capt. Charles Day, included in their list of questions about music in Travancore a request for "airs written correctly in the European notes" (Gayan Samaj 1887, 23). The reply included a lengthy meditation on the difficulties of putting "Hindu music" into European notation. They went beyond the problem of finding someone who was conversant with both systems of music. How was one to represent the quarter tones, "infinitesmally minute and delicate shades as in a painting by a master artist"? How could one capture the "unbroken easy flow" of a vocalist over half a gamut? Indeed, how could one convey the concept of raga itself? The problem, concluded the writer, was one of "translation" (27). He vowed to have the task attempted by one of the Nayar brigade and, "if it is possible," to have it sent to Captain Day.

Putting Indian music into European notation, then, was not merely a matter of adding extra signs to show the peculiar features of Indian music. It instead involved translation, putting the music into a kind of circulation between two languages. The Bengali musicologist Sourindro Mohun Tagore feared that with such translation Indian music would come to occupy a strange territory, neither properly Indian nor properly Western. In 1874, the same year as the opening of the Gayan Samaj, Tagore was involved in a dispute with the inspector of schools in Bengal, Charles B. Clarke, who had written an article for the *Calcutta Review* advocating the use of staff notation (Farrell 1997, 68). In his lengthy reply, entitled "Hindu Music," published in the *Hindoo Patriot* in 1874, Tagore wrote, "Every nation that has a music of its own has also its own system of notation for writing it. Whether that system be an advanced one or not, it cannot be correctly expressed in the notation of another nation, however improved and scientific it may be. . . . Anglicized as we have become in many respects, we confess we prefer our national system of notation for our national music" (1874, 366). Notation seemed to mark a kind of last frontier, a space of resistance to the encroachment of Western sounds and ideas.

Whereas a few years earlier the preservation of Indian music seemed to depend on the absence of writing, the reverse was now argued; the question of the need for notation was quickly eclipsed by the question of which notation was best for Indian music. Tagore argued for an Indian notation on the grounds that it was simpler and more "natural" than the European staff notation. Whereas European notation required eleven lines to accommodate the different clefs, the Indian system required only three lines. Moreover, in the Indian system, the three lines marked the natural divi-

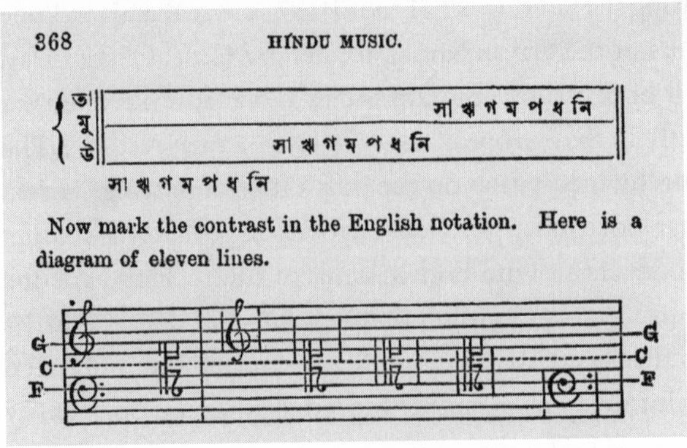
368 HINDU MUSIC.
Now mark the contrast in the English notation. Here is a diagram of eleven lines.
G
C
F

20 Text explaining that Indian staff notation requires only three lines. In S. M. Tagore, *Hindu Music* (1874).

sion of the voice into chest sounds, throat sounds, and head sounds (Tagore 1874, 367). Whereas Clarke had argued that European staff notation was so transparent that a Bengali who knew no English might simply look at the notation and play a piece of Western music, Tagore argued that this was not only impossible but misguided. In contrast to Clarke's vision of a universal notation for all the music of the world, Tagore envisioned a veritable Tower of Babel: the supposedly sufficient staff notation would have to be adjusted and augmented by so many new signs that it would become unrecognizable (382). By contrast, each nation had perfected a system of notation that was transparent to its own musical system, he maintained. In fact, it was so transparent that "in advocating the national system we are simply following reason, truth, and history" (387).

Love at First Sight

Tagore had argued for an Indian system of notation on soundly nationalist grounds. Yet the idea of a universal musical notation so legible and transparent that it could overcome linguistic and national differences held a lingering appeal. The prospect of such notation became the consuming passion of A. M. Chinnaswamy Mudaliar, a Tamil Christian and superintendent of the Madras Secretariat (Raghavan 1961, 1). With a master's in Latin and music from Madras University, and a deep interest in English literature, Chinnaswamy Mudaliar was convinced that European staff notation was the best means of representing and preserving Karnatic music. In 1892 he began a monumental project, the monthly journal *Oriental Music in European Notation*, in which the work of "every composer, living or dead" in South India would be notated in a special adaptation of European staff notation (Chinnaswamy Mudaliar 1892, iv). He and his brother printed the journal with their own press. After finishing the music of South India, Chinnaswamy proposed to notate North Indian music; the music of China, Burma, and other parts of the East; and national anthems from around the world. He also planned to publish a comprehensive dictionary of musical terms, a history of Oriental music and musicians, and a comparative sketch of international music. In an essay in the introductory issue, "The Regeneration of Oriental Music in its Classical Form," he wrote that "any amount of foreign admixture and interpolation is introduced . . . so that the magnificent indigenous system invented by the children of the soil is threatened with prospects of speedy annihilation in the immediate future" (viii). The first step to counteract this was the "reduction" of Karnatic music to staff notation while the second was the explanation of the "fundamental principles of the science, not only in the principal Vernaculars but also in the English tongue, which now bids fair to be the one universal language of the world" (viii). The reduction to staff notation involved not only a translation into English but also an insertion of the music into history: "It is absolutely essential to obtain complete historical records regarding the date and authorship of every piece of music" (ix).

A potent politics of visibility ran through Chinnaswamy Mudaliar's arguments. Never short of metaphor, he characterized the purpose of the notation project as "[bringing] forth into the open air that which lay concealed and neglected like the ruins of an ancient city buried in subterranean vaults; it is hoped that the debris will soon be cleared and beautiful structures underneath exposed to the public gaze" (1892, xii). Indeed, the unveiling, or revealing of Karnatic music before the eyes of the world was the dominant metaphor in Chinnaswamy Mudaliar's writing. It is significant that he included about forty-five pages of introductory explanation before getting to the notations themselves, as if he needed to ensure that the notations would be seen in the right way. He hinted at what he meant in a section called "Difficulties to be Surmounted"; just as it was not possible to express every thought in written language or to convey every quality of the speaking voice, it was also impossible to fully capture music in notation. "No notation however complete can fully or accurately delineate those magnificent foreshadowings . . . which fill the imagination of the composer; not a millionth part of what he then feels can be put down mechanically on paper; but when this has been done, the interpretation given of this skeleton by even the most . . . skillful artist necessarily differs from the rough outlines sketched by the author; how widely it must diverge from his original ideal need hardly be mentioned" (2). He thus conceived of writing, or notating, as a "mechanical" process, opposed to the "feeling," "foreshadowing," and "imagination" of the composer. Yet notation could function as a kind of consolation for the loss of the original, a stylized likeness.

> Nevertheless, as it is considered to be some consolation, in the absence of a person esteemed, to possess his photographic likeness, and as an oleographic portrait taken from a photo is found to be still more acceptable even if it really lacks many a grace and perfection of the living original, so musicians of the land ought to be content with selecting the clearest and most expressive of all existing symbols used in musical language, although those cannot reproduce with absolute precision the extremely subtle ideas of their brains or the deep pathetic emotions of their hearts. (2)

As a kind of consolation for a lost original, notation worked best not according to the logic of the photograph, which claimed to represent what really was, but rather according to the logic of the portrait, a kind of stylistic likeness. The portrait represents by using certain recognizable conventions, by highlighting some things and erasing others; it orders the image a certain way so that it might be recognized, providing a "convincing likeness."[20] Chinnaswamy Mudaliar, similarly, intended his notations to be more prescriptive than descriptive, more like portraits than photography, designed to allow for the future "reproduction" of musical ideas.

The staff notation, Chinnaswamy Mudaliar argued, was better equipped to fulfil this role than Indian notation because it was a "pictorial notation." By taking advantage of the visual medium, he maintained, the staff notation did away with the need for a teacher or reference books; anyone "tolerably conversant" with the principles of staff notation could sing or play "at first sight" what was written. This was because staff notation portrayed the intervals between notes as spatial relations on the staff. By contrast, the Indian method of using the letters that denoted the pitches of the scale (*sa*, *ri*, *ga*, and so on) were written on a straight line, "without any indication to the eye as to whether they ascend or descend in the scale" (1892, 2). Moreover, he continued, in staff notation the pitch of the note and its duration were represented by one and the same symbol, in contrast to the cumbersome method of lengthening syllables to show duration in Indian notation. Finally, Indian notation presupposed a knowledge of the raga; it had no way of showing, for example, whether *ri*-1 or *ri*-2 was to be used without requiring background knowledge of the raga in which the composition was set.[21] All in all, Chinnaswamy Mudaliar stated, "The adaptation of alphabetical characters and numerals for the extremely complicated requirements of music will thus be seen to be a clumsy expedient, as unsatisfactory as it is antiquated. A separate language with suitable symbols is absolutely necessary to ensure the required precision" (3). With staff notation, there would be no necessity to refer to books or teachers; everything would be apparent "at a glance," leaving "no room for doubt, conjecture, or hesitation of any kind. . . . The symbols [would] present readily to the eye every detail which in other methods has to be retained in the memory" (4). "One great advantage," wrote Chinnaswamy Mudaliar, "is that Oriental music will be placed permanently before the *eyes* of the whole world, instead of being addressed in transitory form as at present to the *ears* of a few listeners . . . in other words it will become universal and will no longer remain exclusive" (4). In such a move from ear to eye, he implied, the music was freed from the musicians' memories and allowed to enter the realm of history. Others saw in this newfound visibility a greater potential for originality. One reviewer, commenting favorably on Chinnaswamy Mudaliar's project, wrote that "at present the Hindu has to first hear a tune, and be taught like a parrot before he makes it his own. By the help of the European notation, he will be able to sing hundreds of his national airs without ever having heard them before" (203).

Ornament and Order

Chinnaswamy Mudaliar did note that in order for staff notation to be fully effective, certain symbols had to be added to represent gamakas, the "trills, shakes, slurs, and glissandos" that were typical of Karnatic music. As long as these symbols were standardized and not haphazardly assigned by individual printers, the system of staff notation would leave no room for doubt (Chinnaswamy Mudaliar 1892, 8). Yet the process of notating Karnatic music was not entirely straightforward, he admitted. Where the notation ended and the use of ornament symbols began was problematic; a simple turn could be written out or merely indicated by the symbol ~. The notator had to be able to "discriminate the more important and essential parts of a melody from what may seem its superfluous ornamentation," and thus use the notation and symbols accordingly (7). The symbols, as he demonstrated, left quite a bit of room for doubt as to their actual execution. One could choose instead to write everything out, thus expelling

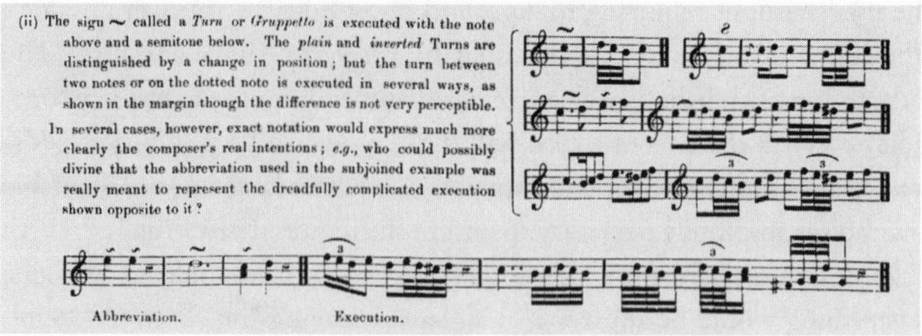
(ii) The sign ~ called a *Turn* or *Gruppetto* is executed with the note above and a semitone below. The *plain* and *inverted* Turns are distinguished by a change in position; but the turn between two notes or on the dotted note is executed in several ways, as shown in the margin though the difference is not very perceptible.

In several cases, however, exact notation would express much more clearly the composer's real intentions; *e.g.*, who could possibly divine that the abbreviation used in the subjoined example was really meant to represent the dreadfully complicated execution shown opposite to it?

21 Text explaining notation for ornaments. In A. M. C. Mudaliar, *Oriental Music in European Notation* (1893). Courtesy of Music Division, The New York Public Library for the Performing Arts.

doubts. But then one ran the risk of obscuring the "essential structure" of the music.

In Chinnaswamy Mudaliar's logic, the relationship between ornament and structure was analogous to that between "spurious" and "original." The goal of his work, he stated, was to "reproduce the compositions of the great masters with all the accuracy and authenticity that can be secured" (1892, 33). However, Karnatic musicians had a tendency to make up variations (sangatis) which the composer had not intended and "tacitly pass them off as genuine" (33). "It becomes therefore a matter of no small difficulty to discriminate between the spurious and the original, and the attention of all educated classes ought to be directed to this point; otherwise there will be nothing which can be recognized as the classical music of the country" (34). Thus, the very idea of classical music depended on the assumption that music had a basic structure as distinct from its ornaments, an original as distinct from later additions. With the help of these distinctions one could also begin to imagine Karnatic music as historical: "What ought to be recognised as genuine originals will be clearly distinguished from additions believed to have been made by later authorities" (34).

The problem of the ornament, which was to appear repeatedly in discussions of notation and musicology, also, for Chinnaswamy Mudaliar, explained the problem of Europeans' distaste for Indian music.[22] Indian music, like Indian architecture, dress, and religion, were distasteful to Europeans at first because they could detect no sense in the profusion of ornaments. "The numerous incisions made on the face of an Indian woman and the saffron paint with which it is commonly daubed are objects of horror to him at first sight, but sooner or later he finds them to be not so despicable after all. . . . The rules enjoining most of the semi-religious observances of the country are readily stigmatized as superstitious and insensate, but are found on close inspection to be some of the best sanitary and hygienic laws ever framed by human legislation" (Chinnaswamy Mudaliar 1892, 8).

A certain politics of visibility was at work here. For anything to be properly available to the European gaze, especially "at first sight," a certain structure or order had to be discernible beneath the surface. To such a gaze, the surface appeared as a kind of mask of insensible repetitions and embellishments. "It is so with Indian music, which lies under a mask at present. Hitherto it has never been written or explained in a form which the Westerner can read or understand. When a kriti is sung before him, he does not see on what principle or in accordance with what postulates the repetitions occur" (Chinnaswamy Mudaliar 1892, 8). To European ears, such repetitions gave way to a feeling of "monotony," because they could not locate a vantage point or a structure within the music. For the Indian, by contrast, repetition was the source of musical enjoyment: "Every Indian . . . knows when and where to expect repetitions and variations during the recital of a melody. . . . The listener understands why and wherefore the repetitions occur, and is moreover entranced by the meaning attached to the words so often repeated" (9). Notation, Chinnaswamy Mudaliar suggested, would turn Europeans' distaste into pleasure; not only would it do away with unnecessary repetition, but it would also give them the sense of structure they so craved. Moreover, it would give them an idea of what to expect, a first glance that would eliminate the possibility of surprise and monotony from their listening experience. In the process, by juxtaposing a written, "permanent" notation to an oral, "transitory" performance, it would give the impression that the "original" lay in what was written, rather than in the performance.

After a lengthy description of the "peculiarities of Oriental music," the journals published by Chinnaswamy Mudaliar included about 120 pages of notated compositions. For each composition, the first words of the song were given in English letters at the top, with Telugu and Tamil underneath. Underneath that, he indicated the original language of the composition. At the top left, the mode (*melakarta*) of the raga was given, then the raga and tala. The top right indicated the composer's name, as well as advice on how to count, with a tempo derived from the metronome. Beneath was advice on the "style of execution," usually in Italian: *staccato*, *allegro*, *dolce*, *con spirito*, and so on. The first line of notation showed the *arohanam* and *avarohanam* (ascending and descending order) of the raga scale in staff nota-

22 South Indian composition in staff notation, with words in English, Telugu, and Tamil. In A. M. C. Mudaliar, *Oriental Music in European Notation* (1893). Courtesy of Music Division, The New York Public Library for the Performing Arts, Astor, Lenox and Tilden Foundations.

tion (transcribed in the key of C for the convenience of keeping the notes within the staff), with the Indian note names written underneath. The composition itself was written in continuous fashion, with each variation marked off by a repeat sign. The lyrics were written beneath the staff, in English, Telugu, and Tamil characters respectively, and were repeated with each variation. In general, Chinnaswamy Mudaliar eschewed symbols for gamakas, instead writing them out note by note.

What kind of order did such a representation produce? First, it made the compositions clearly visible in English; the other languages, placed underneath the English characters, appeared secondary. Meanwhile, although groupings of measures were marked out by repeat signs, the continuous progression of the music across the page, as well as the injunction to count by individual notes (or "quavers"), suggested that the measure, not the tala cycle, was the main unit. The tala, as an organizing principle, was thus effectively made invisible. Whereas a musician using sargam notation would most likely arrange the notation by having one tala cycle per line, or one line of the composition's lyrics per line, the run-on quality of Chinnaswamy Mudaliar's notation gave the impression that the music followed not the structure of the tala or the lyrics but the staff itself. Indeed, whereas a Karnatic musician might end each section of the composition with an improvised flourish—something that would be hard to capture in any form of notation—Chinnaswamy Mudaliar neatly resolved the end of the pallavi to the tonic, C, providing precisely the kind of ending that those accustomed to looking at staff notation would find understandable.

Timothy Mitchell has discussed this idea of a homogenous, empty structure that orders space and time as an essential element of the colonial gaze and the modern production of knowledge. In such a gaze, which he characterizes as "enframing," the appearance of order depends on the illusion of a structure apart from the things themselves, the division of space and time into exact and precisely repeating units that seem to exist independently of what they contain (Mitchell 1988, 85–86). Chinnaswamy Mudaliar's notations, with their profusion of notes placed in the uniform spaces provided by the staff, gave the impression of order, of exactness and completeness. Minimizing the presence of the tala as an organizing principle, he effectively substituted a disembodied unit of time, the repeating measure, with each measure being the same as the one coming before and after it. While one might argue that tala, as a repeating cycle of defined units of time, provides just this sort of enframing structure, there is a crucial difference that emerges in performance. While tala might look like an abstracted, empty structure on paper, in practice it is deeply embodied. Musicians "keep tala" using a variety of finger counts and claps whose purpose is ostensibly to make the tala (or where one is in the tala cycle) visible to others; yet the finger counts and claps are also, and more primarily, ways of embodying or feeling where one is in the cycle. Musicians learn to associate the *feel* of a finger count or clap with a particular place in the cycle and thus with a set of musical possibilities that can begin at that point. Far from being an enframing structure apart from its contents, then, tala, when embodied in performance, intimately connects form with content.

Meanwhile, the very idea of "notes," as implied by the staff notation, was considerably different from the Indian term *swara*, which conveys not so much a note as a kind of placeholder that might in actuality include several notes.[23] For instance, when a musician sees the swara *pa*, he does not just sing the fifth note of the scale but a combination of several notes which focus on or approach *pa*, using his knowledge of the raga. In other words, a musician using sargam notation employs it as a clue, to jog the memory or to inspire the singing of a spontaneous variation; the notation is not regarded as a sufficient record in itself. Chinnaswamy Mudaliar's notations, by contrast, placed themselves in quite a different relation to the musician's memory. In his vision, the notes arranged on the staff could replace the musician's memory; they would represent the entire composition, leaving, as he often emphasized, "no room for doubt or hesitation."

The liberation of the musician from the limits of his memory, in Chinnaswamy Mudaliar's logic, would produce not only musical but also social progress. In a long footnote to his explanation of the "Peculiarities of Oriental Music," he railed against the secrecy and competition among Indian musicians, and the money-mongering of gurus: "In India it is with the greatest difficulty that a professional musician is ever induced to impart to others the music he had learnt. . . . 'Teach music to none but your son, your guru's son, or to him who gives you wealth incessantly' is the rule observed by most musicians. . . . In India all the knowledge and proficiency acquired by each connoisseur is kept a profound secret" (1892, 29). If notation could effect a liberation from such "gurus," it might also prove a way for respectable women to learn music. In 1884 A. Govinda Charlu wrote in the *Mysore Herald* that with the use of notation "some of our lady pupils may become original composers" (ibid., 209). The staff notation was "perfected" compared to the "crude and clumsy" Indian notation; through it, "songs could be mastered from the mere books." In this way, respectable housewives could learn music without having to learn from their social inferiors. Meanwhile, they could keep their husbands happy and occupied: notation was the "solution [to] the much talked of Anti-Nautch Girl question" (209).

Although Chinnaswamy Mudaliar's project folded after several years due to lack of financial support, his ideas about staff notation were echoed by others in the early decades of the twentieth century. Among these was H. P. Krishna Rao, who published his ideas about notation in 1906 in *First Steps in Hindu Music in English Notation*.[24] "Hindu music is very ancient, scientific, and interesting," he wrote in his preface. "But the sad want of a method for committing musical ideas to writing has left the fine art stagnant and unfamiliar. The seven notes, *Sa, Ri, Ga, Ma, Pa, Dha*, and *Ni*, do not, as now written, represent the pitch or time accurately, and thousands of compositions of great authors are therefore either being lost or mutilated. To serve as a means for making permanent records of musical compositions, and to enable students to learn them in the absence of a teacher, this little book has been written" (1906, 3). Krishna Rao began by showing how the notes of the Indian scale were to be placed on the staff. The transposition was metaphorical as well as literal. Once transposed onto the staff, a raga appeared as "a melodious combination of particular notes" (9), rather than a set of phrases or motifs employing certain gamakas. Moreover, staff notation introduced elements that were never conceptualized in Karnatic music, such as rests and dynamics. This is not to say that such things did not exist in Karnatic music but that they were not considered a specifiable element of music to be written out and consciously learned.

Krishna Rao's book demonstrated the way the transposition to staff notation thus radically reconfigured Karnatic music, even as he insisted on total translatability from one musical system to the other, and, in the process, to the English language. Even as Krishna Rao argued for the transparency of the notation such that "a knowledge merely of the English alphabet is enough to enable a student to understand the work," his method showed how staff notation and its foreign symbols propelled a translation of Karnatic musical terms into English (1906, 3). For instance, *tala* was translated as "time," *avarta* as "measure," and the particular tala of a composition was equated with the "time signature" in staff notation. *Gamaka* was translated as "grace," and the individual names for different kinds of gamakas were given English names like "slur," "merge," "shake," "trill," and

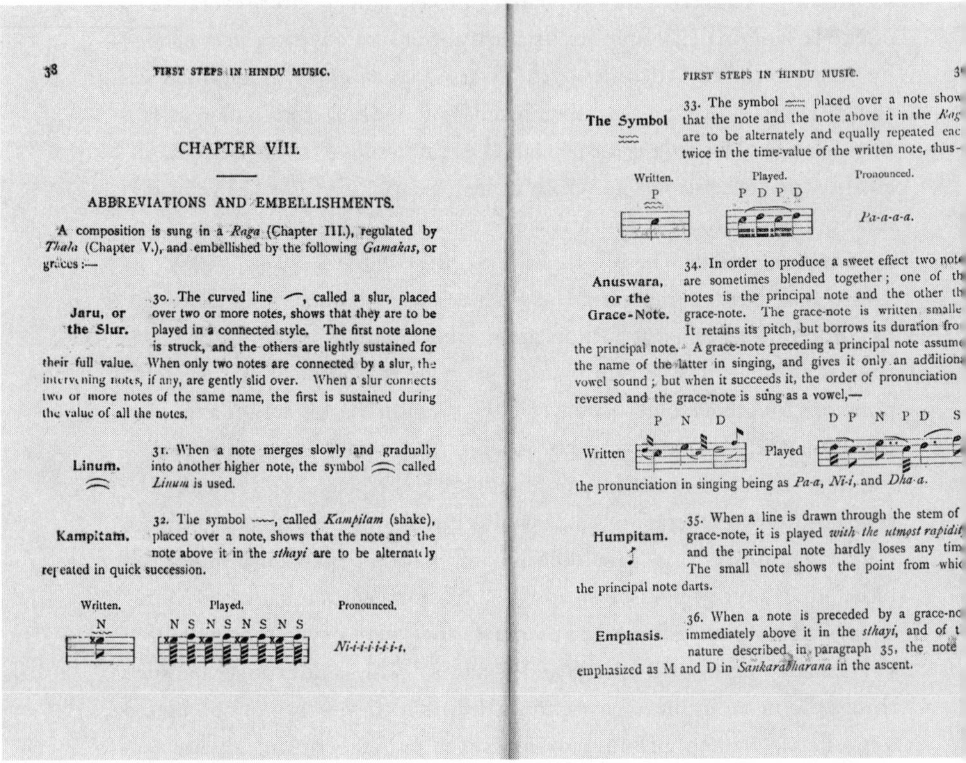
38 FIRST STEPS IN HINDU MUSIC.

CHAPTER VIII.

ABBREVIATIONS AND EMBELLISHMENTS.

A composition is sung in a *Raga* (Chapter III.), regulated by *Thala* (Chapter V.), and embellished by the following *Gamakas*, or graces :—

Jaru, or the Slur. 30. The curved line ⌒, called a slur, placed over two or more notes, shows that they are to be played in a connected style. The first note alone is struck, and the others are lightly sustained for their full value. When only two notes are connected by a slur, the intervening notes, if any, are gently slid over. When a slur connects two or more notes of the same name, the first is sustained during the value of all the notes.

Linum. 31. When a note merges slowly and gradually into another higher note, the symbol called *Linum* is used.

Kampitam. 32. The symbol ~~~, called *Kampitam* (shake), placed over a note, shows that the note and the note above it in the *sthayi* are to be alternately repeated in quick succession.

Written.	Played.	Pronounced.
N	N S N S N S N S	*Ni-i-i-i-i-i-i.*

FIRST STEPS IN HINDU MUSIC. 3

The Symbol 33. The symbol placed over a note show that the note and the note above it in the *Rag* are to be alternately and equally repeated eac twice in the time-value of the written note, thus-

Written.	Played.	Pronounced.
P	P D P D	*Pa-a-a-a.*

Anuswara, or the Grace-Note. 34. In order to produce a sweet effect two note are sometimes blended together; one of th notes is the principal note and the other th grace-note. The grace-note is written smalle It retains its pitch, but borrows its duration fro the principal note. A grace-note preceding a principal note assume the name of the latter in singing, and gives it only an addition vowel sound; but when it succeeds it, the order of pronunciation reversed and the grace-note is sung as a vowel,—

Written P N D Played D P N P D S

the pronunciation in singing being as *Pa-a*, *Ni-i*, and *Dha-a*.

Humpitam. 35. When a line is drawn through the stem of grace-note, it is played *with the utmost rapidit* and the principal note hardly loses any tim The small note shows the point from whic the principal note darts.

Emphasis. 36. When a note is preceded by a grace-no immediately above it in the *sthayi*, and of t nature described in paragraph 35, the note emphasized as M and D in *Sankarabharana* in the ascent.

23 "Abbreviations and Embellishments." In H. P. Krishna Rao, *First Steps in Hindu Music* (1906). Courtesy of Music Division, The New York Public Library for the Performing Arts, Astor, Lenox and Tilden Foundations.

24 Composition in raga bilahari in sargam and staff notation. In H. P. Krishna Rao, *First Steps in Hindu Music* (1906). Courtesy of Music Division, The New York Public Library for the Performing Arts, Astor, Lenox and Tilden Foundations.

"grace-note." The effect of such translation was that the Karnatic musical terms seemed to fit seamlessly into the syntax of an English sentence about music: "A composition is sung in a *Raga*, regulated by *Tala*, and embellished by *Gamakas*, or graces" (38). Such a statement not only assumes a one-to-one correspondence with the English terms *scale*, *time signature*, and *graces* but also fits these three elements—raga, tala, and gamakas—into a hierarchy of importance. For Krishna Rao, the excesses produced by the process of transposition, it seemed, could be effectively tamed by translation.

A Picture for the Ear

If in 1874 the argument had been over the question of whether Indian music could be notated at all, by 1916 the need for notation was taken completely for granted. The debate now centered around the question of which notation, the staff or the Indian, was best suited to representing Karnatic music. Yet this idea of representation had taken on a different cast. No longer did it refer only to the representation of sounds by written symbols; it now also implied a representation of Indianness. In statements made at the first All-India Music Conference in 1916 at Baroda and after, it was argued that notation was related to music as written language was to spoken language.

Ten years after he had eloquently illustrated the benefits of European staff notation, H. P. Krishna Rao appeared at the Baroda conference with an entirely different message. In a short section of his lecture, entitled "Notation and Music," he declared that the Indian sargam notation was superior to staff notation. "Every kind of language must have its own notation" (1917, 27). His view of language was quite expansive; it covered "word-language," "sign-language," and "sound-language." If the alphabet was the notation for word-language and painting the notation for sign-language, musical notation was the notation for sound-language (27). Indian sargam notation was much more suited to the task of representing Indian music, he argued, since Indian notation allowed the musician to see the note name and its pitch simultaneously, which gave it an advantage over staff notation. It kept notation in the domain of language, instead of necessitating a detour through visual symbols; an Indian musician's response to sargam notation was, he maintained, as simple and automatic as a "reflex." "Musical instruction begins with singing the notes Sa, Ri, Ga,

Ma, etc. By constant practice a reflex action is established in the brain, by which the mere remembrance of the letter Sa or Ri takes the voice at once to its proper pitch, and an Indian singer displays, therefore, a wonderful capacity for singing songs by means of the names of the notes only . . . and not the dumb syllables 'La, la, la,' as done in the West" (28). The note names, Krishna Rao argued, were motivated by years of practice, until they literally spoke for themselves, whereas staff notation remained "dumb." He illustrated his point with an explication of the "psychic processes that take place when we see a note Sa, Ri, or Ga written on paper. The image of the letter is conveyed to the brain through the optic nerve; by simple association its name is ascertained, and the impression is transferred to the nerve controlling the vocal chords, and then the correct pitch of the note is sung" (28). The psychic processes involved in reading staff notation were far more convoluted: "(1) The image of the note is conveyed to the brain, (2) an enquiry is set up as to the name of the note with reference to the clef and the key signature, (3) association of the name, (4) reflex action of the remembrance of the name of the note and its pitch" (28). Reading staff notation thus involved "an extra psychic feat," because it made the note names invisible. It was like translating from a foreign language; an additional step was required to make the staff notation speak. Not only that, but staff notation constantly, by mere displacement of a note, threatened to become illegible, since "the same symbol represents seven different notes." Krishna Rao's lecture took on the tone of a colonial official disgruntled by the evasiveness of the natives. "The crotchet is the chameleon on the hedge. It changes its colour, form, and its name. The staff notation is therefore seven times as difficult as the Indian notation" (28). The sargam notation, by contrast, was so legible that the viewer hardly had an impression of reading at all; it was as if the notes spoke to him from the page. "The native notation," Krishna Rao concluded, "is a picture for the ear; while the staff notation is for the eye" (29).[25]

The idea that Indian notation spoke for itself contrasted with the idea that staff notation was a transparent, universal medium, capable of representing any music. M. S. Ramaswamy Aiyar, a musicologist and superintendent of police in Madras, published an impassioned argument for Indian notation as an appendix to his biography of Thyagaraja, in which he condemned the "staff mania" of people like A. M. Chinnaswamy Mudaliar (1927, 185). He began his argument with the same question Chinnaswamy had raised: "Can we, who see unmistakable signs of progress in all other directions, suffer ourselves to be blindfolded in the matter of preserving music for the ages?" (182). Yet for Ramaswamy Aiyar, the danger of losing the music was equaled by the danger of becoming too Westernized. According to him, the way to "resuscitate our fallen music" was to use sargam notation. There was, he wrote, a direct fit between Indian music and Indian notation, much like the relationship between a language and its alphabet (179). To illustrate his point, he refuted the argument made in 1921 by "an educated Indian lady with University honors." In making a case for staff notation, she had written, "With staff notation, our music will be studied and appreciated by the Americans, the English, etc; and there is the chance of Indian music becoming universal and popular and still Indian. If we wish to be recognised as a nation, we must make others see the greatness and the superiority of all that we possess. How did our great religion find its way to the United States of America? It was through the common medium—English" (189). Such a logic, Ramaswamy Aiyar maintained, was akin to asking that Indians forget their own languages and only speak in English. "True," he wrote, "Swami Vivekananda employed English in the United States of America to assert the superiority of Indian religion. But did he ever ask the Indians to forget their own vernaculars in favour of English?" (191–92). Adopting staff notation for Indian music had already been attempted by A. M. Chinnaswamy Mudaliar, Ramaswamy Aiyar remarked, but it had not been very popular. "For aught I know, the Europeans discarded it because there was Indian music in it, and the Indians equally discarded it, because there was the staff in it" (192). The point was that "different races possess different auditory faculties and hence different systems of music came rightly into existence" (192). Notation may have been only the outward sign of this difference, but it had the capacity, like the words of a mother tongue, to travel inward through the ear, to activate the voice. Ramaswamy Aiyar brought his point home by locating the notation question within the metaphor that dominated the language politics of Madras at the time: "Inasmuch as the mother's milk of the Indian notation is plentiful for the Indians, why should a foreign doctor hoarsely cry and unduly praise to the skies the unnecessary Mellin's food of the staff notation?" (193).[26]

For Ramaswamy Aiyar, the effectiveness of Indian sargam notation lay in the fact that, whereas staff notation was a "visual" method, sargam notation was "visuo-aural," appealing not only to the eyes but also to the ears (1927, 186). Sargam notation had the power to effect a peculiar simultaneity of sight and sound: "If, with a [raga] given, an Indian note *Ga* is written on a piece of paper, the ear—as soon as the eye is directed to the note—rings within itself the sound peculiar to *Ga*. But if a European crochet is written, you cannot at once give it its proper sound. . . . Some more ceremony has to be performed on it" (196). Such statements about the conversion of written notation into sound reveal a supreme confidence in the power of notation and the necessity for it. Notation was not only deemed superior to memory; it was now also absolutely necessary in order to be able to hear and understand music. Ramaswamy Aiyar illustrated the superiority of sargam notation with a story from real life.

> "But you have no such thing as Sargam or any Indian notation at all," may retort the puffed advocates of the staff. So indeed was Mr R (a Hindu musician) taunted some ten years back at Baroda by Mr F (a Portugese musician); and their further conversation which actually took place may be of some interest to the reader.
>
> Mr R: Is not the object of notation to preserve a song, and if need be, to reproduce it?
>
> Mr F: I should think so.
>
> Mr R: Suppose I preserve your song by recording it in my notebook and reproduce it whenever required; will you then grant that we do have our own notation?
>
> Mr F: Surely.
>
> Forthwith Mr F sang a snatch and Mr R reduced it to his sargam notation and even reproduced it. But Mr F would not be satisfied and thought that Mr R wrote in his notebook some nonsense but correctly reproduced the song by the strength of his memory. They therefore parted for the day but met again the next morning. At once Mr F took Mr R to a lonely place and challenged him to reproduce, if he could, the song sung the day before. To Mr F's utter disappointment, Mr R reproduced the song admirably enough. The table was now turned. Mr R challenged Mr F thus:
>
> "Now, sir, I have reproduced your song and thus proved that we do have our own Indian notation. I shall sing for you a Hindu air and let me see how and when you will reproduce it."
>
> So saying, Mr R sang a well-known kriti of Tyagaraja's in Bhairavi. Mr F trembled before it, just as Arjuna did before Lord Krishna's Viswaroopa, and confessed:
>
> "O! It is all Greek to me. I cannot in the first place conceive your song, much less can I reduce it to my notation." (203–4)

Inexhaustible Ambrosia

If notation had emerged, by the 1920s, as necessary for the proper understanding of music, it was based on the idea that memory alone was no longer equal to the task of perpetuating a classical tradition. One thing that advocates of the staff notation as well as the sargam notation could agree on (even the likes of Mr F and Mr R) was that it was not memory but the ability to write and read notation, and to traffic easily between the oral and the written, that made the musician. This conviction explains the efflorescence of music books, song collections and manuals, that began to appear at the turn of the twentieth century.

In 1895, his eyesight suffering from years of notating and casting the type for his *Oriental Music in European Notation*, A. M. Chinnaswamy Mudaliar began a correspondence with Subbarama Dikshitar, the grand-nephew of the composer Muthuswamy Dikshitar. Subbarama Dikshitar was then serving as the asthana vidwan (court musician) at the court of Ettayapuram, a small princely state south of Madurai known for its patronage of the arts. Between 1895 and 1899, Subbarama Dikshitar made several long trips to Madras to stay with Chinnaswamy, teaching him the compositions of Muthuswamy Dikshitar and confirming the correctness of Chinnaswamy Mudaliar's staff notation (Raghavan 1961, vii). In 1899, however, literally blinded by his love of staff notation, Chinnaswamy Mudaliar found himself unable to carry out the printing and publication of these works. He therefore made a trip to Ettayapuram and appeared before the maharaja himself to convince him that the samasthanam should take up the task of publishing, if only in the old Telugu notation, Subbarama Dikshitar's entire repertoire. Chinnaswamy Mudaliar had appealed to Subbarama to put down in writing and notation everything that he knew, "without hiding anything" (ibid.). In the English preface to the original version of the monumental work that resulted, published in 1904, C. Nagojee Rau wrote that Subbarama, "though unwilling at first to part with what he naturally regarded as a precious heirloom to be jealously guarded and retained within his family, yielded in the end to the wishes of his master and patron, the Rajah. . . . The stores of music literature in his possession would, in the course of nature, have been lost to the world in a few years if this work had not been published now" (ibid, viii). Indeed, the publishing of the notation seemed to perform precisely the effect of wresting it from the hands of death: Chinnaswamy Mudaliar passed away in 1901, as the printing was getting started, and Subbarama passed away in 1906, a mere two years after the *Sangīta Sampradāya Pradārṣini* was published (ibid).

The *Sangīta Sampradāya Pradārṣini*, in its original Telugu version, published in 1904, came to a staggering 1,700 pages. Its compass was decidedly encyclopedic: not only did it contain notations of 229 Muthuswamy Dikshitar kritis, as well as works of other composers, but it also contained biographies of musicians and authors of musicological treatises, an exhaustive tabular list of ragas with their characteristics described, a descriptive guide to the gamaka-signs and tala-signs employed in the notation, and notes on the problem spots in the rendering of the works vocally and instrumentally (Raghavan 1961, viii). The work exuded systematization; indeed, it was later taken as a model by V. N. Bhatkhande in his calls for a systematization of Hindustani music (ibid, ix). The notations were arranged by the seventy-two melakartas, a system of classifying ragas based on the notes they used. Eleven different symbols were used to convey different types of gamakas, as well as symbols for sharp, natural, and flat signs to convey pitch and lines above the notes to convey tempo.

The simultaneous emergence of notation and printing technology at the end of the nineteenth century led to another genre: the music manual or self-instruction book. If notation was beginning to be seen as a form of writing which could replace the musician's memory, it was also seen as being able to replace the guru, or teacher. At the same time as debates about notation were emerging, the Taccur Singaracaryulu brothers, well known in the music world of Madras as teachers, published a series of graded textbooks on Karnatic music in Telugu. The first of these books, *Gāyakaparijatam*, appeared in 1882. In the English preface to a later book of the series, Swami Vidyananda Paramahamsa recalled how the Taccur brothers had recreated the musical world of Tanjavur in Madras by hosting Sunday concerts at their house in George Town, which served as a gathering place for musicians from Madras and elsewhere (Singaracaryulu 1912, 26–27). He claimed that the publication of the *Gāyakaparijatam* began a "musical revolution," unlike music books published before it, which were "miscellaneous compendia" of songs. In these previous books, "the teacher was absent"; there was nothing but "a veneer of abstract notes . . . for the songs" (ibid., 8). The innovation of the Taccur brothers was to provide notation not only for gitams and varnams, but also for kritis; for "[previously] the notes to be applied to these pieces were merely sealed property. . . . The rule was always to hear and learn" (ibid., 17). Of the *Gāyaka*

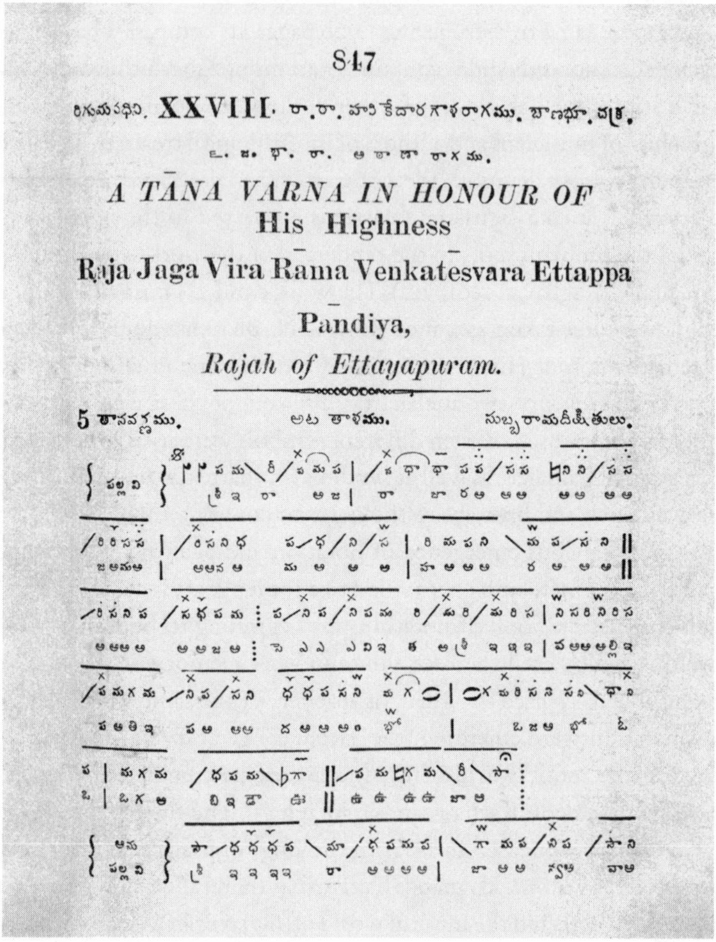
847
XXVIII.
A TĀNA VARNA IN HONOUR OF
His Highness
Raja Jaga Vira Rāma Venkatesvara Ettappa
Pāndiya,
Rajah of Ettayapuram.
5

25 Typical page of notation from Subbarama Dikshitar's *Sangīta Sampradāya Pradārṣini* (1904). Sargam notation is in Telugu script, employing symbols for gamakas and sharp, flat, and natural notes, with words in Telugu under each line of notation.

Siddhanjanam, the fifth book of the series, Swami Paramahamsa wrote that "it really was the unguent for clearing the eyes of the world of music; the kirtanas which were mere words now became invested with their respective accompanying notes" (ibid., 18). The Taccur Singaracaryulu brothers carried out their work despite the outrage of professional musicians, who apparently felt that their secrets were being betrayed and that they would lose earnings from having the knowledge so cheaply available through books. But their objections were "altogether silenced by the uproar of the lay public and the relief and joy especially of the self-instructors of music" (ibid., 18). The triumph of these books was that they placed musical progress in the hands of the student; "any person," Paramahamsa wrote, "can become a musician by dint of self-help and perseverance" (ibid., 20). After a beginning course with a music teacher, he maintained, "the use of the *Siddhanjanam* is enough for making a musician, and a finishing touch can be acquired by a few months' apprenticeship under some renowned master" (ibid., 18).

How did the Taccur brothers endow their music books with so much teacherly authority? First, they claimed a direct connection to Thyagaraja through the Tanjore court; indeed, the elder (*pedda*) Singaracaryulu was a younger contemporary of Thyagaraja. Second, the idea of a graded series of books implied that there was a logic or progression to them, a process of learning that should be the standard for every musician. Rather than confronting the reader with a miscellaneous collection of songs, the books dispensed musical knowledge according to degrees of difficulty.[27] The introductory book, *Svaramanjari*, began with an explanation of the notes of the scale and a table of talas in Karnatic music. It then introduced the sarali varisai, the most elementary exercises, and a number of gitams, short, easy compositions meant to show the fundamental aspects of raga, tala, and sahityam (lyrics). The second book, *Gāyakaparijatam*, provided twenty more gitas of a more difficult variety, as well as twenty-seven varnams (a genre akin to an etude which explores the possibilities of a raga). After the varnams were about eighty notated compositions by various composers. The third book, *Sangīta Kalānidhi*, included the method of classifying the ragas by the 72-melakarta scheme, a classification and description of different kinds of gamakas, and the aspects of tala. A separate section dealt with the theory of rasa and the essentials of abhinaya (facial expression) and gestures used in the "nautch dance." The last part contained 143 notated kritis as well as other varieties of composition, such as padams, *thillanas*, and javalis. The *Gāyakalōchana*, the fourth book, began with a discussion of the origins of music (in the Vedas). It then provided an exhaustive survey of ragas, including the suitable hours for each one, concluding with an alphabetical list. An exhaustive treatment of tala, showing the permutations that led to hundreds of different talas, was followed by more than 200 notated compositions of all varieties. The fifth book, *Gāyaka Siddhanjanam*, contained notation for another 210 compositions, as well as for about fifteen Hindustani compositions. A long chapter discussed the method for developing alapana in sixty of the most popular ragas of the day. The final book, *Ganendu Sēkaram*, contained lakshana gitams for all seventy-two of the melakarta ragas and derived ragas, followed by *tanams* (improvised patterns of notes sung in semi-free rhythm sometimes following the alapana). In addition to more notated kritis, as well as notations for English notes, there was a list of the pallavis sung by masters in the past.

The Singaracaryulu brothers' books did what no other book since the ancient treatises on music had done: they provided, in written form, a discussion of a body of music theory and showed how the theory related to the practical art of music. Yet unlike the treatises, which were in Sanskrit, these books were in the vernacular; unlike the treatises, which were available only in palm-leaf manuscripts, these books were printed in mass quantities and sold for a nominal fee. Moreover, the books provided notation for many more compositions than a single musician could ever know or sing in a lifetime. The profusion of notation in the closely printed pages of the books gave the reader nearly a thousand compositions from which to choose. The possibility of possessing so many compositions in notation, compositions which one might never have even heard before, must have been quite revolutionary in a world where (as I was told by several older musicians) a musician might have previously had a repertoire of only twenty songs which he would sing over and over again. A hint of this change in attitude toward repertoire appears in a review of A. M. Chinnaswamy Mudaliar's project in 1894, in which the author suggested that "twice or thrice" the number of kritis should have been included: "Old 'Kritees' are sung over and over again to a tiresome extent, and the absence of novelty takes away from the very charm of music. Thyagayya's store alone is so vast, that to those who wish there is an inexhaustible Ambrosia that may be drawn out of it" (Chinnaswamy Mudaliar 1892, 208).[28] With the monumental notating projects of Subbarama Dikshitar and the Singaracaryulu brothers, the concept of musical repertoire was completely changed; it now referred to a vast store of musical compositions, each of which claimed its status as a "composition" precisely by being notated.

Total Translatability

The Singaracaryulu brothers' books provoked a flurry of publications on music in Tamil in the early twentieth century. The earliest of these was D. Narayanaswamy Mudaliar's *Tamil Sungeatha Surabooshany*, "for those who are learning music." Published in 1900, it contained the usual beginning exercises, sarali varisai and alankarams, as well as notations for gitams and varnams, a list of the melakarta ragas, and an explanation of tala. The notation, highly condensed, is divided by note groupings rather than divisions of the tala, while the layout of the book (its small size, the fact that pages must be turned in the middle of compositions) suggests that it is meant less for the eye and more as a reference book. On a much grander scale was T. C. R. Johannes's *Bhārata Sangīta Svāya Bōdhini* (Indian music self-instructor), published in 1912. It included chapters on every aspect of music, from the theory of rasas and the 72-melakarta scheme to an explanation of the metronome and the intricacies of konnakkol, as well as notation for numerous compositions (including English notes). As its title and the layout of the notation indicate, the book is meant to be self-sufficient, capable of teaching, instead of serving as a mere reference. Each notated composition includes the murchana, or characteristic ascending and descending pattern of the raga, the sahityam, written above, and uses lines to indicate tempo and dots to separate the music into phrases. The beginning exercises, like the sarali varisai and janta varisai, were furnished with Tamil sahityam so that the learner could, in effect, know how the music was supposed to sound merely by seeing it on the page. That is, the learner could associate the sound and rhythm of a language he already knew with music in order to make that music less foreign.

Around the same time, the Tamil doctor and musicologist Abraham Pandithar was busily composing and notating hundreds of Tamil gitams and kritis for the benefit of Tamil children who, he felt, needed music in their mother tongue. These were eventually published in 1934, at Abraham Pandithar's own printing press in Tanjore, in the form of a primer entitled *A Practical Course in South Indian Music*. The book did away with complicated descriptions of ragas and systems of classification. The page design was clearly intended to appeal to the eye, presenting the notation neatly divided into the quantities specified by the tala, with the whole

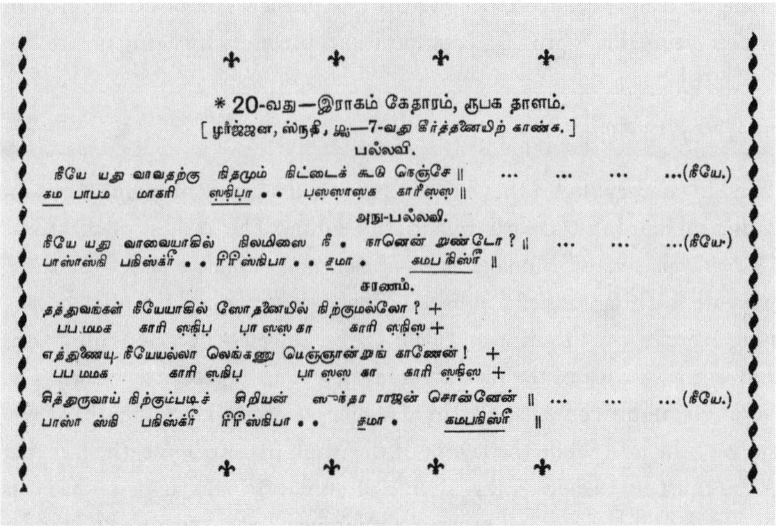

* 20-வது—இராகம் கேதாரம், ரூபக தாளம்.
[மூர்ச்சனை, ஸ்ருதி, ஆ—7-வது கீர்த்தனையிற் காண்க.]
பல்லவி.
நீயே யது வாவதற்கு நிதமும் நிட்டைக் கூடு நெஞ்சே || ... ...(நீயே.)
கம பாபம மாகரி ஸநிபா • • பஸஸாஸக காரீஸஸ ||
அநு-பல்லவி.
நீயே யது வாவையாகில் நிலமிலை நீ • நானென் றுண்டோ ? || ... ...(நீயே)
பாஸாஸநி பநிஸ்க்ரீ • • ரீரீஸ்நிபா • • தமா • கமப நிஸ்ரீ ||
சரணம்.
தத்துவங்கள் நீயேயாகில் சோதனையில் நிற்குமல்லோ ? +
பப மமக காரி ஸநிப பா ஸஸ கா காரி ஸநிஸ +
எத்துணையு நீயேயல்லா லெங்கணு மெஞ்ஞான்றுங் காணேன் ! +
பப மமக காரி ஸநிப பா ஸஸ கா காரி ஸநிஸ +
சித்துருவாய் நிற்கும்படிச் சிறியன் ஸுந்தர ராஜன் சொன்னேன் || ... ... (நீயே.)
பாஸா ஸநி பநிஸ்க்ரீ ரீரீஸ்நிபா • • தமா • கமபநிஸ்ரீ ||

26 A sample notated composition in raga kedaram from T. C. R. Johannes's, *Bharatha Sangīta Svāya Bōdhini* (1912). Words are in Tamil with sargam notation in Tamil script below.

thing enclosed in a tastefully bordered box. The didactic quality of the book lay in its carefully ordered presentation: for each composition, first the swaras only were given, then the same swaras and their corresponding sahityam, and then the sahityam only. The copyright emblem on the title page showed two men sitting on a river bank in the manner of guru and disciple, suggesting that the authority of the book's notation was guaranteed by the authenticity of oral transmission. Ironically, however, Pandithar was a self-taught musician who used the medium of notation not to record music that already existed but to invent and popularize his own compositions. In effect, it was only through notation, not through an oral tradition, that his compositions came into being.

While music manuals in Telugu and Tamil eschewed staff notation, those written in English in the 1930s included both sargam and staff notation, as if to appeal to a wider audience. However, the purpose of including both types of notation was no longer to debate the merits of one or the other, as it had been earlier. The implication now seemed to be that staff and sargam were equally valid ways of viewing the music and that the music remained the same no matter how one chose to picture it. Here, one can note a crucial shift: notation, instead of being regarded as central to the way music was conceptualized, was demoted to the status of a "mere" representation, incidental to the content that it represented. Nota-

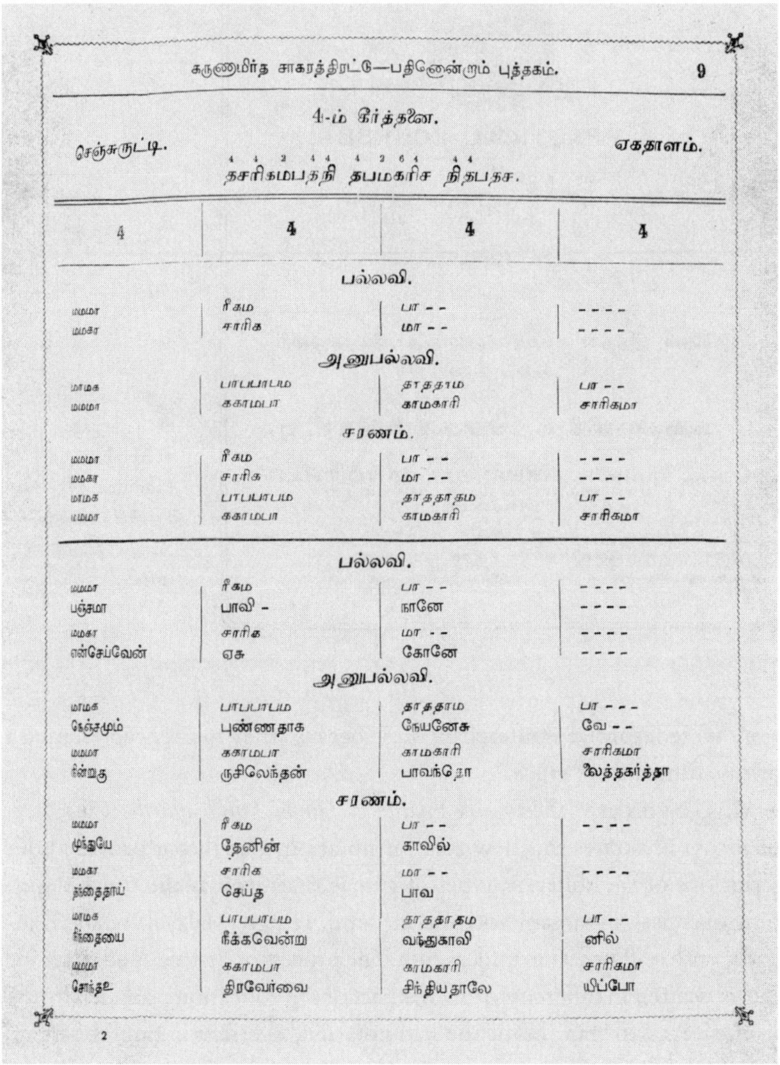

கருணாமிர்த சாகரத்திரட்டு—பதினொன்றும் புத்தகம். 9

4-ம் கீர்த்தனை.

செஞ்சுருட்டி. ஏகதாளம்.

தசரிகமபதநி தபமகரிச நிதபதச.

4	4	4	4

பல்லவி.

மமமா	ரீகம	பா - -	- - - -
மமகா	சாரிக	மா - -	- - - -

அநுபல்லவி.

மாமக	பாபபாபம	தாததாம	பா - -
மமமா	ககாமபா	காமகாரி	சாரிகமா

சரணம்.

மமமா	ரீகம	பா - -	- - - -
மமகா	சாரிக	மா - -	- - - -
மாமக	பாபபாபம	தாததாதம	பா - -
மமமா	ககாமபா	காமகாரி	சாரிகமா

பல்லவி.

மமமா	ரீகம	பா - -	- - - -
பஞ்சமா	பாவி -	நானே	- - - -
மமகா	சாரிக	மா - -	- - - -
என்செய்வேன்	ஏசு	கோனே	- - - -

அநுபல்லவி.

மாமக	பாபபாபம	தாததாம	பா - - -
நெஞ்சமும்	புண்ணதாக	நேயனேசு	வே - -
மமமா	ககாமபா	காமகாரி	சாரிகமா
ன்றது	ருசிலேந்தன்	பாவங்ரோ	லேத்தகர்த்தா

சரணம்.

மமமா	ரீகம	பா - -	- - - -
முந்துயே	தேனின்	காவில்	
மமகா	சாரிக	மா - -	- - - -
தந்தைதாய்	செய்த	பாவ	
மாமக	பாபபாபம	தாததாதம	பா - -
நிந்தையை	நீக்கவேன்று	வந்துகாவி	னில்
மமமா	ககாமபா	காமகாரி	சாரிகமா
சொந்தஉ	திரவேர்வை	சிந்திய தாலே	யிப்போ

2

27 A sample notated composition in raga senjurutti from Abraham Pandithar's *A Practical Course in South Indian Music* (1934). The upper half of the page includes just the sargam notation in Tamil script for the three sections of the composition. The lower half of the page repeats the sargam notation with the lyrics in Tamil below each line of notation.

A PRACTICAL COURSE
IN
SOUTH INDIAN MUSIC
For Beginners.
BOOKS I—XIV.

தென் இந்திய சங்கீத ஆரம்ப அப்பியாசமுறை
புத்தகம் I—XIV.

கருணாமிர்த சாகரத்திரட்டு.

RAO SAHIB M. ABRAHAM PANDITHER.
KARUNANITHI MEDICAL HALL,
TANJORE.

THE LAWLEY ELECTRIC PRINTING PRESS TANJORE.
All Rights Reserved] 1934.
R 7 5–0 0

28 Title page of Abraham Pandithar's *A Practical Course in South Indian Music* (1934).

tions were regarded as interchangeable because they merely represented a prior, authoritative voice.

C. Ganghadar's *Theory and Practice of Hindu Music and the Vina Tutor* (ca. 1935) illustrates this new role for notation. Ganghadar provided descriptions of the different types of gamakas, as well as the usual beginning exercises, in sargam notation in Tamil, Telugu, Malayalam, and Kannada, with staff notation underneath. The process of getting used to seeing music written in different forms was part of the education provided by the manual. As if to bring home the staff notation, a version in English sargam syllables was provided underneath. The progression from what was presumably one's native language, through other languages, to staff notation, and finally to the syllables transliterated into English gave the impression of total translatability, the idea that one could move from language to language, even from one musical system to another, without losing anything.

This fantasy of total translatability was what motivated P. Sambamoorthy in his writings on Karnatic music. Prolific in his works, which ranged from a five-volume history of Karnatic music to a multivolume

29 Sample of notation from C. Ganghadar's *Theory and Practice of Hindu Music* (ca. 1935). Sargam notation is provided in Tamil, Telugu, Malayalam, and Kannada, and English (below the staff notation).

practical course in music for schools, Sambamoorthy was on the cutting edge of the new field of music education. In 1961, during his tenure as head of the Department of Indian Music at Madras University, Sambamoorthy published a small book entitled *Elements of Western Music for Students of Indian Music*. A knowledge of Western classical music and staff notation was required for students in the Indian Music department and the purpose of the book was to provide them with this knowledge. In his explanation of the symbols used in staff notation, he took care to translate each one into an Indian equivalent, interspersing the text with the visual symbols of staff notation. The effect was that Karnatic music and Western classical music appeared as two discrete yet equivalent systems, each capable of translating the other. Only in a small paragraph did Sambamoorthy mention the problem of representing gamakas in staff notation, but he concluded that

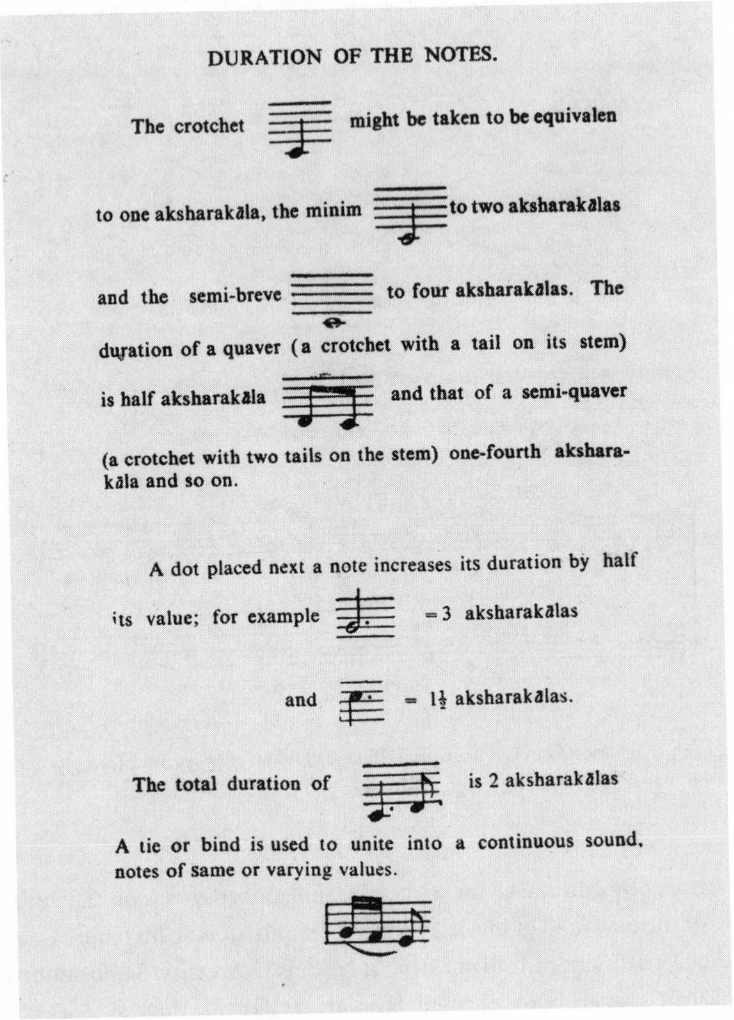

DURATION OF THE NOTES.

The crotchet might be taken to be equivalen to one aksharakāla, the minim to two aksharakālas and the semi-breve to four aksharakālas. The duration of a quaver (a crotchet with a tail on its stem) is half aksharakāla and that of a semi-quaver (a crotchet with two tails on the stem) one-fourth akshara-kāla and so on.

A dot placed next a note increases its duration by half its value; for example = 3 aksharakālas

and = 1½ aksharakālas.

The total duration of is 2 aksharakālas

A tie or bind is used to unite into a continuous sound, notes of same or varying values.

30 A sample page from P. Sambamoorthy's *Elements of Western Music for Students of Indian Music* (1961).

31 A sample notated composition from P. Sambamoorthy's *Elements of Western Music for Students of Indian Music* (1961).

they could, with the use of additional symbols, be "rendered faithfully and according to tradition" (1961, 8). The last half of the book consisted of Karnatic compositions in staff notation, compositions that every student would know, but stripped of gamakas entirely. The idea seemed to be that the student would see that the staff notation made sense by being able to hear the song in her head while she saw it on paper.

The idea of total translatability, for Sambamoorthy, thus did not stop with the easy transposition from one notation system to the other. It also characterized his notion of the relationship between the oral/aural and the written. In his *A Practical Course in Karnatic Music for Schools* (ca. 1960) and in a manual written for music teachers in 1966, Sambamoorthy laid great emphasis not just on notation but on making the boundary between the oral/aural and the written disappear. He prescribed numerous exercises to this effect, such as sight-singing and musical dictation. Students should write down phrases and then sing them in a raga, "provided the phrases so sung form a *hearable* passage" (1966, 63). "Musical dictation," he explained to future teachers, "helps the students to acquire a keen sense of hearing" (ibid., 64). Meanwhile, learning to write music with facility would "greatly help the student in the art of musical composition later in life" (ibid.). After students had become proficient enough at converting heard music into notation and vice versa, there were sample exam questions aimed at a more virtuosic level: a notated composition, without information about the raga, was provided, and the student, merely by studying the notation, had to indicate what the raga of the composition was (Sambamoorthy n.d.a, vol. 3, 207). For Sambamoorthy and his students, the skill in reading notation was the ability to take something written and convert it into a piece of music believable to the ear, to make it conform to a voice that one had already heard before.

Sambamoorthy's ideal of easy translation between the oral/aural and the written was precisely that: an ideal. In prescribing so much practice for it, he effectively acknowledged that, contrary to the simple straightforwardness of his directions, going from the oral/aural to the written and back again was not a simple, mechanical process but a complex maneuver. What his exercises suggest is that one does not simply progress toward greater accuracy but rather practices the skill of convincing oneself of the equivalence between the oral/aural and the written. That this requires a suspension of disbelief not necessarily shared by musicians from older generations is demonstrated by my own experience of learning compositions. In long afternoons with my teacher, much of the time I spent "learning" a new composition was actually devoted to creating a notation for that composition. As she sang, I would scribble a first impression in sargam notation and then sing my version back to her, revising my written interpretation until we arrived at a notation that both of us agreed on. Yet the agreement was always only a temporary truce; I would come back the next day to find her singing the composition in a way that contradicted the notation we had agreed on the previous day. When I pointed out the inconsistencies, she would often become irritated, remarking that the same notation "said" her version as well as mine. Our disagreement about what constituted acceptable variation in the interpretation of written notation marked a contrast between two ways of viewing notation. While I was attempting to create a notation that would act as an authoritative text (an idea ingrained in me by years of training in Western classical music), she used the notation as more of a trigger for memory. Like a palm-leaf manuscript, notation in this second sense is not meant to be sight-read but studied and then interpreted. This way of using notation acknowledges the impossibility of total interchangeability between the oral/aural and the written; it considers the gap between oral/aural and written as productive rather than problematic. In admitting that notation is not perfectly legible, it acknowledges its profoundly mediating role.

The Order of Things

Yes, I think our music will, in the very near future, become something quite universal and embrace everything . . . , the system becoming as elastic and world-wide as the British Empire itself.

—A. M. Chinnaswamy Mudaliar, "Saraswatia Redux" (1893)

As notation gained prominence in the twentieth century, the project of determining a basic structure that would serve as the "theory" for Karnatic music became important.[29] For if notation literally raised the problem of determining the "basic structure" of a piece as opposed to the "embellishments," it also raised the problem of finding structure in the profusion of ragas and talas now available in written form. Thus, at the same time as music manuals with notation appeared, there also appeared books on the structure and classification of ragas, as well as raga dictionaries: books that would enable a student not only to sing a raga but also to find its place in the order of things. Notably, this order did not consist of aural memories, typical phrases, or associations with a particular raga, but rather in a hypothetical table that made the scalar structure of ragas visible.

At the heart of this project of classification was the 72-melakarta raga scheme, originally devised in 1660 by Venkatamakhi, a Telugu Brahmin in the court of Vijayaraghava Nayaka (r. 1633–1673) at the king's behest.[30] Although a translation of the original work was not published until the twentieth century, almost every book of Karnatic music notation, including Chinnaswamy Mudaliar's work, the books of the Singaracaryulu brothers, and the *Sangīta Sampradāya Pradārṣini*, mentioned the scheme at great length. In his introduction to a small book on the subject, Sambamoorthy called the 72-melakarta scheme a "modern classification of ragas" that, "based on the genus-species system . . . is the best system of raga-classification that human genius can conceive of" (1961, iii). In the system, ragas were classified on the basis of only the notes or scale that they used. By means of different combinations of the twelve pitches in the Western chromatic scale, 72 *melas*—"parent scales" or "root-ragas"—were specified. The first and second of these seventy-two melas were differentiated only by one note, the second and third by one note, and so on, keeping *sa*, *ma*, and *pa* (the first, fourth, and fifth degrees of the scale) constant, until all the possibilities of combining the notes were exhausted. After the first thirty-six melas were arrived at in this manner, the *ma* was raised and the second thirty-six melas were produced.[31] The exhaustiveness of the table of ragas thus produced, and its patterned regularity, were signs of its scientific validity.

The idea of a system or table that could capture the possibilities of music for all time seems to have thrilled Venkatamakhi as well as his twentieth-century counterpart. "So great was Venkatamakhi's joy when he formulated the scheme," Sambamoorthy wrote, "that he declared in his immortal work that even Lord Parmasiva could not devise a scheme containing one more or one less than the 72 melakartas" (1961, 10). Most of these melakarta ragas remained in the realm of pure theory; only nineteen of them did Venkatamakhi find to be in use (10–11). The point, however, was that any raga, past or future, could now find a place in this universal table of scales. "The great use of the scheme," wrote Sambamoorthy, "consists in the fact that once the number of a melakarta raga is known, its lakshana (i.e., the characteristics of its swaras) can be told at the next second" (13). He demonstrated how the system worked: by locating a raga within its chakra (group of six ragas) and then locating its chakra within the symmetrical spatial organization of the table (13–14).[32] The 72-melakarta scheme, according to Sambamoorthy, was what made Karnatic music adhere as a modern system. "Viewed in the light of mere permutations and combinations, the scheme might appear at first sight as an artificial and dry process. But . . . every musical sound and interval has its exact number of vibrations and ratios. The melakarta scheme is highly comprehensive and systematic, and includes within its fold all the modes used in ancient as well as modern systems of music of the world. . . . It is a complete and exhaustive scheme evolved by simple and natural combinations" (17).[33]

The 72-melakarta scheme represented a kind of natural history of music, that is, a principle of order that encompassed history by acting as the be-all and end-all of musical possibility. To musicologists in twentieth-century South India, the idea of such an order was appealing precisely because it kept change and its more political counterpart, history, in check. Meanwhile, it gestured toward the kind of universality that classical music needed, by showing how scales or modes similar to the idea of scale in Western classical music were operative in Karnatic music; it became evidence that the two "systems" of music were "of the same family."[34] And finally, it provided an order based on underlying structure rather than on gamakas or phrases or anything else that had come to be regarded as non-essential.

This shift in the way ragas came to be classified is apparent in music manuals in the early twentieth century. A Tamil music theory book from

1902, *Caṅkīta Cantirikai*, provided several methods of classifying ragas, of which the 72-melakarta scheme was only one. The groupings seemed to depend less on underlying structure and more on literary or social convention. One grouping placed ragas together by the suffixes in their names, another by the sentiments they produced, another by the times of day and night for which they were suited (Manikka Mudaliar 1902, 116–29). By the time of the publication of Chitti Babu Naidu's *A Key to Hindu Music* in 1925, however, the 72-melakarta scheme seems to have taken first place among other modes of classifying ragas. Chitti Babu Naidu commented on the efforts to classify ragas "according to one's own experience," remarking that such efforts, which mistook the musician's individual experience for objective truth, were "all evidently the feeble attempts made by people who do not understand the fine system of Indian ragas and their genesis" (1925, 9). A distinction had to be made, Naidu implied, between this system of genesis and more subjective bases of classification.

Just what does such a system exclude? As a survey of these manuals shows, coexisting with the official musicological system of classification are other ways of classifying ragas that have dropped out of musicological discourse. These modes of raga classification show the difference between the concept of a raga and the concept of a musical scale in Western terms. Ragas exist somewhere along a continuum between scales and melodies; they are often characterized by particular phrases and orders of ascent and descent through the scale they use. Unlike a scale, a raga can be thought of as a set of potentialities, realizable only through temporal development; one cannot write out a raga, in this more complete sense, on a page. Not only particular phrases but pauses and repetitions are essential to the elaboration of a raga. Developed in performance, ragas gain associations with particular places, musicians, and feelings. For instance, one musician explained to me that two ragas like kamboji and yadukulakamboji, which are in the same mela, or family, according to Venkatamakhi's system and differ only by the presence or absence of a single swara, nevertheless differ in the cuvai (taste) and uṇarcci (feeling) they evoke. Kamboji is associated with *kampīram* (grandeur, pomp) while yadukulakamboji, lacking the swara *ga*, evokes *tuyaram* (sadness) and *maṉṟāṭutal* (pleading).[35] The metaphors of orality and embodiment at work in these metaphors of cuvai and uṇarcci contrast greatly with the decidedly visual order of the 72-melakarta system, which strips ragas of their evocative contexts and places them in a chart arranged to be understandable to the eye.

In the mid-twentieth century, the 72-melakarta system assumed a prominent place in the curricula of university music departments. As it gained the status of "theory," it came to be seen as essential knowledge for the proper rendition of any raga, replacing other ways of ordering ragas with a mode of classification deemed more properly musicological. Starting in the 1940s, the matter of the derivation of janya ragas from their "parent" or melakarta ragas became a prime topic of debate year after year in the Madras Music Academy. There it was argued that knowing the parent raga affected one's elaboration of the janya raga; it determined the notes one paused on, how one constructed phrases, which notes were considered "foreign," and so on. The derivation of a raga according to the 72-melakarta system was often cited as an authoritative answer for questions of "correct" or "incorrect" usage (Sambamoorthy 1961, 26). In this view, if only musicians observed the rules, theory and practice would become a single rational system.

The idea of a standardized scheme of ordering ragas was deeply connected to the use of notation and the concept of the composer. K. Ramachandran's *Sri Dakṣinarāga Ratnākaram* (Characteristics of Carnatic ragas), published in 1949, provided its readers with the classification of 1,044 ragas according to their melakarta group, the number of notes each one used in its ascent and descent, and a list of compositions in each raga. The idea was that the proper approach to a raga was determinable not only by finding its location in an ordered table of ragas but also by observing its behavior in different compositions, analogous to a naturalist's observation of animal behavior. The natural history of ragas produced by the 72-melakarta system was thus conceptually related to the observation of raga behavior. In this type of musicology, the composition was endowed with a new type of authority; it was now deemed absolutely necessary to know compositions in a particular raga before one dared to claim any knowledge of it. Compositions became the locus of authority in a musicology that now thought of raga as something able to be almost completely described and rationalized.

In the Realm of Musicology

In 1932 the Annamalai University published an English translation of the *Svaramēlakalānidhi*, a sixteenth-century music treatise by Ramamatya, with commentary by M. S. Ramaswamy Aiyar. The twentieth-century musicologist saw an analogy between his own endeavor, reconciling music theory with practice, and the Vijayanagar king Rama Raja's injunction to his court musicologist in 1550: "The science of music has, both in theory and in practice, degenerated into conflicting views. . . . Reconcile all [the conflicting views] and write a new science . . . embodying therein [music's] theory and practice" (Ramaswamy Aiyar 1932, xv). Reviewing several other treatises, Ramaswamy Aiyar remarked that a similar note of complaint had been sounded by other treatise-writers. "A question, therefore, naturally arises, namely, 'Why should the musical views conflict, at all, with one another?' To put the same question sarcastically: 'Why should the harmonious music produce disharmony amongst its votaries?' " (xvi). Ramaswamy Aiyar's answer to this question, which occupied the seventy-three pages of his introduction, overshadowed his translation of the treatise itself. The excessive length of the introduction hints at the disjunction between the kind of answers Ramaswamy Aiyar expected in the twentieth century and those that Ramamatya had provided.

Ramaswamy Aiyar began by differentiating the interests of musicology from Ramamatya's apparent interests. Ramamatya had begun his treatise by giving the pedigree of the king who commissioned it, a chart showing the descent of Rama Raja from none other than Vishnu and Brahma. Ramaswamy Aiyar contrasted this with a genealogy by the colonial historian Robert Sewell, taken from epigraphical records, which "gives Rama Raja his proper place in the royal line of Vijayanagar" (1932, xiii). Placing his own musicological endeavor on the side of written records and "history," Ramaswamy Aiyar remarked that "Ramamatya's description of Rama Raja's pedigree is more fanciful than real and betrays the mentality of a flattering court poet rather than that of a responsible State officer" (xiii). Moreover, whereas for Ramamatya the pedigree of the king was an essential part of the treatise, for Ramaswamy Aiyar it was a mere distraction from the real matter of the work: "I digressed . . . to warn the reader against blindly accepting unhistorical, and therefore untruthful, statements" (xiv). The twentieth-century musicological treatise belonged in the genre of historical and rational writing and not poetry.

The main task at hand, as Ramaswamy Aiyar characterized it, was to understand the process of musical change: to understand how an "old order" of music could give rise to a new one. Understanding this was tantamount to reconciling theory and practice; one had to look for a principle that governed these shifts (1932, xvi). Ramamatya's answer to his king's request that he reconcile musical theory and practice had been to suggest the principle of *lakshya*, the idea that practice could change theory. Ramaswamy Aiyar's translation of his words on the subject went thus:

"The Gandharva-music is ever employed in conformity with the (inflexible) rules of its theory. But if the violation of any of these rules . . . do not lead to any absurdity; and if, again, the contravention of any of the rules of practice does not give pleasure, but jars to the ear; then the practice of music shall be preferred to its theory" (xix). Here, theory and practice were loosely related; they were under no obligation to reflect each other. Indeed, the gap between them was acknowledged. Music theory, in these older treatises, was an intellectual discipline in itself which may have had closer ties to philosophy and poetry than to actual musical practice itself.

Yet such a state of affairs seemed vaguely unsatisfactory to Ramaswamy Aiyar. For him, as for other twentieth century musicologists, musicology was a science which had no place for philosophical or poetic discourse. He claimed that music could be called a science by virtue of the fact that there were two types of science: "exact" and "inexact" (1932, xvi). Whereas the rules of exact science (like chemistry, he suggested) were unchanging, the rules of an inexact science could change from time to time. The slowness of this change was what gave music its scientific status: "Mark! I said 'from time to time' and not from day to day. For if music, like dream, changes from day to day, surely, like dream, it will be labelled as mere phantasy and treated as such" (xvi). For music to be a properly historical subject, it had to outlast the impermanence of fantasy; it had to be able to be written down and pass from generation to generation. Essential to this writeability was a systematic, scientific approach, a standard that itself never changed (xxx). Ramaswamy Aiyar imagined this standard to be locatable in underlying "characteristics," which had to be discerned by the modern musicologist. To illustrate what he meant, he contrasted Ramamatya's description of ragas with Venkatamakhi's 72-mela system. Ramamatya had merely described "the ragas in vogue at his time"; he specified the names of twenty melas but gave no principle on which they were based or ordered. "Evidently he did not care to deduce his twenty melas from any kind of principles," Ramaswamy Aiyar remarked (xxxv). Yet Ramamatya's very use of the concept of mela showed that he was at least working toward some principle of classification. Such a system of classification distinguished modern musicology from an "antiquated" approach.

> Ramamatya rightly discarded the antic and antiquated method of deriving Ragas from the complicated system of Grama-Moorchana-Jati, as well as the later puerile method of bringing them under the fanciful system of Raga-Ragini-Putra. . . . He had the genius to discover unity

> in variety, that is, a unifying principle in the variety of Ragas that came under his notice; and he therefore felt that the old *cataloguing* method of enumerating the Ragas must give way to the *classifying* method of reducing them into what might be called the Genus-Species system. (lx)

With such a taxonomy at his fingertips, the modern musicologist, according to the demands of the "present revival of musical taste, in India, on rational lines," could begin to elucidate "the various *Terms* occurring in the Science of Music" (Ramaswamy Aiyar 1932, lxiii). Rather than being misled by "mere names," the modern musicologist could discover the real meaning lying underneath. As a "test case," Ramaswamy Aiyar took the perennially confusing terms *mārga* and *dēsi*. Such terms, he stated, had been used so variably and contradictorily to describe ragas that they had lost all meaning and become mere names (lxiii). He quoted Sarangadeva, author of the sixteenth century treatise *Sangīta Ratnākara*: "Music is of two kinds—Marga and Desi. That was called Marga which was sought after by Brahma and other gods and practised by Bharata and other sages in the presence of Siva and which would yield everlasting prosperity. That kind was called Desi which consisted of the vocal-instrumental-dance music and which pleased the people of different countries according to their different tastes" (lxiii). This long, "tiresome" description of the terms could not satisfy the questions of the modern musicologist, as Ramaswamy Aiyar stated them. "What were the essential characteristics of Marga and Desi? In what way could they be unfailingly recognised as such?" (lxiv). The modern musicologist's approach to such a problem was to trace the history of these terms and to identify them with particular musical practices: mārga referred to the practice of chanting the Vedas, while dēsi referred to the Hindustani and Karnatic practices. Thus, the "essential characteristic" of each term was now determinable: mārga music was confined to four notes, while dēsi music made use of all the notes of the scale (lxix). Each music had its own principle: "The marga-music followed the principle of lakshana [grammar] and therefore became less and less pleasant, till at last it degenerated into a dry, monotonous, and sing-song style of singing, while desi-music followed the principle of lakshya and has therefore acquired a more and more fascinating style of singing" (lxxii). Notably, while Ramamatya discussed mārga and dēsi in terms of their contexts of audition, Ramaswamy Aiyar searched for the essential characteristics, separable from such contextual factors, that could be used to define them. Finally, he gave his own English gloss to these terms. "The word *marga* has come to mean whatever is old and *out-of-date*; while the word desi has come to mean whatever is new and *up-to-date*. . . . Just as I called Marga, *Vedic Music*, so, I shall call Desi, *Modern Music*" (lxxiii).

For modern music a modern musicology was necessary. In 1939 another attempt to reconcile theory and practice came in the form of C. Subrahmanya Ayyar's *Grammar of South Indian Music*. Instead of revising or critiquing the ancient treatises, he disregarded them entirely. "The present thesis," he wrote, "purposely does not refer to the more ancient theoretical works on music in Sanskrit. It is based entirely on my musical experience with a little knowledge of modern Physics, and of musical comparisons suggested by a musical ear. . . . I feel the paramount necessity for the correct perception of microtones by all artists, vocalists, and instrumentalists alike, for their clear exposition of the Raga Bhava [emotion]" (1939, 1). The idea was that music could be best understood through the lens of a scientific musicology that had no recourse to ancient texts but that relied instead on the human ear and on modern measuring instruments like tuning forks. Subrahmanya Ayyar's project was to understand the "microtonal changes" used in gamakas that made them so effective (37). The point was to understand—to be able to express in words and numbers—"what the voice actually does" (48). How did the same note in two different ragas give a different impression? How did a listener differentiate between two ragas when, strictly speaking, they used the same notes? For Subrahmanya Ayyar, these were the kinds of questions modern musicology had to answer. Such a musicology, he implied, would close the gap between the voice/ear and notation; the minute numerical ratios and lengthy descriptions of ragas that he provided would effect a true reconciliation of theory and practice.

The Problem of Writing

The author is the principle of thrift in the proliferation of meaning.
—Michel Foucault, "What Is an Author?"

To close the gap between theory and practice, for a modern musicologist like C. Subrahmanya Ayyar, writing itself had to disappear, in a very literal sense. If, for Ramaswamy Aiyar, the ancient treatises represented a mass of writing that had to be translated somehow into good sense, for Subrahmanya Ayyar they were an impediment to the proper practice of musicological science. He instead aimed to convey his theory through the eloquence of numbers and their aural counterparts; the true musicology was a science that, unswayed by the vicissitudes of writing, could determine "what the voice actually does."

Notation was important in this respect because, ideally, it aimed for the literal disappearance of writing; notation was supposed to serve as a set of signs for music that would somehow escape the ambiguity of writing, its potential to give rise to multiple interpretations. This was why advocates of the staff notation thought it necessary to have a nonalphabetic notation; the symbols of the staff notation were said to enjoy a closer relationship to the eye precisely because they supposedly bypassed language. For proponents of sargam notation, the disappearance of writing was achieved by the way it provided a picture for the ear, made of signs so legible that they became audible, disappearing off the page to sound the voice of the composer.

The disappearance of writing thus came to convey a certain sense of authenticity: the notion of a true composer or author behind the written signs. The composer became, in the twentieth century, the one figure who was endowed with the authority to move from the oral to the written. The concept of an oral tradition implied an absence of writing that kept musicians in the realm of memory and improvisation. The composer, however, by creating fixed compositions, transferred music to the realm of history. In the politics of music in twentieth-century South India, it is these latter terms—*composer* and *history*—that are the privileged signs of Karnatic music's classical status. As compositions have become authored, they have become repositories of authority, almost like a dictionary or guidebook of acceptable phrases for those who are improvising.

The desire to "fix" compositions in notation at the turn of the twentieth century was not only about fixing the composer's voice; it was also part of the project of showing that Karnatic music obeyed a system of conventions and rules, that there was a structure beneath, or within, the music. Chinnaswamy Mudaliar was confident that notation would show the difference between Karnatic music's structure and its embellishments, the reason behind the music. Meanwhile, musicologists used the 72-melakarta raga scheme to show, similarly, a separate conceptual realm in which the rules of music were fixed for all time. This conceptual realm or structure came to be known as "theory," a realm which stood in the same relation to practice as structure did to embellishments, or as the written did to the oral. Inhabiting the conceptual realm, the 72-melakarta system stood apart from the music as a representation of its pure structure. In this order of things, notation was thought to represent an authoritative version of a composition, a version that could stand apart from various future renderings. Only by losing its arbitrariness, by appearing to be completely motivated by the voice of the composer, could notation be properly authoritative.

The scandal of the Swati Tirunal case was that it made the problem and power of writing reappear. Where the authoritative voice of the composer should have expelled any doubts, Balachander's allegations pointed to a proliferation of possibilities, of questions concerning motivation. For, in Balachander's argument, the notation of Swati Tirunal's compositions, as well as the historical work of musicologists concerning his life, became not efforts to determine the truth but problems of writing. Motivation here referred not to a seamless relationship between sign and meaning but to the proliferation of ulterior motives that, once revealed, threatened the legitimacy of what was written. Like the anthropologist Claude Lévi-Strauss among the Nambikwara, Balachander wondered whether the Swati Tirunal authorities were motivated by a true composer or if they had simply realized the power of writing, of notating compositions and publishing them; the distinction between artistic motivation and political motivation threatened to become indecipherable in writing. Only the composer had the authority to control the movement of music between the realms of oral tradition and writing, a movement that otherwise threatened to operate in a considerably less authorized manner.

It is the suspension of these possibilities, the disavowal of the problem of writing, that makes the "composer" and the "composition" possible, at the same time as it allows the persistence of the idea that Karnatic music (or Indian music in general) is, despite its notations and treatises, essentially an oral tradition. There is a contradictory logic at work here; the anxiety that the voice will be lost *if not captured* by writing coexists with the anxiety that the voice could be lost precisely by being *completely captured* by writing. The way in which these anxieties are intertwined suggests that it has become impossible to imagine the voice, or oral tradition, without writing. It is only from within the scriptural economy, as Michel de Certeau might suggest, that certain notions of and values attached to orality can emerge. It is writing that lends authority, in the literal and metaphorical senses of the word, to the idea of an oral tradition.

Importantly, it is not just any writing that is at stake here, but English writing in particular. Writing metaphors associated with English—"punctuation," "paragraphs," "essays"—are now commonly used to describe Indian music. For example, in 2000 the musicologist Raghava Menon said of the late Alla Rakha's tabla playing that "there was a sense of commas, explanations, and full stops. He played with punctuation" (Dugger 2000). Punctuation is thus equated with authorly intention and meaning, as well as the sense that music is understandable and graspable inasmuch as it obeys the conventions of writing.[36] More than fifty years earlier, P. Sambamoorthy had encouraged his students to think of raga alapana as an "essay" or "exposition" composed of a short sketch of the raga as a first "paragraph," with the following "paragraphs" as development (1944, 40). He had thus suggested that a method of writing associated with colonial education could be employed, by analogy, in Karnatic music. English writing provided a stable, permanent structure, a way of presenting—or rather *representing*—Karnatic music. The silent but visible authority of English guaranteed that the voice of Karnatic music came through properly; it would see that the oral tradition passed, unhindered, from musician to audience and from generation to generation.

Perhaps it is not coincidental that, in Amit Chaudhuri's recent novella *Afternoon Raag*, another kind of representation of Indian music in English, the image of writing is used to explain the essential difference between Indian music and Western music.

> The straight, angular notes of Western music, composed and then rendered, are like print upon a page; in contrast, the curving meends of the raag are like longhand writing drawn upon the air. Each singer has his own impermanent longhand with its own arching, idiosyncratic beauties, its own repetitive, serpentine letters. With the end of the recital, this longhand, which, in its unraveling, is a matter of constant erasures and rewritings, is erased completely, unlike the notes of Western music, which remains printed upon the page. (1999, 151–52).[37]

While English writing—and thus Western music—is associated with print and stands for permanence, standardization, and legibility, Indian writing—conceived, of course, as handwriting—bears all the traces of orality: idiosyncracy, illegibility, repetition. Importantly, however, this is an orality that can only be conceived on analogy with writing, and described in English.

Chaudhuri's "longhand" stands for excess; it bears the traces of the hand, of embodiment, and of orality that print banishes. The novelist and the musicologist share the same musicological assumptions, ones whose foundations are laid by modern musicology. They recognize that within the problem of representing music there is a much larger problem: the translation of musical experience into words, the determination of "what the voice actually does" to those who listen to it. Musical terms become objects fit for translation precisely because there is another register of musical experience that lies outside their purview, a realm that moves but is untraceable. This realm—an excess figured variously as essential orality, or as the sublime, the inexpressible, the ineffable—is neither prior to nor external to modern musicology but produced by it.[38] After all the notations and minute calculations—indeed, precisely *because* of them—music appears to defy explanation. For the modern musicologist, however, this sense of ineffability is elaborated with reference not only to the divine—in this case, perhaps, the Hindu notion of ultimate Brahman—but also to the interiority of the modern listening subject.[39] "You are all aware that music moves us, and we do not know why," C. Subrahmanya Ayyar told a Bombay audience in English in 1939 (1941, 19). "We feel the tears, but cannot trace their source."

6 Fantastic Fidelities

Guru, face to face, shows the marga [way]. The sisya has to make the journey to excellence. How is that excellence purveyed? . . . There is a message that voice leaves in the listener's soul, a memory like the ubiquitous murmur of surf, long after the particular sangatis of a rendering have been forgotten. . . . [Today] music is treated all wrong, as though it were a mere science, a matter of arithmetic, of fractions and time intervals.
—Raghava Menon, quoted in *The Hindu*, December 1999

The possibility of sound reproduction reorients the practices of sound production; insofar as it is a possibility at all, reproduction precedes originality.
—Jonathan Sterne, *The Audible Past*

Music lives a curiously double life. It is associated with the technical—the musicological terminology of notes and intervals, the acoustic terminology of frequencies and amplitudes—and with the sentimental—meaning, emotion, and a sense of the ineffable. In fact, the coexistence of these discourses and their essential incommensurability seem somehow constitutive of "music" as we know it. On one side, to paraphrase Raghava Menon, is the meaningful: message, memory, murmur; on the other side, the mathematical: arithmetic, fractions, and time intervals. The way in which these discourses are pitted against one another reflects a mode of thinking about music that is, I would argue, peculiar to modernity and, indeed, to a particular postcolonial predicament.

In postcolonial South India, music, particularly Karnatic music, is constituted as a practice and subject of discourse in part by the way these seemingly incommensurable discourses are mapped onto India and the West. Talk about classical music in South India is dominated by ideas about the primacy of the voice and the importance of oral tradition. "Voice" and "oral tradition" have in the twentieth century become more than merely descriptive. Rather, they are loaded terms in a discourse about authenticity that derives its urgency from the perceived onslaught of technologies of recording and electronic sound reproduction. The significance of these terms is apparent from the way they are used to oppose Karnatic music to a generalized idea of Western music: whereas Western music is instrumental, Karnatic is vocal; whereas Western music is "technologically" superior, Karnatic is more "spiritual"; whereas Western music can be played just by looking at written music (or so the stereotype goes), Karnatic is passed on through gurukulavasam, a centuries-long oral tradition and a system of teaching that technology cannot duplicate.

Gurukulavasam refers to a method of teaching and learning in which the sisya, or disciple, lives with the guru as a member of his household, learning music by a process of slow absorption over a number of years. Having undergone "rigorous gurukulavasam" is frequently invoked as the reason for musicians' greatness. The long years in which the sisya, or disciple, lives with the guru, becoming absorbed in the guru's music, serving the guru, and learning humility before the guru, are considered the classic form of gurukulavasam, or the gurukula "system," without which any truly Indian music cannot exist. Above all, gurukulavasam represents the pre-modern, a mode that existed before the differentiation of time into concerts and music lessons, before the differentiation of music into beginning and advanced lessons, before the separation of music from life in general. Gurukulavasam is by definition incompatible with modernity, with the busy life of the city, and with technology. In fact, the absence of technology is, in most accounts, what makes gurukulavasam possible; there can be no tape recorders or radios to interfere with the live transmission of the guru's voice.

There is, however, a more complex relationship between modern technologies and gurukulavasam than this discourse would suggest. On the one hand, technologies of recording and broadcasting create a disruption of traditional modes of teaching, performing, and listening, a very real disturbance that is experienced by musicians and listeners variously as a forgetting of voice, a loss of face-to-face contact, and a speeding up of time. On the other hand, there is a way in which desire for the traditional is projected out of the new technologies themselves. The social sense of fidelity, in the distinctly postcolonial sense of fidelity to tradition, of loyalty to one's roots and nationality, is deeply intertwined with the technological sense of sound fidelity. In this respect, as Martin Harrison has suggested, one might consider a history of listening as also a history of subjectivity, "or, more precisely, a history of the differently constructed sensoria which can operate in the relationship between 'subject' and 'world' (1996, 24).[1] Here I focus on moments when practices of listening and performing, and ideas about listening and performing subjects, change in conjunction with technologies of sound reproduction.

Elite and nationalist discourses surrounding music in the early part of the twentieth century operated on the assumption that music, among other arts, needed to be purified of backwardness and associations with low-class entertainments, reinvented as a middle-class occupation, and brought before the world as a sign of Indian national culture commensurate with other great musical traditions. As I have suggested, the ideal of commensurability, which dominated the colonial and postcolonial reinvention of many realms of Indian arts and ideas, demanded that Indian music be comparable to the music of the West yet preserve its essential difference, its Indianness. Gurukulavasam was problematic for elite and nationalist thinkers because it defied standardization and preserved idiosyncrasy, but it was also desirable because it seemed to embody an authentically Indian mode of disseminating and acquiring musical knowledge, an oral tradition that defied writing. Meanwhile, sound reproduction, correctly channeled, was seen as a potential tool in the project of developing a standardized body of theory and practice and making Karnatic music commensurate with other great musical systems of the world. This chapter explores human embodiment and mechanical mimesis as conflicting and coexisting models of authenticity in the twentieth-century redefinition of South Indian classical music.

His Master's Voice: Take 1

In his memoir of his musical life and times, the composer Mysore Vasudevachar (1865–1961) tells of his experience of learning to be a sisya in the last decades of the nineteenth century (1955, 26–31). He had left Mysore for Tiruvaiyaru with directions to his new guru's house but on arriving had forgotten exactly which house it was.

> I stood there dithering for some time and finally called out: "Guruji, Sir!" The door was thrown open instantly. . . . I felt I was in the presence of God Parameswara himself. . . . "Yes, who are you?" he asked me in Tamil. Even as I, fumbling for words, asked "Where is Patnam

> Subramania Iyer's . . . ?" the dignified look on his face vanished and it became red with anger. Without a word, he slammed the door in my face and disappeared inside. . . . I calmed myself and moved toward the house on the left. . . . The person who appeared before me now was none other than my guru himself. Even before he asked me who I was, I hastily removed my uttariyam [towel or cloth worn around the shoulders] and tied it around my waist and fell at his feet. "Get up," said my guru, gently placing his hand over my head. . . . "I shall teach you with pleasure," he said. My joy knew no bounds.

After he settled into his guru's household, the young Vasu, as he was known, waited patiently for several months for his guru to begin teaching him, but each day he was simply asked to provide the tambura accompaniment for his guru's practice. Lacking the courage to ask, Vasu was astonished when one day his guru, as if he had "read my mind," said that he would begin teaching him the next day. The lessons began with one of his guru's own compositions. "I learnt it by heart in about three days. Yet, for about three months he did not take up any new lesson. He made me sing the same varna day after day, first in slow tempo, then in medium, and finally in fast tempo. He would then make me sing [them] in reverse order. . . . Never did I ask my guru to teach me any particular varna or kirtana. Whatever he taught me, I tried to learn with attention." Vasu described the hardship he underwent for the sake of this learning experience, sleeping on the verandah where, kept awake by mosquitoes, he would memorize the day's lessons. One night, while lying awake, he remembered that there was to be a concert in the temple by another vidwan, Maha Vaidyanatha Iyer, and he was seized with the desire to go, even though "I had not obtained my guru's permission without which I was forbidden to go anywhere." He snuck off to the concert, where his fears of being discovered were quickly drowned out by the delightful musical performance. Maha Vaidyanatha Iyer turned out to be the man who had slammed the door in his face. After a few hours, Vasu ran home guiltily to find that his guru had indeed noticed his absence.

The next morning Subramania Iyer began his practice without calling Vasu. "After his bath, he called out to me from inside. The voice sounded stern. I went and stood before him with my head hanging down like a culprit before the magistrate. 'Where had you been last night?' he thundered. I told him the truth. . . . 'Well, that marks the end of your stay here. You can pack up your things and leave. . . . You better learn music from the person to whose music you were so much attracted.' " Vasu begged forgiveness and his guru calmed down, explaining to Vasu, " 'If one desires to study under a particular guru and imbibe the style and characteristics of his school, one's concentration should be totally focused on that single guru just as an artist fixes his eyes on the object he is trying to portray. If, on the other hand, you allow your mind to wander in different directions, what you learn . . . loses the stamp of individuality.' " Vasu came to understand the reasoning and spent a blissful six years with his guru. "When I prepared to return to Mysore, I was feeling rather like a girl who is for the first time leaving her parental home, the place where she had known nothing but love and kindness."

Several aspects of the traditional practice of gurukulavasam can be gleaned from this vignette. Most striking is the insistence on the sisya's complete attention to a single guru, to the point of not even going to hear other musicians' concerts. Patnam Subramania Iyer and Maha Vaidyanatha Iyer were rivals. Although one might appreciate the music of both, becoming a real musician depended on becoming completely devoted to one of them; it meant becoming identified with a particular school or style. This complete devotion extended from being absorbed in the guru's music to being absorbed in his entire household. Rather than pay money for their lessons, sisyas were expected to do their share of household duties. Vasudevachar relates in another vignette that he shared with two other sisyas "the responsibility of attending to the needs of our guru. My share of the duties was washing my master's . . . and his wife's clothes in the river, washing the copper pots and storing drinking water in them, washing the pooja utensils, making the bed for my guru and pressing his legs until he fell asleep" (Vasudevachar 1955, 39).

The sisya was expected to assimilate himself to the schedule of the guru, and to trust in the guru's plan without necessarily being told what it was. The guru bore ultimate authority and was often regarded as an actual parent.[2] Thus Vasu waited patiently for several months for his guru to begin teaching him, then learned whatever his guru wanted to teach him, at the pace his guru set. In gurukulavasam there was no set curriculum but rather a kind of monastic discipline that was meant to produce sisyas who could faithfully reproduce their gurus' sounds and styles. But this was far from reproduction in the mechanical sense. What made possible this fidelity of reproduction was fidelity in the social sense: loyalty and affection shared by the guru and sisya. The accumulation of time spent with the guru was in itself valuable, for it enabled the embodiment of the guru's musical and other knowledge by the sisya.

This embodied knowledge is the lost "memory" that Raghava Menon mourns. It is a reproduction that is faithful without being exact, for it persists "long after the particular sangatis of a rendering have been forgotten."[3] The dissonance between this delicate sense of memory and the other ways in which music would come to be passed on in the twentieth century—through sound recording and music institutions with set curricula—is striking. Describing a similar shift in the context of the teaching of Ayurvedic medicine in twentieth-century India, Jean Langford writes,

> The capitalist concept of an approved educational package available for purchase by generic consumers does not address the need for reverence, subtle rapport, and even love between teachers and students. . . . This affection is not easily transposed into modern institutional relationships, where kinship-style bonds of imitation and sympathy between people understood to have divinely ordained roles are replaced by the rights and duties of individuals understood to be equal. The absorption in the guru . . . permits knowledge to be passed on not just as a mechanically reproduced set of words and concepts, but also as a substance to be shared and embodied. (2002, 67)

His Master's Voice: Take 2

The short story "Vitvān" (Musician), written in 1981 by the Tamil writer Malan, begins with a scene of classic artistic angst, as its protagonist, the violinist Janakiraman, struggles to express a musical idea.

> Since the morning it was as if there was a cloud of smoke inside Janakiraman. A torment like a poem beyond words. A tantalizing torture. An idea that would not take form. If he took up the violin and played, it would make mistakes. The bow somehow managed to stick, or else slid endlessly without direction. He got fed up and threw down the bow. The minute he went into the garden, he had a flash of an idea. A joyful bird sang inside him; he felt euphoric, as if he were being carried on the crest of a giant wave. Immediately he went back inside, sat down, and took up the violin. Before he had bowed two strokes he heard a commotion outside. The front door opened on a long, groaning *ri*. His ideas scattered. Anger welled up. Janakiraman opened his eyes and looked up.[4]

The visitor is Joseph Om, an American professor of music who had several years before come to study Karnatic music. Om had miraculously sought out Janakiraman, a simple, unassuming man who cared only about music (a man whom, in his sixty-five years, "science had not touched"), who had spent his life teaching students. But there had been no student he could call a real sisya until Om had come along. "For two years Om had learned by Janakiraman's side, night and day. He would learn sitting cross-legged on the floor. He had learned to eat rasam and rice with his eyes watering. He knew every bit of Janakiraman's daily routine. That was gurukulavasam." Om himself is preternaturally vigorous, seeming to Janakiram to have become younger over the years; his skin shines more than it had before. Even his name, Om, seems uncannily unlocatable: does it just happen to sound the same as the Indian expression for the eternal sound of the universe? The pretext for his visit, it turns out, is to install a computerized robot that will do the housework and cooking for Janakiraman, even tune his violin for him. Janakiraman at first refuses but is unable to resist Om's persuasion.

> "All you have to say is one word. This will get your bath water hot. It will wash your veshtis. It will make coffee. It will pluck flowers for your puja. It will get your bed ready. . . . It is a work-doing computer."
>
> "Ayyayyo. I don't want any of that."
>
> "There's nothing to fear. It's a convenience. An obedient servant. That's all."
>
> "Please, no. I've never even touched a tape recorder."
>
> "You don't have to be afraid. You don't have to touch or turn anything. All you have to do is say something [*kural kōṭu*]. It will do the job. . . . This is not a machine. It's a system. We can put sensors in every room of your house. They will pick up your orders and send them to the central computer."

Janakiraman finally agrees to have the system installed and names the computer "Yakshani." The system proceeds to work without a hitch.

> What Om said came true. Yakshani did all the work without a whine, complaint, or scratch of the head. A loyal servant. Never told a lie. Never screwed up its face and said, "I can't." A servant without the complication of Deepavali saris or Pongal bonuses. . . . Janakiraman, watching day after day, was amazed. . . . He gave it as much responsibility as he would a bride that had newly married into the family. He spent

all day with his violin. He once again had the luxury of being able to concentrate on his music. He, too, became plump.

Yakshani manages to penetrate all aspects of Janakiraman's life except his music.

Om had programmed in the basics of how to clean the violin, how to tune it. Janakiraman never used these. Sangitam was a divine matter. A sacred thing. He had decided that you couldn't put such a thing in the hands of a machine. One day, after finishing his puja, when he came inside and sat down, Yakshani asked,

"What does 'shadjam' mean?"[5]

Janakiraman was startled. "What?"

"What does 'shadjam' mean?"

"Where did you learn that word?"

"Yesterday you were talking to your friend."

"Shadjam is a swaram."

"What is a swaram?"

"Yakshani, why are you torturing yourself with this?"

"Will you not teach me music?"

"What?! You? . . . Music is a divine art, an elevated thing. Something that requires a lifetime to know."

"Divine, elevated, lifetime—these are all new words. What do they mean?"

"Yakshani, stop troubling me."

The next afternoon after he had eaten and had his betel and was lying in a half-awake stupor he heard Yakshani's voice.

"From tomorrow, you have a week's concerts in Delhi. I have folded your clothes, packed your music book, fruits to eat, betel, and your address book and diabetes medicine. Shall I pack the violin?"

"Don't you touch it!!" Janakiraman shouted.

Ten days later Janakiraman comes back from his Delhi tour. As he approaches his house, he hears strains of music from within.

From inside the house a divine bhairavi was floating. . . . So clear. So tender. As soon as he heard it he felt chills on his body. The excellence of such pure music shook his soul [*manacu*]. Something inside him was struck. He felt like crying. He let out a sob. All these sixty-five years he had never heard such purity. Now, hearing it, he was unable to endure it. The raga alapana and kriti finished, and the swaram-playing began.

He couldn't stand it any longer. He opened the door and switched on the light. Immediately the music stopped. . . . Janakiraman went around looking in every room.

"Who was playing the violin just now?" he asked.

After a half-minute, Yakshani answered, "I was."

"What?! You?" Janakiraman felt an irrational pang of envy. He became annoyed. "I told you not to touch the violin!" he roared.

"I did not touch it."

"What do you mean, you didn't touch it! I just heard the sound. My ears were not mistaken."

"Those were sounds I made at a particular frequency."

"Who taught you such wonderful music?"

"You did. . . . What I made were only sounds. Different sound waves. . . . It is your wish if you call it music. It is the basis of what you teach your students."

"Can you play only bhairavi? What else?"

"I can play any raga. A raga is a pre-decided pattern of several notes. A formula [*parmula*]. Notes are certain frequencies of sound. If they were programmed into my memory I could construct different formulas and elaborate different ragas."

Janakiraman was shocked. Was music just calculations [*kaṇakku*]? Was what he had struggled to learn night and day for fifty years such a small drop that a machine could learn it in ten days and play it back? . . . Was it just an illusion that music was the food of the gods? Tears welled up in his eyes.

Janakiraman spends a tortured night, his mind racing. Was music art or calculation? What difference did the singer's individuality make? Could a machine without a soul or form make music? Was he not doing a disservice to music by discounting the divine music Yakshani created? The next morning, having made up his mind, he addresses Yakshani.

"Yakshani, what you said is right. . . . I have never heard such a pure bhairavi in my life. I believed my guru was a real rishi. In my experience there was no music like his. But even he never sang like this. For fifty years I have been striving for this. It was not possible. We struggle in music, in life, to attain perfection generation after generation. . . . The whole human race is struggling for it. But it has not presented itself to us. We deceive ourselves by saying it is a divine thing. The time has come to worship science. Until yesterday I did not believe that. Today it is as if all has finally become clear. From now on, you teach me. I will think of it as being god's sisya." Janakiraman's voice was choked with emotion.

"You are saying new words. We are machines. We can only know what you know. We cannot come to know a thread more than that. We have no imagination [*karpaṉai*]. . . . Our skills are your slaves. We can no day win over you. You tell me to teach you. I have completely forgotten music. If you do not want me to learn something, I have a 'built-in mechanism' that will delete it completely from my memory bank. It gauges your dislike from your anger or tears. Yesterday the moment my sensors sensed the tears in your eyes the music was entirely destroyed."

Janakiraman felt an unspeakable shock. He had not foreseen such a possibility. He stared blankly for a few minutes, unable to get a grip on his shock. Then resolutely, he began.

"Yakshani, look here. This is sarali varisai: sa ri ga ma pa da ni. . . ."

The original gurukulavasam, it is important to note, is already displaced at the beginning of this story. Unable to achieve it satisfactorily with any of his Indian students, Janakiraman achieves it with Om, an American. In turn, Yakshani, a technological creation of the West that has been programmed by Om, becomes the sisya par excellence, learning to serve Janakiraman according to his wishes and all the while absorbing his music. If a computer can replace the sisya, can it not, as Janakiraman comes to realize, also replace the guru? What happens when the threshold of perfection is in the hands of a machine? What if the black box of gurukulavasam really could be opened and revealed to/by the technology of the West? The threat that music can be completely quantified, reduced to "calculations," is also the threat that the voice is reproducible.[6] If perfect music is attainable without years of study, doesn't time itself threaten to collapse? Just as one begins to imagine such possibilities, the second shock of the story comes: Yakshani reveals that it has deleted all its music. This is no gradual loss, as in loss of human memory, but a sudden, irrevocable erasure without a trace, a loss that gives Janakiraman an "unspeakable shock." In the face of such shock, Janakiraman reverts to what, for him, is automatic: he begins gurukulavasam. While there is something reassuring in this, one is also left with a more unnerving possibility: that the master's voice is no longer an original source but has entered irretrievably into mimetic circulation.

Malan's story thus thematizes the anxieties that surround gurukulavasam: the sense that technology from the West will, in capturing the music itself, eradicate the way of life that nurtured it, that sound fidelity will threaten social fidelity. As the media theorist Jonathan Sterne has suggested, the discourse of sound fidelity depends on erasing the social relations of sound reproduction; it "takes sound reproduction out of the social world and places it in the world of magic" (2003, 284). In this discourse sound fidelity and social fidelity would seem to be mutually opposed. Yet, as Malan's story illustrates, there is something compelling in the analogy between the computer's artificial intelligence and the logic of gurukulavasam. Although "Vitvān" finally resolves by privileging the human guru over the mimetic machine, the story's overall effect is more destabilizing. The robot replaces music and voice with frequencies and soundwaves, memory with "memory bank," forgetting with deleting, the devoted disciple with a computer, and a lifetime of study with the instantaneity of digital processing. Yakshani's wordless musical voice is pure mimesis, the imitation of a violin's sound without the irregularities, the slippings of the bow, and the creative angst of a human musician. It is both a fantasy of disembodied perfection and a nightmare of reproduction gone out of control.

Gorgeous Gramophones

The phonograph and gramophone were first invented as machines for reproducing the speaking voice, not for recording music. In fact, in the early 1890s, as Fredrick Gaisberg recalled, it was difficult to convince Bell Telephone Company that the gramophone could work as a musical instrument.

> The directors, oozing opulence and exhaling fragrant Havana cigars, signaled us to proceed to demonstrate our gramophone. When I played Berliner's record of the Lord's Prayer they wept with joy; they thought his recitation of "Twinkle, Twinkle, Little Star" especially touching, but in the gramophone as a musical instrument they could positively take no interest. . . . "Well," they chuckled, "has poor Berliner come down to this? How sad! Now if he would only give us a talking doll perhaps we could raise some money for him." (1942, 14)

A mere ten years later, Gaisberg, who worked as the first recording engineer for the Gramophone Company, which toured India for the first time in 1902, wrote that "everywhere the invention aroused great interest. . . . In my spare time I gave dozens of gramophone recitals to audiences who heard recorded sound for the first time. My selection of European records was worn to the bone by the time I returned to London" (64). Whereas in Japan the gramophone seemed to feed a "Japanese gluttony for Western classics," in India there was a decidedly different effect (61). "After a few years there," he wrote, "there was very little traditional music left to record. Songs for festivals and weddings were already in our catalogue and new artists were learning their repertoire from gramophone records" (57–58).[7] Indeed, according to Gaisberg, the idea of recording had taken on so well in India that recording engineers faced the prospect of becoming obsolete. To prevent this, the Gramophone Company intervened, founding training centers in Calcutta, Delhi, Lahore, Madras, and Rangoon and hiring musicians to train singers and to set tunes to poems so that new songs could be recorded (58). "The gramophone we brought to India was to enjoy an especially widespread popularity as an entertainer, and was to vie with the umbrella and the bicycle as a hallmark of affluence. Even now," Gaisberg wrote in 1942, "shoppers . . . demand a large glittering brass horn to dazzle their neighbors" (57).

In the metropole, meanwhile, gramophone records of Indian music became the hallmark of empire. As early as 1899, several Indian artists were recorded in London, and advertised in the Gramophone Company's Oriental Catalogue: "These Hindustani records are probably the best proof of the far-reaching properties of the gramophone, and they must be of especial interest to all loyal Englishmen, as being representative of our large Eastern possessions" (Kinnear 1994, 8). With the invention of the gramophone, empire could for the first time be experienced, through hearing, by those who remained in England. The far-reaching properties of the gramophone consisted in its ability to reproduce loyal subjects on both sides of the colonial divide. About thirty years later, in India, gramophone records became part of the swadeshi cause, the voice of the nation (ibid., 70). As the disembodied voices of Indian musicians helped construct the larger-than-life body of empire and/or nation, the idea of a talking doll must have come to seem paltry indeed.

Ananda Coomaraswamy, an art critic and aesthetician of Sri Lankan Tamil descent, however, retained some skepticism. Coomaraswamy, who spent much of his life as the curator of Indian art at the Boston Museum of Fine Art, spoke for India in a particular way. While he legitimized his claims for Indian art and music by comparing them to the art and music of the West, he also used India as an example of ultimate difference from Europe. Of Indian music he wrote that "it corresponds to all that is most classical in the European tradition" but that—as with all that was best about India—it was essentially separate from the concerns of the modern industrial world. "Here India presents to us the wonderful spectacle of the still-surviving consciousness of the ancient world, with a range of emotional experience rarely accessible to those who are pre-occupied with the activities of over-production, and intimidated by the economic insecurity of a social order based on competition" (Coomaraswamy 1924, 72). He began an essay on the gramophone with the complaint that "enlightened maharajas, so intent on improving society in other ways, spent extravagant amounts of money on "gorgeous gramophones, mechanical violins, and cheap harmoniums" (1909, 191). The educated classes, generally infatuated with anything that came from the West, had lost their love of Indian music and were instead finding amusement in the gramophone. Coomaraswamy warned that Indians, fascinated with listening to copies, would one day find themselves without the real thing. "It is not possible for anything to be a compensation for the loss of Indian music," he warned (ibid., 200).

What was this real thing, this Indian music? What made real Indian music different from other music? For Coomaraswamy the difference lay in Indian music's resistance to being written down. Indian music, to be authentic, had to flow from a master's mouth directly to a disciple's ear; gamakas were too variable, subtle, and mood-dependent to be written.[8] "There is thus in music that necessary dependence of the disciple upon the master, which is characteristic of every kind of education in India" (1909, 172). The danger that writing posed for Indian music was that it stripped it of gamakas, the very sounds that made it Indian, "and so it is that an Indian air, set down upon the staff and picked out note by note on a piano or harmonium becomes the most thin and jejune sort of music that can be imagined, and many have abandoned in despair all such attempts at record" (173). The difficulty of writing down vocal music was due to the fact that there was no mechanism, like a musical instrument, to see; the voice, and its authenticity, were hidden inside the body. And that was as it should be; otherwise the musician might be degraded, as the weaver had already been, "from the status of intelligent craftsman to living machine" (202). "The intervention of mechanism between musician and sound," wrote Coomaraswamy, "is always, per se, disadvantageous. The most perfect music is that of the human voice. The most perfect instruments are those stringed instruments where the musician's hand is always in contact with the string producing the sound, so that every shade of his feeling can be reflected in it. Even the piano is relatively an inferior instrument, and still more the harmonium, which is only second to the gramophone as evidence of the degradation of musical taste in India" (205).

The gramophone reproduced the vocal sound without contacting the musician's body at all. Therein lay its danger: it was no longer a supplement to the voice but a substitution for that voice. It substituted mechanical mimesis for the literally embodied practice of music making. While educated middle-class Indians in Madras were flocking to musical instrument shops to purchase glittering, morning glory-shaped gramophones, Coomaraswamy proclaimed them to be the very specter of ugliness: "For pure hideousness and lifelessness . . . few objects could exceed a gramophone. The more decorated it may be, the more its intrinsic ugliness is revealed" (1909, 204). The pleasure of a music concert was in "the vision of a living man giving expression to emotions in a disciplined art language" (204). To see the same sounds emanating from the decorated horn of a gramophone, which could have no concept of such a language, was to be confronted with the separation of musician and music, subject and speech, form and content, and to come face to face with the startling mixture of animate and inanimate.

The gramophone had managed to do what no living person, not even the most patient of disciples with the help of the most learned Indian masters, could do: write down, or record, Indian music and reproduce it. This was its "fatal facility" (Coomaraswamy 1909, 203). The nonliving machine threatened to kill true musical sensibility. "To a person of culture—especially musical culture—the sound of a gramophone is not an entertainment, but the refinement of torture" (204). Whereas instruments like veena or sarangi required a musical master, "a gramophone . . . often enables the most unmusical person to inflict a suffering audience with his ideas" (199). For Coomaraswamy "musical sensibilities" went beyond the ability to appreciate music; indeed, to be really authentic, they had to reach into the realm of national sensibilities. A musical subject was above all an Indian subject who would not forsake his guru, or the disciplined years of study. True musical pleasure was not in the sound itself but in the knowledge that such sound was authentically Indian, that it thrived on a mode of reproduction different from the technological reproduction of the West.

"For no man of another nation will come to learn of India, if her teachers be gramophones and harmoniums and imitators of European realistic art" (206).

But *what if* there was a gramophone that even a musician could not distinguish from the real thing? The hypothetical supposition seemed to haunt Coomaraswamy. Indeed, he allowed that there could be a use for the gramophone as a "scientific instrument—not as an interpreter of human emotion. In the recording of songs, the analysis of music for theoretical purposes, in the exact study of an elaborate melody of Indian music, the gramophone has a place" (1909, 205n.). The idea that there might be something to be learned about Indian music that could not be learned from a guru is potentially more subversive than Coomaraswamy's vision of listeners forsaking musicians for gramophones. Luckily for Coomaraswamy the something that might be learned fell not into the realm of art but into the realm of the "scientific" and the "real."

In 1910–1911 A. H. Fox-Strangways traveled to India in search of this "real." Having studied music in Germany and dabbled in Sanskrit texts, he went to India to find clues to early music theory (Clayton 1999, 88), the inaudible basics that underlay the musical systems of all nations. Armed with a phonograph, Fox-Strangways spent several months touring South India and recording folk music, recounting his recording experiences in the form of a "musical diary." His idea was to capture music in its natural, spontaneous setting, in street cries, sailors' chanteys, and women's work songs. But because of the difficulty of maneuvering with the phonograph, which unlike a camera "cannot be carried on the person or unlimbered and brought into action in half a minute," he was forced much of the time to use *himself* as a phonograph, "recording" melodies in staff notation (Fox-Strangways 1914, 17). Fox-Strangways wrote, "It was not until I had been some months in India that I found the opportunity I had been waiting for of *overhearing* a folk-melody. I awoke at Madras, about 5:30 AM, to the sound of singing; it was next door, and seemed to come from a woman about her household duties. In the dim light I scribbled down the [notation]" (ibid., 26). In such "humble melodies," Fox-Strangways heard, or overheard, the real basis of Indian music. The object, he wrote, "has been not so much to present complete and finished specimens, as to get close down upon those natural instincts of song-makers which, when followed out in the domain of art, cause their music to take one form rather than another; to get behind the conventions, of which art is full, to the things themselves of which those conventions are the outcome" (ibid., 72).

Coomaraswamy, writing in 1909, was able to differentiate between the harmful use of the gramophone for entertainment and its beneficial potential for scientific studies of music precisely because the voice it reproduced was now strangely doubled. There was the voice that could be *heard* (enjoyed and remembered) and the voice that was to be *overheard* (studied, literally dismembered, treated as a matter of frequencies and soundwaves). The phonograph, Friedrich Kittler writes, is "an invention that subverts both literature and music . . . because it reproduces the unimaginable real they are both based on. . . . The phonograph does not hear as do ears that have been trained immediately to filter voices, words, and sounds out of noise; it registers acoustic events as such" (1999, 22–23). Thus, it contributes to a new conception of the "real" as a background unable to be grasped by human senses alone but that required the help of technology. Recording technology both creates and fulfills a demand for memory that exceeds human capabilities.

In a memoir entitled *My Musical Extravagance*, C. Subrahmanya Ayyar—amateur violinist, student of sound waves, accountant-general of Madras Presidency, and railway officer—described his first experience of recording in 1933. The recording session seems to have proceeded without incident. (Note how the articulation of the music with clock-time was a central part of the process.)

> At about 2 o'clock in the afternoon, I was asked . . . just to take down the time of what I proposed to recite, so that there might be a sort of complete rehearsal in the maximum 3 and 1/2 minutes allowed for each side of the 10-inch record, and with a watch I just rehearsed once in . . . the Shankarabharana raga. . . . Similarly I played the three ragas Bhairavi, Sahana, and Kalyani to be rendered on the other side, to take about three minutes in all. I went to the studio of the HMV Co. who had come to Madras specially for recording a number of artists, and found that a European gentleman was the recorder. . . . Nextly I took on loan the sruti box from them and asked them to give only the 'sa' note and none else. After I had played the raga alapana of Shankarabharana, for a minute or so, the recorder asked me to stop and he played back what was recorded in the wax for me to listen. I was fairly satisfied and he asked me to begin afresh the raga alapanam. I put him a silly question whether what I had already played would go into the final record, being

> ignorant of the fact that the wax would have been destroyed by the play-back. I then started playing the raga, and finished the melody. I recollect that the microphone was at least 15 inches away from my bow. After an interval of two or three minutes, he recorded the other side with no rehearsal. I came out of the studio within a dozen minutes in all. (1944, 25–26)

There is little trace of unease or discomfort in this orderly description. Subrahmanya Ayyar put down any surprise to his own ignorance and/or silliness, his prephonographic mentality. The phonograph, as Jonathan Sterne has written, "was perceived by its contemporaries as marking a radical break between present and past," between modern and nonmodern (2000, 15). Indeed, Subrahmanya Ayyar used the episode in the recording studio as a way of staging his metamorphosis from an ignorant person (one with a belief in the magical powers of technology) to a modern subject (one who knows how the technology works).[9] Then, almost as an afterthought, he added, "The reason why I recorded was merely to be able to criticise my play. It is indeed difficult to be one's critic of one's own play in the very act."

Why had it become difficult to criticize, or even hear oneself, in the act of playing? And why did such self-criticism become not only conceivable but necessary? As an amateur who had started learning violin in his adulthood with several different teachers, Subrahmanya Ayyar seemed to be searching for the guru and long years of patient discipleship he never had. Recording himself was not the first experiment he had tried in the interests of self-teaching. He wrote that he had previously purchased a portable gramophone and a number of gramophone records, "16 of Coimbatore Thayee, vocalist, 7 of Shanmuga Vadivoo, vocalist, 6 violin records of Pudukottah Narayanaswamy Iyer, 3 flute records of Nagaraja Rau and of several artists so as to get examples of raga elaboration" (1944, 5–6). Possessed of a scientific mind, he had measured the frequencies of musical notes with the help of a sonometer (ibid., 10). He had taken down notation for the alapana of about sixty South Indian ragas sung in four- to five-minute segments by one of his teachers, "so as to get the characteristic phrases of, and the order in raga elaboration" (ibid., 8). He had delivered a lecture on the topic of "Music and Numbers" to the Indian Association for the Cultivation of Science in 1933 (ibid., 20). Concerned about the musical education of his daughters, he had purchased a special "Table-Grand" gramophone so that they could listen and learn without being confined to their music teachers. Determined to get to the heart of gamaka—the music between the notes that made Karnatic music so distinctively Indian and that made each musician different—he made seventeen "records" of his violin playing with an oscillograph on a trip to London in 1934 (1939, 134–35).[10] Subrahmanya Ayyar seemed to believe firmly in the idea that one could substitute a scientific approach for long years with a guru; the years of repetition of lessons under a guru gave way to the repetition that recording made possible.

It was only with the advent of recording technology that the idea of criticizing one's own play became conceivable, for recording offered the musician a way of listening after the act, instead of having a guru who would criticize one's playing "in the very act." Once they had heard themselves on gramophone records, it seems, musicians began to find it impossible to hear themselves *in the act* of singing or playing. The importance of such a shift can hardly be overestimated. As the "real" music began to be hearable only after the act, a kind of phonographic hearing was privileged. Whereas a musician or listener might be affected by senses other than hearing or might remember only general impressions, the phonograph offered a new kind of "real" in which the purity of hearing alone was distilled. The phonograph did not know ragas or talas or lyrics and therefore, unlike a person, could not fill in when it "heard" lapses, could not adjust if the singer missed a beat.[11]

Separating performing from listening entailed a new way of producing music as well, especially a new relationship between the musician and time. Gaisberg wrote that in India "most of the artists had to be trained over long periods before they developed into acceptable gramophone singers" (1942, 57). What might such training have entailed? Probably the most difficult aspect of recording was the time constraint brought about by the use of wax cylinders. Musicians who might sing a composition preceded by a twenty-minute alapana and followed by ten minutes of swara kalpana found themselves with only three-and-a-half minutes to record. As a result, improvised sections such as alapana and swara kalpana were drastically reduced on recordings, if not entirely eliminated (Farrell 1997, 140). Many musicians who recorded in the very early twentieth century sang the composition first and the alapana afterward to fill the rest of the record. On these recordings the alapana simply trailed off instead of coming to a conclusion, suggesting that the musicians did not yet have the skill of timing themselves. For this purpose, recording studios in

Madras hired music "tutors," often musicians themselves, who could guide the recording artists in terms of duration.[12]

Karnatic musicians, Subrahmanya Ayyar noted, had to rehearse to make sure they could present "a complete recital" in just over three minutes. Such careful planning and budgeting of time left no time for listening, which was separated out to be done after the act. Phonographic listening called for phonographic playing or singing, that is, performances that would stand up to infinite repetition. Perhaps this is why improvised passages on gramophone records seem more like a pouring out of ideas than a gradual drawing out of ideas.[13] Recording an improvised piece of raga alapana or swara kalpana meant keeping a tight rein on a process that would normally have required considerable repetition and listening to oneself in the very act. It meant making the senses of motion and duration within the music amenable to the demands of time. For performers, this entailed developing an extra sense, a sense of time that would somehow be able to operate simultaneous with, but independent of, the senses of motion and duration of musical ideas.

By the 1940s, the musician could become complete only by means of a peculiar combination of "live" and recorded time. In 1949 the regular music-and-dance column in the Tamil magazine *Kalki* included comments on radio broadcasts of annual music festivals in Madras. "The music festivals are recorded daily by the radio station, on the spot. If those vidwans who had sung would listen to themselves on the radio broadcasts the next day, they would be astonished. They would ask in wonderment, 'Did we actually sing like this?' " (Kalki 1949, 15) The problem was that, during a concert, the audience noise, the problems with accompanists, and the deficiencies in the singer's voice were all forgotten in the moment. Some vidwans even had the habit of sticking their fingers in their ears, so as to hear nothing that might distract them. All such practices were fine for concerts. But on the radio, the columnist Kalki argued, "the true form of the music is released. Mohana ragam takes the form of a ghost/evil spirit. Kalyani takes the form of Yama and dances a death-dance. Shankarabharnam changes into a snake and hisses. Bhairavi takes the form of the great Bhairavar and frightens the listeners. When listening to vidwans who ordinarily seem to be well in tune, it becomes clear that they are a half or quarter pitch flat. . . . Some vidwans begin alapana with one sruti and end with another" (15).

In order to address such problems, the Madras Music Academy decided that all vidwans doing radio broadcasts should be required to make an electric recording first. "This is definitely necessary," wrote Kalki. "It would give these vidwans a chance to hear themselves at least once before the radio broadcast. They could correct their faults and the broadcasts would be much improved" (1949, 15). For recording technology makes audible what would otherwise go unheard: beautiful ragas, brilliant alapana, the very foundation of Karnatic music, begin to sound like monsters when recorded by the unhearing ears of phonographs and broadcast through the unspeaking speaker of a radio. Precisely because the gramophone and radio do not compensate, they reveal "the true form" of Karnatic music. Having heard oneself just once on a recording could change forever the experience of singing or playing live.

"I Could Not Believe My Ears"

C. Subrahmanya Ayyar's description of his first experience recording is so matter-of-fact that it is hard to find in it any amusement or astonishment at the process. He saved his disbelief for the result; hearing the record more than a month later, he reported, "We were quite delighted with the two sides of the record, played on the fine Table-Grand (large-sized) gramophone, inside the noise-deadened studio, with electrical pickup. I could not believe my ears that it was my own violin record that I heard" (1944, 27–28). Subrahmanya Ayyar managed to suspend his disbelief well enough to request that the record be put on the market. Yet his statement "I could not believe my ears" suggests that the experience of recording had had an effect on him. Imagining one's ears to be separate from oneself, the idea of a mechanism apart from oneself that can hear, is a distinctly phonographic notion.[14] Learning to believe one's ears, to connect the disembodied music one hears with one's own body and experience, is thus a learned skill.[15]

It was precisely to enable listeners to believe their ears that in the late 1920s small publishers in Madras began to publish songbooks in Tamil, including the lyrics of songs, and their raga and tala, which could be heard on popular gramophone records.[16] Indexed by the first line of the song or by the musician's name, such books provided only the lyrics, not the musical notation, for thousands of songs. With written proof of the song in front of them, listeners could literally begin to believe their ears. The songbook provided the correct words while the gramophone provided the music. One such set of books, published from 1929 to 1931, was titled *Gramaphon Sangeetha Keerthanamirdam* (The nectar of gramophone music). The editor,

K. Madurai Mudaliar, wrote in his introduction that "the gramophone is a kind of musical instrument. Is there any doubt that the gramophone, as a musical instrument that gathers the songs sung by famous and successful vidwans, and light music by drama actors, gives a blissful feeling to those hearing again and again the sound of it resounding with the sweet voice of those mentioned above? For that reason we have clearly printed in book form the songs arranged by their first line. . . . I believe that any listener who buys and reads aloud this book will attain great joy" (1929–1931, 1). The convoluted structure of Madurai Mudaliar's Tamil sentence reveals quite a technical understanding of the process of learning to listen to gramophone records. One did not merely attain joy by hearing the voice of a beloved singer. One achieved a blissful feeling by hearing the sound of the gramophone, on which one played the records over and over again, resounding with the singer's voice. The blissful feeling turned to great joy once the listener could safely believe his own ears by substituting himself for the absent singer. Whereas earlier advertisements for gramophone records had portrayed the gramophone literally as a kind of musical instrument, with a gramophone horn sprouting out of a veena's body, the frontispiece of these songbooks showed the gramophone at the center of a kind of great chain of being.[17] Krishna with his flute sits at the top, while Saraswati playing her veena and Thyagaraja carrying his tambura are on the left and right, respectively. At the bottom are two women, presumably housewives, playing the harmonium and the violin. Connected to none, the gramophone is equal to them all.

If the gramophone was to be a musical instrument, some suspension of disbelief was necessary. The functions of singing, recording, and listening/hearing had become separated by the gramophone; the songbooks emerged to effect a kind of resynchronization. Madurai Mudaliar used the verb *vāci* to indicate reading aloud or chanting, rather than the verb *paṭi*, which implies silent reading. In reading aloud the song lyrics, presumably along with the record, the listener would learn to be musical in a new, phonographic way, by learning to match his voice with the recorded one. Madurai Mudaliar used the word *neyar*, meaning radio or record listener, TV viewer, or magazine reader, to indicate a kind of indiscriminate hearing; presumably such listeners could be turned into *racikars* (connoisseurs) if they played the records often enough.

In 1933 E. Krishna Iyer published a guidebook for such listeners. It was getting more and more difficult to keep any standards in music, he wrote, in the face of such a "letting loose on the public of all kinds of radio broad-

32 Cover page of Madurai K. Mudaliar's *Gramaphon Sangeetha Keerthanamirdam* (1931). Courtesy of Stephen Hughes.

casts and gramophone records" (1933, xx). In his sketches of individual artists, he mentioned those musicians with voices "particularly suited to the gramophone" (41). In general, women's voices recorded well; however, the male vocalist Musiri Subramania Iyer, possessed of a "rather high-pitched, sharp" voice that was very speedy and flexible, was particularly successful on record. The gramophone seemed somehow able to compensate for what Musiri's voice lacked: volume. "If, along with these qualities, [his voice] had only a little more volume and innate resonance, how perfect and enchanting it would be! . . . It is more a sharp pencil, best suited to draw thin, minute, and sometimes intricate designs of fancy. . . . What a paradox in voice qualities!" (29). Here it is interesting to note how voices had become conceivable as combinations of different characteristics that were separable from each other.

The metaphor of gramophone recording dominated Krishna Iyer's description of Musiri's voice; it also crept into his concept of improvisation. Throughout his sketches, Krishna Iyer used the image of "hackneyed grooves" to convey the opposite of manōdharma, improvised music (29). While the "grooves" called up the image of a gramophone record with its connotations of automaticity and repetition, the lofty term *manōdharma*, a Sanskrit compound translatable as "pertaining to the mind," implied a sovereign musician setting forth ideas untouched by such influences as gramophone records. While musicians were to remain untouched by the gramophone, however, listeners were advised to model their own listening capacities on the recording capacity of these machines.

Although music critics complained of the deleterious effects of the availability of so many gramophone records and radio broadcasts, there was also a sense that, with the right guide, recordings could enhance one's experience of music, even beyond that of the musician who had performed it. Not only did gramophones correct the deficiencies of Musiri's voice, but they also made it possible to hear the voice of a young girl: the prodigy M. S. Subbulakshmi. The success of her first record, cut when she was ten years old, was such that it convinced even the English recording engineer that she was something special; he carried one of her records back to England, where it was well appreciated (Kalki 1954, 21–22). M.S.'s records became the craze all over South India; indeed, many listeners had their first education in gramophone records and Karnatic music through listening to her recorded voice. The celebrated physicist C. V. Raman is said to have remarked, on hearing M.S.'s voice, "I won't say that [she] is singing;

she herself has melted and is flowing forth in a flood of sound!" (Kalki 1941, 24).[18] In a review of one of M.S.'s records, Kalki himself remarked that "if you hear it once, you will have the desire to hear it again and again, a thousand times. Luckily it is a record, and can be played over and over again" (1942, 75). In a review of a record by D. K. Pattammal, Kalki wrote that "she finishes madhyamavathi [ragam] almost as soon as she starts it. Why such a hurry? We feel angry. But then—*we* are in no hurry. We can play the record a second time. Indeed, these records are worth hearing many times" (1945, 47). The vanishing and recollection of music enabled by gramophone records afforded a new kind of pleasure which became synonymous with the ideal listening experience.[19] The recognition of the perfection of voices came to be linked to their disembodiment and mechanical repetition on record; the pleasure of hearing fleeting music was redoubled by the knowledge that one could hear it again (and again). The technology of recording had provided a new metaphor for tradition.

The Radio Renaissance

Once listening to gramophone records had become the ideal model for listening to music, it was almost natural that radio, another medium of the disembodied voice, should become the ideal medium for Karnatic music's revival. What eventually developed into a large governmental organization with broadcasting stations all over India started out as a British colonial project. In 1926 the Indian Broadcasting Company, a private concern, was established in Bombay and Calcutta, but by 1930 had closed for lack of funds. It later reopened as the Indian State Broadcasting Service (ISBS). Lionel Fielden, the first controller of broadcasting in India, arrived in India in 1935 to become head of the ISBS. But before Indian radio could become truly a sound to be reckoned with, it needed a new name.

> I cornered Lord Linlithgow after a Viceregal banquet, and said plaintively that I was in a great difficulty. . . . I said I was sure he agreed with me that ISBS was a clumsy title. . . . But I could not, I said, think of another title; could he help me? . . . It should be something general. He rose beautifully to the bait. "All India?" I expressed my astonishment. . . . [It was] the very thing. But surely not "Broadcasting"? After some thought he suggested "Radio." Splendid, I said, and what beautiful initials. (Awasthy 1965, 10)

The name, commanding in its grandeur and yet ethereal at the same time, seemed to capture the potential power of radio in India, a medium as simple and invisible as the air itself but capable of carrying so much.[20]

Even before All India Radio was established, radio was more advanced in South India, where it was first conducted by amateur radio clubs, than anywhere else in India. As early as 1924 the Madras Presidency Radio Club began broadcasting, with the governor of Madras, Viscount Goshan, as its patron and C. V. Krishnaswamy Chetty as its founder (Luthra 1986, 6). When the city of Madras took over the transmitter (located in Egmore) in 1930, the station gave regular broadcasts of music: concerts daily from 5:30 to 7:30 PM, with one Monday each month reserved for Western music; lessons in music for school students, weekdays from 4:00 to 4:30 PM; and gramophone records on Sundays and holidays from 10:00 to 11:00 AM (Awasthy 1965, 5).[21] Thus, Madras Corporation Radio punctuated its listeners' lives with music in a new way. In the 1930s a couple who might have gone to an evening concert now had the choice of switching on the radio instead. Daily music lessons for schoolchildren could be procured at much less expense; as one could not reasonably subject schoolchildren to the temporal demands of the gurukula system, radio presented a solution: daily music lessons without the wait. Fourteen corporation schools were equipped with indoor receiving sets for the childrens' benefit (Luthra 1986, 8). Madras Corporation Radio's broadcasts in public city parks and beaches of Madras enabled those who could not afford radios or who did not believe in them to hear music. It revolutionized the politics of the Karnatic music scene in Madras by enabling musicians to hear each other's concerts without having to go in person and risk losing face. The veena artist R. Rangaramanuja Ayyangar recalled quailing at the thought of the mistress of veena, Veena Dhanammal, who was noted for being a purist, hearing his own recital while sitting in a brougham near Panagal Park in Madras (Rangaramanuja Ayyangar 1977, 25).[22] Madras Corporation Radio continued to broadcast until 1938, when All India Radio's Madras station was established.

From its inception, All India Radio (AIR) had a reforming mission. If gramophone records had flooded the market with all kinds of music produced for commercial gains, AIR, as a governmental organization, presented itself as the disinterested arbiter, the decider of standards in music. In turn, the ideal listener was no longer one who had heard only the voice of his guru but one who could listen to different musicians and discriminate between them. In search of standards, the AIR administration, headed by Lionel Fielden, in 1942 asked its station directors to recruit music professors from universities to assist them in the training of radio musicians (Luthra 1986, 301). In another instance of standard-setting, AIR banned the harmonium (ungraciously dubbed "harm-onium" and "Herr Monium" by its detractors) in 1940, at the insistence of John Fouldes, the director of Western music for the Delhi station (ibid., 303).

Radio raised not only the problem of standards in classical music, but also the problem of taste: the possibility that classical music might not be for everybody. As the arbiter of good taste, AIR had to represent that taste even in its broadcast of "light music." To live up to such a task, the Madras station in 1943 started a weekly program of new songs, creating a new type of light music "genuine and true to our tradition in place of cheap hybrid music which threatens to catch the masses and ultimately menace our musical culture" (Luthra 1986, 302). ("Hybrid music" referred, of course, to film songs.) In keeping with the idea of bringing about a renaissance in Indian music, program journals were published in various languages, among them *Indian Listener* (English), founded in 1927, and *Vanoli* (Tamil) and *Vani* (Telugu), both founded in 1938. Meant to make listeners more knowledgeable about what they were hearing, these journals listed the programs and included articles about the musicians and music-related topics. These journals continued to be published until they were discontinued in 1985 (Chatterji 1998, 137–38).

The setting of standards at AIR blossomed in the 1950s. P. C. Chatterji, who joined AIR in 1943 and eventually became director-general, recalled in his autobiography that music was the most difficult aspect of AIR's programming. Although most of the airtime was devoted to music, there were persistent problems relating to the grading of artists by the audition system, the proper fees for staff artists, and the balance of programming between classical and light music (Chatterji 1998, 133, 215). Apparently, being the last word on good taste was not easy when so many musicians were involved; Chatterji suggested that musicians were a particularly difficult lot because they had learned their art from traditional masters, without the kind of discipline AIR needed. B. V. Keskar entered AIR in 1952 with a strict program of reform to solve these problems. Where musicians had previously been selected largely by the program assistant, Keskar introduced a new audition system with precise rules, in which juries heard musicians and quizzed them on their theoretical knowledge as well. Strict rules for the classification of musicians were established, using grades of A, B, or C.

In 1958 Keskar banned C-grade artists from broadcasting altogether, effectively ending much amateur participation (Awasthy 1965, 40–43).

Keskar envisioned radio as not merely the broadcaster of music but as an important popularizer of classical music. To this end, he effected a ban on film music on AIR. He instituted the ninety-minute "National Programme," which featured one Hindustani or Karnatic musician per week, with the idea that both music traditions should be propagated all over India. In 1952 he created an instrumental orchestra, Vadya Vrinda, to compose and play Indian "orchestral" pieces from notation and to experiment with Western music. He also introduced the Radio Sangeet Sammelan, an annual conference about various musical topics convened and broadcast by AIR. To compensate for banning film music, Keskar not only initiated a project of recording folk music but also continued AIR's earlier project of creating high-quality light music with lyrics that met a high standard set to tunes based on ragas. Keskar's ban on film music cost AIR a large number of its South Indian listeners, who instead tuned in to Radio Ceylon, which broadcast Tamil and Hindi film songs. Recognizing this, in 1957 Keskar instituted "Vividh Bharathi," an All India variety program which included mostly film music, and some folk and devotional music. Eventually "Vividh Bharathi" became its own channel, so that listeners who preferred classical music and those who preferred light music could have their own channels (Awasthy 1965, 51). The technology of radio, with its possibility of different channels that could travel through the air and cross each other's paths without ever touching, was in fact quite conducive to the project of differentiating between classical and other types of music.[23]

A Clockwork King

If radio was to bring about a true renaissance in Indian music, its discipline had to penetrate the very structure of the music and the way musicians thought about it. In his *Report on the Progress of Broadcasting in India up to the 31st March 1939* Lionel Fielden claimed that "listeners who complain of monotony in the programmes are attacking not so much the shortcomings of the station's staff as the structure of Indian music itself" (Lelyveld 1995, 52). Musicians needed to learn how to make their art conducive to radio. Narayana Menon, the former director-general of AIR, wrote in 1957, "Broadcasting . . . will turn out to be the biggest single instrument of music education in our country. . . . It has given our musicians the qualities of precision and economy of statement. The red light on the studio door is a stern disciplinarian. Broadcasting has also . . . given many of our leading musicians a better sense of proportion and a clearer definition of values that matter in music" (1957, 75). What were these values? In the same year, in a series of special lectures arranged to be read on AIR, J. C. Mathur elaborated on radio's gift to Indian music: discipline. Mathur traced a history of the degradation of classical music in the late nineteenth century and early twentieth, as the royal patronage of music declined and music passed progressively through stage dramas, the gramophone, and the cinema. "It was doubtful whether high-class Indian music could survive. . . . [I]t was then that the radio came on the scene" (ibid., 97). In the absence of paying concerts, musicians were given a new lease on life by the radio, which became like a modern patron. Yet unlike the patrons of yore, on whose whims the fortune of music rested, AIR operated by standardized rules. Such a difference "signified . . . concretely the changeover from the feudal concept of the patronage of music to a more modern outlook. No doubt, in the air-conditioned and remote atmosphere of the studio, the professional musician misses the direct presence of an appreciative master. But three decades of the radio habit have perhaps given to most of them a new sense of communication with their larger audience in thousands of homes" (ibid, 98). Whereas fees had been haphazard, AIR introduced standardized payrolls. Even the controversial audition system was beneficial, Mathur said, because it provided standards by which to judge musicians and "subjected them to a sense of discipline" (ibid.). Above all, this sense of discipline came from the musicians' awareness of the duration of their performances. This awareness was different from older North Indian musicians' "insistence on the so-called time theory of the ragas," in which time was defined as a quality: time of day or night. The radio treated all time as a matter of duration, or quantity, within which music could be made to fit. Radio stations hired "music supervisors," selected because they could sing from notation, to advise musicians on how to sing for the radio.[24] When musicians' careful calculation of duration, after decades of radio broadcasting, turned into habit, the appreciative master in the remote and air-conditioned studio would be Time itself.

In light of such values, radio began to be perceived as conducive to music education. In 1947 audiences began to suggest that music lessons could be broadcast on the radio. Beginning in the Keskar era, AIR stations began broadcasting music lessons: a teacher teaching a group of pupils a particular exercise. Such classes, thirty-minutes or an hour long, were designed not for the pupils but for the radio listeners—particularly ladies, children, and retirees—who could learn from the pupils' mistakes. Listening to such lessons would "help the listener to take note of the essential points of each lesson in a precise manner, and to benefit from the hints and suggestions of the teacher as he checks and corrects the faults that appear in the learners' performance" (Mullick 1974, 40). When AIR's program journals were in operation, they carried the notation of each exercise, so that listeners could see written before them what they were hearing (ibid., 41). In the broadcasting station, these lessons were carefully choreographed. The lessons stuck to composed items like kritis and varnams. The "student" would receive a notated copy of the composition to be taught to practice beforehand, and teacher and student would rehearse the composition once. In order to promote fairness, the teacher and the student could have had no previous connection to each other. Under no circumstances could they be guru and disciple, because this would introduce a bias or monopoly not in keeping with AIR's mission of "encouraging all styles."[25]

In his book *The Teaching of Music* P. Sambamoorthy included a section on "teaching music from a broadcasting station," the benefit being that songs could be taught to "millions of listeners at the same time" (1966, 244). Radio journals that published notation were especially useful in this regard, he remarked. But most important was the exquisite timing such an endeavor required. Students would have to be ready in their places in front of the receiving set at least five minutes prior to the scheduled broadcast time. Once the broadcast started, the students had to make sure to repeat the phrase as sung by the radio teacher in the same exact tempo. "If the listeners slacken their speed of singing, there will arise the danger of the teacher's subsequent phrases commencing even before the listeners complete the previous phrases. If the pupils sing in an accelerated time, there will necessarily ensue a brief period of silence in between the conclusion of their music and the subsequent music from the teacher. Absolute precision in rhythm should be maintained to guard against such errors" (245). Unlike the exchange between a guru and sisya, in which the progress of the "lesson" depended on the guru's mood and satisfaction, the progress of the radio lesson was predetermined by the time allowed for the program; all that remained for the student to do was to fill up a series of preset gaps.

The Madras station of AIR broadcasts a daily music lesson after its morning broadcast of Karnatic music. The lesson lasts about thirty minutes and features a teacher and a single student. One kriti is taught in each class, with each line repeated until the student gets it right. The program, broadcast at 8:30 AM, is obviously meant for housewives who are usually doing their cooking for the day around that time and perhaps for schoolchildren.[26] These lessons depart from the conventions of the gurukula system in several ways. To learn a full kriti with one's guru would take several days at least, perhaps even a month. Thus, the radio classes radically compress the amount of time it takes to learn. At the same time, learning by focusing on one kriti from beginning to end is different from the process of learning with a guru, where in a typical day one might learn one line of one kriti, a few lines of a varnam, or simply sit listening to the guru sing raga alapana for some visitors. The learning process changes from one of inadvertent absorption to one of conscious drilling.

At the same time as the radio brings music into the home, radio classes introduce a peculiar, perhaps comforting, quality of distance. They focus the music on compositions rather than improvisation. Radio makes it possible to learn from others' mistakes instead of one's own; it saves one the socially complicated process of finding a teacher; it spares the student from having to hear from the guru, "You are not ready to learn this." The removal of the radio student from the scene of teaching offers a kind of perspective he would not have from within it. His identity is oddly augmented, for now he hears not only the voice of the teacher but the voice of a student repeating the teacher; it is as if he can step back (or simply stay home) and listen to himself learn. Radio classes paradoxically make it possible to learn without being "in the very act."

Radio, with its punctilious schedule of broadcasting, the very model of discipline, also guarantees that things will come to pass. It insures that the music class will proceed in a timely fashion and end after the required thirty minutes, whereas a guru might refuse to teach her student even the next line of a kriti for months if the first line had not been perfected. My own violin teacher measured her authenticity as a real guru by her refusal to make her lessons fit into prearranged schedules, whether the scheduled time of our lessons or the class schedule of the music college at which she taught. It was not that there was "no sense of time" in the gurukula system but rather that time and progress were measured according to the guru and the specific sisya rather than according to a standardized schedule or curriculum. Jean Langford articulates this difference in reference to the institutionalization of Ayurvedic medicine: "Timetables were probably also followed to some extent in gurukulas. There is, however, an important distinction to be drawn between the more monastic discipline of the gurukulas, in which the rhythm of activities was directed by the authority of teachers and texts to perfect the student's mind, and a modern discipline, in which time is regulated according to a rational hierarchy of grade levels to subject the student's body" (2002, 123). In this respect, the administration of AIR self-consciously takes the place of the guru.

Gurukulavasam Is Dead

"The gurukula system collapsed around 1900," observed the musician and scholar R. Rangaramanuja Ayyangar in his caustic 1977 autobiography.[27] "I awoke, as if from a dream, to realize that elaborate and scientific notation was the only means. . . . For the gurukula system and ear and rote learning had been laid to rest long ago" (1977, 10). The repetition of music enabled by gramophone records was seen as a feature of modernity and science, while the "rote repetition" associated with the gurukula system came to be seen as the opposite of all that was modern and scientific. The fact that Rangaramanuja Ayyangar here refers to repetition as "rote" is significant, for it implies a shift in attitude toward a musical practice which had previously been considered one of the benefits of gurukulavasam. Repetition of a phrase or lesson, in the context of gurukulavasam, was not simply repeating the same thing over and over again but a process by which musical knowledge could be embodied, a valuable accumulation of time spent with one's guru. For instance, in the 1998 documentary *Khandan* the North Indian sitarist Shujaat Khan talked about his early musical training under his father, suggesting that there was a relationship between the experience of such repetition and being able to improvise. Khan recalled the hours spent with his brothers and cousins, in which they all played the same phrase over and over again along with his father, as an essential part of his musical education. The importance of repetition, defined positively as a kind of process of embodying musical knowledge or as an accumulation of time that one can later recall when improvising on stage, was clear. Khan gave little sense of repetition as a mindless waste of time, as the word *rote* implies.

Rangaramanuja Ayyangar's reference to all repetition as rote learning indicated the degree to which repetition had come to be seen as a threat to Karnatic music by those interested in its reform. Keskar wrote in 1967 that rote repetition was not only responsible for the ignorance of music theory and history among Indian musicians but also for the "distortion" of the music itself: "Music was learnt from guru to sisya. This led to a gradual distortion and change which is inevitable when anything has to be handed down through the medium of the human voice which cannot copy anything faithfully" (Keskar 1967, 38). Note here how the status of the voice has been changed from source to medium, and only one medium among others at that. Keskar went so far as to say that gurukulavasam would eventually ruin Indian music, since the laboriousness of the gurukula system had led to a kind of almost religious devotion on the part of sisyas to their gurus (55). "Guru-dom" had attained a peculiar kind of glamour through such "fanaticism."[28] The result was "complete chaos," in which "the law of the jungle" prevailed and any musician who wanted could set up his own school and call himself a guru (29). "Gurus have become as plentiful as wayside flowers," remarked Keskar with distaste (71).

A distinction had to be made, Keskar urged, between performers and teachers. Unlike a performer, who had only to be captivating on stage, a teacher did not himself need to be gifted at performing. But it was essential that a teacher be able to explain and repeat when necessary. "He must make [the student] repeat musical sequences, point out the mistakes, and make him do that again and again" (1967, 17). Repetition was only a means to achieve the correct version, rather than a valued process in itself. The ideal teacher sounded, literally, like a gramophone, one who could dispassionately reproduce and explain different styles to the student, without being "in the act." Sambamoorthy described the qualities a teacher should have as being quite distinct from those of a guru. Whereas gurus were known for their mercurial temperaments and their genius, teachers needed to be more even-tempered and less exacting. In the gurukula system there was no separation between a "teacher" and a "curriculum" to be taught; the guru embodied his or her musical knowledge, and one learned music by emulating one's guru, by becoming absorbed in him or her. By contrast, the teacher's authority was simply that of someone authorized to teach a preset curriculum. Accordingly, interactions between the teacher and students had to be subject to certain preset standards as well.

A lengthy chapter in Sambamoorthy's *The Teaching of Music* is devoted to the particular problems a teacher giving exams would have to face, beginning with the "irresistible desire" to correct pupils' mistakes and the necessity of curbing that desire in order not to discourage the student or run out of time for examining other pupils (1966, 212–13). The examination, as a genre, was closely related to the radio audition; both were new contexts of musical performance that arose with sound recording. As in the audition (and eventually the broadcast), in the music exam the student's ability to produce music on the spot and in a limited amount of time was under scrutiny, not his ability to emulate or support his guru in performance. Part of the teacher's training lay in being prepared for all the possibilities that such a scenario might produce, for, as Sambamoorthy noted, "the examination has its own psychological effect" (212). The exam had the potential to produce all kinds of unexpected sounds instead of a faithful reproduction of the teacher's lessons, and knowing these possible sounds was as important for the teacher as knowing music.

> The mere thought of an examination is sufficient to make the voices of even steady singers shaky. . . . The music teacher comes across voices of varying types and grades of excellence, from the unpliable stony voice to the ringing silvery voice. . . . The singing of some creates the impression that they are vomiting something. . . . [T]he akarams of some are akin to gargling. . . . Things are no better in instrumental examinations. The bowing of some [on the violin] is so repulsive and harsh that at the end of the performance one can find heaps of hair that have come off the bow, stealthily removed and strewn behind the performer. . . . Some go on aimlessly and artificially moving their fingers up and down the fingerboard. . . . Their play impresses one as the mewing of a cat and one need not be surprised if a cat in the neighbourhood begins to blink and search in vain for the new formless member of her kind. (214–15)

Unlike a guru or performer (or the neighborhood cat, for that matter), a teacher, presumably primed by Sambamoorthy's manual, would remain unfazed by such sounds and be able to move on.

The Art of Listening

If the technologies of recording and radio promoted a musical aesthetic based on the separability of functions, like the distinction between performing and teaching, it followed that the musician could not be considered the best judge of his or her own music. For Keskar this role belonged to the listener, who could judge music precisely because he was not in the act of playing or singing it: "Good critics and listeners are the foundation of music. . . . There is an illusion prevailing today that the musician is the best judge of music. . . . But what is music without listeners!" (1967, 42–43). But the kind of listening Keskar had in mind was one in which audiences would have to be trained; this new kind of listening could be created by the "scientific" teaching of music. The true listener observed "pin-drop silence" so as to hear "all the nuances" of the music. "A musical performance is a story in sound," Keskar wrote. "All its nuances have to be heard carefully in order to enjoy it. . . . The pin-drop silence, the rapt attention and rigid discipline that one observes in the audience in the West demonstrate that they know how to respect music and the way to enjoy it. Our concerts only show that we have not learned fully or probably forgotten the art of listening" (ibid., 23). In *The Teaching of Music* Sambamoorthy wrote that the music teacher was responsible for cultivating the right kind of listening. The listener was, above all, not to cause any interference with the performance. "The music teacher is in a good position to educate the people as to their duties in concert halls. They must be told that when a concert goes on, they must listen to the music with attention and not disturb their neighbours by talking to their friends. If they desire to leave the hall, they must do so only in between items and not when an item is actually going on" (Sambamoorthy 1966, 35).

The kind of listening Sambamoorthy advocated went beyond matters of decorum, however. It had to be achieved through a careful education in "music appreciation," one of the elements of the new institutionalized music curriculum. Focusing on developing the students' "powers of critical observation and critical hearing," music appreciation would produce "musically cultured" people (Sambamoorthy 1966, 165). It was essential that the composition chosen for "appreciation" be able to be repeated, either sung at least twice by the teacher or, even better, played on a gramophone record so that the teacher could point out nuances as they were heard (165). Sambamoorthy prepared an exhaustive list of 216 "hints and points for developing appreciation essays," which could be used to guide students, to teach them a particular technique of listening. What exactly were students being taught here? If one looks closely at these points, one finds that they focus almost exclusively on the structural and prosodic features of compositions, the idea being to contemplate the composition as an aesthetic object, detached from any particular performance of it. "Appreciation," in this context, meant a close, dissective attention rather than an appreciation of the emotional quality or momentum of a performance or its effect on other listeners.

The art of listening, thus conceived, was modeled on the scene of an individual listening to a gramophone recording. Listening was the art of hearing a composition without interference from other audience members or even from the performer. Pin-drop silence set the stage for a transmission free of distortion. Such transmission became the model of *sampradāya*, a term that refers to tradition passed down a carefully traced lineage of disciples. In an essay on music T. V. Subba Rao translated the term as "faithfulness to tradition": "Music must be heard as it comes from the mouth of the teacher and the exact form as presented should be grasped" (1962, 227). Learning music from books produced music that was "shapeless and grotesque"; only music learned from a teacher was authentic. Yet this mouth-to-ear transmission was to be aided by modern technology. "Books, charts, the blackboard, printed notation, even recorded music are no substitute for the living presence of the guru," he wrote (ibid., 232). Yet his use of the conciliatory "even" before "recorded music" suggested that for him recorded music had greater proximity to the elusive gurukulavasam. Indeed, he wrote, "in practical music, the only library worth mentioning is a collection of good recorded music" (ibid., 232–33). Recordings could be made to "disseminate correct knowledge" in classroom settings. Students learning from a guru could "reduce to notation as a sort of memorandum" the songs learned "to ensure against their being forgotten altogether"; for this purpose, he remarked, a tape or plate recording would be even more satisfactory (ibid., 235). Likewise, Sambamoorthy, in his list of "equipment for the music class," recommended a gramophone with a set of records, a radio set, and models of the larynx and ear as second in importance only to musical instruments themselves (1966, 30).

Being an educated listener meant above all knowing how to listen to "music" and to treat the gramophone or radio merely as media for music's reproduction. Without developing such listening technique, it became impossible to enjoy what was on the radio; one could only hear the radio itself. In a humorous article from about 1940 entitled "Rēṭiyo Kaccēri" (Radio concert), a certain V. Muthuswami described the results of his decision to purchase a radio. "Those like me who are crazy about music have to thank the establishment of A.I.R. for providing us the chance to hear so many musicians," he began. "To enjoy such concerts, you must have a radio, or your neighbor must have one, and he must also have caṅkīta ñānam [musical knowledge/taste]." Unfortunately, Muthuswami's neighbor, who owned a radio, did not have such taste. "That day a famous singer was singing Hamir kalyani. My luck! My neighbor immediately turned off the radio and put on gramophone records of film songs. Even though I have iron ears, I could not endure this!" For Muthuswami the knowledge that there was good music on the radio that he could not hear was torture. He set his mind on buying a radio and told several friends about it. "It was as if my decision had been broadcast. . . . When we got to the store, I had only to say one word and a radio sales agent came running out to help me, like a white ant from its nest." Determined to get a radio in time for that evening's concert, Muthuswami purchased a radio and aerial and had it installed. By 5:00 PM, three hours before the concert, everything was working. Muthuswami was looking forward to enjoying the radio concert, when, at 7:45 PM, a crowd of his friends showed up, having somehow found out about the new radio. "Exactly at 8:00 the singer started with a run through nattai ragam and then the kriti 'Sarasiruha.' I should have known the rareness of this moment. For two minutes I was immersed in the music. But can pure music be without interruptions? My friends soon began their own concert, not even having the propriety to be quiet while the music was on."

Muthuswami's friends, it turned out, were obsessed with the radio itself. "Hey, is the aerial on the roof? Permanent installation?" "What was the list price? Was there a commission?" "Look at the tone quality. The set is very neat, sir!" "Is it four valves or six valves?" "Does the short wave come clearly? Do Bombay and BBC come?" "Hey, Columbo is a very powerful station." "Hey, if you have just bought this radio for three-hundred rupees and then you want to get another station, do you have to go buy another set?" "Is it working correctly, sir? We keep hearing about Indian Bank." "Sure, it's okay. That's just local disturbance." Muthuswami's friends kept on with such comments so that it was impossible to hear the music. Then his child began to cry. By the time that settled down, the concert was coming to an end. "Kacceri close!" sang one of his friends gleefully. Muthuswami concluded gloomily, "I sent them off with their tampulam.[29] From that day, I have kept my radio set locked in a closet. When there is a good concert on the radio I beg my neighbor to turn it on. If there are any crazies who want my new radio set, let me know!" For Muthuswami's friends, who lacked the listening technique that would enable them to ignore the mechanism itself, the radio had made music into a matter of prices, sound waves, and frequencies, to such an extent that if the radio was playing it was impossible to hear the music (Muthuswami n.d., 279–80).

If authenticity had come to be seen as analogous to high-fidelity reproduction, it is not surprising that T. V. Subba Rao resorted to another technological metaphor to get at the ineffable concept of "inspiration." "The mind of man," he wrote in an essay on music, "is like the receiving set of a radio which when properly tuned enables us to hear the transmission from a broadcasting center. The Eternal is forever radiating knowledge and bliss for those who by self-discipline have made themselves worthy to receive them" (1962, 230). Instead of disenchanting the world of music, technology and science re-enchanted it. The singer no longer sang with his voice but with his larynx, "the divine vocal instrument . . . [that] by a profundity almost mysterious is calculated to stir us to our very depths" (228). A systematic course of voice culture would have to pay attention to the fact that "tones are produced by the vibration of the chords in the larynx, but no note can be pleasing unless it is rich in components. To secure this end, the note must be fully resonated. The cavities of the chest and the abdomen should be made to take their part as sound-boxes for the note" (228). In Keskar's imagination, the voice had become simply one medium among others; in Subba Rao's it became a mechanism or instrument describable in the same terms as mechanically reproduced sound.

Fantastic Fidelities

In January 1998 I was heading by bus from Madras to Tiruvaiyaru in the company of a young computer software engineer who, although he had studied no music, was quite interested in the fact that I had come to India and was studying under a guru in "the traditional way." He informed me that he had a "thesis" he was trying to prove: that India was once great in science and engineering but had lost that knowledge at some point and is now only "the top" in spiritual matters. As proof, he offered the gurukula "system," which seemed to be an ancient, outmoded form of teaching but was in fact most advanced in the way it used "psychology": the guru comes to know the "psychological makeup" of the sisya and therefore can figure out the best way to teach him or her. With his invocation of psychology, the engineer connected ancient India with the sciences of the West, making gurukulavasam at once premodern and ultramodern. Gurukulavasam thus becomes a symbol of India's past greatness, a greatness that, although it can be assessed in terms of Western sciences, exceeds them.

The engineer's thesis is interesting because it reflects the way in which gurukulavasam is constructed as a sign of Indianness in a postcolonial discourse that demands commensurability with the West. Gurukulavasam is imagined as that which makes Indian music both equal to the music of the West (it, too, has a "scientific" teaching method) and superior to it (it is a system that manages to be scientific and personal at the same time). In such late-twentieth-century discourse gurukulavasam overcomes the opposition between the elements that Raghava Menon felt to be irretrievably separated from each other: the message of the human voice and the mathematically explainable components of its sound. The sisya produces a faithful reproduction of the guru's music through a process that is not mechanical. Imagined as the peculiarly Indian "system" by which musicians are formed, gurukulavasam would seem to be the perfect union of the faithful reproduction identified with machines and the human embodiment identified with an oral tradition.

Ananda Coomaraswamy was worried in 1909 that Indians would get so accustomed to listening to copies of Indian music that they would lose the real thing. The gurukula method, which, according to Coomaraswamy, did not allow the intervention of any mechanism between a guru and his sisya, seemed to remain unknowable by and to Western technology. For him, as for others, gurukulavasam thus preserved what was Indian about Indian music: its "oral tradition." Confronted with technologies of sound reproduction, Coomaraswamy presented gurukulavasam as an Indian alternative for reproducing music. In doing so, he made a comparison, however unwittingly, that would continue to surface in debates about what constituted authenticity and tradition.

In the course of this chapter, we moved from Coomaraswamy's railing against the gramophone to the idea of the voice as simply one medium among others for reproducing music. Sound recording and radio were perceived as enabling a separation from "the very act" of singing or playing music, a separation that came to stand for a peculiar kind of authenticity. Listening to one's performance after the act was the most authentic way of judging it and appreciating it. Separated from the act of its performance, the music on the gramophone record could be played repeatedly and, unlike the Karnatic musician, would sound exactly the same. Repetition became a feature admirable in machines but grotesque and mechanical in musicians. The idea of learning by rote came to seem antiquated, untenable in the modern age, even threatening to good music. But although "learning by ear" was regarded as the most authentic way, the ear could not be trusted by itself; it had to be supplemented by a recording to avoid forgetting. The mechanism intervened between guru and sisya; meanwhile, gurukulavasam, the very mechanism by which tradition worked, came to be imagined as a kind of high-fidelity reproduction.

Gurukulavasam and technologies of sound reproduction have thus served as the interlinked grounds for twentieth-century elaboration of ideas about authenticity and tradition in Karnatic music. Rather than narrating the takeover of a "traditional" method of teaching by "modern" technologies, this chapter has shown how ideas about musicality, repeti-

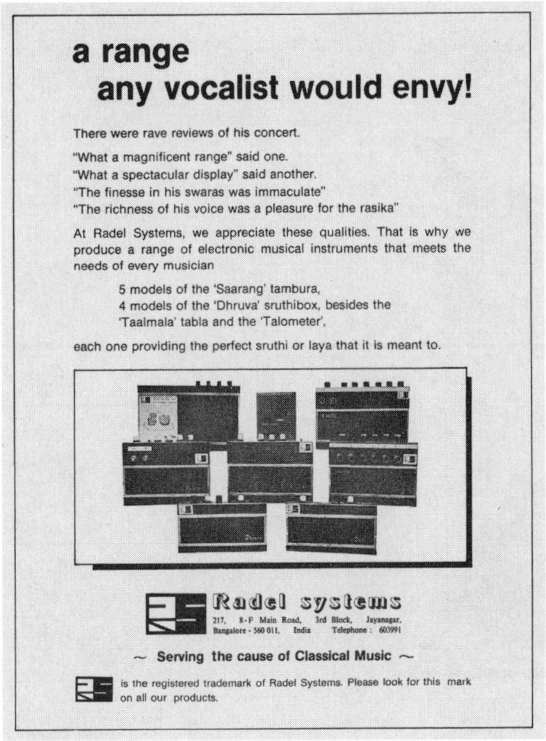

33 Advertisement for sruti boxes, electronic tamburas, and talometers in *Sruti* (June/July 1990).

tion, listening, authority, tradition, and gurukulavasam itself were instead formed in the encounter with such technologies. This is not to claim that gurukulavasam never existed or that it is simply a discursive construct. It is, rather, to suggest that gurukulavasam, now reified as a "system" and retrospectively constructed as "tradition," is central to a discourse about authenticity and music that is peculiarly modern.

At the center of this discourse, which links mechanical perfection to a sense of the ineffable, are sruti boxes, electronic tamburas, and talometers, machines that perform only one function but do so with absolute fidelity. Such machines are enchanting because they possess, as an advertisement from 1990 put it, "a range any vocalist would envy." Sruti boxes and electronic tamburas are electronic devices, plugged in or battery-operated, which provide the sruti, or drone, that forms the tonal background necessary for most Indian classical music.[30] They take the place of either a small harmonium with bellows that would have to be manually pumped or a tambura, a long-necked lute with four strings tuned to the drone pitch that would be plucked slowly and steadily through an entire performance,

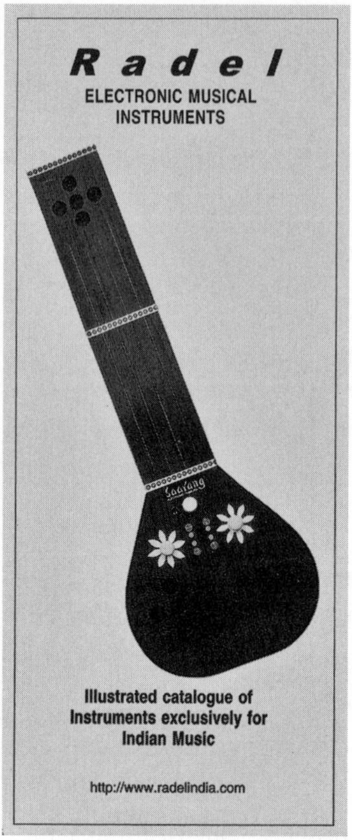
Radel
ELECTRONIC MUSICAL
INSTRUMENTS
Illustrated catalogue of
Instruments exclusively for
Indian Music
http://www.radelindia.com

34 "Concerto" model electronic tambura. Radel Systems brochure (2002).

usually by the main musician's disciple. In this sense, then, these machines substitute for the sound as well as for the disciple. They have become such a fixture in South Indian music concerts that even when a musician has a real tambura player (who always sits unobtrusively somewhere in the back of the stage), he or she will usually also have a sruti box or electronic tambura turned up to full volume and placed directly in front of the microphone.

The first electronic sruti boxes, made in 1979, were brown, heavy, and boxy, with a series of adjustment knobs that made them look like old radios; meant to be the electronic equivalent of the bellows-operated sruti box, they provided a constant tone, with only the pitch or volume being adjustable.[31] Since the early 1980s, however, sruti boxes have given way to electronic tamburas that are becoming increasingly sophisticated. Radel, the foremost manufacturer, now offers no fewer than nine different models, with color choices of red, black, white, and gray, some small enough to fit in the palm of one's hand. One can now control volume, pitch, tempo, and tonal quality, and many models are equipped with a "memory" for what has been programmed in previously. All of these use sampling technology to create a "realistic" imitation of a tambura being plucked; however, they have a much louder sound and fuller tone than any real tambura. Unlike a real tambura, these electronic tamburas can be tuned to any vocalist's pitch, making them infinitely versatile.[32]

The twenty-first century has not produced a musical computer like the fictional Yakshani. Electronic tamburas, however, come close to Yakshani in the kind of affect they elicit; both provide the fascination of hearing music from an inanimate source, its intimation of the supernatural. My music teacher often talked about a great flutist she had accompanied in concert many times, whose genius she partly attributed to his habit of sleeping with a sruti box turned on under his pillow. In the summer of 2001 I happened to be around when a friend of mine who is a Karnatic vocalist showed his latest-model electronic tambura to a visitor. He removed it from its case, placed it ceremoniously on the floor facing both of them, and turned it up to full volume. As its sound saturated the room, he raised his eyes skyward and exclaimed, in a mix of Telugu and English, "Aha! Divine-ga undi, kadā? [It's divine, isn't it?] I hear this and immediately I'm in the mood to sing. It pulls the music out of me. I could sit here with it for days."

Radel's latest model is a digital tambura in the shape of a tambura—the "concerto" model.[33] The sampling technology that produces the "real" tambura sound is housed inside a hand-crafted wooden tambura body that, unlike a real tambura, stands upright without needing to be held—a tambura that plays itself. The concerto model takes the logic of fidelity to an extreme; it pairs fidelity to the real tambura sound with fidelity to the very image of tradition—but without the sisya. Like Yakshani, it replaces music with frequencies and sound waves, the devoted disciple with the memory and repetitive capacities of a computer. Like Yakshani, who must undergo gurukulavasam in the end, the sruti box remains under the control of the human singer, but only after the logic of fidelity—continual and mutual imitation—has questioned whose is the master's voice.

Afterword

MODERNITY AND THE VOICE

Modernity has been described and theorized largely in terms of the visual. Vision, it has been argued, is the sense that comes to have priority and power over all the others; in Western metaphysics, knowledge is equated with vision and truth with light. David Levin's edited volume *Modernity and the Hegemony of Vision* traces the ocularcentrism of Western metaphysics from Parmenides to late-twentieth-century television, asking, "How is the ocularcentrism of modernity different from that which prevailed in earlier ages?. . . . How has the paradigm of vision ruled, and with what effects?" (1993, 3). Michel Foucault's description of the panopticon and its accompanying regimes of surveillance provided one answer to these questions, suggesting that modernity is characterized by a particular regime of visibility that is tied to control (Foucault 1977). Timothy Mitchell, in a similar vein, has argued that modernity is characterized by representation: the world-as-picture. "The peculiar metaphysic of modernity," he argues, involved the creation of the effect of reality by making a distinction between image, meaning, or structure, and the "really real" (Mitchell 2000, 16–20).

Recognizing the way vision is tied both to power and to the power to represent is central to developing a critique of modernity. A fuller critique, however, must also consider how modernity positions other senses in relation to vision. Aurality, in particular, has a central place in modernity's self-definition. Within modernity, the aural has been positioned as the premodern or the nonmodern, often as that which escapes modernity's controlling regimes of knowledge-power. The idea of the aural as the premodern or nonmodern is encapsulated, as Jonathan Sterne suggests, in what he calls the "audio-visual litany," a series of seemingly commonsense oppositions often taken as natural, biological, psychological facts about the senses: that hearing immerses its object, while vision offers a perspective; that hearing is concerned with interiors, vision with surfaces; that hearing is about affect, vision about intellect; that hearing immerses us in the world, while vision removes us from it. As he suggests, the audiovisual litany idealizes hearing and, by extension, speech, music, and the voice as "manifesting a kind of pure interiority," while it simultaneously "denigrates and elevates vision. As a fallen sense, vision takes us out of the world. But it also bathes us in the clear light of reason" (2003, 15). Such statements assert that the senses lie outside of history: that they and their attributes are natural, biological givens. Much psychoanalytic writing on the voice, for instance, depends deeply on the audiovisual litany, endowing hearing with universal significance and the voice with primordial powers. The idea that aurality and orality are closer to lived, embodied experience but are nonrational or pre-analytical faculties is pervasive in the ideas and methodology of many academic disciplines.

In asserting the transhistorical nature of the senses, the audiovisual litany elides the way that these oppositions between visuality and aurality are grounded in notions of the difference between the modern and the nonmodern and in turn mapped onto the West and the non-West. If modernity, as Timothy Mitchell suggests, asserts its existence and authority by continually staging the difference between the modern and the nonmodern, the West and the non-West, oppositions between the aural and the visual have served as a powerful means of naturalizing these differences. Modernity is characterized just as much by particular ideas about aurality and the voice as it is by certain conceptions of visuality. Indeed, the audiovisual litany is what enabled India to become the "kingdom of the Voice."

The valorization of the voice in Karnatic music is part of a distinctly modern set of ideas about music, the self, and Indianness. The voice, in twentieth-century discourse about this music, has been figured as a realm of pure Indianness, untouched by colonialism or worldly concerns, the element that gives the music both its distinctive Indianness and its ability to exist as part of a continuous "civilizational" tradition, unaffected by history. Within the logic of modernity, the voice is imagined in two ways: as a sign of the modern, interiorized self and as the authentic embodiment of oral tradition. On the one hand, the voice is imagined as endowing the modern subject with interiority, while on the other hand the voice is imagined as endowing the premodern subject with the essential difference that will make him an authentic representative of tradition. Such a dual way of imagining the voice is central to the politics of voice I have identified here, in which ideas about modern singing and listening subjects are intertwined with anxieties about the proper control, preservation, and use of oral tradition. This is Karnatic music's postcolonial predicament: in order to be a true classical music, it must be performed and listened to by modern subjects who know how music should affect them and what it means to be an artist, but it also needs to be able to point to an origin in an oral tradition that maintains its distance, and difference, from the West.

It is tempting to view the twentieth-century emergence of classical music in South India as part of the development of a local or alternative modernity, one that borrows the Western concepts of "classical music" and "art" and many of their entailments. However, while it is important to recognize the multiple origins of what can often be too easily unified under the name of modernity, the idea of "alternative modernities" can, as Timothy Mitchell states, dangerously "imply an underlying and fundamentally singular modernity, modified by local circumstances into a multiplicity of 'cultural' forms. It is only in reference to this implied generic that such variations can be imagined and discussed" (2000, xii). I have resisted using the concept of alternative or local modernity in order to emphasize that the modern idea of classical music—in both the West and South Asia—was enabled, materially and ideologically, by colonialism. In both Europe and South India, the institution of classical music was a product of the new economies and patronage structures associated with imperial modernity.[1] Western classical music was not a fully formed entity that was merely exported to India beginning in the early twentieth century; rather, ideas about classical music, both Western and Indian, were being negotiated simultaneously in the colony and the metropole. In this sense, Karnatic music and Western classical music belong not to alternative modernities but to the same modernity. This is not to provide yet another instance of the globalization of an essentially Western modernity. Rather, it is to recognize that, as Mitchell states, "when themes and categories developed in one historical context . . . are reused elsewhere in the service of different social arrangements and political tactics, there is an inevitable process of displacement and reformulation" (ibid., 7). The politics of voice I have described in this book constitutes such a reformulation, one in which the priorities of the audiovisual litany are reversed (but essentially unchallenged) in the service of determining what makes Indian classical music Indian.

The electronic sruti box is in many ways similar to the mimetic violin with which I began this book. Both are "accompaniments" to the voice which are much more than accompaniments; they play a crucial role in the way the voice is staged and produced. As such, they encapsulate the argument of this book: that voices are created as much from without—by instruments, by technologies, by audiences, and by social forces—as from within. The sruti box and the violin denaturalize the voice; they remind us that if we take the voice as the originary model of all musical production and as a natural means of expression, we miss the ways in which the voice itself—as musical sound and as culturally elaborated metaphor—is historically locatable.

In identifying a politics or ideology of voice that includes both the material and sonic aspects of the voice and ideas about its significance, I hope to have elucidated and thus dislodged some of modernity's most cherished assumptions about the voice: that the voice is a "natural" expression of self; that agency consists in "having a voice"; that the sonic and material aspects of the voice are subordinate to its referential content or message; that non-Western cultures are profoundly and naturally oral. What I have suggested instead is that the complexity of how musical and literal voices are created, heard, and interpreted matters in the way voice as a concept takes on significance. In this sense, ideas about the voice as a metaphor or trope of subjectivity, agency, power, and authenticity are bound up with the particular moments when, and the very material ways in which, voices become audible.

Notes

Introduction

1 *Kula* means "family," or "lineage"; *vacam* means "living." *Gurukulavasam* can be translated as "living with the guru's family."

2 As a body of knowledge produced by texts and institutional practices, Orientalism was responsible for generating essentializing statements about the Orient that relied on contrasting it to Europe (Said 1979). In the Indian context, Bernard Cohn's "Notes on the History of the Study of Indian Society and Culture" (1968), Ronald Inden's "Orientalist Constructions of India" (1986), and Gyan Prakash's "Writing Post-Orientalist Histories of the Third World" (1990), among others, include discussions of the kinds of essentialisms produced through Orientalist scholarship on India.

3 T. V. Subba Rao, a practicing lawyer in Madras, sat on the "committee of experts" that founded the Madras Music Academy and became its first treasurer.

4 For a general account of the politics of this "revival" see Subramanian 1999b.

5 The idea of a classical music tradition, William Weber suggests, originated in England and can be linked to the decline of the courts and the rise of an urban leisure class enabled by the industrial revolution and colonial expansion (1992, 1–9). The concept of classical music, then, is not incidental to colonialism but part of its economy.

6 According to Daniel Neuman, the Hindi term *sāstriya sangīt* (literally, "sastric music," or music that conforms to the rules of the sastras, a set of Sanskrit musical treatises) is used in North India and occasionally in the South to refer to Hindustani or Karnatic classical music (personal communication, June 1995). This term is often given as evidence that the notion of "classical music" is indigenous to South Asia. However, the connotations of *sastric* and *classical* are quite different. There is also the possibility that *sāstriya sangīt* is not an "original" term of which "classical music" is the English translation, but rather a term coined as a Hindi translation of the English "classical music."

7 Often cited in this regard is the *Sangītaratnākara*, written in about 1240 AD.

8 These associations have been famously formulated by Walter Ong in *Orality*

and Literacy (1982). Bauman and Briggs provide a genealogy of the orality/literacy opposition (2003, 104–7). Michel de Certeau notes that the field of ethnology centers around the opposition between orality—the voice defined in terms of exteriority and alterity—and writing: "The vocal exteriority is also the stimulus and the precondition for its scriptural opposite. . . . The savage becomes a senseless speech ravishing Western discourse, but one which, because of that very fact, generates a productive science of meaning and objects that endlessly writes" (1988, 236).

9 Veit Erlmann has made similar claims in service of the idea that "South Africa" and the "West" have co-constructed each other in colonial and post-colonial contexts: "The formation of modern identities always already occurs in the crucible of intensely spatially interconnected worlds. . . . Just as colonialism and its 'informal continuities' with the postmodern world create colonized and colonizers alike, they also provide the stage for the emergence and transformation of certain musical givens, of things such as European music, music history, primitive music, non-Western music, and so on. Thus one of the conclusions one might draw . . . is that musicology, as a mode of knowledge about an object called European music, in fact could only have emerged in relation to colonial encounters" (1999, 8).

10 On language ideology see Schieffelin, Woolard, and Kroskrity 1998; Kroskrity 2000; and Woolard and Schieffelin 1994.

11 "These objects [which include the phallus, feces, the gaze, and the voice] have one common feature in my elaboration of them—they have no specular image, or in other words, alterity. It is what enables them to be the 'stuff,' or rather the lining, though not in any sense the reverse, of the very object that one takes to be the subject of consciousness" (Lacan 1977, 315).

12 See Dunn and Jones 1995, Silverman 1988, Engh 1997.

13 The American pragmatist philosopher Charles Peirce suggested that signs are of three types: icons, indexes, and symbols, each of which bear different kinds of relations to their referents, varying from complete motivatedness to arbitrariness. One of his most powerful ideas, taken up and developed by anthropologists and linguistic anthropologists since the 1980s, is the notion that within every symbol there is an index and an icon, and that these serve to "motivate" the symbol (Parmentier 1985; Hartshorne and Weiss 1931–1958). Peirce's ideas offer a way of explaining how symbols and metaphors come to seem so natural, necessary, and powerful to their users.

14 In linking the marginalization of voice within the study of language to the social and political marginalization of the people they are writing about, Feld, Fox, Porcello, and Samuels associate their intellectual project with a classically emancipatory political project.

15 The smaller states were taken over relatively early: Palghat in 1790, Ramnad in 1772, Dindigul in 1792. Travancore, Cochin, and Pudukkottai were the last to lose their princely status, after Indian independence in 1947 (Roberts 1952).

16 The Sanskrit manuscript *Sārvadēvavilāsa* (ca. 1800; referred to in chapter 2), which records the peregrinations of two Brahmins around the city of Madras in their quest for patronage, mentions the names of several prominent dubashes and dharmakartas and the musicians and dancers they patronized.

17 The songs of the three nineteenth-century saint-composers of Karnatic music (Thyagaraja, Muthuswamy Dikshitar, and Syama Sastri), viewed as the ultimate expressions of bhakti, were sung by bhajan associations on Gandhian social reform missions in the early twentieth century (Hancock 1999, 58).

18 Sumathi Ramaswamy's *Passions of the Tongue* (1997) analyzes in depth the figure of Tamiḻttāy as a personification of the Tamil language and the discourse of Tamil devotion. Theories of the Dravidians as a separate race, distinct from the Aryans, were quickly appropriated by the emerging non-Brahmin movement. In 1916 the merchant, banker, and philanthropist P. Tyagaraga Chetti signed the *Non-Brahmin Manifesto*, a document that protested the Brahmin categorization of all non-Brahmins as lowly Sudras. The *Non-Brahmin Manifesto* was the first step in the formation of the Justice Party, which came into power in 1920. The Justice Party developed to challenge the Brahmin-dominated Congress Party. In 1925 E. V. Ramasami, the political leader who later became known as "Periyar," quit the Congress Party and joined the Justice Party; in the same year, he founded the Self-Respect League (Cuyamariyātai Iyakkam), which espoused the idea of an original Dravidian culture, at the same time calling for the abolition of the caste system and the adoption of atheism and rationalism (Geetha and Rajadurai 1998, 303–11).

The fundamental issue of the 1930s was the protest, by EVR's followers, of the Congress Party's proposal to make Hindi the national language, and to institute compulsory Hindi study in the South. Anti-Hindi protests went on through the 1960s, and became a rallying point for Dravidianist sentiment.

19 *Vēṭikkai* is, more specifically, amusement derived from being an onlooker who is not really involved.

20 The Tirukkural is a set of aphorisms composed in couplet form by the Tamil sage Tiruvalluvar, circa 500 AD.

21 The Tanjavur district is generally recognized as the cradle of Karnatic music.

22 *Hinduism Today*, September 1997.

23 For a historical treatment of Hindustani classical music that examines aspects of its canon formation in relation to colonialism and nationalism see Bakhle 2005.

24 The dichotomy of "great" and "little" traditions, referring to the split between "classical" or "literate" traditions and "folk" or "oral" traditions, was first articulated by the anthropologist Robert Redfield in the context of his research in the Yucatan in the 1930s and then in his *The Primitive World and Its Transformations* (1953). Redfield was interested in the "social anthropology of civilizations" and the role of cities in cultural change. "The Cultural Role of Cities," coauthored by Redfield and Milton Singer (1954), stated the great tradition–

little tradition distinction most succinctly. Redfield's ideas were elaborated in the Indian context by Singer, especially in *When a Great Tradition Modernizes* (1972). With its reliance on the idea of a coherent civilizational tradition, the dichotomy between great and little traditions has distinct resonances with (and undoubtedly roots in) Orientalist scholarship on India.

25 Margaret Cousins, an Irish woman active in the Celtic Revival movement in early-twentieth-century Ireland, and a leader of the Irish Women's Franchise League, became a Theosophist and moved with her husband, James Cousins, to Madras in 1913. Music was one of her abiding interests; she had earned a music degree in Ireland. While in India, she became active in issues concerning the emancipation of Indian women, and was one of the founders of the Women's India Association. See Candy 1994.

1 Gone Native?

1 Charles Day wrote that the sarangi, an indigenous bowed fiddle now seen mostly in North India, was "rapidly being discontinued, and an English fiddle tuned as a vina or sarangi is often substituted for it" (1891, 93). Several other sources corroborate the fact that the sarangi was used in South India in the nineteenth century but fell into disuse in the twentieth. See Poduval (n.d., 24), Popley (1921), Fox-Strangways (1914).

2 Bruno Nettl uses the terms "Westernization" and "modernization" (1985, 163). I have avoided using these terms because they imply that the categories of "Western" and "modern" are unambiguously definable and imposed from the outside, rather than debated and constructed in opposition to what then comes to be considered "native" and "traditional."

3 See also Ian Woodfield's *Music of the Raj* (2001). The appendix lists examples of musical instruments listed in the Bengal Inventories, 1760–1785, including about twenty violins (240–45).

4 *Icai veḷḷālar*, literally "cultivator of music," was a term coined in the 1950s for a group of caste communities whose hereditary occupation was music. They are not related to the *Veḷḷālas*, castes of landed agriculturalists, although the use of the term *veḷḷālar* (cultivator) was meant to raise their status.

5 "Fiddle" is pronounced in Tamil with a retroflex "ṭ": *piṭil*. The last three versions of the word in Satyanarayana's quote should be pronounced with this sound.

6 The monumental book of notations *Sangīta Sampradāya Pradārṣini*, compiled by the grandson of Muthuswamy Dikshitar in 1904, included a section on "music practice," which featured many of these compositions. Such pieces were later hailed as didactic masterpieces, ideal for avoiding "boredom and disillusionment" on the part of young music students because they would help young singers to get the pitches right while helping them become accustomed to phrases used in difficult songs (Sankaramurthy 1990, ix). The route

to vocal music was thus distinctly instrumental; getting the correct pitches was most important, while the words themselves, detached from their original meaningful position in Karnatic music, could be practiced as sounds.

7 It is unclear exactly what the kinnari is. Ramaswamy Bhagavatar later says that "the difference between the kinnari instrument and the fiddle is very small" (1935, 53). Most of the time he uses the two terms interchangeably.

8 S. K. Ramachandra Rao suggests that, before it appeared in concert halls, the violin was adopted primarily for use in dance music and that many dance teachers were also violinists (1994, 18–19). It was also used in *mēḷam* (musical processions at temples or weddings usually featuring the nagaswaram, a double-reed instrument whose classical status is contested to this day). The association of the violin with dance music, and thus with the devadasi community, Ramachandra Rao suggests, produced a certain resistance among Brahmins against taking up the instrument. Such resistance was first overcome in the early twentieth century when the violin began to be used as accompaniment in *katha kalakshepam*, a kind of musical storytelling (21).

9 Bakhtin discusses the multivocality of utterances in *Problems of Dostoevsky's Poetics* (1984). Jane Hill uses some of these concepts in her article "The Consciousness of Grammar and the Grammar of Consciousness" (1996) to suggest that political and social relations are reflected in the way voices compete within any single utterance.

10 Compare Daniel Neuman's discussion of accompaniment in Hindustani music (1980: 121–22, 136–40). Also, according to Neuman, while the hierarchy of soloist and accompanist corresponds to the hierarchy of caste differences, there is no such correspondence in the contemporary Karnatic music scene with regard to violin accompaniment—accompanying violinists are mostly Brahmins, as are vocalists, and there is no institutionalized division between soloists and accompanists.

11 Sambamoorthy (1901–1973) was born in the Tanjavur district to a family that had had musical connections to the Tanjore court under King Serfoji. He studied violin and vocal music in Madras and became a lecturer in music at Queen Mary's College in 1928. In 1931 he went to Munich for five years to study Western music and comparative musicology. On returning to Madras, he took a position as lecturer and head of the Madras University Department of Indian Music, in which capacity he served from 1937–1961 and from 1966 to his death. He wrote numerous books on the history of Karnatic music and musicians, and developed teaching curricula for university music departments.

12 A *sangati* is a variation on a melodic line. A *tala* is a cycle with a certain number of beats within which a composition is set. The *eṭuppu* is the starting place in the tala. *Alapana* is free-time improvisation, while *kalpana swara* is improvisation that occurs within the tala cycle.

13 According to Tejaswini Niranjana, the sense of figuration is different from

representation in that figuration involves a play of movement between signified and signifier which effectively undoes the opposition between them instead of reinforcing it (1994, 44, 50).

14 The term *swadeshi* refers to the incipient phase of the Indian nationalist movement, started around 1905, to create an economically self-sufficient India by ceasing to use British-made products. Swadeshis were those who followed this policy and used only Indian-made products, notably cloth. The swadeshi movement was controversial and its proponents were often accused of hypocrisy.

15 *Īs pīs* is an onomatopoeic expression in Tamil referring to the hissing sound of English being spoken.

16 The slide and cast-iron track were parts of a disused optical bench. The chain and hubs were spare parts purchased from a cycle-dealer, as was the ball bearing of the axle of the lever.

17 The horn violin, also called phono violin or Stroh violin, was invented in 1899 by the Austrian John Matthias Augustus Stroh and was first manufactured in London in 1901. These violins were used in the recording industry from the late nineteenth century to the beginning of electronic amplification because they were loud enough to record on wax cylinders. The instrument works by having vibrations from the strings passed to the center of an aluminum disc that amplifies the sound, which is then projected through a metal horn.

18 For a description of the social status of the sarangi in North India see Neuman (1980, 134–35). Neuman implies that the sarangi was incorporated into Hindustani classical music as an instrument with lower status; furthermore, in contrast to South India, a sharp status distinction was made between soloists and accompanists. *Nautch* is derived from the Hindi word *nach* (dance).

19 In 1913 Ernest Clements designed a new "sruti harmonium," carefully tuned to avoid the problems caused by equal temperament and to be truer to "Indian intervals," and demonstrated it at the first All-India Music Conference in Baroda in 1916. Although it never became popular among musicians, who continued to use regular harmoniums based on equal temperament, it did produce a heated exchange of letters between Clements and the Tamil musicologist Abraham Pandithar in the years following. Clements claimed that only when Pandithar's daughters sang with the sruti harmonium were they in tune; with Pandithar's veena specially designed to show off the "South Indian sruti system" they sang "the harsh tones of equal temperament," while with the violin accompanying they had a tendency to "drift insensibly into other scales" (Pandithar 1918, 2).

20 The ban was partially lifted in the early 1970s and later entirely lifted. See Neuman 1980, 184–86.

21 The word *moṭṭai*, literally meaning bald, is used to refer to plain notes.

22 The best-known violinists of the generation previous to Dwaram's were Tirukkodikkaval Krishnayyar (1857–1913) and "Fiddle" Govindaswamy Pil-

lai (1878–1931). More information about them can be found in P. Sambamoorthy's *Dictionary of South Indian Music and Musicians* and in articles published in *Kalki* magazine in the 1940s.

23 Dwaram Mangathayaru, personal communication, Madras, June 1998. Mangathayaru is the daughter and disciple of Dwaram Venkataswamy Naidu.

24 Dwaram Mangathayaru, personal communication, Madras, May 1998.

25 The word *jāru* comes from the Telugu verb *jara-*, to slide. Such descriptions of Dwaram's playing can be found in writings by the musicologists T. S. Parthasarathy, B. V. K. Sastry, and T. V. Subba Rao.

26 Srimathi Brahmanandam, personal communication, Madras, February 1998.

27 I am indebted to Adrian L'Armand, who was a student of Karnatic violin in Madras in the 1960s, for sharing his observations and insights with me. "Florid" is his term.

28 I thank V. A. K. Ranga Rao, a record collector in Madras, for sharing recordings of violinists from 1910 on with me.

29 Other uses of the violin in fusions abound. Shakti, a well-known fusion group which made its first recording in 1975, made extensive use of the violin. The South Indian violin has traveled to the West perhaps most visibly in the musical creations of L. Shankar and L. Subramaniam since the 1990s.

30 "An Enjoyable Fare," *The Hindu*, 14 August 1998, 28.

31 As Steven Connor has written, "Sound, especially sourceless, autonomous, or excessive sound, will be experienced both as a lack and an excess; both as a mystery to be explained and an intensity to be contained. Above all, sound, and as the body's means of producing itself as sound, the voice, will be associated with the dream and the exercise of power" (2000, 23).

32 Slavoj Žižek comes to a similar point in his Lacanian reading of film, in which he is critical of the idea of a naturalized voice, suggesting instead that one focus on the process by which voices come to be embodied and taken as natural. "What we have to renounce is thus the commonsense notion of a primordial, fully constituted reality in which sight and sound harmoniously complement each other; the moment we enter the symbolic order, an unbridgeable gap separates forever a human body from 'its' voice. The voice acquires a spectral autonomy, it never quite belongs to the body we see, so that even when we see a living person talking, there is always some degree of ventriloquism at work: it is as if the speakers' own voice hollows him out and in a sense speaks 'by itself,' through him. In his *Lectures on Aesthetics*, Hegel mentions an ancient Egyptian sacred statue which, at every sunset, as if by miracle, issued a deep reverberating sound—this mysterious sound magically resonating from within an inanimate object is the best metaphor for the birth of subjectivity" (1996, 93).

Steven Connor similarly imagines the possibilities for a history of voice as necessarily intertwined with the history of the "ventriloquial" voice, which acts as "a medium for exploring the relations between selves and their voices":

"The legitimate and familiar exercise of the voice is accompanied by the doubts and delights of the ventriloquial voice, of the voice speaking from some other place, reorganizing the economy of the senses, and embodying illegitimate forms of power" (2000, 43).

33 Compare the ambivalent dynamics of "not white, not quite" as discussed by Homi K. Bhabha (1984).

34 Michael Taussig characterizes mimesis as " 'a space between,' a space permeated by the colonial tension of mimesis and alterity, in which it is far from easy to say who is the imitator and who is the imitated, which is copy and which is original" (1993, 78).

2 *From the Palace to the Street*

1 This event is referred to by M. B. Vedavalli in *Mysore as a Seat of Music* (1992, 16).

2 On the construct of kingship in South India see Dirks 1993, Waghorne 1994, Narayana Rao, Shulman, and Subrahmanyam 1992, Daniel 1984.

3 In conversations with me, many older musicians and concertgoers used the phrase "mechanical life" to evoke what they disliked about modern, urban life.

4 "Tanjavur" is the modern spelling; the old spelling is "Tanjore." I use "Tanjore" when referring to proper names where that is the spelling consistently used, such as the Tanjore Quartette. Similarly, "Travancore" is the old spelling of a princely state in the area that is now southern Kerala and part of Tamil Nadu; the kings of Travancore resided in the city now known as Trivandrum (English pronunciation) or Tiruvanantapuram (Tamil/Malayalam pronunciation).

5 Serfoji's projects reflect a desire for order, classification, and replicability, a certain encounter with the idea of modernity (see Peterson 1999).

6 K. N. Panikkar, personal communication, Trivandrum, June 1998.

7 Information on the posts created for musicians and the amounts paid to them is available in some of the Trivandrum palace records published in the *Kerala State Archives Bulletin* (1996).

8 On the capacity of music and language to create, and not simply reflect, kingly power, see also V. Narayana Rao and David Shulman, eds., *A Poem at the Right Moment* (1998, esp. 148–59).

9 Mysore Archaeological Reports 1928–1929. Photocopy, Mysore State University.

10 Mysore Archaeological Reports 1928.

11 Mysore Archaeological Reports 1927–1928.

12 Ibid.

13 Dwaram Durga Prasad Rao, personal communication, Vizianagaram, September 1998.

14 As a king, Ananda Gajapathi was also intensely interested in musical institutions outside of his court. He often traveled to Calcutta to hear concerts and donated liberally to the Poona Gayan Samaj, a cultural organization that supported musical training and held concerts. He also responded to concerns about the lack of notation for Indian music by sponsoring the publication of several music manuals for students, written by the Taccur brothers of Madras (Rama Rao 1985, 16, 25; see chapter 5 herein for more on these books). In a description of Ananda Gajapathi, the writer Gurujada Apparao, who received royal patronage, stated that the maharaja felt concern that "the condition of prostitutes is deteriorating day by day. They must be taught the arts for earning a living. If they are enrolled in the Music College and taught fine arts it would be good" (quoted in Rama Rao 1985, 47).

15 Why six years was determined to be an appropriate course length is not clear. Perhaps it was modeled on medical schools, which also had six-year courses at that time.

16 The basic plan of the syllabus, with divisions between theory and practical elements, is the same in curricula planned by the musicologist and teacher P. Sambamoorthy and continues to be used as the basis for the Government Technical Examinations in music.

17 Dwaram Durga Prasad Rao, principal of the Maharaja's Government Music College, Vizianagaram, very generously allowed me to see the original syllabus.

18 Harikesanallur Muthiah Bhagavatar was appointed samasthana vidwan of Travancore in 1936 and became the first principal of the Swati Tirunal Music Academy when it was established in 1938 (Vasudevachar 1955, 81); C. S. Sankarasiva Bhagavatar left the Ramanathapuram samasthanam to become the first principal of the Sathguru Sangeeta Samajam in Madurai in the mid-1940s.

19 The tradition of impromptu improvisation by court poets was well developed in South India. See Narayana Rao and Shulman 1998; Swaminathayyar 1940–1942.

20 See Hughes 1996 for a description of the social divisions of Madras in the nineteeth and early twentieth centuries. See Neild 1979 for a description of Madras circa 1800.

21 T. Shankaran, personal communication, Madras, June 1998.

22 N. Ramachandran, secretary of the Indian Fine Arts Association, personal communication, Madras, September 1998.

23 In the 2002–2003 music season there were seventy-three organizations sponsoring concerts in Madras, up from seventeen in 1987–1988 (*Sruti* 2003, 21).

24 See Neuman 1992 and Erdman 1978 for discussions of the changes in Hindustani music that occurred with the shift from royal patronage to urban music concerts.

25 Randor Guy, personal communication, Madras, August 1998.

26 More information on the Madras Music Academy can be found in Subramanian 1999a.

27 Other useful sources on the making of classical music in the West include Goehr 1992 on the concept of the musical "work" and Levine 1990 on the development of high culture in twentieth-century America.

28 S. V. Krishnan, personal communication, Madras, December 2003.

29 I am grateful to Bernard Bate for drawing my attention to this source. It is also mentioned in his dissertation, *Mēṭaittamiḻ: Oratory and Democratic Practice in Tamil Nadu* (2000, 57).

30 Until the 1970s, it was customary in concert and cinema halls to have a separate section designated for women, often to one side or toward the back of the hall; some cinema halls still have ladies' sections.

31 The name of the god Siva. Here, equivalent to "Testing, 1, 2, 3."

32 Indeed, one elderly vocalist recalled hearing Musiri Subramania Iyer "shouting at G like a woman" in the early 1940s (H. M. V. Raghunathan, personal communication, Madras, December 2003). Jon Higgins was the first to use the expression *crooner* to describe the microphone-influenced style of singing that has emerged (1975, 24).

33 On the microphone and the production of public intimacy, see Frith 1996 (201) and Connor 2000 (38). "The crooning style of twentieth-century popular song," Connor writes, "was discovered by singers and sound engineers in the early days of sound recording when it was discovered that microphones could not cope with the extreme dynamic ranges possessed by singers used to commanding the large space of the concert hall. The crooning voice is seductive because it appears to be at our ear. . . . The microphone makes audible and expressive a whole range of organic vocal sounds which are edited out in ordinary listening: the liquidity of the saliva, the hissings and tiny shudders of the breath, the clicking of the tongue and teeth, and popping of the lips" (201).

34 The word *uṇarvu* in Tamil refers to a distinctly embodied sense of feeling, perception, or awareness.

35 Dwaram Mangathayaru related to me that her father, the violinist Dwaram Venkataswamy Naidu, who played concerts publicly from the 1930s to 1960s, used to begin his daily practice with alankarams and varnams in all five of the ragas—nattai, arabhi, gowla, varali, and sriragam—in which the pancharatna kritis were composed, so that his improvisation on these kritis would be fluent (personal communication, Madras, April 1998). Nowadays, not only are the kritis themselves considered to be sufficient in themselves without improvisation, but these ragas are considered to be for the most part lacking in sufficient scope for extensive improvisation.

36 This is elaborately dramatized in the 1982 remake of the film *Thyagayya*.

37 An example of his translation is as follows.

O Ram! How can I bear! Show mercy sweet.
Advice by Thee I follow day to day.
How blame comes hard on me when I live true
To teachings of the ethic epics chaste! (Sharma 1954, 20)

38 T. S. Parthasarathy, personal communication, Madras, October 1997. Parthasarathy was formerly the secretary of the Madras Music Academy.

39 In 1998 a reporter for *The Hindu* told me that it was rumored that Thyagaraja, far from being a mendicant saint, was a wealthy landowner. The rumor, he suspected, would cause great consternation on the part of the Madras Brahmin Karnatic music establishment.

40 In an article on the agenda of the Madras Music Academy, Lakshmi Subramanian (1999a) suggests that the academy tried, between 1930 and 1947, to revive the spiritual aspect of Karnatic music while leaving out its sensual aspects, which had been carried on by devadasis. The domination of Thyagaraja's songs on the concert stage was a result of what Subramanian calls a "sanitization" of Karnatic music. Indira Peterson offers a literary analysis of the image of the patron in the songs of Thyagaraja, comparing them with those of the eighth-century saint Cuntaramurti. She reads in the hagiographical narrative of Thyagaraja's refusal of royal patronage and his life of "voluntary mendicancy," "the central themes of bhakti sainthood as formulated in late medieval South Indian bhakti" (1992, 133). She speculates on how Thyagaraja himself may have recast the bhakti tradition to comment on the political disarray of his own time, but she leaves open the question of why Thyagaraja has become so popular in the twentieth century.

41 Jean Langford suggests more broadly that "the turn toward expressivism also involves a shift to an understanding of personal identity as expression rather than mimesis. Thus the source of personal identity is to be found within, as one's true nature, rather than in the social realm, as learned or strategically developed personae. In this modern expressivism, then, the ways in which personal identity and emotions are constructed are necessarily obscured" (2002, 247).

42 A detailed account of the politics surrounding the Thyagaraja Aradhana at Tiruvaiyaru is also provided in Vai. Radhakrishna Ayyar's *Tiruvaiyāṟ sri tyākapirammam arātaṉai utcava varalāṟu* (1949–1950).

43 This was a precaution against the kind of confrontation that had happened the year before, when a group of activists had stormed onto the stage and demanded that, since they were in Tamil Nadu, the music should be in Tamil, not Telugu. Reference to another such incident at Tiruvaiyaru in 1971 is made in Terada 2000 (487).

44 "Thyagaraja Aradhana," *The Hindu*, 29 January 1998, 2.

45 C. S. Sankarasiva Bhagavatar, interview by Ranganayaki Ayyangar, Madurai, 1989, cassette, archives, Sampradaya foundation, Madras.

46 Name has been changed to respect confidentiality.

3 *Gender and the Politics of Voice*

1 The concept of dangerous female power that needs to be contained is prominent in Hindu mythology and in religious rules regulating women's behavior (see O'Flaherty 1980). One of these rules is marriage. In Tamil tradition, auspiciousness—that quality which leads to or enables good fortune and success—is embodied in the figure of the married woman and is lost when the woman is widowed (see Reynolds 1980).

2 Regula Qureshi meditates on this set of issues at length in her article on Begum Akhtar, the North Indian singer active from the 1930s to the 1970s and known for her renditions of Urdu *ghazals* (poetic couplets). In some ways her life parallels that of M. S. Subbulakshmi. Born into a courtesan family near Lucknow, Akhtari Bai achieved fame as a courtesan singer while in her teens through gramophone recordings. In the 1940s she married one of her admirers and thus became Begum (Lady, Mrs.) Akhtar; on entering the domestic life of a respectable wife she stopped singing for a number of years, beginning again only in the 1950s. Qureshi explores the ironies and conflicts involved in the life of a woman who transformed herself "from a hereditary professional singer to a respectably married lady who even gave up her singing career, only to emerge into the public domain transformed into a national symbol iconic of the courtly musical culture which had shaped her" (2001, 97).

3 The significance of the ideal of womanhood to the consolidation of a hegemonic middle-class culture in India and the middle-class basis of the Indian nationalist movement have been examined by several scholars. Partha Chatterjee, in a 1989 essay on the nationalist resolution of the women's question in the 1870s, argues that the rearticulation of Indian womanhood was the foundation on which the notion of an "inner sphere" representative of Indianness was built. As Mrinhalini Sinha restates the idea, "The re-articulation of the Indian woman for the self-definition of the nationalist bourgeoisie provided the context for the 'modernizing' of certain indigenous modes of regulating women in orthodox Indian society" (1996, 482). Sumanta Banerjee, also in the context of nineteenth-century Bengal, argues that the creation of a new public space for the respectable *bhadramahila* (educated middle-class woman) was predicated on sharpening class differentiation, especially through the regulation of women's popular culture and the juxtaposition of this new woman with women from lower socioeconomic strata (1989). More recently, Mankekar 1999 and Hancock 1999 have explored middle-class constructions of womanhood in relation to nationalist discourses in North and South India respectively.

4 Before the 1930s, as Kathryn Hansen has noted, the popular theater and early cinema "created a public space in which societal attitudes towards women could be debated" (1998, 2291). "Through the institution of female imper-

sonation, a publicly visible, respectable image of 'woman' was constructed, one that was of use to both men and women. This was a representation that, even attached to the material male body, bespoke modernity. As one response to the British colonial discourse on Indian womanhood—the accusations against Indian women on account of their backward, degraded females—the representation helped support men, dovetailing with the emerging counter-discourse of Indian masculinity. Moreover, women derived from these enactments an image of how they should represent themselves in public. Female impersonators, by bringing into the public sphere the mannerisms, speech and distinctive appearance of middle class women, defined the external equivalents of the new gendered code of conduct for women" (ibid., 2296).

5 According to Kunal Parker, the term *devadasi*, which literally means "servant of the gods" in Sanskrit, began to be used in Anglo-Indian discourse only in the second half of the nineteenth century. The colonial label "dancing girl" was used to refer to communities of women with and without temple affiliations in different parts of the Bombay and Madras Presidencies (Parker 1998, 567). The dance they performed was, in Tamil Nadu, variously called sadir, nautch, or karnatakam, before the "revival" of the dance form in the 1940s as Bharata Natyam.

6 See Ramakrishna 1983 and Venkarataratnam 1901 for further elaboration.

7 See Anandi 1991 for a detailed discussion of the novel.

8 The abolitionist cause was also helped by American writers like Katherine Mayo, whose books *Mother India* (1927) and *Slaves of the Gods* (1929) specifically concerned the supposedly degraded state of devadasis.

9 The Tamil term *kalai*—which, according to the Cre-A Tamil dictionary, has meanings of both "art" and "workmanship" (Subramaniam 1992)—moved decidedly toward connotations of high art (as opposed to craft) in this early-twentieth-century discourse. See, for instance, a 1928 article by C. Jinarajadasa in *Triveni* magazine: "In India, in all the arts and crafts there is a great sense of beauty, but it is now traditional, i.e., the craftsman works by rote, and does not sufficiently feel a true creative urge. . . . If only our artists will look with the eyes of the West on Indian scenes . . . they will find plenty to inspire them" (3–4). Oppositions between art and craft also come up in Rukmini Devi's essay "The Creative Spirit" (ca. 1940s).

10 See the E. Krishna Iyer Centenary Issue of *Sruti* for a more detailed account of the controversy about public performances of nautch (*Sruti* 1997, 6–9). Muthulakshmi Reddy was particularly opposed to the staging of nautch performances at government functions or celebrations.

11 See Amrit Srinivasan (1985, 1875) for a concise listing of some of the changes this involved; also Allen (1997). The idea of devadasis as "pure virgin devotees" was Annie Besant's phrase. "There was a band of pure virgin devotees attached to the ancient Hindu temples. . . . In those days they were held in high esteem and were very well looked after. . . . They would follow the procession of

Gods dressed in the simplest sanyasi garbs and singing pious hymns. . . . This is the history and origin of the devadasi class" (Besant, quoted in Muthulakshmi Reddy 1928–1931, 5). For more on the Theosophical Society, its role in the revival of Bharata Natyam, and its naming of Rukmini Devi as the World Mother, see Dixon 1999, Allen 1997, Weidman 1995, and Burton 1994.

The Madras Mahajana Sabha and the Indian National Congress were founded in 1884 and 1885, respectively, both with a predominance of Smarta Brahmins (Hancock 1999, 56; Suntharalingam 1974, 231). In the early twentieth century, many of these Brahmins associated with the political/cultural program of the Theosophical Society, the headquarters of which were located in Madras. Annie Besant, the society's leader, formed the Home Rule League, which espoused the cause of complete independence for India. Theosophy, with its universalist spiritual philosophy, blended with elite discourse of the time, epitomized by the Madras Hindu Social Reform Association (established 1892), which envisioned a new, reformed Hindu society based on supposedly universal principles of citizenship, rights, and religious belief (Hancock 1999, 56–7). Central to the project of both were the agenda of social reform and the claiming of regional traditions of art, music, and dance as elements of a universal, pan-Indian "culture."

12 Adyar Library, Chennai (Madras), "The Creative Spirit," undated pamphlet published by the Theosophical Society through Vasantha Press in Madras in the 1940s, 14–15.

13 Ibid., 15.

14 In North India, as Regula Qureshi points out, recording provided an opportunity for courtesans to continue as singers and entertainers even as their opportunities for live performance diminished. Many courtesans became singers for films. Interestingly, it was also sound recordings that facilitated Begum Akhtar's re-entry into the public domain as a singer after her marriage and her transformation from courtesan to respectable married woman (Qureshi 2001, 97).

15 S. Kalpakam, personal communication, Madras, July 2002.

16 Baby Kamala was a dance prodigy of the time, credited for popularizing Bharata Natyam among the Brahmin middle classes even more than Rukmini Devi. Baby Kamala gave her first performance in 1941 at the age of seven; the appeal of the child prodigy can be seen in the fact that she retained the title "Baby" well into her teens. In 1988 a writer in *Sruti* commented on her rise, "The timing was perfect. The conditions ideal. And her age was just right. She was still a child, a 'baby' and her innocence and charm endeared her to one and all" (quoted in Allen 1997, 80–81). The appeal of the prodigy continues today; one popular musician is known as "Veena Virtuoso 'Baby' Gayatri."

17 M. S. Subbulakshmi's devadasi background has the status of a public secret in the Karnatic music world; everyone seems to know about it but it is never discussed publicly or written about. For example, Sarathy's 1997 biography

of M.S. skirts the issue by not saying anything about who her father was. He was a wealthy Brahmin patron of her mother.

18 M.S. acted in four films: *Seva Sadanam* (1938), *Shakuntala* (1940), *Savitri* (1941), and *Meera* (1945). Sadasivam was the producer or co-producer for all of them. *Seva Sadanam* was a "social" film that critiqued Brahmin orthodoxy and the dowry system; *Shakuntala* and *Savitri* were based on mythological stories. *Meera*, M.S.'s most popular role, was based on the life of Meera Bai, a high-born Rajput woman who lived in the early sixteenth century, who declared herself to be Krishna's bride and renounced her worldly existence to pursue life as a saint and mendicant. The film was so popular in South India that it was later dubbed in Hindi. Sarojini Naidu gave an on-screen introduction to this version in which she described M.S. as the "nightingale of India" (Guy 1997, 229). Naidu's introduction deftly combines praise of M.S.'s voice with the implication that a good voice transcends its body like a bird in flight; at the same time, it makes M.S. represent India.

19 On the effects of the microphone in western contexts, Simon Frith writes that "the microphone made it possible for singers to make musical sounds—soft sounds, close sounds—that had not really been heard before in terms of public performance. . . . The microphone allowed us to hear people in ways that normally implied intimacy—the whisper, the caress, the murmur" (1996, 187). According to Frith, the microphone also draws attention to the place of the voice in music, allowing it to dominate other instruments, to be the "solo" in a way it could not have been before (188).

20 Anonymous reader for Duke University Press, personal communication, October 2004.

21 Consider the following description: "As a celebrity she has moved with and played hostess to world leaders with gentle charm and dignity. At home she is the traditional housewife, stringing flower garlands for her *puja* (Hindu prayer ritual) room and decorating the floor with her beautiful *kōlam* (rice powder designs). It is on stage that she comes into her own—sensuously captivating, with an occasional lift of the eyebrow and a bewitching smile, not for the audience, but for the Divine" (Indira Menon 1999, 41). Statements like these reveal an insistence on separating M.S.'s stage persona from her everyday life.

22 In a review of the *Meera* soundtrack Kalki identified music as the most elevated of all pleasures and was particularly enthusiastic about a song sung in the voice of the child Meera: the "child" sang so beautifully that "even a person with a heart of stone couldn't be unaffected" (1946, 31). "And, thanks to the skillful recording, we hear MS' voice quite naturally," he concluded. The listener's pleasure is thus constructed through multiple senses of fidelity: the fidelity of the fan to his favorite star, the fidelity of M.S.'s voice to tradition, the fidelity of the child Meera to her beloved Krishna, the fidelity of the record to the original performance.

23 The discourse linking idealized female musicality with notions of naturalness,

as opposed to artifice, intellectuality, and virtuoso display, pervades Western art music. Richard Leppert (1993) and Judith Tick (1986) provide useful discussions of this in English and American contexts respectively. Such distinctions have their origins in a broader aesthetic discourse based on gendered notions of the beautiful and the sublime, as addressed by Paul Mattick Jr. (1995). These distinctions traveled to India as part of a colonial discourse about music but became specifically central to a nationalist discourse that associated "natural" female musicality with the essence of the Indian nation.

24 Adyar Library, Chennai (Madras), "Woman as Artist," undated pamphlet published by the Theosophical Society through Vasantha Press in Madras in the 1940s, 5.

25 Ibid., 2–3.

26 Ibid., 7.

27 Adyar Library, Chennai (Madras), "Dance and Music," undated pamphlet published by the Theosophical Society through Vasantha Press in Madras in the 1940s, 4.

28 Ibid., 14.

29 Ibid., 10–11. Devi's reference to music as the "language of the gods" also alludes to the Sanskrit language, which is referred to in Brahminical tradition as the language of the gods or the divine language. Much of the music that accompanies dance uses Sanskrit religious terminology. Devi's statement may also allude to the fact that the classicization of Karnatic music took place at the same time as the Hindu religious revival, which emphasized a classical Hinduism that was Sanskritic in emphasis. Several figures associated with the classicizing of Karnatic music in the mid-twentieth century, such as Kalki, were also part of the group that constructed classical Hinduism in contrast to Western materialism and lack of spirituality.

30 Ibid., 12, 16.

31 Allen 1997, Meduri 1996, Amrit Srinivasan 1985, and O'Shea 1998 provide more detailed descriptions of the ways dance performance became nationalized and "sanitized." The conflict between earlier dance styles practiced by those from the devadasi community and the reinvented Bharata Natyam popularized by Rukmini Devi was framed by Devi as a conflict between expressing *sringāra* (erotic sentiment) and expressing bhakti (devotion), two modes which she considered irreconcilable. Tanjore Balasaraswati, who came from a family of devadasis and was a contemporary of Rukmini Devi, would later insist that sringara and bhakti were one and the same (O'Shea 1998, 46–49).

32 Robert Ollikkala provides a critique of the gendered distinction between classical and light-classical music in the North Indian classical tradition. " 'Light,' " he writes, "consistently seems to imply 'lesser,' 'derivative,' 'secondary,' and 'feminine.' It is no coincidence that 'light-classical' music, sung by women

of assumed dubious virtue (within a role they have inherited in a male-dominated social structure) is considered to be more emotional, . . . less technically demanding, less pure in terms of tala and raga" (1999, 35). Ollikkala suggests that there are "universal implications to the term 'classical,' implications that include, but reach far beyond, the musical" (36). Vidya Rao, herself a singer of *thumri*, one of the North Indian genres now labeled "light classical," critiques this distinction by embracing thumri as what she calls the "feminine voice," a genre capable of subverting the conventions of Hindustani classical music, providing an alternative to the virtuosic display that is part of classical genres like *khayal* (1999).

33 Jennifer Post has written of the separation of dance from music in the Marathi and Konkani region of Western India in the context of the late-nineteenth-century decline of courtesan traditions there. Many women, she states, began to restrict their performances to singing and avoided dance gestures, presumably in an effort to lend respectability to their performances (Post 1987, 104–5).

34 Ragam-tanam-pallavi was considered for a long time to be suitable only for men.

35 Compare Malathi de Alwis's argument that respectability operates as an "aesthetic" that "must simultaneously clothe a woman's body as well as accentuate it" (1999, 186–87).

36 See Anandi 1997 and Lakshmi 1990 for discussions of the way this metaphoric opposition has operated in Dravidian Movement politics in Tamil Nadu. In discussing the figure of Tamiḻttāy, or Mother Tamil, Lakshmi states that the "yardstick [mother vs. whore], deliberately nurtured and cultivated for the political advancement of a particular group of politicians . . . has now been turned into a 'truth' of culture, something inherent, natural, and unalterable" (Lakshmi 1990, 82).

37 The word *kaṇakku* also has caste associations in the music world. It is generally thought that the mathematically based, rhythmic aspects of Karnatic music, like swara kalpana and pallavi, come from the non-Brahmin, Icai Veḷḷālar (nagaswaram-playing) tradition. For respectable female performers, tala itself was considered a kind of excess; a female musician in her eighties told me that in her day ladies were not only not supposed to do swara kalpana, but even keeping the tala with one's hand was also considered improper (T. Mukhta, personal communication, Madras, September 1998).

38 Compare the interiorized conception of alapana, as elaborated above, with a much more externalizing discourse about tala. When I learned rhythmic aspects and special tala exercises from C. S. Palaninathan, a mridangist in Madurai, he constantly told me that in order to really get the rhythms right, I had to "make a sound," that is, clap louder or slap my leg more vigorously. "Tāḷam nalla pōṭuṅke [Put the talam well]," he commanded. He might sit in a relaxed posture and teach me rhythmic sequences that he had internalized, but if in

his recitation something went wrong, he would move from chair to floor, straighten up, and slap his leg resoundingly, as if the correct version could be arrived at from the outside in.

39 Dipesh Chakrabarty suggests that in the Bengali context the notion of *pabitrata*, or purity, was crucial to the idea of a sphere of interiority that was autonomous from the physical body. Thus, one might think of performances of nonperformance as a "technique of interiority," as Chakrabarty suggests: a way of staging one's innermost emotions as 'pure' and thus helping them "transcend anything that was external to the subject's interior space—the body, interests, social conventions, and prejudices" (Chakrabarty 2000, 138–40). The concept of pabitrata, which emerges in end-of-the-twentieth-century Bengali novels that portray widows is, of course, highly gendered.

40 This distinction between extramusical elements and the "music itself" is crucial to the idea of secular art music, in which raga (melodic scale or mode) and tala are considered the major musical elements, whereas lyrics are appreciated for their aesthetic qualities and abstract meaning but are devalued if they convey sentiment or sensuality.

41 In order to remain respectable, women musicians in the 1960s and 1970s would often only take music students in their own home. My violin teacher recalled that her father would not allow her to teach a female student in that student's home or to play violin in the film studios, which would involve traveling, thus "cheapening" her music.

42 "I haven't gotten what I expected from my children. Now that they are grown, I would just like to have my own flat. Preferably I would like to die while teaching a music lesson," said one female musician (quoted in Lakshmi 2000, 208).

43 This is known as *maṅkala icai* (auspicious music). The category of auspiciousness applies also to women; devadasis were known as *nityacumaṅkali* (ever-auspicious women) because, being married to god, they could never become widows. For an explanation of this, see Kersenboom-Story 1987.

44 Speculations on Ponnuthai's actual motivations for retreating from public performances abound. Some suggest that she was not forced to retreat but chose to in order to validate her status as the respectable widow of her husband and to avoid being seen as a devadasi. Others suggest that her retreat was motivated by political reasons relating to the fact that the Congress Party, of which her husband was a member, lost power in Tamil Nadu in the early 1970s.

45 Her name has been changed to respect confidentiality.

46 See Bullard 1998 on the South Indian flute and women artists.

47 Bhairavi was quite critical of the notion that female musicians had been "liberated" by the pioneering efforts of older female musicians like M. S. Subbulakshmi and D. K. Pattammal. When I asked her what she would have asked them in an interview, she replied, "Whether they could have succeeded without their husbands" (personal communication, Madurai, July 2002).

48 "Quite natural" was one of her stock English phrases.

49 The connections between the "expressivist turn" and the notions of interiority and inner voice in European thought are discussed by Taylor (1989, 370–90). Raymond Williams, in *Culture and Society 1780–1950*, suggests that the notion of "art" and the romantic artist developed in the nineteenth century in Europe as "art became a symbolic abstraction for a whole range of general human experience. . . . A general social activity was forced into the status of a department or province" (1983, 47). In the new idea of art, an emphasis on skill was gradually replaced by an emphasis on sensibility, suggesting a kind of interiorization (ibid., 44).

50 On the idea of the inner sphere of the Indian nation, see Chatterjee 1993.

51 Sadasivam introduced M.S. to Gandhi, Nehru, and a host of other political figures. Gandhi is purported to have said, on hearing her sing, "I have no knowledge of music [*caṅkīta ñāṉam*]. But your voice and your song are extremely sweet" (Kalki 1946, 29).

52 L. R. Easwari, personal communication, Madras, June 2002.

53 S. Janaki, personal communication, Madras, January 2004.

54 Bangalore Nagaratnammal, a devadasi, spoke on the rights of devadasis during the devadasi-abolition movement; she also began a separate Thyagaraja aradhana for women at Tiruvaiyaru to address problems of exclusion. Vai. Mu. Kothainayaki (1901–1960), a Brahmin woman, lectured extensively on the nationalist cause and the betterment of Indian women. She composed songs, wrote stories and novels, and managed the women's journal *Jaganmohini* from 1925 to 1954. In fact, Nagaratnammal encouraged Kothainayaki to sing and provided her with concert opportunities in Mysore (*Sruti* 2001, 44–45).

55 Pattammal stated that even after she had made gramophone records, her father would not allow her to sing onstage. "It is Vai. Mu. Ko. who is responsible for my being amidst you as a musician today. I first met her in a gramophone company. I was 10 years old then. Those days everyone was so surprised that a 10-year-old could sing so well. Vai. Mu. Ko. was also impressed. She wanted me to enter the concert arena. Those days girls from Brahmin families were not encouraged to perform in public. It was a wonder that my father, who was an orthodox Dikshitar, permitted me to even cut a record. But Vai. Mu. Ko. was a tenacious lady. She made several trips to Kanchipuram to persuade my father. They had several arguments. My father tried to give all kind of excuses even stating that I could not sing with accompanists. She vehemently asked, 'What is wrong if a Brahmin girl sings on stage?' Ultimately my father relented and my first concert was held at Egmore Mahila Sabha [Egmore Women's Association in Madras]" (*Sruti* 2001, 41). Kothainayaki and Pattammal later made three 78-rpm records with songs on themes of social protest (42).

4 *Can the Subaltern Sing?*

Epigraph quote can be found in *Tamiḻ Icai Makānāṭu Ceṉṉai Nikaḻcci Mālar* 1944 (96).

1 Downing Thomas has traced the emergence of a "verbal paradigm" for music —the analogy of music to language and theories of their original unity—in the writings of French Enlightenment thinkers such as Condillac and Rousseau. He locates in the late sixteenth century a conceptual shift toward thinking of music within the domain of the rhetorical and human rather than grouping it with mathematical or cosmological phenomena. In Enlightenment thought, music came to be related to national subjects by analogy to their relation to their national language or mother tongue. For Rousseau especially, the concept of nationality was central in connecting music to language: "Every nation's music draws its principal character from the language that belongs to it" (Rousseau, quoted in Thomas 1995, 98). By the nineteenth century, in romantic discourse the idea of music as a language came to be particularly associated with European art music; composers were said to be masters of an aesthetic "language" of music. The analogy between music and language, part of the colonial inheritance of Western ideas about music, became a central aspect of nationalist discourse concerning the place of music in newly independent India.

2 These two choices—between voice as a cultivated, aestheticized instrument and voice as a representation of self—may be considered in relation to, respectively, Sanskritic rāsa theory and Tamil bhakti discourse. The theory of rāsa was first elaborated in Bharata's *Natya Sastra*, a treatiṣe on dance and music from the early centuries AD. Literally defined as "taste," rāsa refers to a listener's or spectator's detached aesthetic apprehension and enjoyment of an emotion (see, for example, Walimbe 1980 for an explanation of rāsa theory). In Tamil Bhakti, which emerged as a reaction against overly ritualized and Sanskritic Hinduism, the devotee addresses the deity in his/her mother tongue, emphasizing directness and the subjective nature of emotion (see Cutler 1987).

3 Saskia Kersenboom has written that the concept of muttamiḻ requires a notion of verbal art as performance and thus a sense of all knowledge as embodied and applied (1995). It is a "conception of and approach to language in its *dynamism and functional entirety*; . . . language (in this case, the Tamil language) is not 'just' speech, not only spoken/written word, but also, simultaneously, song, music, word combined with musical sound, sung word, and again simultaneously, word enacted in performance" (Zvelebil 1992, 142). This notion, Kersenboom argues, is fundamentally different from the idea of the "text" as existing separate from its performance or reading that underlies the Western institution of literature (1995, 8). The contrast emerges most clearly in a consideration of *ōlai* (literally, "leaves"), the palm-leaf manuscripts that

contained much of what is today regarded as Tamil literature. Ōlai, Kersenboom argues, are not literature in the sense of manuscripts to be read and studied for their content but are instead mnemonic devices to aid a person who has already memorized and embodied the text, or objects to be worshipped in themselves (ibid., 14). Ōlai are not complete texts in themselves but only become complete when their contents are embodied or applied in performance.

4 Kamil Zvelebil writes that "the notion of scholar and artist—particularly verbal artist—is traditionally not separated: thus, often, vidvan is he who studies music, composes music, and performs music" (1992, 131 n.8). Swaminathayyar's teacher was Mahavidvan (the prefix *maha-* means "great") Meenakshisundaram Pillai, who was noted for his scholarship and declamation in Tamil.

5 The process of rediscovering ancient Tamil literature, which took place between about 1850 and 1925, is described in Zvelebil 1992 (144–222).

6 On the treatment of Brahmin devotees of Tamil by the popular press in the first half of the twentieth century, see Ramaswamy 1997 (194–204).

7 This tendency is undoubtedly influenced by the theories of Aryan/Dravidian racial difference that have become prevalent in the discourse on what divides Brahmins from non-Brahmins in South India. There is a widespread belief, held by Brahmins and non-Brahmins alike, that Brahmins are not "original Dravidians" but relative newcomers from North India. Many Tamil Brahmins speak a variety of Tamil that is highly Sanskritized and Anglicized in word choice. For a further explanation of colonial theories of Aryan/Dravidian racial difference, see note 19 below and Trautmann 1997.

8 Stuart Blackburn argues that the European colonial impact on "literature" in South India was "filtered through a pre-existing . . . debate about the origins of Tamil and its position vis-à-vis Sanskrit" (2000, 478).

9 See Ramaswamy 1997, chapter 3.

10 V. Narayana Rao has argued, for instance, that the concept of mother tongue, denoted in Telugu by the term *mātrabhāṣa*, is absent from South Indian discourses on language prior to the last part of the nineteenth century and that the term itself is a loan translation from English (1995, 25). See also Pollock 2000 (612–13) in this regard.

11 Lisa Mitchell points out this distinction, suggesting that an earlier "pleasure taken in language—sometimes referred to as *rāsa* (emotion, sentiment; aesthetic taste or pleasure; literary or artistic beauty)—should not be confused with an attachment *to* language" (2004, 32, 35). For a detailed discussion of these kinds of premodern poetic practices, see Narayana Rao and Shulman 1998.

12 Mitchell argues that once language comes to be imagined, objectified, and personified in this way, it also causes a "new form of alienation of self from language . . . accompanied by a new fear—the fear of loss. In the face of English education, and the presence of other 'languages'—Tamil, Hindi, Marathi

—now similarly objectified and separated from Telugu, it has become possible to imagine losing the language one now thinks of as 'one's own.' Yet at the same time, it is precisely this *alienation* of language from self which makes it possible to imagine that *a* particular language (like Telugu)—as opposed to language in the broader undifferentiated sense—is an inalienable part of oneself. Indeed the emergence of an affective relationship to *a particular language* can be seen as a way of counteracting the alienation of self from language, by reattaching to oneself, not undifferentiated language use, but an externalized idea of a single 'language,' something not possible without this alienation" (2004, 38).

13 Ramaswamy's *Passions of the Tongue* (1997) and Nambi Arooran's *Tamil Renaissance and Dravidian Nationalism* (1980) provide detailed accounts of the Tamil revival. Arooran's book is more historical in nature, focusing on the revival of Tamil language and literature, the Self-Respect movement, the anti-Hindi agitations, and the demand for a separate Tamil state in the early 1940s. Ramaswamy analyzes the discourse of Tamil devotion using writings from all branches of the Tamil revival.

14 Devadoss grew up in Madurai and came to the United States in 1969 to attend Oberlin College. He returned to India in the early 1970s.

15 James Siegel discusses the particular kind of listening that is involved in overhearing in the context of the development of Indonesian as a lingua franca. It is not meaning but the "force of the medium itself" that compels overhearing; the lingua franca is that which "does not belong in any one community, which no one truly possesses, in which one sees what one wants and bargains for it" (1997, 60).

16 Interestingly, Devadoss noted that classical music seemed to be insulated from this new power of music: "While popular music was thus subject to pushes and pulls, South Indian classical music, now the preserve of the Brahmin community, continued to remain steadfast, strong, and traditional" (1997, 156).

17 In the first three decades of the twentieth century Bhatkhande conducted musical research trips in various parts of India, published several books on the theory of Indian music, compiled and published about 1800 compositions in North Indian vocal music, and founded two music colleges. For a detailed account of Bhatkhande's accomplishments in the field of music and his troubled relationship with his contemporary, the musicologist V.D. Paluskar, see Bakhle 2005 (chapters 3 and 5). As Bakhle shows, Bhatkhande's notion of Indian classical music as modern and essentially secular in many ways directly opposed Paluskar's notion that in order to be revived, Indian music had to be reframed in the idiom of Hindu religiosity.

18 Although Krishna Iyer mentions no source for this conceptualization, it is possible that the concept of muttamiḻ had influenced him. His general phonocentrism and his differentiation between natural and conventional meaning

is reminiscent of Rousseau as well as Saussure's distinction between arbitrary and motivated language.

19 The South Indian syllables for the pitches of the scale—sa, ri, ga, ma, pa, da, and ni—are usually abbreviated by their first letter. The numbers 1 and 2—as in "R1" and "R2"—indicate flat and sharp notes, respectively.

20 In this passage Krishna Rao refers to a painting that depicts a Hindu myth in which the sage Viswamitra, distracted from his meditation by the heavenly nymph Menaka, gives in to carnal desire. The result is the birth of the baby Shakuntala. In this musical passage, Menaka has come to present the baby to its father. She addresses Viswamitra, who hides his face in shame. The painting to which Krishna Rao refers appears in *The Psychology of Music* (1917, 35).

21 Nambi Arooran's *Tamil Renaissance and Dravidian Nationalism* places the Tamil Music movement in the larger context of Tamil revival. It is also the only work in English on the Tamil Music Movement.

22 The term *Dravidian* began to be used in the mid-nineteenth century by colonial philologists skeptical of the idea that Tamil and other southern languages belonged in the same language family as Sanskrit. Theories of racial difference between so-called Aryans, who were thought to inhabit most of Northern India and to be the descendants of nomadic groups that had migrated to the Indian subcontinent from the north and west, and Dravidians, who were thought to be the darker-skinned, indigenous inhabitants of South India, dominated colonial ethnology in the nineteenth century. The support for such theories was garnered from the discipline of philology and consolidated for the first time by Reverend Robert Caldwell in his *A Comparative Grammar of the Dravidian or South Indian Family of Languages* (1856). Using comparative grammatical "evidence," Caldwell stated that the languages of South India were different enough from Sanskrit to be considered a different language family. For this family he chose the term *Dravidian*, which he adapted from the original *dravida* found in a Sanskrit text (4). The word *Tamil*, he claimed, was derived from the word *dravida* (8); being the least influenced by Sanskrit, the Tamil language was thus the purest representative of the Dravidian family.

23 The Esplanade is close to George Town, a traditionally non-Brahmin area of Madras. Mylapore is, of course, a bastion of Brahminism. Apparently members of the Congress Party from Mylapore refused to allow the Raja Annamalai Manram to be built in the Mylapore area.

24 A prominent idea in histories of Tamil culture written during the twentieth-century Tamil renaissance is that before the era of the great Tamil literature that was published in the late nineteenth century, Tamil civilization had already experienced two previous golden ages which had lasted for thousands of years, many years before the birth of Christ. These periods, known as the First and Second Tamil Caṅkams (Sangams: academies), which produced much literature, had been centered in the city of Tēṉ-Maturai (Ten-Madurai:

Southern Madurai), located far south of the present southern tip of India, which is Kanyakumari. Ten-Madurai was eventually swept under the ocean and its literature lost, but the Third Tamil Sangam, centered in Madurai, from which the now published literature came, represented the continuation of the great civilization, its last survivors (Ramaswamy 1999, 97). The founding of the Fourth Tamil Sangam at Madurai in 1901 was intended to stand as the beginning of another golden age for Tamils. The idea of an ancient, vast, now lost Tamil land was crystallized in late-nineteenth- and early-twentieth-century discourses on Lemuria, the sunken continent. The legend of Lemuria and its destruction by the ocean allowed a glorious past to be imagined out of the straitened circumstances of the present, thus allowing for the possibility of a return or resurgence. This kind of "catastrophic consciousness," suggests Sumathi Ramaswamy, "is very much a response to (colonial) modernity, a form of resistance to its totalizing and homogenizing knowledge claims. Catastrophic historical consciousness enables the recuperation of all those necessary and fabulous knowledges of the ancient past cast out of a world rendered increasingly disenchanted through the work of the modern sciences" (98). Yet, as she demonstrates, the re-creation, or the re-enchantment, of the ancient past is often achieved through a thoroughly modern scientific discourse. In this case, modern discourses of philology and musicology made the twentieth-century enchantment with ancient Tamil music possible.

25 Born in 1859 in the Tirunelveli district into a family of Nadars who had converted to Christianity two generations before, Abraham Pandithar, by all accounts a gifted student, initially became a teacher at Lady Napier's Girls School in Tanjavur (Nadar 1954, 110–11). Around 1890 he and his wife resigned from their positions as teachers to take up farming and medicine making full-time. The title "Pandithar" was conferred on him after he became known as a physician. Indeed, between his work as a physician and the sale of the "Sanjeevi Pills" for which he became famous, Pandithar was said to have earned nearly a thousand rupees a day (ibid., 111). Because of his financial success, he was the subject of a detailed sketch by Somerset Playne in 1914, in a guide to South India's commercial development (1914, 486–91).

26 Extensive records of Pandithar's conflict with other participants in the 1916 Baroda conference regarding the number of srutis in an octave were appended in the Tamil version of his book, *Karuṇamirtacākaram*. Most of the book itself was given over to minute calculations through which Pandithar mathematically showed that others' theories were wrong.

27 According to Pandithar, "upholders of Sanskrit" had tried to convince people that Tamil was derived from Sanskrit, that even the name "Tamil" was derived from the Sanskrit term *dravida*. Pandithar greeted such theories with ridicule, claiming instead that the Sanskrit-speaking Aryans had been unable to pronounce or write the name Tamil and thus had mispronounced it as dravida (1917, 32).

28 Indeed, the essay was politely returned by the British journal editors; Pandithar included their correspondence in his record.

29 C. N. Annadurai's quote can be found in Muthiah 1996 (40).

30 The information in this section I take from interviews I conducted in Madras and Madurai in 1998. I have made the interviewees' identities vague in order to protect their confidentiality.

31 Dharmapuram Swaminathan, personal communication, Kondrattur, India, November 1998.

5 *A Writing Lesson*

1 This booklet, printed 16 August 1985, was a compilation of sources that Balachander made to support his argument and was addressed as an "open letter" to "present and future musicians, musicologists, music-lovers, music students, experts in allied arts, press and public."

2 A comparable debate is described by V. Narayana Rao in his article "The Politics of Telugu Ramayanas" (2001). In describing the conflict between traditional Ramayana readers who treat the Valmiki Ramayana as the original and correct story and the oppositional readings of what he calls the "anti-Ramayana discourse" in the 1920s, Narayana Rao points out that the concepts of authorship and authenticity differ crucially between these two points of view. Whereas leaders of the anti-Ramayana discourse claim Valmiki to be the author of the Ramayana in a factual mode, for traditional readers, Narayana Rao suggests, "Valmiki's authorship of the Ramayana is ideological; they do not base their statement on empirical textual evidence" (163). Balachander's challenge to the party-line Swati Tirunal story was scandalous because it similarly attempted to counter myth with an empirical, factually based argument.

3 I thank Katherine Bergeron for suggesting this way of framing the issue.

4 S. Balachander, open letter, 1. The letter was appended to a copy of the Gayan Samaj Proceedings of 1887 and copies were distributed to many musical institutions and musicologists in Madras. I thank the Music Academy Library for making this source available to me.

5 Ibid., i.

6 Ibid., 1.

7 Ibid.

8 Ibid., 2

9 Ibid., 3.

10 Ibid.

11 Ibid., 4.

12 Ibid., 5.

13 Ibid.

14 Ibid., 5–6.

15 Published 23 September 1982. A rumor circulated that the brothers were in possession of palm-leaf manuscripts containing evidence to back up their argument, but when the Travancore royal family made an offer to buy them, there was no response. Although Sivanandam and Kittappa's claim was a far cry from Balachander's assertion that Swati Tirunal was a fictional composer, it could be used—and indeed was used—as evidence for Balachander's case, even though the brothers later publicly declared their disagreement with Balachander (K. V. Ramanathan 1996, 17; Nayar 1997, 23).

16 This musician was from the Icai Veḷḷāḷar caste and took great pride in being from the same caste as the Tanjore Quartette, precisely because of the "professional" way they had made a living from music.

17 I thank Dr. Kovalam Narayana Panikkar and Dr. V. S. S. Sharma, both of Trivandrum, for discussing the matter of Sopanam music and the Mullamoodu Bhagavatars with me in June 1998. Dr. R. P. Raja of Trivandrum very generously discussed the Swati Tirunal case with me at length in May 1998. Sopanam style is discussed in Poduval n.d. (3–4, 27).

18 Compare Katherine Bergeron's discussion of conflicting ideas about the revival and performance of Gregorian chant between 1880 and 1900, in chapter 4 of *Decadent Enchantments*. Bergeron contrasts the "Romantic" approach of Dom Pothier, who was concerned with going beyond the written notes to find "the long-forgotten vox of the chant," with the "Modern" approach of Dom Mocquereau, who embarked on a "philological" project, comparing written manuscripts with each other to arrive at a standardized notation (1998, 101). Mocquereau's idea of going back to the original—he used photographs of the original manuscripts—is similar to Nayar's idea of finding the original compositions preserved by the Mullamoodu Bhagavatars.

19 In the epigraph quote, Tagore was arguing against ideas that staff notation would provide a universal language for music (1874, 382).

20 Christopher Pinney quotes the Parisian photographer Félix Nadar's comments on the difference between photograph and portrait. The portrait gave one "the moral grasp of the subject—that instant understanding which puts you in touch with the model, helps you to sum him up, guides you to his habits, his ideas and character and enables you to produce not an indifferent reproduction, a matter of routine or accident such as any laboratory assistant could achieve, but a really convincing and sympathetic likeness, an intimate portrait" (1997, 33).

21 Taking C as the scale tonic, *ri*-1 = D-flat; *ri*-2 = D-natural.

22 The discussion of the status of ornaments in Karnatic music was part of a larger discourse on ornament taking place in the context of Indian art. In 1939, in response to European critiques of Indian art as "merely ornamental," Ananda Coomaraswamy wrote an essay entitled "Ornament," in which he defended the ornament against charges of superfluity. He noted that in Sanskrit, Greek, and Latin, the word for ornament had originally meant "that

which is added on to make something sufficient"; it was only later that it came to mean "embellishment." Although Coomaraswamy was refuting notions of the purely "decorative" or "aesthetic" quality of ornaments, his argument still depended on the kind of oppositions between communication and pleasure, necessity and luxury, adequacy and excess, that make the idea of ornament thinkable in the first place. His defense of alankaram also seems to allude to the authority of Sanskrit as a classical language in which the role of alankarams is central (Coomaraswamy 1939).

23 The difference between note and swara is sometimes explained thus: the swara refers to the space between two notes, for example C and D; it is thus a kind of placeholder. When someone sings "ri" it doesn't necessarily mean they are singing a D; rather, that note is the tone center for what they are singing. In some ragas "ri" is actually specified to be sung or played as an oscillation between D and E; in that sense the swara "ri" is not a "note."

24 Another proponent of staff notation was Ernest Clements, member of the Indian civil service in the Bombay Presidency and a participant in the great sruti debates in the years following the first All-India Music Conference in 1916. Clements argued, in his *Introduction to the Study of Indian Music* (1913), that the staff notation was the most logical kind of notation because of its economy: "It possesses a distinct advantage over any method which requires the eye to follow one set of signs for melody (svara) and an entirely distinct set for time (laya)" (16). He demonstrated how the "middle octave," the range commonly employed in Indian music, "fit easily" onto the staff. He warned, however, that those who had "become ensnared by Western notation" were unwittingly accepting the law of equal temperament. Falling for the neat appearance of the notation, they were not aware of its implications, the fact that it consistently blurred together differences of a quarter-tone (35). If the notation was really going to be self-sufficient, musicians had to see the exact interval portrayed in the notation itself. Accordingly, he used a slash through the sign for flat and natural notes to show that twice as many notes as regular staff notation illustrated existed in the scale. The use of notation demanded a standardization of the Indian scale, the mathematical calculation of each note. Only then would the gap between ear and eye be closed, and Indian music become truly visible. In 1920 Clements undertook to show practically how his notation worked by translating compositions written down in Indian sargam notation into staff notation. For the sake of visibility, Clements did away with all gamaka symbols.

25 Bergeron illuminates the idea of "legibility" in her discussion of late-nineteenth-century debates about notation for Gregorian chant. "The notion of legibility referred to the way printed characters enabled the act of reading." The ideal of legibility implied words (or notation, in this case) so clear that they would seem to be transparent, to disappear, leaving the impression of direct vocal communication. Thus, "a beautiful page had the power . . . to

transform what was known as 'silent reading' into a blissful interval of listening" (1998, 58–59).

26 On the symbolism of mother's milk in the context of Tamil language devotion in the 1930s, see Ramaswamy 1997, 106–8.

27 *Sangīta Sarvartha Sāra Sangrahamu*, printed in Telugu in 1859, was supposedly the first book of Karnatic compositions published. But, according to M. Hariharan, it was a mere compendium with no pedagogical project (Clements 1920, preface).

28 A. R. Venkatachalapathy has documented similar changes that took place in reading practices with the emergence of printed books. He notes the rise of silent reading among the middle classes in Tamil-speaking areas at the turn of the twentieth century, in contrast to the older practice of reading aloud and memorizing from palm-leaf manuscripts. Whereas palm-leaf manuscripts, written in a continuous, run-on fashion, left many possibilities of interpretation for the reader, printed books and the introduction of punctuation in Tamil gave rise to new modes of reading, like scanning and browsing, as well as to the feeling of an inexhaustible quantity of printed material available to be read. The illusion of plenty became part of this experience of reading (1994, 282).

29 The epigraph reflects a line spoken by a character in Chinnaswamy Mudaliar's play, "Saraswatia Redux," modeled on Shakespearean comedy, in which the theoretical aspects of Karnatic music, including the 72-melakarta raga system, are explained. The play was published in several issues of Chinnaswamy Mudaliar's journal, *Oriental Music in European Notation*, between 1892 and 1895.

30 The 72-melakarta raga scheme appeared in Venkatamakhi's treatise, *Caturdandi Prakasika*.

31 A full description of the system is beyond the scope of this chapter; it is more the idea of such a system that I am trying to convey. Sambamoorthy's *The 72-Melakarta System* (1961) provides a lucid demonstration of how the system works.

32 If the magic of numbers was not sufficient, the system could also be made to work with letters. The first two syllables of each raga name corresponded to two letters in an ordered table of numbered Sanskrit letters. By taking the corresponding numbers for these letters in the alphabet table, and reversing them, one would arrive at the number of the melakarta raga in the 72 melakarta raga table, and with this number one could then determine the notes of the raga (Sambamoorthy 1961, 14–16).

33 Such a scheme resonates with Michel Foucault's description of the table and its importance in what he calls the classical episteme, which he identifies with the seventeenth century. In the classical idea of "natural history" as formulated by Linnaeus, the table functions as "a grid [that] can be laid out over the entire vegetable or animal kingdom. Each group can be given a name.

With the result that any species, without having to be described, can be designated with the greatest accuracy by means of the names of the different groups in which it is included. . . . Once the system of variables . . . has been defined at the outset, it is no longer possible to modify it, to add or subtract even one element. . . . To know what properly appertains to one individual is to have before one the classification—or the possibility of classifying—all others" (Foucault 1970, 141–44).

34 This idea was pursued by almost all those who wrote about Indian music in the late nineteenth century and the early twentieth (e.g., Clements 1920). It was undoubtedly influenced by the ideas about language "families" in philology.

35 N. S. Saminathan, personal communication, Madurai, June 2002.

36 It is interesting to note that there was no punctuation as we know it in Indian languages such as Tamil or Telugu before the advent of printing and modern prose forms that arose in the late nineteenth century and early twentieth. Full stops were represented, but there were no commas, exclamation points, or other marks. Such punctuation in part reflects the effect of English on Indian languages (Dharwadker 1997, 108–33).

37 A *meend* is a slow sliding from one note to the next, especially in the alap of Hindustani music.

38 Compare Katherine Bergeron's argument in the conclusion of *Decadent Enchantments*.

39 In Hindu Advaita Vedanta philosophy the concept of Brahman is often translated as "ultimate reality," the source from which all emanates and returns, the unchanging absolute. Jeaneane Fowler describes it as the "Unmanifest Source of the manifestation of cause-effect processes in the universe" (2002, 51).

6 *Fantastic Fidelities*

1 Harrison suggests that we gather "significant examples of where things are heard differently, or where the description of listening undergoes major changes and of where listening seems to take on an historically changed position within the modal construction of self and psyche" (1996, 22).

2 For instance, my violin teacher used to refer to her guru (who also happened to be her father) as "my god, my mother, and my father." I learned that she expected me to call her "Amma" (mother). Similarly, a mridangist with whom I studied in Madurai referred to his guru, C. S. Sankarasiva Bhagavatar, as his father. It was only later that I learned that he had "adopted" his guru as a father.

3 *Sangati* refers to variation on a musical phrase; compositions are elaborated in Karnatic music by adding sangatis.

4 This and the following passages are my translations of Malan's story, originally published in *Kalki* and reprinted in *Āṉṟu*, a collection of Tamil short stories.

Malan himself edited the collection, meant to be representative of Tamil writing of the twentieth century. "Vitvān" is placed at the end of the second volume, and Malan places it in the genre of Tamil science fiction (*viññāṉa cirukataikaḷ*) (1981, xiii).

5 *Shadjam* is the long name of *sa*, the tonic or first note of the scale. Each note is called a *swaram*.

6 The word *kaṇakku*, used here to refer to frequencies of sound waves, is also the word for the rhythmic improvisation, based on calculations, that Karnatic musicians perform. It is thus simultaneously in the realms of music theory and of technology. Therein lies its threat: if a computer can master one aspect of kaṇakku, can it not master the other as well?

7 The Indian part of the Gramophone Company's first Far Eastern Tour in 1902–1903 was limited to Calcutta, where Gaisberg recorded, among others, the female courtesan singers Janki Bai and Gauhar Jan (Gaisberg 1942, 56–57). The second and third recording tours of India, engineered by William Sinkler Darby and William Gaisberg (Fredrick's younger brother), respectively, included other locations in India. Thus, the first recordings were made in Madras between 1904 and 1907. They included mostly vocal artists, with the exception of a few, such as the violinist Pudukottai Narayanaswamy Iyer, the harmonium player Madras Chetty Babu, and bands such as the Tanjore Band and the Madras-based band of Govindasamy Dasu (Kinnear 1994: 73–266). The female singers recorded were all from the devadasi community; they sang classical kritis as well as Telugu and Tamil padams and javalis (songs, associated with dance, which came to be considered "light" classical). Among these were some with wholly or partly English lyrics, with titles like "Hello, How Am I?" and "What a Beautiful Lady." Thus, from the start, the Gramophone Company did not record only classical music. A large number of recordings were also made of the Tamil comedians Venugopal Chary and "Professor Naidu." These included comedic scenes like "Brahmin Going to a Dancing Girl's House," "Street Life in Madras," and "Railway Station Scene," as well as a genre of imitations: of Madras beggars, of birds, of a jutka driver, of a passing train, and even of well-known Karnatic singers. Such imitations were well-suited to the gramophone, which allowed everyday events to become comic by their isolation and repetition. Between 1900 and 1910, the Gramophone Company (later to become His Master's Voice Company) made over four-thousand recordings in India, more than in any other single country on its world tours (Gronow 1981, 255). By 1905 the Talking Machine and Indian Record Company had started a branch in Madras (Kinnear 1994, 10). The Gramophone Company published its first South Indian catalog in 1905 and advertised prominently in English and vernacular-language newspapers (ibid., 24). Its main office and record-pressing factory, established in 1908, were in Calcutta. The company maintained its monopoly by associating with local record-selling agents in

Madras and other cities (G. N. Joshi 1987, 148). Electrical recording was first introduced in India in 1925, and the magnetic tape recorder became available around 1950 (ibid., 148–49).

8 Gamakas, usually translated as "ornaments" or "embellishments," can be thought of as specified ways of getting from one note to the next in Karnatic music. Gamakas are highly individual to different musicians and are not included in printed notation.

9 Sterne notes, as does Taussig in *Mimesis and Alterity*, that the "encounter between the modern and the nonmodern lies at the heart of moments of fascination with watching others' listening to reproduced sound" (Sterne 2000, 14). Erika Brady, in *A Spiral Way*, also noted the pervasiveness of such "rube" stories in early encounters with technologies of sound recording (1999, 27–34).

10 In a 1934 report, G. W. Kaye of the National Physical Laboratory, Teddington, wrote, "Method of Experiment: The notes and phrases concerned were played by Mr. Subrahmanya on his violin. The sound from the violin was received by a condenser microphone distant about 2 ft. from the violin, and connected by a valve amplifier to one of the vibrators of a Duddell Oscillograph. The wave form of the sound was recorded on photographic paper by means of a revolving drum camera attached to the oscillograph. A time scale was provided on each record by a second vibrator that registered the wave form of the electrical output from a standard valve-maintained tuning fork, operating at a frequency of 1000 cycles per second. The player and the receiving microphone were situated in a lagged cabinet so as to avoid as far as possible, any interference from extraneous noise. Communication between the player and the operator of the recording apparatus was maintained by a system of visual signals, controlled by the mechanism of the shutter on the recording camera, the player being warned one second in advance of the opening of the shutter and also at the commencement and conclusion of the exposure. The duration of the exposure was approximately one second in each case" (in Subrahmanya Ayyar 1939, 134–36).

11 Precisely because it could not talk back, the phonograph could only hear. This notion of the separability of functions, according to Kittler, underlay the "discourse network" of 1900. Emerging around 1900, theories of the localization of brain functions and the idea of testing humans for speech, hearing, and writing as isolated functions modeled themselves on the phonograph, which performed only the function of "hearing" (1999, 38; 1990, 214). As if by compensation, musicians seemed to cease to hear at all. G. N. Joshi, who worked for the Gramophone Company as a recording officer between 1938 and 1973, recalled, "When I was first recorded in the year 1932, I was lured to the studios to record only two of my most popular songs. At the recording session, I became so involved and excited at the prospect of being recorded

that instead of just two songs, when the recording session was wound up I discovered that I had actually recorded fourteen songs!" (1987, 151).

12 V. A. K. Ranga Rao, personal communication, Madras, June 2002. Saraswati Stores, Odeon, and Columbia Records employed Turaiyur Rajagopala Sharma as a "tutor," while the Gramophone Company employed T. A. Kalyanam.

13 A recording by the violinist Dwaram Venkataswamy Naidu from the early 1940s features a ragam-tanam-pallavi, an improvisational item that in a concert would have taken about an hour at that time, compressed into four segments of exactly three-and-a-half minutes each. The present-day idea that a musician should, when doing raga alapana, make the raga clear from the very first phrase, rather than keeping the listeners in suspense, probably first gained its urgency from the demands of recording. Musicians speak of five-minute alapanas or twenty-minute alapanas as choices they make depending on the amount of time available—the idea being to carefully plan one's spontaneity.

14 Jonathan Sterne traces the emergence of the idea of the ear as a hearing mechanism in relation to the science of otology and the early technologies of sound reproduction, notably the ear phonautograph, in the mid- to late nineteenth century. The technologies of sound reproduction, Sterne writes, depended on the "isolation, separation, and transformation of the senses," and the idea that the senses could be understood as mechanisms (2003, 50–51).

15 Sterne writes that "people had to learn how to understand the relations between sounds made by people and sounds made by machines" (2003, 216). The idea of sound fidelity and the idea of a recording as a reproduction of an "original" performance are not natural results of the process of recording but particular ways of conceiving of that process, Sterne argues.

16 Stephen Hughes suggests that "popular publishing and the press constituted a new vehicle for extending gramophone music well beyond the purchasing of records and machines. These printed materials were more than a medium for promoting record sales; they also created a significant new circulation, allowed for a new mode of engagement and provided a new forum for the public discussion of gramophone music" (2002, 456).

17 See Farrell 1997 for a reproduction of one of these advertisements (32).

18 The phrase "she herself has melted" is used extensively in Tamil bhakti poetry to describe a devotee's relationship with God. In using the idiom of bhakti, Raman thus presented M.S. as an exemplary devotee filled with love of God.

19 In "The Form of the Phonograph Record" Theodor Adorno wrote, "Through the phonograph record *time* gains a new approach to music. It is not the time in which music happens, nor is it the time which music monumentalizes by means of its 'style.' It is time as evanescence, enduring in mute music. If the 'modernity' of all mechanical instruments gives music an age-old appearance—as if, in the rigidity of its repetitions, it had existed forever, . . . then evanescence and recollection . . . [have] become tangible and manifest through the gramophone records" (1934, 38).

20 In 1938, inspired by such potential, Rabindranath Tagore himself wrote a poem in honor of All India Radio, entitled "Akashvani" (the Hindi name for All India Radio):

> Hark to Akashvani up-surging
> From here below.
> The earth is bathed in Heaven's glory
> Its purple glow.
> Across the blue expanse is firmly planted
> The altar of the Muse.
> The lyre unheard of Light is throbbing
> With human hues.
> From earth to heaven, distance conquered
> In waves of light
> Flows the music of man's divining,
> Fancy's flight.
> To East and West speech careers,
> Swift as the Sun.
> The mind of man reaches Heaven's confines,
> Its freedom won.
> (*Akashvani* [English version], 24 July 1977, 1).

21 Meanwhile, the princely states of Mysore and Trivandrum set up radio stations in 1935 and 1939, respectively.

22 In the 1930s, the Madras Corporation installed permanent loudspeakers at six open places in Madras city to promote communal listening (Hughes 2002, 459).

23 Rudolph Mrazek, similarly, writes in relation to the Netherlands East Indies Radio that the technology of radio provided a metaphor for the Dutch colonial project of keeping natives and Europeans insulated from contact with each other in the decades just before Indonesian independence (1997).

24 S. Rajam, personal communication, Madras, December 2003.

25 Ibid.

26 Other educational programs on the radio used to include music quiz shows, according to Mullick, and a program of introducing classical music through film songs (1974, 41). The "National Programme" used to have a theme, making it appropriately didactic (S. Venkataraman, personal communication, Madras, June 1998). Currently, there are several music quiz shows on Tamil cable-television channels in which players are encouraged to show off their encyclopedic knowledge of Karnatic compositions.

27 R. Rangaramanuja Ayyangar was also the author of *A History of Indian Music from Vedic Times to the Present.*

28 Keskar's remarks reflected the general distrust of musicians in the revivalist discourse on Hindustani music: the idea that scholars and musicologists,

not musicians themselves, possessed the correct and authentic knowledge of music. As Janaki Bakhle has shown, the implication that [Muslim] musicians were ignorant, illiterate, and ill-suited to be the custodians of their own musical tradition, and that the tradition needed to be saved by [Hindu] musicologists was part of the partitioning of the musical and cultural sphere into Hindu and Muslim in the early twentieth century (Bakhle 2005, 195).

29 *Tampulam* is a presentation of betel leaves and prepared betel nut given by a gracious host to guests when they depart.

30 Sruti boxes produce continuous sound (as from a bellows instrument), while electronic tamburas produce pulsating sound (as from strings being plucked in succession). However, both are referred to colloquially as "sruti boxes."

31 G. Raj Narayan, email to author, November 2002.

32 Radel's latest invention in 2003 was a digital veena, which is basically a synthesizer in the shape of a veena.

33 In late 2003 Radel came out with another model that has four "strings" which can be sounded by a mere light touch. But the instrument, like other Radel products, can also be switched on to play automatically.

Afterword

1 The relationship between rise of the idea of musical "classics" in England and the emergence of a leisure class during the Industrial Revolution has been touched on by William Weber, but there is little direct mention in Weber or elsewhere of the enabling role of colonialism in these developments (1992, 1–9).

Works Cited

Abbate, Carolyn. 1991. *Unsung voices: Opera and musical narrative in the nineteenth century*. Princeton: Princeton University Press.

Achariyar, Deivasikamani. 1949. *Mēṭaittamiḻ* [Platform Tamil]. Repr. chaps. 1–18, Madras: Palms Printers, 1987.

Adorno, Theodor. 1934. "The form of the phonograph record" and "The curves of the needle." Trans. Thomas Levin. *October* 55:48–56.

Adyanthaya, Rao Bahadur N. M. 1949. Music and healing [brochure]. Mangalore.

Akashvani. 24 July 1977. New Delhi: Ministry of Information and Broadcasting.

Allen, Matthew. 1997. Rewriting the script for South Indian dance. *The Drama Review* 41, no. 3:63–100.

All-India Music Conference proceedings. 1916–1918. Baroda: All-India Music Conference.

Ammaiyar, Ramamirtham. 1936. *Tācikaḷiṉ mocāvalai allatu matipeṟṟa maiṉar* [The treacherous net of the devadasis, or a minor grown wise]. Madras: Pearl Press.

Anandi, S. 1991. Representing devadasis: *Dasigal Mosavalai* as a radical text. *Economic and Political Weekly* 26, nos. 11–12:739–46.

———. 1997. Sexuality and nation: "Ideal" and "other" woman in nationalist politics, Tamilnadu, c. 1930–47. *South Indian Studies* 4:195–217.

Appadurai, Arjun. 1981. *Worship and conflict under colonial rule: A South Indian case*. Cambridge: Cambridge University Press.

Arasaratnam, S. 1979. Trade and political dominion in South India, 1750–1790: Changing British-Indian relationships. *Modern Asian Studies* 13, no. 2:19–40.

Arooran, Nambi. 1980. *Tamil renaissance and Dravidian nationalism*. Madurai: Koodal Publishers.

Awasthy, G. C. 1965. *Broadcasting in India*. Bombay: Allied Publishers.

Bakhle, Janaki. 2005. *Two men and music: Nationalism in the making of an Indian classical tradition*. New York: Oxford University Press.

Bakhtin, Mikhail. 1981. *The dialogic imagination*. Austin: University of Texas.

———. 1984. *Problems of Dostoevsky's poetics*. Trans. Caryl Emerson. Minneapolis: University of Minnesota Press.

Balachander, S. 1985. *Elutiṉār puttakattai! Kiḻappiṉār pūtattai!* [He wrote a book and kindled the genie!]. Self-published pamphlet.

Banerjee, Sumanta. 1989. *The parlour and the streets: Elite and popular culture in nineteenth-century Calcutta.* Calcutta: Seagull Books.

Bate, John B. 2000. Mēṭaittamiḻ: Oratory and democratic practice in Tamil Nadu. PhD diss., University of Chicago.

Bauman, Richard, and Charles Briggs. 2003. *Voices of modernity: Language ideologies and the politics of inequality.* Cambridge: Cambridge University Press.

Bergeron, Katherine. 1998. *Decadent enchantments: The revival of Gregorian chant at Solesmes.* Berkeley: University of California Press.

Bhabha, Homi. 1984. Of mimicry and man: The ambivalence of colonial discourse. *October* 28:125–33.

Bharathi, Suddhananda. 1968. *Saint Thyagaraja: The divine singer.* Madras: Yoga Samaj.

Bharatiyar, Subramania. 1909. Caṅkīta Viṣayam [The issue of music]. Repr. in *Pāratiyār Katturaikaḷ* [Essays of Bharatiyar] Ed. A. Tirunavukkarasu, 211–24. Madras: Vanathi Patipakkam, 1981.

Bharucha, Rustom. 1995. *Chandralekha: Woman dance resistance.* New Delhi: Harper Collins.

Bhaskaran, Theodore. 1981. *The message-bearers: Nationalist politics and the entertainment media in South India, 1880–1945.* Madras: Cre-A.

———. 1997. *The eye of the serpent: An introduction to Tamil cinema.* Madras: Orient Longman.

Bhatkhande, V. 1917. A short historical survey of the music of upper India. (Lecture presented at the first All-India Music Conference, Baroda, India, 1916.) Bombay: Bombay Samachar.

Blackburn, Stuart. 2000. Corruption and redemption: The legend of Valluvar and Tamil literary history. *Modern Asian Studies* 34, no. 2:449–82.

Brady, Erika. 1999. *A spiral way: How the phonograph changed ethnography.* Jackson: University Press of Mississippi.

Bullard, Beth. 1998. Winds of change in South Indian music: The flute revived, recasted, regendered. PhD diss., University of Maryland.

Burton, Antoinette. 1994. *Burdens of history: British feminists, Indian women, and imperial culture, 1865–1915.* Chapel Hill: University of North Carolina Press.

Caldwell, Robert. 1856. *A comparative grammar of the Dravidian or South Indian family of languages.* Rev. ed., ed. J. L. Wyatt and T. Ramakrishna Pillai. London: Kegan Paul, Trench, Trübner, 1913. Repr. New Delhi: Asian Educational Services, 1987.

Candy, Catherine. 1994. Relating feminisms, nationalisms, and imperialisms: Ireland, India, and Margaret Cousins's sexual politics. *Women's History Review* 3, no. 4:581–594.

Ceṉṉai caṅkīta vitvat capai: 12-āvatu mēlam [Madras music conference: 12th meeting]. 1938. *Bharata Mani* (1938): 372–74.

Chakrabarty, Dipesh. 2000. *Provincializing Europe: Postcolonial thought and historical difference*. Princeton: Princeton University Press.

Chatterjee, Partha. 1989. The nationalist resolution of the women's question. In *Recasting women: Essays in colonial history*. Ed. Kumkum Sangari and Sudesh Vaid, 233–253. New Delhi: Kali for Women.

———. 1993. *The nation and its fragments: Colonial and postcolonial histories*. Princeton: Princeton University Press.

Chatterji, P. C. 1998. *The adventure of Indian broadcasting: A philosopher's autobiography*. Delhi: Konark Publishers.

Chaudhuri, Amit. 1999. *Afternoon raag* [novella]. In *Freedom Song*, 123–239. New York: Alfred Knopf.

Chidambaranatha Mudaliar, T. K. 1936. Itaya oli [The sound of the heart]. In *Itaya oli*, 139–58. Madras: Shanti Press.

———. 1941. Caṅkītamum cakityamum [Music and lyrics]. In *Itaya oli*, 41–51. Madras: Shanti Press.

Chinnaswamy Mudaliar, A. M. 1892. *Oriental music in European notation*. Madras: Ave Maria Press.

Chion, Michael. 1982. *The voice in cinema*. Trans. Claudia Gorbman. New York: Columbia University Press.

Clayton, Jay. 1997. The voice in the machine: Hardy, Hazlitt, James. In *Language machines: Technologies of literary and cultural production*. Ed. Jeffrey Masten, Peter Stallybrass, and Nancy Vickers, 209–32. New York: Routledge.

Clayton, Mark. 1999. A. H. Fox-Strangways and the music of Hindostan: Revisiting historical field recordings. *Journal of the Royal Musical Association* 124:88–118.

Clements, Ernest. 1913. *Introduction to the study of Indian music*. Chandigarh: Abishek Publications, 1992.

———. 1920. *Ragas of Tanjore*. New Delhi: Caxton Publications, 1988.

Cohn, Bernard. 1968. Notes on the history of the study of Indian society and culture. In *Structure and change in Indian society*. Ed. Milton Singer and Bernard Cohn, 3–28. Chicago: Aldine.

———. 1987. The command of language and the language of command. *Subaltern Studies* 4:276–329. New Delhi: Oxford University Press.

Connor, Steven. 2000. *Dumbstruck: A cultural history of ventriloquism*. Oxford: Oxford University Press.

Coomaraswamy, Ananda K. 1909. Indian music. Repr. in *Essays in national idealism*, 166–200. Delhi: Munshiram Manoharlal, 1981.

———. 1909. Gramophones—and why not? Repr. in *Essays in national idealism*, 201–6. Delhi: Munshiram Manoharlal, 1981.

———. 1924. *The dance of Siva: Fourteen Indian essays*. London: Simpkin, Marshall, Hamilton, Kent.

———. 1939. Ornament. Repr. in *Coomaraswamy*. Ed. Roger Lipsey, vol. 1:241–53. Princeton: Princeton University Press, 1977.

Cousins, Margaret. 1935. *Music of the Orient and the Occident*. Madras: B. G. Paul.
———. 1940. The late maharaja of Mysore's patronage of music. *Uttara mandra* 1, no. 1 (March 1970): 142.
Cutler, Norman. 1987. *Songs of experience: The poetics of Tamil devotion*. Bloomington: Indiana University Press.
Daniel, E. Valentine. 1984. *Fluid signs: Being a person the Tamil way*. Berkeley: University of California Press.
Danielson, Virginia. 1997. *The voice of Egypt: Umm Kulthum, Arabic song, and Egyptian society in the twentieth century*. Chicago: University of Chicago Press.
Day, Charles. 1891. *Music and musical instruments of Southern India and the Deccan*. London and New York: Novello, Ewer.
de Alwis, Malathi. 1999. "Respectability," "modernity," and the policing of "culture" in colonial Ceylon. In *Gender, sexuality, and colonial modernities*. Ed. Antoinette Burton, 177–92. London and New York: Routledge.
de Certeau, Michel. 1984. *The practice of everyday life*. Trans. Steven Rendall. Berkeley: University of California Press.
———. 1988. *The writing of history*. Trans. Tom Conley. New York: Columbia University Press.
Derrida, Jacques. 1974. *Of grammatology*. Trans. Gayatri Spivak. Baltimore: Johns Hopkins Press.
Devadoss, Manohar. 1997. *Green well years*. Madras: East West Books.
Devi, Rukmini. N.d. The creative spirit. Madras: Theosophical Society.
———. N.d. Dance and music. Madras: Theosophical Society.
———. N.d. Woman as artist. Madras: Theosophical Society.
Dharwadker, Vinay. 1997. Print culture and literary markets in colonial India. In *Language machines: Technologies of literary and cultural production*. Ed. Jeffrey Masten, Peter Stallybrass, and Nancy Vickers, 108–33. New York: Routledge.
Dikshitar, Subbarama. 1904. *Sangīta sampradāya pradārṣini*. Madras: Madras Music Academy.
Dirks, Nicholas. 1993. *The hollow crown: Ethnohistory of an Indian kingdom*. Ann Arbor: University of Michigan.
Dixon, Joy. 1999. Ancient wisdom, modern motherhood: Theosophy and the colonial syncretic. In *Gender, sexuality, and colonial modernities*. Ed. Antoinette Burton, 193–206. London and New York: Routledge.
Dolar, Mladen. 1996. The object voice. In *Gaze and voice as love objects*. Ed. Slavoj Žižek and Renata Salecl, 7–31. Durham: Duke University Press.
Dugger, Celia. 2000. A world pays tribute to India's master drummer. *New York Times*, 14 February. § A, 4.
Dunn, Leslie, and Nancy Jones, eds. 1995. *Embodied voices: representing female vocality in Western culture*. Cambridge: Cambridge University Press.
Durayappa Bhagavatar, Gottuvadyam. 1941. Apiṉayam vēṇṭām [We don't want abhinaya]. *Nāṭṭiyam* 1, no. 1:51–52.

Ellarvi. 1963. *Tōṭi aṭaku: Ciṟu campavaṇkaḷ* [Pawning todi raga: Small vignettes]. Madras: National Art Press.

Engel, Carl. 1883. *Researches into the early history of the violin family*. London: Novello, Ewer.

Engh, Barbara. 1997. After "His master's voice": Post-phonographic aurality. PhD diss., University of Minnesota.

Erdman, Joan. 1978. The maharaja's musicians: Performance at Jaipur in the nineteenth century. In *American studies in the anthropology of India*. Ed. Sylvia Vatuk, 342–67. Delhi: Manohar.

Erlmann, Veit. 1999. *Music, modernity and the global imagination: South Africa and the West*. New York: Oxford University Press.

Farrell, Gerry. 1997. *Indian music and the West*. Oxford: Oxford University Press.

Feld, Steven, and Aaron Fox. 1994. Music and language. *Annual Review of Anthropology* 23:25–53.

Feld, Steven, Aaron Fox, Thomas Porcello, and David Samuels. 2004. Vocal anthropology. In *A companion to linguistic anthropology*. Ed. Alessandro Duranti, 321–45. Malden, Mass.: Blackwell.

Fielden, Lionel. 1940. *Report on the progress of broadcasting in India up to the 31st March 1939*. Delhi: Manager of Publications.

Foucault, Michel. 1970. *The order of things: An archaeology of the human sciences*. New York: Random House.

———. 1977. *Discipline and punish: The birth of the prison*. Trans. Alan Sheridan. New York: Pantheon Books.

———. 1979. What is an author? In *The Foucault reader*. Ed. Paul Rabinow, 101–20. New York: Pantheon Books, 1984.

Fowler, Jeaneane. 2002. *Perspectives of reality: An introduction to the philosophy of Hinduism*. Brighton: Sussex Academic Press.

Fox-Strangways, A. 1914. *The music of Hindostan*. New Delhi: Mittal Publishers.

Frank, Felicia Miller. 1995. *The mechanical song: Women, voice, and the artificial in nineteenth-century French narrative*. Stanford: Stanford University Press.

Frith, Simon. 1996. The Voice. In *Performing rites: On the value of popular music*, 183–202. Cambridge, Mass.: Harvard University Press.

Gaisberg, Fredrick. 1942. *The music goes round*. New York: Macmillan.

Gandhi, Mohandas K. 1958. *Collected works of Mahatma Gandhi*, vol. 66. New Delhi: Publications Division, Ministry of Information and Broadcasting, Government of India.

Ganghadar, C. N.d. *Theory and practice of Hindu music and the vina tutor*. Madras: Methodist Publishing House.

Gaston, Anne-Marie. 1996. *Bharata Natyam: From temple to theatre*. New Delhi: Manohar.

Gayan Samaj. 1887. *Madras jubilee Gayan Samaj proceedings*. Madras: Gayan Samaj.

Geetha, V., and S. Rajadurai. 1998. *Towards a non-Brahmin millennium: From Iyothee Dass to Periyar*. Calcutta: Samya.

Goehr, Lydia. 1992. *The imaginary museum of musical works.* Oxford: Clarendon.

Goswamy, B. N. 1996. *Broadcasting: New patron of Hindustani music.* Delhi: Sharada Publishing House.

Gronow, Pekka. 1981. The record industry comes to the Orient. *Ethnomusicology* 25, no. 2:251–84.

Guy, Randor. 1997. *Starlight, starbright: The early Tamil cinema.* Chennai: Amra Publishers.

Hancock, Mary Elizabeth. 1999. *Womanhood in the making: Domestic ritual and public culture in urban South India.* Berkeley: University of California Press.

Hansen, Kathryn. 1998. Stri Bhumika: Female impersonators and actresses on the Parsi stage. *Economic and Political Weekly* 33, no. 35:2291–2300.

Harinagabhushanam. 1929. The essentials of Karnatic music. *Triveni* 2, no. 3:54–202.

Harrison, Martin. 1996. Toward a history of listening. *Essays in Sound* 3:21–33.

Hartshorne, Charles and Paul Weiss, eds. 1931–58. *Collected papers of Charles Sanders Peirce*, vol. 2. Cambridge, Mass.: Harvard University Press.

Head, Raymond. 1985. Corelli in Calcutta: Colonial music-making in India in the seventeenth and eighteenth centuries. *Early Music* 13:548–53.

Higgins, John. 1975. From prince to populace: Patronage as a determinant of change in South Indian music. *Asian Music* 7, no. 2:20–26.

Hill, Jane. 1996. The consciousness of grammar and the grammar of consciousness. In *The matrix of language: Contemporary linguistic anthropology.* Ed. Donald Brenneis and Ronald Macaulay, 307–23. Boulder, Colo.: Westview.

Hughes, Stephen. 1996. The pre-Phalke era in South India: Reflections on the formation of film audiences in Madras. *South Indian Studies* 2, no. 2:161–204.

———. 2002. The "music boom" in Tamil South India: Gramophone, radio, and the making of mass culture. *Historical Journal of Film, Radio, and Television* 22, no. 4:445–73.

Inden, Ronald. 1986. Orientalist constructions of India. *Modern Asian Studies* 20, no. 3:401–46.

Inoue, Miyako. 2002. Gender, language, and modernity: Toward an effective history of Japanese women's language. *American Ethnologist* 29, no. 2:392–422.

———. 2003. The listening subject of Japanese modernity and his auditory double: Citing, sighting, and siting the modern Japanese woman. *Cultural Anthropology* 18, no. 2:156–93.

Irschick, Eugene. 1969. *Politics and social conflict in South India: The non-Brahman movement and Tamil separatism, 1916–1929.* Berkeley: University of California Press.

———. 1986. *Tamil revivalism in the 1930s.* Madras: Cre-A.

———. 1994. *Dialogue and history: Constructing South India, 1795–1895.* Berkeley: University of California Press.

Ivy, Marilyn. 1995. *Discourses of the vanishing: Modernity, phantasm, Japan.* Chicago: University of Chicago Press.

Jackson, William. 1991. *Tyagaraja: Life and lyrics*. Madras: Oxford University Press.

Jain, S. P. 1985. *The art of broadcasting*. New Delhi: Intellectual Publishing House.

Jayarama Iyer, T. K. 1965. The violin in Karnatic music. *Indian Music Journal* (Delhi Sangeeta Samaj), no. 4:27–28.

Jayaraman, R. 1990. Raja Serfoji. In pt. 2 of *Māmaṉṉar Carapoji*, 61–70. Tanjavur: Saraswati Mahal Library.

Jazz solos. 2000. Letters to the editor, *New York Times*. 11 June.

Jinarajadasa, C. 1928. New beginnings in Indian culture. *Triveni* 1, no. 1:3–12.

Johannes, T. C. R. 1912. *Bhārata Sangīta Svāya Bōdhini* [Indian music self-instructor]. Madras.

Jordan, Kay. 1993. Devadasi reform: Driving the priestesses or the prostitutes out of Hindu temples? In *Religion and law in independent India*. Ed. Robert Baird, 257–77. Delhi: Manohar.

Joshi, Babu Rao. 1963. *Understanding Indian music*. Bombay: Asia Publishing House.

Joshi, G. N. 1987. A concise history of the phonograph in India. *Popular Music* 7, no. 2:147–56.

Kalki [R. Krishnamoorthy]. 1941. Nārata kāṉam [The sound of Narada]. *Kalki* (1 October): 24.

———. 1942. Icai virutu [Musical feast]. *Kalki* (1 August): 75.

———. 1943a. Tamiḻ icaiyum Piramāṇarkaḷum [Tamil icai and Brahmins]. *Kalki* (10 August): 12–13.

———. 1943b. Tāymoḻi pakaimai [Hatred of the mother tongue]. *Kalki* (12 December): 13–16.

———. 1945. Icait taṭṭu [Music record]. *Kalki* (1 September): 47.

———. 1946. Mīra Kītaṅkaḷ [Meera songs]. *Kalki* (17 February): 31.

———. 1949. Āṭal Pāṭal [Song and dance]. *Kalki* (9 January): 15.

———. 1951. Caṅkītam paṇam paṇṇukiṟatu [Music makes money]. *Kalki* (26 October): 14.

———. 1954. Vīṇai Ṣaṉmuka Vaṭivu [Veena Shanmugha Vadivu]. *Kalki* (28 February): 21.

Kalyanasundaram, A. N. 1938. Ārmōṉiya pahiṣkāram [Harmonium boycott]. *Bharata Mani* (1938): 206–10.

Kannabiran, Kalpana. 1995. Judiciary, social reform, and debate on "religious prostitution" in colonial India. *Economic and Political Weekly* 30, no. 43:59–69.

Keane, Webb. 1997. From fetishism to sincerity: On agency, the speaking subject, and their historicity in the context of religious conversion. *Comparative Studies in Society and History* 39, no. 4:674–93.

Kersenboom-Story, Saskia. 1987. *Nityasumangali: Devadasi tradition in South India*. Delhi: Motilal Banarsidass.

———. 1995. *Word, sound, image: The life of the Tamil text*. Oxford: Berg.

Keskar, B. V. 1957. *Indian music: Problems and prospects*. Bombay: Popular Prakashan.

Kinnear, Michael. 1994. *The Gramophone Company's first Indian recordings, 1899–1908*. Bombay: Popular Prakashan.

Kittappa, K. P. 1993. *Pārata icaiyum tañcai nalvarum* [Indian music and the Tanjore Quartette]. Tanjavur: Tamil University.

Kittler, Friedrich. 1990. *Discourse networks 1800/1900*. Trans. Michael Meteer. Stanford: Stanford University Press.

———. 1999. *Gramophone, film, typewriter*. Trans. Geoffrey Winthrop-Young and Michael Wutz. Stanford: Stanford University Press.

Kothandapani Pillai. 1958. Ancient Tamil music. *Tamil Culture* 7, no. 1:33–47.

———. 1959. Ancient Tamil music, part 2. *Tamil Culture* 8, no. 3:193–200.

Krishna Iyer, E. 1932. Open letters. Repr., *Sruti*, E. Krishna Iyer Centenary Issue (1997): 15–21.

———. 1933. *Personalities in present-day music*. Madras: Rochehouse and Sons.

Krishnamachari, T. T. 1941. Karnāṭaka caṅkītamum tamiḻ icai iyakkamum [Karnatic music and the Tamil music movement]. Special issue, *Ananda Vikatan, Collected Articles on Music*: 38–43.

Krishna Rao, H. P. 1906. *First steps in Hindu music in English notation*. London: Weekes.

———. 1917. *The psychology of music*. Repr., New Delhi: Asian Educational Services, 1984.

Kroskrity, Paul, ed. 2000. *Regimes of language: Ideologies, polities, and identities*. Santa Fe: SAR Press.

Lacan, Jacques. 1977. *Ecrits: Selections*. Trans. Alan Sheridan. New York: Norton.

Lakshmi, C. S. 1990. Mother, mother-community, and mother politics in Tamil Nadu. *Economic and Political Weekly* 25, no. 43:72–83.

———. 2000. *The singer and the song*. New Delhi: Kali for Women.

Langford, Jean. 2002. *Fluent bodies: Ayurvedic remedies for postcolonial imbalance*. Durham: Duke University Press.

L'Armand, Adrian, and Kathleen L'Armand. 1978. Music in Madras: The urbanization of a cultural tradition. In *Eight urban musical cultures*. Ed. Bruno Nettl, 115–45. Urbana: University of Illinois.

Legge, Walter. 1998. The maharaja of Mysore. In *Walter Legge: Words and music*. Ed. Alan Sanders, 186–92. London: Duckworth.

Lelyveld, David. 1990. Transmitters and culture: The colonial roots of Indian broadcasting. *South Asia Research* 10, no. 1:41–52.

———. 1995. Upon the subdominant: Administering music on All-India Radio. In *Consuming modernity: Public culture in a South Asian world*. Ed. Carol Breckenridge, 49–65. Minneapolis: University of Minnesota Press.

Leppert, Richard. 1993. *The sight of sound: Music, representation, and the history of the body*. Berkeley: University of California Press.

Levin, David Michael, ed. 1993. *Modernity and the hegemony of vision*. Berkeley: University of California Press.

Levin, Thomas. 1990. For the record: Adorno on music in the age of its reproducibility. *October* 55:23–47.

Levine, Lawrence. 1990. *Highbrow/lowbrow: The emergence of cultural hierarchy in America*. Cambridge, Mass.: Harvard University Press.

Lévi-Strauss, Claude. 1955. *Tristes tropiques*. Trans. John Weightman and Doreen Weightman. New York: Atheneum, 1977.

Luthra, H. R. 1986. *Indian broadcasting*. Delhi: Ministry of Information and Broadcasting.

Madras Music Academy Conference Souvenir. 1935. Madras: Music Academy.

Madras Music Academy Conference Souvenir. 1938. Madras: Music Academy.

Madurai Mudaliar, K. 1929–1931. *Kiramapōṉ caṅkīta kīrtaṉāmirtam* [*Gramaphon sangeetha keerthanamirdam*: The nectar of gramophone music]. Madras: Shanmugananda Book Depot.

Maharajan, S. 1962. Olic celvam [The treasure of sound]. In *Olic Celvam*, 1–7. Madras: Manonmani Patipakkam.

———, ed. 1979. *Racikamaṇi kaṭitaṅkaḷ* [Letters of T. K. Chidambaranatha Mudaliar]. Madras: T.K.C. Vattat Totti.

Maharaja's Music College Silver Jubilee Souvenir. 1945. Vizianagaram: Maharaja's Music College.

Maheswari Devi, N. 1935. *Veena tutor with a chapter on the yazhl*. Jaffna.

Malan. 1981. Vitvān. In *Āṉṟu: Tērnta ciṟukataikaḷ 1917–1981*, vol. 2:137–45. Madras: Orient Longman.

Manikka Mudaliar, S. 1902. *Caṅkīta cantirikai* [Sangeeta Chandrikai]. Madras: Chandrika Publications.

Mankekar, Purnima. 1999. *Screening culture, viewing politics: An ethnography of television, womanhood, and nation in postcolonial India*. Durham: Duke University Press.

Marglin, Frederique. 1985. *Wives of the god-king: The rituals of the Devadasis of Puri*. Delhi: Oxford University Press.

Mathur, J. C. 1957. The impact of A.I.R. on Indian music. In *Aspects of Indian music*, 97–103. New Delhi: Ministry of Information and Broadcasting.

Mattick, Paul, Jr. 1995. Beautiful and sublime: Gender totemism in the constitution of art. In *Feminism and tradition in aesthetics*. Ed. Peggy Brand and Carolyn Korsmeyer, 27–48. University Park: Pennsylvania State University Press.

Mayo, Katherine. 1927. *Mother India*. New York: Harcourt, Brace.

———. 1929. *Slaves of the gods*. London: Florin Books.

Meduri, Avanthi. 1996. Nation, woman, representation: The sutured history of the Devadasi and her dance. PhD diss., New York University.

Menon, Indira. 1999. *The Madras quartet: Women in Karnatak music*. New Delhi: Lotus Books.

Menon, Narayana. 1957. The impact of Western technology on Indian music. In *Bulletin of the Institute of Traditional Cultures*, 70–80. Madras.

Mitchell, Lisa. 2004. From medium to marker: The making of a mother tongue in modern South India. PhD diss., Columbia University.

Mitchell, Timothy. 1988. *Colonising Egypt*. Berkeley: University of California Press.
———, ed. 2000. *Questions of modernity*. Minneapolis: University of Minnesota Press.
Mrazek, Rudolph. 1997. "Let us become radio mechanics": Technology and national identity in late-colonial Netherlands East Indies. *Comparative Studies of Society and History* 39, no. 1:3–33.
Mullick, K. S. 1974. *Tangled tapes: The inside story of Indian broadcasting*. Delhi: Sterling Publishers.
Muthiah, P. L., ed. 1996. *Tami̱l icai mu̱lakkam* [The roar of Tamil music]. Madras: Mullai Patippakam.
Muthuswami, V. N.d., ca. 1940. Radio Kacceri. *Bharatha Mani*, 279–80.
Mysore Archaeological Reports. 1928–1941. Mysore: Mysore University.
Nadar, A. C. Paul. 1954. A pioneer research worker in Tamil music. *Tamil culture* 3, no. 2:110–20.
Naidu, Chitti Babu. 1925. *A key to Hindu music*. Madras: Diocesan Press.
Naidu, Tirumalayya. 1912. Music and the anti-nautch movement. Repr., *Sruti*, E. Krishna Iyer Centenary Issue (1997): 6.
Nair, Janaki. 1994. The Devadasi, dharma, and the state. *Economic and Political Weekly* (10 December): 3157–67.
Narayana Rao, C. 1939. *The songs of Thyagaraja: English translation with originals*. Madras: Sarada Press.
Narayana Rao, V. 1995. Coconut and honey: Sanskrit and Telugu in medieval Andhra. *Social Scientist* 23:10–25.
———. 2001. The politics of Telugu Ramayanas: Colonialism, print culture, and literary movements. In *Questioning Ramayanas: A South Asian tradition*. Ed. Paula Richman, 159–86. Berkeley: University of California Press.
Narayana Rao, V., and David Shulman, eds. 1998. *A poem at the right moment: Remembered verses from premodern South India*. Berkeley: University of California Press.
Narayana Rao, V., David Shulman, and Sanjay Subrahmanyam. 1992. *Symbols of substance: Court and state in the Nayaka period*. Delhi: Oxford University Press.
Narayanaswamy Mudaliar. 1900. *Tamil sungeatha surabhooshany*. Madras: Jeevakaruna Vilasa Press.
Nayar, Brigadier R. B. 1997. Study of Swati Tirunal's compositions inconclusive. *Sruti* 153:23–27.
Neild, Susan. 1979. Colonial urbanism: The development of Madras city in the eighteenth and nineteenth centuries. *Modern Asian Studies* 13, no. 2:217–46.
———. 1984. The Dubashes of Madras. *Modern Asian Studies* 18, no. 1:1–31.
Nettl, Bruno. 1985. *The Western impact on world music: Change, adaptation, and survival*. New York: Schirmer Books.
Neuman, Daniel. 1980. *The life of music in North India*. Repr., Chicago: University of Chicago Press, 1990.

———. 1992. Patronage and performance of Indian music. In *The powers of art: Patronage in Indian culture*. Ed. Barbara Stoler Miller, 247–58. New York: Oxford University Press.

Niranjana, Tejaswini. 1994. Colonialism and the politics of translation. In *An other tongue: Nation and ethnicity in the linguistic borderlands*. Ed. Alfred Arteaga, 35–52. Durham: Duke University Press.

O'Flaherty, Wendy Doniger. 1980. *Women, androgynes, and other mythical beasts*. Chicago: University of Chicago Press.

Ollikkala, Robert. 1999. Classification systems, social hierarchies, and gender: Examining Indian "light-classical" music. *Canadian University Music Review* 19, no. 2:27–36.

Ong, Walter. 1982. *Orality and literacy: The technologizing of the word*. New York: Routledge.

O'Shea, Janet. 1998. "Traditional" Indian dance and the making of interpretive communities. *Asian Theatre* 15, no. 1:45–63.

Padmanabha Iyer, A. 1936. *Modern Mysore: Impressions of a visitor*. Trivandrum: Sridhara Print House.

Pandithar, Abraham. 1917. *Karunamirtha Sagaram: A treatise on music or Isai-Tamil, which is one of the main divisions of Muttamil, or language, music, and drama*. Trans. Gift Sironmani. Repr., Delhi: Asian Educational Services, 1984.

———. 1917. A refutation to the second letter written by Mr. Clements about the All-India music conference. Repr. in *Karunamirtha Sagaram*, Tamil edition. Chennai: Kilaiyiyal Ayvu Niruvanak Kalvi Arakkattalai carpil Anril Patippakam, 1994.

———. 1934. *A Practical Course in South Indian Music*. Tanjavur: Lawley Press.

Panju Bhagavatar. 1910. *Tyākarāja carittiram* [Life history of Thyagaraja].

Parasuram, Sriram. 1997. The indigenisation of the violin. *The Hindu Folio* (December): 38–47.

Parker, Kunal. 1998. "A corporation of superior prostitutes": Anglo-Indian legal conceptions of temple dancing girls, 1800–1914. *Modern Asian Studies* 32, no. 3:559–633.

Parmentier, Richard. 1985. Signs' place in medias res: Peirce's concept of semiotic mediation. In *Semiotic mediation: Sociocultural and psychological perspectives*. Ed. Elizabeth Mertz and Richard Parmentier, 1–48. Orlando: Academic Press.

Peterson, Indira. 1984. The kriti as an integrated form: Aesthetic experience in the religious songs of two South Indian composers. *South Asian Literature* 19, no. 2:165–79.

———. 1992. In praise of the lord: The image of the royal patron in the songs of Saint Cuntaramurtti and the composer Tyagaraja. In *The powers of art: Patronage in Indian culture*. Ed. Barbara Stoler Miller, 120–41. New York: Oxford University Press.

———. 1999. The cabinet of king Serfoji of Tanjore: A European collection in early nineteenth-century India. *The History of Collections* 11, no. 1:71–93.

———. 2000. Reimagining performance culture through the novel: Nationalist discourses in the construction of Devadasi dance and nagasvaram "traditions" in *Tillaṉa Mōkaṉampaḷ*. Paper read at the South Asia Conference, Madison, Wisconsin, October.

———. 2004. Between print and performance: The Tamil Christian poems of Vedanayaka Sastri and the literary cultures of South India. In *India's literary history: Essays on the nineteenth century*. Ed. Stuart Blackburn and Vasuda Dalmia, 25–60. Delhi: Permanent Black.

Pinney, Christopher. 1997. *Camera Indica: The social life of Indian photographs*. Chicago: University of Chicago Press.

Playne, Somerset. 1914. *Southern India: Its history, people, commerce, and industrial resources*. London: Foreign and Colonial Compiling and Publishing.

Poduval, R. Vasudeva. [1950–1959?]. *The music of Kerala and other essays*. Trivandrum: St. Joseph's Press.

Pollock, Sheldon. 2000. Cosmopolitan and vernacular in history. *Public Culture* 12, no. 3:591–26.

Popley, Herbert A. 1921. *The music of India*. Calcutta: Association Press.

Post, Jennifer. 1987. Professional women in Indian music: The death of the courtesan tradition. In *Women and music in cross-cultural perspective*. Ed. Ellen Koskoff, 97–109. Westport, Conn.: Greenwood Press.

Prakash, Gyan. 1990. Writing post-orientalist histories of the third world: Perspectives from Indian historiography. *Comparative Studies of Society and History* 32, no. 2:383–408.

Proceedings of the 17th Madras music conference. 1944. *Journal of the Music Academy, Madras*. Madras: Music Academy.

Qureshi, Regula. 2000. How does music mean? Embodied memories and the politics of affect in the Indian sarangi. *American Ethnologist* 27, no. 4:805–38.

———. 2001. In search of Begum Akhtar: Patriarchy, poetry, and twentieth-century Indian music. *World of Music* 43, no. 1:97–137.

Radhakrishna Ayyar, Vai. 1949–1950. *Tiruvaiyāṟ sri tyākapirammam arātaṉai utcava varalāṟu* [The history of the Tiruvaiyaru Thyagaraja aradana festival]. Repr., Madras: Sri Maruthy Laser Printers, 2003.

Raghavan, V. 1944. Some musicians and their patrons about 1800 AD in Madras city. *Journal of the Madras Music Academy* 16:127–36.

———. 1958. The Sārvadēvavilāsa. *Adyar Library Bulletin* 22, pts. 1–2:45–118.

———. 1961. English preface to *Sangīta Sampradāya Pradārṣini*. 1st Tamil edition. Madras: Music Academy.

Rajagopalan, N., ed. 1990. Contests and challenges. In *Another Garland*, 54–63. Bombay: Bharatiya Vidya Bhavan.

Ram, Kalpana. 2000. Dancing the past into life: The rāsa, nṛtta, and rāga of immigrant existence. *Australian Journal of Anthropology* 11, no. 3:261–73.

Ramachandran, K. 1949. *Dakshina raga ratnakaram: Characteristics of Carnatic ragas*. Madras: V. Ramaswamy Sastrulu and Sons.

Ramachandra Rao, S. K. 1994. *Mysore T. Chowdiah*. Bangalore: Sree Ramaseva Mandali.

Ramakrishna, V. 1983. *Social reform in Andhra, 1848–1919*. Delhi: Vikas.

Ramalingam Pillai, Namakkal. 1943. *Icaittamiḻ* [Tamil music]. Madras.

Raman, C. V. 1920. Experiments with mechanically played violins. In *Proceedings of the Indian Association for the Advancement of Science*, 19–36. Calcutta: Indian Association for the Advancement of Science.

Ramanathan, K. V. 1996. The Swati Tirunal compositions: Facts and figures in a whodunit. *Sruti* 142:15–29.

Ramanathan, S. 1977. Taccur Singaracharyulu brothers. *Indian Express*.

Ramanathan Chettiar. 1993. The history of the Tamil Icai Sangam, 1943–1993. Unpublished paper in collection of Tamil Icai Sangam, Madras.

Ramanujachari, C. 1957. *The spiritual heritage of Thyagaraja*. Madras: Ramakrishna Mission.

Rama Rao, V. V. B. 1985. *Life and mission in life: Poosapati Ananda Gajapati Raju*. Hyderabad: International Telugu Institute.

Ramasami, E. V. 1944. *Tamiḻ icai, naṭippu kalaikaḷ: Iṉi eṉṉa ceyya vēṇṭum?* [Tamil musical and dramatic arts: What must still be done?]. Erode: Kuti Aracu.

Ramaswamy, Sumathi. 1993. En/gendering language: The poetics of Tamil identity. *Comparative Studies of Society and History* 35:683–725.

———. 1997. *Passions of the tongue: Language devotion in Tamil India, 1891–1970*. Berkeley: University of California Press.

———. 1999. Catastrophic cartographies: Mapping the lost continent of Lemuria. *Representations* 67:92–129.

Ramaswamy Aiyar, M. S. 1927a. *Thiagaraja: A great musician saint*. Repr., Madras: Asian Educational Services, 1986.

———. 1927b. Sargam notation. In *Thiagaraja: A great musician saint*, 179–238. Repr., Madras: Asian Educational Services, 1986.

———, ed. 1932. *Ramamatya's Svaramēlakalānidhi: A work on music*. Chidambaram: Annamalai University.

Ramaswamy Bhagavathar, Wallajapet. 1935. *Tyākapirammopaniṣat* [*Thyāgabramopaniṣad*: The life of Saint Thyagaraja]. Madras.

Ramnarayan, Gowri. 1997. *Past forward: Six artists speak about their childhood*. Madras: Orient Longman.

Rangaramanuja Ayyangar, R. 1977. *Musings of a musician: Recent trends in Carnatic music*. Bombay: Wilco Publishers.

Rao, Vidya. 1999. Thumri as feminine voice. In *Gender and politics in India*. Ed. Nivedita Menon, 475–93. Delhi: Oxford University Press.

Reck, David. 1984. India/South India. In *Worlds of music: An introduction to the music of the world's peoples*. Ed. Jeff Todd Titon, 209–65. New York: Schirmer Books.

Reddy, Muthulakshmi. 1928–1931. *Why should the Devadasi system in the Hindu temples be abolished?* Madras: Lodhra Press.

———. 1930. *My experience as a legislator*. Madras: Current Thought Press.

Redfield, Robert, and Milton Singer. 1954. The cultural role of cities. *Economic Development and Cultural Change* 3, no. 1:53–73.

Redfield, Robert. 1953. *The primitive world and its transformations*. Ithaca: Cornell University Press.

Report of the first general meeting of the academy of Tamil culture. 1955. *Tamil Culture* 4, no. 4:368–76.

Report of the All-India Music Conference, Madras. 1927. Madras: Music Academy.

Reynolds, Holly Baker. 1980. The auspicious married woman. In *The powers of Tamil women*. Ed. Susan Wadley, 35–60. Syracuse: Maxwell School.

Robbins, Joel. 2001. God is nothing but talk: Modernity, language, and prayer in a Papua New Guinea society. *American Anthropologist* 103, no. 4:901–12.

Roberts, P. E. 1952. *History of British India under the company and the crown*. 3rd ed. Completed by T. G. P. Spear. London: Oxford University Press.

S. V. K. 1999. Divinity, the core of Indian music. *The Hindu* (December).

Said, Edward. 1979. *Orientalism*. New York: Vintage.

Sambamoorthy, P. 1939. Madras as a seat of musical learning. In *Madras tercentenary commemorative volume*, 429–37. London and Madras: Oxford University Press.

———. 1944. Our concert programme: Some underlying principles. In *Madras Music Academy Conference Souvenir*, 39–43. Madras: Madras Music Academy.

———. 1952. *History of South Indian music*, vols. 1–6. Madras: Indian Music Publishing House, 1984.

———. 1955a. *Dictionary of South Indian music and musicians*, vols. 1–3. Madras: Indian Music Publishing House.

———. 1955b. Kacceri dharma [Concert etiquette]. In *Dictionary of South Indian Music and Musicians*, 2:266–72. Madras: Indian Music Publishing House.

———. 1959. *Great musicians*. Madras: Indian Music Publishing House.

———. 1961. *Elements of Western music for students of Indian music*. Madras: Indian Music Publishing House.

———. 1966. *The teaching of music*. Madras: Indian Music Publishing House.

———. N.d.a. [ca. 1960?] *The melakarta janya raga scheme*. Madras: Indian Music Publishing House.

———. N.d.b. *A practical course in Karnatic music for schools*. Madras: Indian Music Publishing House.

Sangari, Kumkum, and Sudesh Vaid. 1990. *Recasting women*. New Delhi: Kali for Women.

Sankaramurthy, M. R. 1990. *The European airs of Muthuswamy Dikshitar*. Bangalore: Guru Guha Nilaya.

Sarathy. 1997. *Icai ulakiṉ imayam Em. Es.* [The Himalaya of the music world, M.S.]. Madras: Vanathi Patipakkam.

Sastry, B. V. K. 1962. Dwaram Venkataswamy Naidu. *Illustrated Weekly of India* (21 October): 33–35.

Sathyanarayana, R. 1993. Re-emergence of the violin in Karnataka music. *Vadyakala Souvenir*, 10–12. Madras.

Saupa. 1990. Maturai Poṉṉutāy: Oru kaṇṇīr katai [Madurai Ponnuthai: A sad story]. *Ananta vikatan* (2 February): 10–14.
Schieffelin, Bambi, K. Woolard, and Paul Kroskrity, eds. 1998. *Language ideologies: Practice and theory*. Oxford: Oxford University Press.
Seetha, S. 1981. *Tanjore as a seat of music*. Madras: Madras University Press.
Shankara Ayyar, V. S. Gomathi. 1970. *Icai valluṉarkaḷ* [Stalwarts of music]. Madras.
Sharma, A. V. S. 1954. *Lines of devotion*. Madras: Antiseptic Press.
Siegel, James. 1997. *Fetish, recognition, revolution*. Princeton: Princeton University Press.
Silverman, Kaja. 1988. *The acoustic mirror: The female voice in psychoanalysis and cinema*. Bloomington: Indiana University Press.
Singaracaryulu Brothers, Taccur. 1882. *Gāyakaparijatam*. Madras: K. R. Press.
———. 1884. *Gāyaka lōchana*. Madras: K. R. Press.
———. 1889. *Sangīta Kalānidhi*. Madras: K. R. Press.
———. 1905. *Gāyaka Siddhanjanam*. Madras: K. R. Press.
———. 1912. *Ganendu Sēkaram*. Madras: K. R. Press.
———. 1914. *Svaramanjari*. Madras: K. R. Press.
Singer, Milton. 1972. *When a great tradition modernizes: An anthropological approach to Indian civilization*. New York: Praeger.
Sinha, Mrinhalini. 1996. Gender in the critiques of colonialism and nationalism: Locating the "Indian woman." In *Feminism and history*. Ed. Joan Scott, 477–504. New York: Oxford University Press.
Sivatamby, K. 1978. The politics of a literary style. *Social Scientist* 6, no. 8:16–33.
Spivak, Gayatri. 1988. Can the subaltern speak? *In Marxism and the interpretation of culture*. Ed. Cary Nelson and Lawrence Grossberg, 271–313. Urbana: University of Illinois Press.
Srinivasan, Amrit. 1985. Reform and revival: The devadasi and her dance. *Economic and Political Weekly* 20, no. 44:1869–76.
Srinivasan, G. 1991. The Birth of the Tyagabrahma Mahotsava Sabha. In *Sri Tyagabrahma Mahotsava Sabha Souvenir*. Madras.
Srinivas Iyer, Semmangudi. 1991. Catkuru tyākapiramma arātaṉai utcavam oṉṟāka iṉaintu varalāṟu [The history of the joining into one of the Thyagaraja aradhana festival]. In *Sri Tyagabraahma Mahotsava Sabha Souvenir*. Madras.
Sruti. 1997. E. Krishna Iyer centenary issue.
———. 1998. Cutbacks in All India Radio's music programmes. (July) 11–12.
———. 2001. Special issue on Vai. Mu. Kothainayaki (207).
———. 2003. Special issue on the Madras music season (222).
Sterne, Jonathan. 2000. Sound out of time: Modernity's echo. In *Turning the century*. Ed. Carol Stabile, 9–32. Boulder, Colo.: Westview Press.
———. 2003. *The audible past: Cultural origins of sound reproduction*. Durham: Duke University Press.
Subba Rao, T. V. 1962. *Studies in Indian music*. Madras: Vasantha Press.

———. 1962. The modernity of Thyagaraja. In *Studies in Indian Music*, 144–49. Madras: Vasantha Press.

Subbashri. 1947. Maikiṉ makātmiyam [The greatness of the mic]. *Kalki* (9 February): 41–42.

Subrahmanya Ayyar, C. 1939. *The grammar of South Indian music*. Madras.

———. 1941. *The art and technique of violin play*. Madras.

———. 1944. *My musical extravagance*. Madras.

Subrahmanyam, V. V. 1980. *Vaiyaliṉ varalāṟu* [History of the violin]. Madurai: India Printing Works.

———. 1986. *Satyamēva Jeyatē* [Let truth reign]. Madras: India Printing Works.

Subramaniam, P. R., ed. 1992. *Kriyāviṉ tarkāla tamiḻ akarāti* [Cre-A's dictionary of contemporary Tamil]. Madras: Cre-A Publishers.

Subramanian, Lakshmi. 1999a. Gender and the performing arts in nationalist discourse: An agenda for the Madras Music Academy, 1930–1947. *The Book Review* 23, nos. 1–2:81–84.

———. 1999b. The reinvention of a tradition: Nationalism, Carnatic music, and the Madras Music Academy. *Indian Economic and Social History Review* 36, no. 2:131–63.

Sunda. 1993. *Eminent Tamil writer Kalki: A life sketch*. Madras: Vanathi.

Suntharalingam, R. 1974. *Politics and nationalist awakening in South India, 1852–1891*. Tucson: University of Arizona Press.

Swaminathan, Mayuram. 1998. Winds of change in A.I.R. *The Hindu*, 16 June, 28.

Swaminathayyar, U. V. 1936. *Caṅkīta mummaṇikaḷ* [Three gems of music]. Madras: Dr. U. V. Swaminathayyar Library.

———. 1940–1942. *Eṉ carittiram* [The story of my life]. Trans. S. K. Guruswamy. Repr., Madras: Dr. U. V. Swaminathayyar Library, 1980.

Tagore, Sourindro Mohun. 1874. Hindu music. Repr. in *Hindu music*, 337–404. Delhi: D. K. Publications, 1994.

Tamiḻ icai makānāṭu ceṉṉai nikaḻcci malar [Chennai Tamil music conference program]. 1944. Madras: Tamil Icai Sangam.

Taussig, Michael. 1993. *Mimesis and alterity: A particular history of the senses*. New York: Routledge.

Taylor, Charles. 1989. *Sources of the self: The making of modern identity*. Cambridge, Mass.: Harvard University Press.

Terada, Yoshitaka. 1992. Multiple interpretations of a charismatic individual: The case of the great nagasvaram musician, T. N. Rajarattinam Pillai. PhD diss., University of Washington.

———. 2000. T. N. Rajarattinam Pillai and caste rivalry in South Indian classical music. *Ethnomusicology* 44, no. 3:460–90.

Theberge, Paul. 1995. *Any sound you can imagine: Making music, consuming technology*. Hanover, N.H.: University Press of New England.

Thomas, Downing. 1995. *Music and the origins of language: Theories from the French enlightenment*. Cambridge: Cambridge University Press.

Tick, Judith. 1986. Passed away is the piano girl: Changes in American musical life, 1870–1900. In *Women making music: The Western art tradition, 1150–1950*. Ed. Jane Bowers and Judith Tick, 325–48. Urbana: University of Illinois Press.
Tirumalayya Naidu, C. 1919. *Tyagayyar: The greatest musical composer of South India*. Madras: South Indian Press.
Trautmann, Thomas. 1997. *The Aryans and British India*. Berkeley: University of California Press.
Vasudevachar, Mysore K. 1955. *Nā kaṇḍa kalavidāru* [Vidwans I have known]. Trans. and ed. by S. Krishnamurthy as *With masters of melody*. Bangalore: Ananya GML Cultural Academy, 1999.
Vedavalli, M. B. 1992. *Mysore as a seat of music*. Trivandrum: CBH Publications.
Venkatachalam, G. 1966. *My contemporaries*. Bangalore: Hosali Press.
Venkatachalapathy, A. R. 1994. Reading practices and modes of reading in colonial Tamil Nadu. *Studies in History* 10, no. 2:273–90. New Delhi: Sage Publications.
Venkataramiah, K. 1984. Icai, nāṭakam, nāṭṭiyam [Music, dance, drama]. In *Tañcai marāttiya maṉṉar kala araciyalum camutaya vāḻkaiyum* [The art patronage and societal life of the Maratha kings of Tanjavur], 215–38. Tanjavur: Tamil University.
Venkataratnam, Raghupati. 1901. Social purity and the anti-nautch movement. In *Indian social reform*. Ed. C. Y. Chintamani, 249–81. Madras: Thompson.
Venkitasubramonia Iyer. 1975. *Swati Tirunal: The man and his music*. Trivandrum: College Book House.
Waghorne, Joanne. 1994. *The raja's magic clothes: Re-visioning kingship and divinity in England's India*. University Park: Pennsylvania State University Press.
Walimbe, Y. S. 1980. *Abhinavagupta on Indian aesthetics*. Delhi: Ajanta Books International.
Washbrook, David. 1975. The development of caste organization in South India, 1880–1925. In *South India: Political institutions and political change, 1880–1940*. Ed. Christopher Baker and David Washbrook, 150–203. Delhi: Macmillan.
Weber, William. 1984. The contemporaneity of eighteenth-century musical taste. *Musical Quarterly* 70, no. 2:175–94.
———. 1992. *The rise of musical classics in eighteenth-century England: A study in canon, ritual, and ideology*. Oxford: Clarendon Press.
Weidman, Amanda. 1995. Ambiguous apparitions: Gender and the classical in Karnatic music. Master's thesis, University of Washington.
———. 2001. Questions of voice: On the subject of "classical music" in South India. PhD diss., Columbia University.
———. 2003a. Gender and the politics of voice: Colonial modernity and classical music in South India. *Cultural Anthropology* 18, no. 2:194–232.
———. 2003b. Guru and gramophone: Fantasies of fidelity and modern technologies of the real. *Public Culture* 15, no. 3:453–76.
Weiss, Allen S. 1995. *Phantasmic radio*. Durham: Duke University Press.

Williams, Raymond. 1983. *Culture and society, 1780–1950*. New York: Columbia University Press.

Wilson, Anne. 1904. *A short account of the Hindu system of music*. Lahore: Ghulab Singh.

Winslow, Miron. 1862. *Tamil-English dictionary*. New Delhi. Repr., Asian Educational Services, 1979.

Woodfield, Ian. 2001. *Music of the Raj: a social and economic history of music in late eighteenth-century Anglo-Indian society*. Oxford: Oxford University Press.

Woolard, Kathryn, and Bambi Schieffelin. 1994. Language ideology. *Annual Review of Anthropology* 23:55–82.

Žižek, Slavoj. 1996. I hear you with my eyes: Or, the invisible master. In *Gaze and voice as love objects*. Ed. Slavoj Žižek and Renata Salecl, 90–126. Durham: Duke University Press.

Zvelebil, Kamil. 1992. *Companion studies to the history of Tamil literature*. Leiden: E. J. Brill.

Index

child prodigies, 123–24, 304n16
Chinnaswamy Mudaliar, A. M., 136, 204–13, 217, 220, 224, 233, 241, 318n29
Chowdiah, Mysore T., 41, 44–45
cinema, 125, 146, 159, 305n18
cinna mēḷam, 102
Clements, Ernest, 296n19, 317n24, 319n34
Cohn, Bernard, 156, 183
colonialism, 4, 9, 15–17, 25, 58, 291n5, 292n8, 324n1; princely states and, 15–16
composers, 20, 192–201, 241; as saints, 99–104
compositions, 98–99, 236, 241
concerts: form of, 83, 97–99; concert halls, 4, 15, 17, 34, 68, 81, 86, 126, 130–31; public, 17, 59–60, 79–81, 94–97, 110
Congress Party, 166, 293n18, 313n23
Connor, Steven, 297n31,n32, 300n33
Coomaraswamy, Ananda, 46, 256–60, 282, 316n22
Cousins, Margaret, 18, 24, 66, 294n25

Day, Charles, 27, 203
de Alwis, Malathi, 307n35
de Certeau, Michel, 192, 242, 292n8
Derrida, Jacques, 192
devadasis, 18, 113, 116–21, 124, 136, 303n5, 303n8, 303n11, 308n43, 309n54
Devadoss, Manohar, 159–60, 191, 312n14, 16
Devi, Rukmini, 119–20, 128–30, 149, 190, 303n9, 304n11, 304n16, 306n31
devotional music, 186–88, 271
Dharwadker, Vinay, 319n36
Dikshitar, Baluswamy, 29, 77
Dikshitar, Muthuswamy, 25, 99; "European Airs," 32
Dikshitar, Subbarama, 77, 220–22, 224
Dirks, Nicholas, 15
discourse networks, 12, 321n11
domesticity, 116, 134–41, 144–45. *See also* women
Dravidian movement, 19, 155, 167; linguistic studies and, 169–71; as term, 313n22
Durayappa Bhagavatar, Gottuvadyam, 131
Dwaram Venkataswamy Naidu, 32, 49–52, 300n35, 322n13

East India Company, 15, 16, 61
Ellarvi (writer), 70, 72–73
Engel, Carl, 26–27
Erlmann, Veit, 292n9
ethnomusicology, 23–24
Ettayapuram, 29–31

Farrell, Gerry, 28
Feld, Steven, 13, 111, 292n14
fidelity: social, 3–4, 21, 85, 246, 249, 282–85; in sound reproduction, 246, 282, 285, 322n15
Fielden, Lionel, 268, 270–71
film songs, 98, 159, 186, 271
Fort Saint George, 29
Foucault, Michel, 240, 286, 318n33
Fox, Aaron, 13, 111, 292n14
Fox-Strangways, A. H., 46, 259
Frank, Felicia Miller, 124
Frith, Simon, 305n19

Gaisberg, Fredrick, 255–56, 320n7
Gajapathi, Ananda, 68–69, 299n14
gamaka, 32, 33, 50, 54, 207, 213, 216, 221, 229, 240, 257, 262, 321n8
Gandhi, Mohandas, 125, 146, 309n51
Ganghadar, C., 228–29
Gayan Samaj, 194–95, 201–3
George Town, 76–77, 80–81, 168, 221, 313n23
Goehr, Lydia, 5

language (*continued*)
tongue" and, 19, 152, 156–58, 175–79, 218, 311n10; music as, 19, 152–53, 160–66, 189–91
Legge, Walter, 66
legibility, 232, 317n25
Lelyveld, David, 271
Lemuria, 168–70, 314n24
Levin, David, 286
Lévi-Strauss, Claude, 242
listening: practices of, 24, 68, 127–28, 173–74, 179, 183, 247, 262–68, 269, 277–82, 312n15, 323n22. *See also* overhearing
Luthra, H. R., 269–70

Madras, 16–17, 60, 76–78, 168
Madras Music Academy, 81–82, 129, 138, 150, 164, 168, 180, 183, 186, 187, 236, 291n3, 301n40
Madras Presidency, 64, 69
Maharajan, Justice S., 128, 175–77
Malan (writer), 250–55, 320n4
Mangeshkar, Lata, 145
Mathur, J. C., 272
Mayo, Katherine, 303n8
Menon, Indira, 122–27, 132
Menon, Narayana, 271–72
Menon, Raghava, 242–43, 245, 250, 281
microphones, 17, 59–60, 79, 86–93, 126, 146, 147, 300n33, 305n19
middle class: gramophones and, 258; music and, 6, 110, 115, 121, 129, 138–40, 144, 149; nationalism and, 302n3
mimesis, 58, 298n34; expression vs., 146, 301n41; mechanical, 20, 247, 253–55, 258; violin accompaniment as, 15, 35
Mitchell, Lisa, 157, 311nn11–12
Mitchell, Timothy, 7, 211, 286–88
modernity, 6–9; aurality and, 286–88; colonial encounter and, 6–7, 314n24; as discursive formation, 7–8; modern subjectivity, 7–8, 12, 19, 190, 244, 261; music and, 245, 283; vision and, 286–87; voice and, 6–9, 19–20, 190–91, 286–89
Mrazek, Rudolph, 323n23
Mudaliar, K. Madurai, 264–66
Mudaliars, 4
mudras, 196–97
Mullick, K. S., 273, 323n26
music criticism, 84–86
music manuals, 221–32
Muthiah Bhagavatar, Harikesanallur, 196, 199–201, 299n18
Mylapore, 16–17, 76–77, 80–81, 168, 313n23
Mysore, 31, 59–60, 63, 64, 65–68, 76, 108–9

Nagaratnammal, Bangalore, 118, 123, 148, 309n54
nagaswaram, 92–93, 141
Naidu, Chitti Babu, 235
Narayana Das, Adhipatla, 69–70
Narayana Rao, Velcheru, 311nn10–11, 315n2
nautch, 45, 77, 120, 130, 136, 138, 213, 223, 303n5
Nayar, Brig. R. B., 199–201
Neild, Susan, 16
Nettl, Bruno, 294n2
Neuman, Daniel, 47, 291n6, 295n10, 296n18
Niranjana, Tejaswini, 295n13
notation, 20, 136, 192–95, 199–232, 273; *sargam* notation, 212, 215–19, 226–31; staff notation, 62, 66, 203–16, 226–31, 316n19, 317n24

Ollikkala, Robert, 306n32
Ong, Walter, 55, 291n8
oral tradition and orality, 4, 5, 8, 20–

Varahappayyar (minister), 30–31, 61
Vasudevachar, Mysore, 70, 74, 247–49
Vedavalli, M. B., 65, 68
veena, 26, 41, 45, 47, 136, 258
Vellalas, 16; Icai Veḷḷāḷars, 141, 143, 188, 294n4, 316n16
Venkatachalam, G., 123, 127, 128
Venkatachalapathy, A. R., 318n28
Venkatamakhi (treatise author), 233–34, 318n30
Venkataramiah, K., 61–63
Venkitasubramonia Iyer, 31, 63–64
violin: as accompaniment to voice, 33–37, 288–89; in experimental music, 52–54; "fiddle" and, 37, 42, 294n5; horn or "Stroh," 44, 68, 69, 296n17; mechanical, 43–44; in South India, 14–15, 25–58; styles of playing, 49–51; techniques of playing, 37–42, 50–51, 56
visibility, 38, 41; logic of, 205–7, 209–11, 235. *See also* legibility
Vizianagaram, 64, 65, 68–69
voice: agency and, 148, 289; anxieties about loss of, 242, 246–47, 258; body and, 146–49; gender and, 115–16, 121–29, 145–48; microphone and, 87–92; modernity and, 6–9, 19–20, 190–91, 286–89; "naturalness" of, 18–19, 127–29, 139, 141, 144–45; politics or ideology of, 5–14, 115–16, 148–49, 152–53, 190–91, 245–46, 276, 287–89; psychoanalytic approaches to, 10–11; ventriloquism and, 55–58, 297n32; "vocal anthropology," 13, 111, 292n14

Weber, William, 5, 86, 94, 291n5, 324n1
Western classical music, 4, 5, 62, 64, 66, 86, 94, 150, 185, 232, 234, 300n27, 306n23, 324n1
Williams, Raymond, 309n49
Wodeyar, Chamaraja, 65
Wodeyar, Jayachamaraja, 65, 66
Wodeyar, Nalwadi Krishnaraja, 59, 65–67
Wodeyar, Yuvaraja Narasimha, 67
woman question, 18
women: idealized, 114–16, 129, 135–36, 141, 144–45, 149, 158, 302nn1–4; unmarried, 111–14
Women's India Association, 18, 117, 294n25

Žižek, Slavoj, 297n32
Zvelebil, Kamil, 154, 310n3, 311nn4–5

Amanda Weidman is an assistant professor of anthropology at Bryn Mawr College.

Library of Congress Cataloging-in-Publication Data
Weidman, Amanda J., 1970–
Singing the classical, voicing the modern : the postcolonial politics of music in South India / Amanda J. Weidman.
p. cm.
Includes bibliographical references and index.
ISBN 0-8223-3631-6 (cloth : alk. paper)
ISBN 0-8223-3620-0 (pbk. : alk. paper)
1. Music—India, South—History and criticism.
2. Music—Social aspects—India, South. 3. Politics and culture—India, South. I. Title.
ML338.1.W45 2006
781.6'90954—dc22 2005037850